WANT ME FOREVER

Starry Hills

Book 1

KAYLA CHASE

Mythical Lake Press, LLC

This book is a work of fiction. Names, characters, places, and incidents are either the product of the writer's imagination or are used fictitiously, and any resemblance to actual persons, living or dead, business establishments, events, or locales is entirely coincidental.

Want Me Forever

Mythical Lake Press, LLC

Print Edition

www.KaylaChase.com

Cover Art by Laura Hoak-Kagey of Mythical Lake Design

ISBN: 979-8891560222

To anyone who was ever made to feel lesser

You are amazing and don't let anyone tell you differently

Reader Note

This book contains thoughts, memories, and discussions about childhood verbal abuse, childhood emotional neglect, and the death of a family member. I hope I have treated these items with the care and consideration they deserve.

Chapter One

Sabrina

Today I had the chance to land my dream job and change my life forever.

Well, provided I could calm my nerves and get my shit together.

Which was easier said than done. Not because I wasn't prepared. I was. I was always that person who did twice as much work as everyone else, just in case.

No, my stomach churned and my palms sweated because I would have to face *him* in close quarters again. He was not only the other employee up for the promotion, but he was also the man who made my life hell at work.

The one who'd tried to kiss me against my will.

And if sitting across the conference table from that

bastard wasn't enough to make me nervous, the voice of my long-dead mother also kept trying to break free. The voice I wished I could banish but never quite could.

Still, I had to try. The last thing I need was for her words to ruin everything I'd worked toward over the last five years.

After taking a deep breath, I went to the sink, stared into the mirror, and stated firmly, "I have the knowledge, I have the skills, and I'm going to kick butt in there. The promotion is mine."

For a second, I thought maybe I'd won today. That maybe my mother would stay gone and not make me feel like crap.

However, in the next beat, her words came rushing into my head:

"You're worthless, stupid, and pathetic. You'll never amount to anything so you'd better learn to please a man, or you'll starve on the streets. But you'll have to lose weight first because no one wants a fat bitch in their beds."

I nearly closed my eyes but knew the only way to tune out her voice was to use my own. "I have the knowledge, I have the skills, and I'm going to kick butt in there. The promotion is mine."

Once I'd repeated it a few more times, my mother's voice finally went silent.

For now. Maybe if I was lucky, she'd stay quiet at least until after my meeting was finished.

Squaring my shoulders, I walked out of the bathroom and swung by my office. I worked at a marketing and PR firm in San Francisco, specializing in online social media relations.

But today I wanted to change that and finally become a brand manager.

After taking off my sensible flats and slipping on my lucky black heels with tiny bows on top, I carefully crafted my I'm-a-badass-woman face and headed toward the meeting room. By the time I reached the glass door and walked inside, at least my palms had stopped sweating.

I made myself scan the room and I met the asshole's eyes. His name was Justin Whitmore, and his smarmy, mocking look said payback was coming.

Don't let him win, Sabrina.

I quickly moved my gaze to my boss and smiled before slipping into the seat at her left, across from Justin.

Edwina Jones wore her silver hair in a French twist, a dark-blue dress that probably cost more than my monthly salary, and a black cardigan. She was tough but fair and didn't take anyone's crap.

She also didn't bother with small talk, which I appreciated. After opening her tablet case, she said, "Thank you both for being prompt. As you know, a brand-manager position will open up in a few weeks, and I hope to fill it internally. You two have the best track records with clients, possess strong work ethics, and have shown an interest in this particular job."

Edwina tapped her tablet, and an image appeared on the projector. The website for a place called Wolfe Family Farm and Winery came up.

As I switched into work mode, my doubts and worries faded away.

Right away, I could see the Wolfe family needed help. Their website displayed a picture of rolling hills at sunset, and I couldn't tell if it was a farm or a vineyard, let alone whether they sold wine. Not only that, but there was way too much jargon that your average person wouldn't understand.

I itched to jot down notes but focused on Edwina's next words instead. "For years we've been trying to break into the California winery market. The Wolfe family is located in Sonoma and recently reached out to us for help. Usually, their account would be much smaller than I'd take on. But given how there are hundreds of wineries in Sonoma County—all potential clients—I offered a contract to the Wolfe family to get a foot in the door."

Interesting. I couldn't remember a time when Edwina had agreed to work with anyone who didn't make at least hundreds of millions a year.

When my boss finally met my eyes again, she continued, "It's also the perfect opportunity to determine who will get the promotion." Then she glanced at Justin. "The person who makes the best pitch made after ten minutes will be given the first chance at landing the deal. If for any reason the first person fails, the other will try." She leaned forward. "But let me make it clear—if neither of you gets the Wolfe family to sign, then I'll look outside the company to fill this position." She tapped her nail on the table. "Your ten minutes begin now."

My heart pounded as I opened my portfolio and began writing. I could type faster, but as with all of Edwina's meetings, we were only allowed to bring pens, paper, and to use our phones for research.

The time crunch was a blessing in many ways, mainly because then I wouldn't worry about everything that could go wrong.

Before I knew it, a timer beeped. Justin and I both put down our pens and turned our phones over to hide the screens.

My boss placed her hands together in front of her, fingertips touching, and nodded at Justin. "You go first, Justin."

I made myself look at him as he stood, his expression smug, as if he knew his ideas would always be better.

Asshole.

Justin said, "I'd like the Wolfe family to come into the office to talk about their business. From there, I could send photographers, researchers, wine experts, and a few social media underlings to Starry Hills to help set everything up. Once that's all done and the new website is live, I'd go out and oversee a few in-person events before devising an advertising campaign."

His method was surface-level and impersonal. How was he supposed to find out what made the Wolfe family's wine unique if he didn't spend time with them?

You have a real chance, here, Sabrina. Don't screw it up.

Edwina thanked him and gestured toward me.

Taking a deep breath, I stood and maintained eye

contact with my boss. "I would go out to Sonoma first, visit with them, and learn about their land, their story, and their products. In fact, there's a festival taking place in the nearby town of Starry Hills in a few days where I could check them out incognito, then meet with them formally in person later. After interacting with them for a few days at their farm and winery, I could come back here to work on ideas. I would visit their land as many times as needed until we have the perfect brand identity, feeling, and strategy."

I waited to see what Edwina would say, doing my best not to reveal how my heart thudded.

From the corner of my eye, I noticed Justin rolling his eyes. He probably thought going out to Starry Hills was beneath the position. Well, screw that jackass.

Edwina finally spoke up, her gaze scrutinizing me. "So you'd stay with the client at their winery for a few days to get to know them better? While it wouldn't work with, say, an app company, I think it's perfect for this account."

I blinked. I had meant I'd stay at a hotel and visit during the day, not stay with the Wolfe family itself. But if that gave me the first chance at getting the contract, I'd gladly do it.

My boss tapped her fingers on the table—she often did that to intimidate people—and after probably a minute, she gestured toward me. "You have the first chance, Sabrina."

I mentally jumped for joy but managed to keep my face serious and not make a snarky remark to Justin.

Once I nodded, she continued, "I'll have my

assistant reach out to the Wolfe family and tell them to expect you the day after the festival. When's the event?"

"Valentine's Day."

She nodded. "You'll stay in a hotel the first night, as I want you to do as much research as possible on their competitors."

"Of course. But what about my active accounts?"

Edwina gestured toward Justin. "He'll take them on temporarily."

I risked a glance at Justin, who glared at me.

Well, it was a good thing I'd soon be in Sonoma County and not here.

Edwina stood. "Check in with me via text often and keep me updated. The second they're ready to sign, call me."

She nodded at each of us and left.

I turned toward the door, wanting to tell my best friend the good news. However, just as I placed my hand on the door to push it open, Justin whisper-hissed, "You'll fucking fail, Sabrina. And then I'll swoop in and pick up the pieces."

Probably only because the door was made of clear glass did he not try to corner me and intimidate me further. Drawing courage from the fact that everyone could see us, I looked over my shoulder. "Get used to my extra social media accounts, Justin. Because I'm going to score this deal. You'll see."

With that, I exited the room and kept my shoulders back and my head high until I made it into my office.

As soon as I shut the door, I leaned against it, grateful it was solid wood, and blew out a breath.

Being face to face with that man again had only given me extra incentive to win this promotion. Because then we'd be in different departments, which meant I'd rarely see him.

Pushing aside thoughts of the jerk, I headed toward my desk, sat down, and made a list of everything I needed to do for this assignment.

Sure, charming the Wolfe family was going to be tough. Especially since their winery was family-run and dealing with families had never been easy for me.

Mostly because I'd never really had one.

Not wanting to go down memory lane and risk my mother's voice returning, I opened my laptop and got to work. Valentine's Day was in three days, and I needed to learn as much as possible about Sonoma County and its wines before then.

Because no matter what it took, I was getting the damn promotion. Nothing else mattered.

Chapter Two

Beckett

As the latest people to visit our booth at the Starry Hills Valentine's Festival walked away, I put down the bottle of chardonnay and muttered, "I still don't know why the fuck I'm here."

Aunt Lori raised a dark eyebrow. Even though she was my aunt by marriage and more than a foot shorter than I was, she'd helped raise me and wasn't the least bit intimidated by me or any of my siblings. "Beckett James Wolfe, watch your language."

I snorted. "Says the woman who could out-swear any of us."

Her lips twitched. Aunt Lori's late husband had been my uncle Tim, who'd been in the navy and most definitely a sailor who could make certain people blush.

"After two glasses of wine, maybe. But I haven't touched a drop today." She lightly swatted my arm. "Now, behave. I know your brother Zach usually does these events with me, but trust me—we don't want him here high on painkillers, let alone out in the cold with a broken leg."

"I think he broke his leg just so I'd have to deal with all this sh—er, crap."

Aunt Lori straightened the bottles and tasting cups at our table. "Zach may like to play jokes, but I doubt enduring months of pain and recovery is worth it, even for him." She looked up at me again, strands of her silver-threaded black hair blowing around her face. "Plus, you know how excited he's been to meet with the rep from Edwina Jones and Associates."

Yeah, my brother—I had five siblings, and he fell toward the younger end of them—loved joking with people, making small talk, and doing all the shit I couldn't stand.

I preferred being outside, back on the farm, walking among the vines. I didn't want to sit in front of a computer for hours, let alone talk about websites, social media, or whatever else the rep would say.

But the previous year's harvest had been bad, really bad, and even my stubborn ass had admitted we needed to make some changes if we were to stay afloat.

Before my aunt could go into more detail about how I needed to suck it up, a woman in formfitting dark jeans, black boots, and a gray winter coat walked up to us. I gave a half smile—which was the best I could manage when my balls were about to freeze off—and picked up the nearest wine bottle.

The woman smiled back and glanced around the booth. We had some pictures showing my family from the 1950s to the present day, a few awards, and information about special events, orders, and future tastings.

I didn't usually pay attention to who walked up since it was Aunt Lori's job to handle them. However, I couldn't stop staring at the woman. Her dark-brown hair was pulled back into a tight bun, every hair in place despite the light breeze. The severe style made it so I couldn't help but notice her green eyes and flushed cheeks. Add in her sweet smile, and she was fucking beautiful.

As she shifted in place—probably to stay warm—my gaze traveled down her body. She was full of curves and softness, and the way her jeans hugged her lush thighs made me wonder for a second what she looked like bare, with her legs spread and my head buried between them.

Fuck. Stop it, Beck. You've been without a woman for too long.

She caught me staring, which was my cue to get my head out of the gutter. Doing my best to hide my attraction to her, I offered up the bottle. "Want to try our chardonnay?"

Raising a dark eyebrow, she nodded. "Sure. What should I be noticing?"

"That depends—do you usually drink wine, or are you just trying to sound like you do?"

Aunt Lori scolded me through gritted teeth, "Behave!"

But the woman laughed. "You don't normally get such honesty at these types of events, and I kind of like it."

Aunt Lori glared at me before smiling at the woman. "Even so, excuse my associate. He's a miracle worker when it comes to vines, orchards, or anything that grows. But he's rather lacking when it comes to people. His brother usually helps me out but couldn't tonight. So he's been pouting and being rather grumpy about it."

I nearly rolled my eyes, but I was used to Aunt Lori's spiels.

The woman glanced at me a second and then turned back to my aunt. "I'll admit I haven't drunk a lot of wine in the past. But I'm learning, and if you can be patient and tell me how to do this properly, I'd be super grateful."

Aunt Lori went through her introduction to wine tasting, and I kept my mouth shut, which was best for us all, really. It even gave me a chance to steal a few more glances at the mystery woman without her noticing. I was almost positive she was from the city, and I wondered if she was single or not.

Wait. What? No. I was most definitely not going to ask her to meet up with me later.

Once the woman finished her cup, a drop of wine lingered on her bottom lip. For a beat, I wanted to lean over and lick it off with my tongue.

Damn it. There I went again, lusting after her. I

definitely needed to hit up The Watering Hole in Starry Hills—the local bar—and end my dry spell ASAP.

Still, I couldn't let the woman walk away like that, have someone else point it out, and let her be embarrassed. I tapped my lower lip. "You have wine right here."

She took off one of her gloves and lightly brushed her lower lip. And damn, I couldn't keep my gaze from tracking every little movement. She had the plumpest bottom lip I'd ever seen, one made to be tugged and nibbled.

One that would feel perfect against me as she swallowed my dick.

Grateful for having the table and wine bottles to hide my reaction—I really was acting like a fucking horny teenager tonight—I cleared my throat. "You got it. It's gone."

She sucked her finger clean—fuck, was she trying to kill me?—before lowering her hand and smiling, that alluring dimple showing up again. "Thanks." She turned and asked my aunt, "May I take one of these packets?"

Aunt Lori handed her one. "Of course. Any questions, any at all, just call, and I'll probably be the one you talk with. And if I don't know the answer, my nephews will."

The woman waved and left. Even with her coat covering most of her ass, I still stared at it as she walked away.

Aunt Lori's voice snapped me out of my head.

"You can close your mouth now and wipe the drool off your chin."

"I don't know what the hell you're talking about."

Arching an eyebrow, she said, "I've helped raise you and your siblings for more than fifteen years. I know when you're drooling over a woman."

"I'm thirty-four years old, Aunt Lori. You can stop scolding me at any time now."

She clicked her tongue. "I think you still need them now and again. Hell, you'll probably need them even when you're sixty. And yes, I plan to live forever."

Then she winked, and I chuckled. While I'd give anything to have my parents still alive, Aunt Lori was like a second mother to me. Well, the straight-shooting, occasionally devious mother who always had her nose in other people's business, but I loved her anyway. "How much longer do we have to stay out here? It's fucking freezing."

"Good thing you've never had to live where it actually gets cold."

"Yes, yes, I know. You've lived where snow can be hip deep, and you had to walk three miles each way. But this is Northern California."

My aunt shrugged. "I can manage on my own for the last twenty minutes if you want to leave and warm your tender man parts."

I narrowed my eyes. "There's no way in hell I'm leaving you out here alone at night."

She smirked because she knew I wouldn't abandon her and gestured toward the oncoming couple. "Then smile and try not to insult anyone else tonight, Beckie."

My aunt was the only person in the world I allowed to call me Beckie without complaining. Mostly. She did it to get a rise out of me on purpose. I sometimes thought it was one of her life missions, to irritate the hell out of the Wolfe siblings and ensure we never took ourselves too seriously.

Which we'd needed, after first my dad's death and then later, my mom's.

Not wanting to go down memory lane, I pasted on a fake smile and did indeed manage to stay quiet and not insult anyone else. No other woman caught my eye either.

Despite my better judgment, I kept looking for the finger-sucking woman from earlier, but she never came back.

Once the night wound down and everything was packed up in the truck, I opened the door for my aunt before going to the driver's side. I turned the ignition, put it into gear, and pulled out of the gravel parking lot and onto the road.

I'd been putting off the discussion about tomorrow for as long as possible, but it was time to bite the bullet and get it over with. "I still think Zach should meet with this marketing person, not me."

"Did you check in on your brother at all today?"

Guilt pricked my conscience, but I pushed it away. "No."

"If you had read the group texts, then you'd know Zach is in no condition to speak to anyone outside the family. While his texts were funny, it's clear he can't concentrate well on the pain meds, Beck. It won't kill you to leave the pruning to Carlos and Valerie for one or two days."

"I love pruning the vines," I grumbled.

"Stop sulking. You should've given some of your responsibilities to the staff—or even your brother—years ago, but you never listen to me. It's gotten to the point that I'm this close to giving up."

Silence fell, and I couldn't deny it. But there was a reason I didn't want to share my duties with anyone—I'd promised my father I would keep Wolfe Family Farm and Winery afloat, strong, and still around to pass on to the next generation of Wolfes.

"Fine. I'll help with the marketing person for one day."

"Two days." Though I opened my mouth to argue, she beat me to it. "Two, or I'll start texting every embarrassing emoji I can manage. I haven't used an eggplant or an overheated face in a while."

I groaned. My aunt had forced my siblings and me into a group text a while ago. Well, it included everyone but Zane, who was who the hell knew where on assignment for the navy SEALs.

But the rest of us had to endure her constant teasing. And in the last few months, she'd been using each and every emoji available, as if on a mission to annoy us all to the breaking point.

I turned the truck into the entrance of our property, paying attention to the dark road. When we approached the gate, I punched the code into the keypad. As the gate swung open, I finally replied.

"Fine. I'll help for two days. But only if you promise to never, ever use an eggplant emoji with us ever again."

She laughed. "We'll see. I can promise a week, but if you aren't your charming self with this woman coming to help us, I'm going to be relentless. I might even shock you."

"And to think most people's aunts give them socks at Christmas and twenty dollars in birthday cards."

She snorted. "You love me, Beckie. Don't deny it."

I pulled into my parking spot and leaned over to kiss her cheek. "Despite it all, I do love you, Aunt Lori. But I'd love you even more without eggplant emojis."

My aunt chuckled, and I raced around to open her door. I helped her down because she was ridiculously short and my truck was tall.

I'd parked in the private section, where we lived in the back of the winery's tasting and event rooms, and I unlocked the door and waited for Aunt Lori to enter. Once inside, we headed to the kitchen.

My phone vibrated in my pocket. Since my aunt was busy looking for food in the fridge, I took it out. It was from my younger brother Nolan.

Frowning, I opened it. Nolan was a big-time movie star who lived in Southern California, and he often went silent for weeks or even months at a time for a shoot. He'd been out on one over the last month or two, so getting a message from him in the group text was a big deal. I read it:

Nolan: Is Zach okay?

I scrolled up a few lines and read Zach's messages.

Zach: Why are there spiders crawling on the moon?
Zach: Fuck, they're growing and getting big. Are they spider aliens with superpowers?
Zach: Dude, I don't want a spider alien to probe my ass and study me. Do something.
Zach: Okay. I told them to fuck off and they went. Still, call someone. Eight legs in my ass is too many.

Then there was nothing until Nolan's message.

I sighed. If Nolan had been radio silent, he probably didn't know what had happened to our younger brother. And I didn't blame him for not scrolling through hundreds of texts—mostly from Aunt Lori—to catch up. So I replied:

Me: He's fine. Zach broke his leg and is on pain meds.
Nolan: Do I need to come home?
Me: No, we're fine, brother. Good night.

I put my phone away, mainly because I didn't want Nolan to bring up the beef between us again. I was too tired for that shit. "I'm going up. I'll check in on Zach before hitting the hay."

"G'night, Beckie. And if the bed bugs bite, call an exterminator."

Having heard this many times in the past, I nodded and went upstairs.

When I reached Zach's room, I slowly opened the door. Since Zach and I were the only two siblings who helped with the farm and winery, we both lived at the big house.

I approached the bed and stopped, watching as my little brother slept. Zach was only little because he was younger than me. Out of all my brothers, Zach was the closest to me in height. And maybe if I'd had a few beers, I would admit he was an inch taller.

And while he might not have broken his leg on purpose, I still wanted to know why the fuck he'd been climbing trees in the orchard late at night.

Satisfied Zach would be fine, I left him and went to my room.

Since I usually went to bed earlier—I liked getting up at the ass-crack of dawn—as soon as my head hit the pillow, I fell asleep and had hot, sexy dreams of a certain woman in tight jeans and city-girl boots. One who needed me to lick wine off her lips before eating her pussy and making her scream my name.

Chapter Three

Sabrina

Me: So, this hot guy flirted with me tonight.
Taylor: Ooh, did you hook up with him in his truck?
Me: Um, no. And that just sounds uncomfortable.
Taylor: Not if you put the seat back and recline it enough.
Me: I'm afraid to ask.
Taylor: I'll give you some tips later. Tell me about this guy.
Me: I swear he was undressing me with his eyes.
Taylor: And you didn't ask to go visit his truck? I'm sure he has a truck.
Me: With a stranger? Never. Are you crazy?
Taylor: Hey, I ended up in a car with my hubby not long after I met him.

Me: Which I never thought was a smart idea.
Taylor: <tongue out emoji> If you see the hottie again when in town, maybe ask him out. It's been a while since you got some.
Me: Good night, Taylor.

The next morning, I was in the middle of packing when my phone buzzed. Even without looking, I knew it was my best friend, Taylor Adams.

"Yes, can I help you?"

"Tell me about this sexy long-haired guy who eye-fucked you."

I snorted. "That's not what I said."

"You all but did."

"You know, I could've been sleeping. It's only seven thirty a.m."

"Please, you're awake at five every day. Now, hurry up and spill. I need to leave for work soon, and you were stingy in your texts."

Taylor was the sister I wished I'd had growing up instead of the blood one who'd turned her back on me. "He was cute and tall and had that manly scruff you'd expect of someone who worked on a farm."

"And?"

"Yeah, so he stared at my mouth a beat too long. Not that it matters. He works for the winery I'll be staying at this week, so he's definitely off-limits."

"Hey, if he's just staff, then he's fair game in my book. It's been a while since your ex, Sabrina. Go out and get some."

"I have a drawer at home that can take care of that, thank you very much."

"Your vibrator army can't love you, Sabrina."

"But my vibrator army gives me an orgasm every time, which is a bonus over real men."

Taylor laughed. "It just takes the right one to rock your world. My Ben has an extremely talented tongue." She sighed. "Yes, he definitely knows how to keep a girl happy."

I snorted again. "As you remind me, every chance you get. I'm happy for you, Taylor. I am. But right now, I need to focus on landing this account. And seeing as I'm not good at small talk, I can't afford any distractions, or I might screw it all up. Fantasies of sexy men with talented tongues will definitely have to wait."

I heard her picking up her car keys. "You've got this, Sabrina. When talking with your clients, just pretend they're me. Although maybe don't mention the vibrator army or your dildo gigolos. Who knows what kind of weirdos you might attract. Remember: stranger danger."

I rolled my eyes. "Don't you have to go to work now?"

"Love you, too, Sabrina. Keep me updated on the hottie work guy and his tongue."

"Like that will ever happen. Now, go whip those players into shape and maybe even make them cry a little."

"Mm, I can't wait to get my hands on some hard, knotted muscles today."

Since she was a physical therapist for a major

league baseball team, her job was literally touching a lot of muscled—sometimes even hot—guys.

Laughing, I said, "Bye, Taylor."

I hung up. If only I could channel some of my best friend's energy and outgoing vibes, this entire assignment would be a heck of a lot easier.

But I was definitely an introvert at heart and would have to rely on my other skills.

Namely, being prepared and organized.

I sat down and went over all my notes. I hadn't found out a lot about the Wolfe siblings, unfortunately. One was named Abigail, and she'd been interviewed in an article about a teaching award. There had also been some promotional materials featuring Lori Wolfe, the woman from the night before.

I knew there were five brothers but not much else from my general internet searches, and I wasn't about to hire a PI to dig deeper. I'd find out about them soon enough.

Regardless, next came the hard part—not instantly putting up my guard to protect myself, which always came across as bitchy or cold.

A few hours later, I turned my car into the long driveway leading to Wolfe Family Farm and Winery. The rows of grapevines came into view rather quickly, and I gasped. Even though it was still winter and everything was asleep, the view of rows upon rows of vines set against the rolling hills in the distance was stunning. I could only imagine how beautiful it would be in the summer as the sun set.

If that wasn't enough beauty, I also passed groves that had to be the apple orchard I'd read about. There weren't any leaves yet, but when the apple blossoms were in bloom in the spring, it would be beyond charming.

I'd learned that Sonoma County had once been blanketed in Gravenstein apple trees before being replaced more and more often with grapes. Even though it would've made the Wolfe family more money to take out the remaining trees to plant more vines for the winery, they had kept a small orchard and sold organic apples. They also hosted some special events there too.

They hadn't put much about it on their website, but I'd seen some mentions of family stories from a guided tour review. I would have to take one of those myself.

Before long, the rolling hills and vines were replaced by a large house, one with white stucco walls and a red clay tile roof. It was big, too, but what made it stand out was the veranda that wrapped around the second story. I could just imagine the views from up there as I sipped wine, watching as the sun set behind the surrounding hills. The stars would be bright so far from the city, too, making it magical.

Come to think of it, that was probably why the nearby small town was called Starry Hills.

I pulled into the parking lot, turned off the ignition, and took a deep breath. I'd done my pep talk back in the hotel—the last thing I needed was for the clients to find me talking to myself in the car—but I still needed a moment.

You can do this. Last night, I'd made small talk and survived the festival. I could handle a few more days of the same. And heck, I would get some nice views and maybe learn some more about wine.

Stop stalling and get your butt inside already.

After grabbing my purse and portfolio, I opened the door and exited. The February day was brisk by California standards, and I tightened my cardigan around me. As the wind blew up my skirt, I shivered. I really should've worn a coat.

As soon as I entered the impressive building, a young woman came up to me with a smile. "Welcome to Starry Wolfe Winery. How can I help you today?"

I noticed the logo stitched on the upper left breast of her polo shirt, which was a wolf head with two wine glasses crossed behind it.

I smiled. The image meant the owners probably had a sense of humor, playing on their last names instead of going with something fancy.

I bobbed my head in greeting. "Hello. My name is Sabrina O'Connor, and I have a ten o'clock appointment with Mr. Zachary Wolfe."

The woman gestured. "Mr. Beckett Wolfe had to take over for his brother and is waiting for you in the meeting room. Follow me."

From everything I'd been told, all correspondence between my work and this place had been via Zach Wolfe. Why would they switch contacts now? Did all the brothers work here and share the responsibilities? I mentally added it to my ever-growing list of questions and followed the woman.

Grateful she didn't try to fill the silence, I noticed the tasteful, rustic decor. Oh, it was definitely high-end and had more white than any cabin would ever contain—I'd call it rustic chic—but it seemed like a nice fit. Sonoma and Napa Valley had helped shift the image of wine from snobby and high-class to something a little more laid-back.

So far, everything I'd seen about the Wolfe brand had good bones, and the website could be fixed easily. Still, the initial meeting would show me just how much more work I had ahead of me. Because it was the people behind the business that needed to embrace my suggestions and make the changes.

We reached a door, and the woman stopped in front of it. After she knocked, we entered a small meeting room with a table and some chairs. When I noticed the person inside it, I did a double take and nearly gasped.

Because standing across from me was the tall, rugged hottie from the night before. The one who'd stared at my mouth a beat too long and whom I'd teased by sucking the wine off my finger.

The only main difference was that his long hair danced around his shoulders today, and I couldn't decide if I liked it tied back or loose.

Focus, Sabrina.

Smiling, I opened my mouth, but the man narrowed his eyes at me, clearly pissed. Probably because I hadn't introduced myself the night before.

Well, too bad. I'd merely done my job, and if he

didn't like it, then he must not understand how seriously I took this assignment.

I stood tall, kept my smile in place, and held out a hand. "Nice to meet you, Mr. Wolfe. I'm Sabrina O'Connor from Edwina Jones and Associates."

He didn't shake right away and continued to glare at me.

Not a super-forgiving guy, it seemed. But I was here to help him. His business needed me, and he should realize that soon enough.

Although the longer my hand was out, the more forced my smile was.

Maybe some would just drop their arm and pretend it had never happened. But if we were to work together and succeed, I needed him to accept me as an equal. If I caved now, he'd expect it again in the future. And that way lay trouble.

If Mr. Wolfe wanted to play power games, then bring it. I wouldn't back down. This promotion was too important to me.

Chapter Four

Beckett

Aunt Lori: You can do it, Beckie! <flexing arm emoji> <dancing emoji>
Me: Um, okay.
Aunt Lori: I'm trying to pump you up. There's no cheerleader emoji, though. <sad face emoji>
Me: …
Aunt Lori: <gold medal emoji> <heart emoji> <hug emoji>
Me: ?
Aunt Lori: You're number one, I love you, and I'm sending a virtual hug. You need to get better at this.
Me: Or you could just use English.
Aunt Lori: Come on, you know you want to try. Just one. For me.

Me: <eye roll emoji>

I tugged at my stupid dark-blue polo shirt with the wolf logo on it, ready to get back into my work clothes and into the fresh air. Just staying inside for a few hours was pure hell.

But since Zach had still been asleep ten minutes ago, there was no way I could get out of the meeting with the marketing person. Especially since Aunt Lori needed to finish up the books for last year and wanted to go over them with me later in the day—when she'd reveal just how shitty the harvest had been.

Needing a distraction, I scrolled through the weather forecast on my phone. To some extent, pretty much my entire life revolved around the whims of nature.

Soon, someone knocked and entered. Taking a deep breath, I stood just as our employee, Maggie, opened the door and smiled at me before stepping aside to reveal a woman.

And not just any woman but the one I'd spent all night fantasizing about.

For a second, I thought I must be dreaming. I'd expected some stuffy older person to show up, not a fucking beautiful woman who distracted me to no end.

But then it dawned on me why she'd been at our booth the previous night.

The woman had been spying on us.

Narrowing my eyes, I wondered what other tricks she had up her sleeve. I'd been ambivalent at best about this whole fucking thing, but now I definitely didn't want to deal with her. I didn't like deception. We Wolfes had a lot of issues, but lying wasn't one of them.

She put out her hand. "Nice to meet you, Mr. Wolfe. I'm Sabrina O'Connor."

I stared at her but didn't shake her hand. It was a dickish thing to do, but I needed her to know I was in charge. We were the client, and the agency had assured me that if I had any issues, any at all, I could call them and voice my concerns.

Well, I was already fucking tempted.

The woman named Sabrina cocked an eyebrow and wiggled her fingers. "I don't bite."

I could bark at her to sit down and glower at her until she started talking. Yet the manners instilled in me by my parents and my aunt screamed for me not to be a complete asshole. The wait had done the job anyway.

So I shook her hand for barely a second. Even so, a jolt rushed through me at the contact, and I released my grip as if I'd been burned. *Fuck.* I needed to get over my attraction to this woman. And quickly.

After sitting down, I crossed my arms and made a point not to notice her flimsy dress or how it stretched across her breasts when she sat down. Or how she licked her lips while laying her things down on the table.

Not for you, Beck. Not for you. Irritated at myself, I channeled my inner grump and asked, "Did your spying mission tell you everything you needed to know?"

She calmly opened her portfolio, plucked out a pen, and tapped it against the paper inside. "I take my job very seriously, Mr. Wolfe. I needed to see what you were like in the wild, so to speak, to help me better help you."

"Beck."

She blinked. "Pardon?"

"Mr. Wolfe was my father. Call me Beck."

She nodded. "And call me Sabrina. We'll be working closely together for the next week, so there's no need to be that formal."

If she knew about my dreams and what she'd done to my dick in them, she would know how formality was already out the fucking window.

I grunted. "You'll only have to deal with me for two days, and then you can work with my brother or aunt."

She was unfazed by my gruffness, which kind of annoyed me. "That's fine. My goal is to know everyone involved here, including the land and your production process. What I've already seen is beautiful, and it shouldn't be too hard to entice others to visit."

"I don't want people to visit. I want them to buy wine."

"If all you think about is what you want from the customer and not what they need, then you're doomed to fail."

I frowned. "What the fu—er, what are you talking about?"

"I'm getting ahead of myself. First, I want you and the other members of your family—maybe even some of the staff—to fill out these sheets."

She slid over a stack of papers.

Before I could stop myself, I blurted, "This isn't fucking high school."

Her lips thinned a bit, as if the smile on her face was killing her.

Good. I rather liked annoying her. It was a hell of a lot better than being entranced by her mouth again.

Sabrina replied in an even tone, "I was trying to save time. But if you want me to go around, asking everyone these questions, and filling it out myself, I can."

I stood. "Yes, go ahead and do that. And ask me last. I'll let Maggie know to help you any way she can. Now, excuse me. I need to check on something outside."

Her jaw dropped, but I quickly exited the room and went looking for my aunt.

Because there was no way I could work with that woman.

After last night, I didn't trust her.

My attraction to her was also a big fucking problem. After so many years of being alone and content, focusing on the farm and having casual hookups, why did the one woman I couldn't seem to get out of my head have to be her?

No, it would definitely be safer for Aunt Lori to deal with Sabrina, or even Zach, for that matter.

All I cared about was staying as far away from Sabrina O'Connor as possible.

I found my aunt an hour later, after I'd spent some time pruning the vines and calming my ass down.

Even though I still didn't like Sabrina's deception, Zach had worked his butt off to even get a chance with this marketing firm. They were fancy and usually didn't take on people like us. I'd just have to find a solution that worked for everyone.

My aunt's office was on the second floor, tucked into the corner of the building. I knocked, and she said to enter. Once inside, I shut the door and plopped down in the chair in front of her desk.

Even though Aunt Lori was in her sixties, she usually looked so much younger and full of life. But today, her expression was grim, there were bags under her eyes, and her hair was disheveled.

Leaning forward, I asked, "What's wrong?"

She ran her hands through her hair and kept them in place behind her head. "It's bad, Beckie. We desperately need to shift the older vintages, book more tours and events, and find a way to diversify our income. If the harvest sucks this year, too, the future looks bleak."

Bracing my elbows on the desk, I searched her face. The woman who'd been our rock when first my father died, and later my mother, looked worried.

And that scared the shit out of me. "We've had bad years before."

Sighing, she released her hair, uncaring that it went every which way. "Yes, it's natural to have ups and downs in this business. But sales have dwindled over the years as people shift more to online orders than in-person. We should've listened to Zach sooner."

My younger brother had tried to convince us to set up an online shop and maybe even a wine subscription box. But I'd mostly ignored him. Zach always had grand plans, and most of them were risky.

And even if we both had roles in the business, I was ultimately the decision maker.

I shook my head. "We don't know if his ideas would've helped anyway. He can attend more festivals in the state and maybe a few elsewhere to get more clients and orders."

Aunt Lori's face softened. "Changing how we do things doesn't mean you'll forget or disrespect your father, Beck. All that matters is keeping us afloat."

Fuck. She'd brought that up again.

I stood, needing to pace the room. "I vowed to keep up our traditions, Aunt Lori. And changing things would…"

Well, it would erase the last traces of my dad and mom from the vineyards and orchard.

My dad's dying words to me, right before he died from a heart attack, came rushing back: *Promise me you'll keep this place special, Beck. Keep it for the family. Don't let any of your siblings forget this is home and always will be. Watch over them, son. Protect them.*

He'd died right there in my arms, at the edges of our land, before an ambulance arrived. From that day forward, protecting my four younger siblings had become everything. Not once had I balked at the responsibility or challenges. Not when I was eighteen and certainly not now.

I couldn't—wouldn't—fail them.

But if succeeding meant changing everything my dad had done and erasing his legacy, this place would no longer be special, and I'd feel like I'd failed my father.

It was almost a no-win situation. Logically, I knew my father was gone and my siblings were still alive. But logic warred with my memories and love of my parents, making a mangled mess of my head.

Aunt Lori spoke again, her voice gentle. "Your mom and dad would be proud of you, Beckie. You were so damn young when you took over. All these years, you've shouldered the burden of running this place and taking care of the family." She stood, came to me, and placed a hand on my upper arm. "And I get wanting to be in charge, to control everything, and to live up to your father's expectations. But you're not alone. Zach has all but begged you for years to let him help you. And soon…"

Searching her eyes, I could tell she was keeping a secret. Aunt Lori was many things, but secretive wasn't one of them. "Soon what?"

"First, promise me you won't get mad."

Okay, that didn't sound good. "I'll try my best but can't make any promises. Now, tell me."

She hesitated and then replied, "West is coming home soon, and he wants to help out with the family business."

I blinked, trying to comprehend her words. "West?"

Weston was my eldest brother. At one time, we'd been best friends, nearly inseparable. Then soon after our father died, he married and skipped town, abandoning me when I needed his help the most. I'd barely heard from or seen him since.

"Why the fuck would West be coming home after all this time? Did you have something to do with it?"

"I'm not your enemy, Beck. So stop growling at me."

Taking a deep breath, I counted to five before asking, "Why is Weston coming back, Aunt Lori? Would you tell me, please?"

She searched my gaze and eventually nodded. "Better. Well, you know his wife died a little over a year ago, right?"

I nodded. While I didn't know a lot about West's life, he'd knocked up a girl by accident, married her, and gone to run her father's ranch in the California Central Valley. While they'd lost their first child not long after they married, West currently had two kids and sent a Christmas card every year.

I'd met his wife once, and she was a train wreck—drinking, cheating on my brother, and mostly ignoring her children. If I'd been on good terms with West, I would've had some choice words with her.

Aunt Lori's voice snapped me back to the present. "Well, the details aren't mine to tell, but West had a falling out with his in-laws and wants to get his children as far away from them as possible. Since we have plenty of room, I invited them to stay here until West figures out what to do next."

I frowned. "And you made these decisions without talking to me and Zach?"

She crossed her arms over chest. "Zach knows, but I didn't tell you because I knew you'd overreact and tell him to fuck off. I know he hurt you, Beck. But he's hurting, too, and he needs his family's help."

"Now he needs us, huh? Where was he right after Dad died? Or when Mom got sick? I don't mind helping his kids. But West hasn't even talked to me since that summer they stayed here, and now I'm supposed to just forgive him?"

Aunt Lori's face turned determined, which usually meant she would get what she wanted. "We all deal with grief differently, Beck. You buried yourself in work. West ran away. Hell, Zane joined the navy. Even Nolan put his heart and soul into becoming an actor." She waved a hand around the room. "But this is home to *all* the Wolfe siblings, whenever they need it. I promised your mother I'd keep an eye on you all and kick your butts when necessary. Do I need to kick yours so that you'll listen to me and see some sense? Because I know you'll regret it if you keep West at a distance forever."

Memories of the big brother I'd adored flooded my mind, but I pushed them back. Could I forgive him? Hell, I didn't know. But seeing him again might not be the end of the world.

Aunt Lori continued, "Not only would we be helping West, but you need help, Beck. Zach does a good job on the wine-production side of things, but West could help lift some of the burden from your shoulders in other places." I opened my mouth to protest, but she cut me off. "Give him a trial period at least." She closed the distance between us and looked up at me. "I know you'll dismiss it, but I think you need him as much as he needs you. And his children need us even more."

She was definitely holding something back about my niece and nephew. But that wasn't important right now. "You're guilt-tripping me hard, Aunt Lori."

"Is it working?"

No shame, no coyness—under normal circumstances, I loved it.

But having West around wouldn't be easy, especially if he didn't remember shit about growing grapes. "I can give him orchard duty. It's easier and less risky."

Aunt Lori sighed. "Your stubbornness will cause you more trouble than you can handle one day, Beckie. I swear."

"I'm sure it will. But it's how I've held it together for the last sixteen years, so I see it as a good thing."

My aunt had long ago learned to pick her battles and didn't comment on my last sentence. "Well, as long as West and his kids can stay here with us in the big house, put him to work digging ditches, for all I care."

She knew full well we didn't dig ditches. It was the fucking twenty-first century. "For his kids' sake, he can stay. But if he so much as tries to take charge from me, I'll kick his ass out, Aunt Lori, and he'll be stuck staying in one of the tiny guest houses."

"I'll take it. So, does this mean you'll talk with Zach and West and make plans to run the winery and orchard together? Maybe delegate some more tasks to them? I'm sure after this marketing firm helps us turn things around, you'll need the help."

I cleared my throat. "About that…"

She narrowed her gaze. "What did you do now?"

For a beat, I felt about ten years old. *But fuck that.* It wasn't my fault Sabrina O'Connor had thought deception would be a good first impression.

I explained how the woman from the night before was one and the same, and then added, "How can we trust her now, Aunt Lori? She basically lied to us through omission, which means it might be the norm for her. And if her plan is for us to outright lie to people to drum up business, I won't do it. The Wolfe family has always had their integrity, and I won't compromise that, no matter what. Neither Mom nor Dad would've wanted that."

She raised a dark eyebrow. "You've visited other wineries before, haven't you? To see what they're doing?"

"Yes, but—"

"And did you announce who you were? Or that you were looking for inspiration or judging the competition?"

"No, but—"

"Then why are you judging this woman? Is it because you drooled over her and now feel guilty about it? Worried you won't be able to keep your dick in your pants?"

"Aunt Lori!"

She clicked her tongue. "Don't 'Aunt Lori' me,

Beckie. She hasn't done anything you haven't. And since she'll be staying with us, you'd better patch things up and quickly."

"Wait. What? She's staying here?"

No one had fucking told me that.

Aunt Lori bobbed her head. "To better know us and how we run things. It's better than her driving from Starry Hills every day, wasting time and gas. We have room here for her, even with West and his kids coming." She poked my chest. "So find her, apologize, and give her a guided tour. Oh, and before you go, let me emphasize how much we need her help. If you want a chance to save the orchard, she and her firm are the only way to do it."

My aunt knew exactly where to hit me. That orchard reminded me and my siblings of our mother, of growing up, and of how life had been full of laughter and happiness before death had changed everything.

Running a hand through my hair, I sighed. "Fine. I'll apologize, but she'll have to earn my trust. That's the best I can do."

She patted my arm. "Good lad. Now, check on your brother, and then go look for Sabrina." I'd just turned toward the door when she added, "And invite her to dinner. Abby and Millie will be here, and it'll be great for her to meet them."

Abby was my baby sister, and Millie was her best friend. Although truthfully, Millie was more than that to my family. After all, when her parents had died in a car crash when she was ten, my mom had been made her guardian. So really, she was my other little sister.

And even if I loved them, together they could be trouble. I'd just have to talk to them before dinner to ensure they were on their best behavior for Sabrina.

Because whether I liked it or not, we all had to be fucking nice to that woman. Aunt Lori didn't exaggerate when it came to business and numbers. If she said we needed Sabrina's help, then we truly did.

After murmuring my agreement, I left and went to check on my brother.

I'd bite my tongue and do what needed to be done. However, I hoped like hell Zach was better so he could take over working with Sabrina.

Chapter Five

Sabrina

It had taken hours, but I interviewed all the staff I could find. Apparently, only two of the Wolfe brothers lived on the farm—I called it a farm for shorthand rather than farm and winery—along with the aunt, but she was busy for the morning and would see me later.

No one had shown me to a room, so I ignored my rumbling stomach and was sitting in the same meeting room as before, going over my notes, when the door opened.

Even before looking up, I knew it was *him*, the asshole from earlier.

As he stood in the doorway, his arms crossed and his shoulder leaning against the frame, I could fully admit he was a sexy asshole but a dick nonetheless.

"Yes?"

For a few beats, he merely stared at me.

I didn't shift in my seat. Oh, I would have as a teenager, when I'd barely gotten free from my mother and her narcissistic control shit, but no longer.

However, my stomach rebelled and rumbled loudly enough to echo inside the room.

He frowned. "Are you hungry?"

It was on the tip of my tongue to say, "Of course, asshat. My stomach just shouted it to the world."

But I pasted on my fake smile and replied, "Yes. I haven't eaten yet today."

"Why the fuck not?" When I blinked, he cleared his throat. "I apologize. I'm used to being informal here. Not to mention I'm the older brother and I'm used to taking care of my siblings."

I stared at him, but his brown eyes were unreadable. *What the heck is up with this guy?* He was so hot and cold that it was giving me whiplash.

I said slowly, "Okay."

He stood upright. "Follow me. I'll get you something to eat and then show you to your room."

Gathering my stuff, I asked, "And I can interview you as we eat?"

He nodded curtly. "Fine."

Given his tone, you'd think I was offering to pull his tooth without anesthesia or something. Still, I didn't want him to run away again, especially not until after I had my room.

He gestured for me to follow, and I did. But there was no guided tour or chitchat. No, he strode with purpose, and I had to half jog to keep up, so much so that by the time we reached the kitchen, I was a little out of breath.

My mother's voice came out of nowhere:

"Still a fat bitch, I see."

Taking a deep breath, I mentally repeated, *I am amazing. No one gets to tell me I'm worthless or lesser.*

I didn't realize I'd closed my eyes until I opened them and found Beck staring at me. "Are you okay? Are you going to faint?" He pulled out a stool at the large island. "Sit down."

His being nice to me was weird. But rather than explain that my mother had screwed me up well and good as a child, I merely nodded and sat.

Beck's hand brushed my arm as I slid into the seat, and a jolt of heat rushed through me and shot straight between my thighs.

Growling, he took three steps away, as if he couldn't get away from me fast enough.

Not sure if I was offended or relieved, I cleared my throat and looked around the kitchen. It was simple, with a white subway tile backsplash and light-gray countertops—probably quartz—and stainless steel appliances. Two things stood out, though—a huge fridge and a massive stove.

He must've noticed me staring at the eight-burner stove because he said, "When you have as many siblings as I do, it takes a lot of food and effort just to feed everyone. Add in friends, family, and sometimes even the staff for celebrations, and well, you need oversized sh—er, stuff."

I bit back a smile. For some reason, his almost swearing was adorable, especially since I'd heard far, far worse growing up.

Not wanting to go there, I leaned my forearms on the counter. He quickly turned around to rummage in the fridge and threw back, "What do you want to eat?" He stood and looked at me again, his brows furrowed. "Er, if you're a gluten-free vegan, I have some fruit and veggies, I think."

I tilted my head at the strange statement. "Why would you think I was a gluten-free vegan?"

He gestured. "You're from San Francisco."

A laugh escaped before I could help it. I clamped my hand over my mouth but realized that only drew more attention. So I lowered it and replied, "Not everyone from San Fran is like that. Just as there are stereotypes about farmers and winery owners, there are ones about people from the city. But no, I'm not. I can't really handle caffeine, but everything else is fair game."

He blinked as if being caffeine sensitive was ten times worse than if I'd been a gluten-free vegan. "You can't have caffeine? None?"

My lips twitched. "A single cup of coffee will make my heart race and my head spin, and I won't be able to sit still for like eight hours." I shrugged. "I'm just one of the unlucky ones who can't handle caffeine. Although I can manage a cup of black tea once or twice a day, if you have it."

He ran a hand through his hair—his long dark hair, which was probably soft and smelled like the outdoors.

I wouldn't mind running my hands through it, tugging him close to kiss me, and then…

Stop it. Beck was a client. I could look but nothing else. Edwina had a rule—no dating the clients. And I wouldn't risk this promotion for anything.

Not that I wanted to date Beck. Definitely not.

He sighed. "I don't think we have any tea, just coffee."

His tone made it seem like he was really upset about it.

Was this really the same grump who'd stormed out of the conference room earlier?

"Water's fine."

He plucked a glass from a cupboard, filled it from the filtered water dispenser on the fridge, and placed it in front of me. "You need to eat. So let me make you a fancy grilled cheese. Sound good?"

The thought of warm bread and gooey cheese made my stomach rumble more loudly than ever before.

His lips twitched. "So that's a yes then?"

I nodded and focused on drinking my water, watching Beck as he worked. He wasn't super muscled like the guys who worked out in the gym all the time. Yet his forearms were defined as he worked, and I couldn't stop staring at his shoulders. When he bent over to retrieve something from the cupboard, it highlighted his tight, round ass. One that I wouldn't mind grabbing onto as he thrust into me.

Once he had the sandwich in a pan, he turned

toward me. *Shit.* I did my best to hide the fact I'd been gawking at him.

He seemed oblivious, though. "If you want to ask me those questions now, we can kill two birds with one stone."

Yes, work, work was good. I opened my portfolio, and after jotting down his name, I asked, "If you could describe Wolfe Family Farm and Winery in five words, what would it be?"

He flipped the sandwich before answering. "Family, quality, tradition, home, and amazing."

The last word threw me a little. "Why amazing?"

"Because I only have five words, and it sums up all the remaining feelings I have about this place."

Interesting. "Okay, so now tell me why your wine is a must-try. Why this place? What makes it special?"

He put the grilled cheese onto a plate and cut it in half. Sliding the plate in front of me, he sat on the stool next to me. "First, eat up. Only once your stomach stops rumbling will I answer you."

I didn't like his highhandedness. But the sandwich smelled delicious, so I lifted one half and bit into it. I groaned as the strong, savory cheese hit my taste buds. When combined with the crunchy, buttery bread, it was pure heaven.

After swallowing, I looked up. Beck stared at my mouth for a few beats before meeting my gaze.

Time slowed as I tried to take in the hungry look in his eyes. He had to be jealous of the grilled cheese. Yes, that was it.

I slid the other half toward him. "It's past lunchtime, so we can share it."

Shaking his head, Beck jumped up and moved back to the stove. "No. I'll make one for myself. But we can keep going, until you get all the answers you need."

And for the next half hour, Beck kept his distance from me, focusing on the food.

A small part of me wanted him to sit next to me again so that I could be surrounded by his scent of earth, sky, and pure male.

But since that was my lady parts talking, I kicked that wish aside and focused on the questionnaire. Once it was done and we'd both eaten, he silently took me to my room, told me where everything was, and invited me to dinner.

The door shut before I could utter a reply.

Which was for the best. After all, grumpy, rude Beck was much easier to ignore and treat as a client than the version who'd made me lunch and was upset that he didn't have any tea for me.

Chapter Six

Sabrina

Me: So, he made me lunch.
Taylor: In a grumpy way or a happy way?
Me: What difference does it make? His mood swings are ridiculous.
Taylor: Grumpy means he was doing it because he probably has to. Happy means he wanted to. There's a difference.
Me: Both?
Taylor: That's not helping.
Me: I've only known him a few hours, and he doesn't come with a handbook.
Taylor: Pity, that. <sighing emoji>
Me: <eye roll emoji>
Taylor: Well, I think you want: <wolf emoji> <tongue emoji> <overheated emoji>
Me: I have work to do.

I changed into my comfy work-at-home clothes, compiled all the answers I'd collected from the questionnaires, and dived into filling out my plan of action.

Maybe some would resent being stuck indoors with the beautiful rolling hills of Sonoma just outside. However, I loved working. It was something I could control—most of the time—and I was damn good at my job.

Plus, being in front of my laptop meant I didn't have to be social, friendly, or constantly working on the badass-businesswoman image I tried to keep up.

I was most definitely an introvert at heart, but I could be social for work. Meeting clients, visiting for days, and chatting with people on the ground on a regular basis would be challenging, but I knew I could do it. Even if helping businesses recover or expand wasn't creating world peace, I could make a difference in everyday people's lives as a brand manager, all while never having to worry if I had food to eat or enough money for rent. My entire childhood had been one constant worry and step away from homelessness, and I never, ever wanted to be in that position again.

A timer beeped, ending my break, and I jumped back into my current project. Just as I added items to my brainstorming document, someone knocked on the door.

I finished my sentence, wondered who it could be, and called out, "Come in."

Two women entered the room. One was tall—nearly as tall as Beck—with brown hair and paler skin than I'd expect from someone working outside in the vines or the orchard. I'd seen her picture before—she was Abby Wolfe. The other lady was at least six or seven inches shorter and had dark hair and light-brown skin. They both wore jeans and sweaters, making me self-conscious about my old, shabby clothes.

I resisted tugging on my oversized sweater just as Abby smiled. "Hello. Sorry to just ambush you, but I heard you were here, and I just had to meet you. I'm Abby Wolfe, the youngest Wolfe sibling." She gestured to the other woman. "And this is my sister and best friend, Millie Mendoza. She came to live with us as a kid, but she's as much a Wolfe as I am."

Millie shook her head. "She doesn't need to know our life stories, Abby. We've only just met her."

Abby shrugged. "She's here to get to know our family, so there's no sense in hiding it from her." She tapped a finger against her chin. "You know, I could even make a family tree, if it would help, complete with adjectives to describe my older brothers to a T."

My lips twitched as I imagined what she might say about Beck. I instantly liked the pair of them. "I'll keep that in mind. I'm Sabrina O'Connor, although I'm sure your brother told you that already."

Abby nodded. "I've heard a few things. But Beck's notorious for leaving out the best details, so I'll just get to know you myself."

Er, now I wondered what her brother had said and if it had been good or bad.

Abby leaned forward and fake whispered,

"Although I heard how you irritated the shit out of him, which probably means we'll get along famously."

Millie lightly shoved her sister. "Forgive Abby. She's incorrigible sometimes. We just wanted to meet you and take you down to dinner, since Beck probably didn't show you where the dining room is."

"He didn't, but I'm sure I could've found it eventually."

Millie waved a hand. "You're our guest, so the least we can do is not let you get lost."

"Oh, you live here too? I thought…"

Abby shook her head. "No, Millie and I live on the neighboring lavender farm, which used to be a cattle ranch. Well, technically, it belongs to Millie. But now that I'm back in Starry Hills, I didn't want to live with my brothers again. I love them, but dealing with Millie is way easier than Beck or even Zach."

"I didn't know there were lavender farms nearby."

Millie replied, "Well, it's mainly there for ambiance. I run a wedding and special events business, using the renovated barn on my land for most of it. But a lot of engaged couples love having their pictures taken among the lavender or for their weddings, depending on the time of year. There's always something in bloom, for each season, somewhere on my property." She shrugged. "It's all part of my strategy."

Abby jumped in. "Millie's amazing with business. I only wish Beck would listen to her more. Then he probably wouldn't be in as much trouble as he is right now."

Millie elbowed Abby. "We have a guest, so maybe

don't air out the family laundry in front of her and be nice. Besides, we don't know everything that's going on here, and it's probably complicated."

Rolling her eyes, Abby answered, "You sound like Aunt Lori. But Sabrina's here to get to know the family, so I say be ourselves and don't hide the truth."

"There's sharing the truth, and there's criticizing about things we don't know about."

Abby grumbled. "Maybe."

I couldn't help but smile. It was hard to believe these two ladies were in the same family as Beck. "I won't tell him you said anything. Now, if you'd just give me a minute to change my clothes, then we can head to the dining room."

Abby looked me over. "You're fine. We don't have formal dinners or anything like that. It's just family."

I was wearing faded but super-soft leggings and a long sweater, and they'd seen better days. "Er, no. I should change."

Before they could convince me otherwise, I rushed into the bathroom, put on the slacks and button-up top I'd laid out, and whispered to myself, "You're going to rock this dinner. Just wait and see."

With a nod, I exited the bathroom and followed the two women to the dining room. It didn't take long for Abby to ask, "So, what do you think of Beck?"

I blinked. "Um, I don't know him very well."

Millie's lips twitched. "That's a nice way to say he was an ass earlier."

"I didn't—"

Abby put up a hand. "Oh, you don't have to be

diplomatic with us. Beck can be the biggest grump, but he can also be a big softie. He's more like a dad than a brother to me most of the time. If he hadn't had to take over the winery at eighteen, I think he'd be a little more relaxed."

Beck had taken over at eighteen? I hadn't known that. Although since it wasn't related to my work here, I really should just forget about it.

Millie sighed. "Again with the airing out family stuff. Maybe try to be a little less forthright?"

Abby arched an eyebrow. "After all these weeks of you telling me to have fun and be myself, I do it, and now you scold me?"

Millie and Abby exchanged looks I couldn't interpret. It was probably about more family secrets, I guessed.

I tried to think of how to get out of this awkwardness when the scent of food hit my nose and I heard some noises just up ahead. Millie smiled at me. "Here's the dining room. And later, we'll give you some help, if you need it."

"Help?"

Abby nodded. "Yes. It'll all make sense later."

I didn't have a chance to say another word because we entered the dining room. I spotted Lori Wolfe sitting at the head of the table. Some food had been laid out already—roasted potatoes, grilled asparagus, and of course, wine—but there was no sign of Beck.

Not wanting to think about which version I'd get—the asshole or the nice guy—I smiled at Lori. "Hello."

She stood and smiled back at me. "I'm sorry I had

to cancel our meeting today but something came up. We can meet first thing tomorrow and go over any questions you have. And if there's anything you need, just holler at me, and I'll make sure you get it."

The woman was the shortest of anyone in the room—probably barely five feet—yet she radiated kindness and warmth, and her presence felt so much bigger. The laugh and smile lines around her eyes and mouth told me she probably shared lots of humor and love with her family.

Then Beck walked in, carrying a large platter, and he placed it on the table. I saw it was piled high with steak.

He met my gaze for a beat and said nothing. Then he finally nodded. "Hello again. Sit down, and I'll fetch the wine."

Beck left before I could blink, and Lori motioned toward the chair on her left. "Hurry, and we'll take the biggest steaks before he comes back."

Abby and Millie had already picked their cuts of meat. Lori took one, and then placed one on my plate, leaving the smallest piece on the platter.

Glancing down at more meat than I could ever eat, I shook my head. "I don't need this much food. I should have the smaller one."

Lori dished out some potatoes for herself. "Nonsense. Once it's on your plate, it's yours. That's the rule in this house."

"The rule?"

Abby jumped in. "When we all lived here as kids, we used to always argue about who got what. My mom and Aunt Lori came up with the first-come, first-served rule, and once it touches your plate, no one else can have it."

Millie smiled. "It's definitely weird the first time, but you get used to it. Besides, the best part is watching as someone realizes they're last."

They all shared glances and chuckled.

I wanted to laugh too. But memories of my childhood took center stage, reminding me of how different things had been for me growing up. We'd eaten in silence, not wanting to anger our mom. Because if we did, then our mother would drink and rant and go on about how we had ruined her life.

About how if we hadn't been born, she would be successful, rich, and the envy of everyone.

About how truly unwanted we were and how she only kept us so that she could collect what little child support she could from our fathers.

There hadn't been laughter or love or any sort of kindness—just fear.

Emotion choked my throat, but I swallowed and did my best to push it back.

Lori placed a hand on my shoulder, and I jumped. She quickly removed it. "Are you okay, Sabrina?"

Taking a deep breath, I forced a smile. "Yes. I'm just tired. I think all this fresh air is going straight to my head."

Lori searched my gaze but merely smiled and said, "The city can be fun at times, but I wouldn't want to live anywhere else in the world but Starry Hills. And I can say that with confidence, since I traveled quite a bit with my late husband."

Abby explained, "He was a badass navy SEAL."

"He was. And you left out the best part—the most handsome one of them all."

Abby scrunched her nose. "Ew, no. That's my uncle you're talking about. He looked a lot like my dad, so just no."

Millie whispered, "I'm unrelated, and I can confirm that Tim Wolfe was sexy in a rugged, square-jawed way."

Abby made retching motions just as Beck came in with two bottles of wine. He raised his eyebrows at his sister. "What the fuck are you doing now? If you're about to barf, go outside."

Standing, Abby took one of the bottles of wine from her brother. "They were going on about Uncle Tim again."

Lori waggled her eyebrows. "My navy stud muffin."

Beck and Abby both shuddered, and I couldn't help but laugh. The Wolfe family was turning out to be a lot different from what I'd expected.

Beck worked on opening the wine bottle and muttered, "I'm definitely going to need this to survive dinner with you all."

Abby gently bumped her shoulder against her brother's. "Oh, it could be a lot worse. Especially after how you acted when I was in high school. Five brothers is far too many."

Before I could stop myself, I asked, "What happened back then?"

She switched bottles with her brother, taking the opened one from Beck. "First, do you like red or white? I could go into specifics, but I'm not working in the tasting room right now, and I'm hungry."

Lori snorted. "It's chardonnay or cabernet sauvignon, both from our vineyards. Cab is arguably the best to go with steak, but we're not going to look down on you if you prefer white wine."

Beck popped the other cork. "I might."

Lori tsked. "Stop it, Beckie."

"Beckie?" My lips twitched.

He grunted. "Don't ever call me that, or I won't talk to you."

I cleared my throat, remembering how I needed to stay on Beck's good side. "Noted. And I'll try the red one although not too much. I don't drink very often."

My job required me to occasionally drink with clients, but that was the only time I did it. I didn't want to risk discovering I was an alcoholic, like both of my parents had been.

He came over, took my wineglass, and poured about two inches, which was perfect. As he set it down, he asked, "Do you need a lesson in how to enjoy it to the fullest?"

"Well, last night, I was told to see, swirl, sniff, sip, and savor. Right?"

He grunted. "Then try it."

Everyone's eyes were on me, and I wanted to impress, but I was also practical. "I need to eat something first, or it'll go straight to my head."

Beck frowned at me, but Millie spoke up. "Did you see the present we left for you, Beck?"

His gaze shifted to the platter, and he cursed. "I'm the tallest one here, the one who does manual labor nearly all fucking day, and you give me the tiny-ass steak?"

Millie smirked. "You know the rules. If you'd been smart, you would've left an extra one in the kitchen for yourself, just in case you were still hungry."

He poured wine for everyone else and sat down. Glaring, he stabbed the steak and put it on his plate. "I was busy getting Zach some food. So much for being a nice sibling. It just bit me in the ass."

Lori waved her fork toward Beck. "Mind your manners at the table."

"Yes, ma'am."

It wasn't sarcastic, just automatic. Beck clearly respected his aunt, no matter how much everyone teased one another.

I finished dishing food onto my plate and waited. Even though Millie and Abby were already eating, I didn't want to start before my hosts.

Lori motioned with her hand. "Go ahead and eat, child. You barely have anything on your plate to begin with, and if you want seconds, you'll have to be quick."

Beck sighed. "There's enough food on the table to feed ten people, plus there's dessert."

Raising her eyebrows, Lori replied, "Maybe. But you're the tall, hardworking guy who needs to eat enough for five people, apparently. So I'm being cautious."

He rolled his eyes, and Lori grinned.

A little unsure of my place, I focused on my food. The steak was tender and quite possibly the best I'd ever tasted. After a few bites, I tried the wine—carefully going through all the steps—and was pleasantly surprised at the lingering taste in my mouth. Not long after, I could feel the alcohol doing its magic.

Abby spoke up. "You definitely don't drink often, do you? Your cheeks are already pink after only a few sips."

"Er, not really. Although it's really good." Clearing my throat, I decided to change the topic. Just because I needed to get to know this family didn't mean I would share about mine. "As much as I'm enjoying dinner, I have a few things I need to ask about tomorrow's schedule."

Beck made a hand motion for me to continue as he sipped his wine.

"I'd like to get a tour of the vineyard, the winery, and the orchard. There isn't a lot of information online about any of those places, and I really need to learn as much as possible firsthand so I can judge where to focus our energy in the future."

Beck muttered, "You like spying on us, don't you?"

Ignoring him, I focused on Lori, the more level-headed one. "Would it be possible to do that?"

Lori stopped frowning at Beck and met my gaze. "Of course. Normally, Zach would handle it—he's the most theatrical of us after Nolan—but he has a broken leg and can't get around." She glanced at her nephew. "So Beck will do it and happily."

I expected him to argue, but after sipping his wine again, he shrugged. "After breakfast would be best. I have some actual work to do in the afternoon."

I bit my tongue at his insinuation that anything to do with me wasn't real work. It seemed like the asshole version of him was back.

Lori shared glances with Abby and then Millie before looking back at Beck. "I already took care of that and hired Max King to help us for the week."

Beck frowned a lot, but I thought his latest one was his deepest yet. "Isn't he barely out of high school? Can he even drive?"

"Of course he can drive. Don't be ridiculous. And Max can cart away the vine trimmings, help with the stables, and all around be an extra hand for a few days to lighten your load."

As Beck and Lori stared at each other, I sensed some kind of unspoken battle was going on. And for a beat, I wondered what it was.

But then I reminded myself that learning about their personal issues wasn't part of my job. So I drank my wine and focused on my food.

Abby's voice garnered my attention. "I haven't told you about what happened during high school yet, Sabrina." She put down her knife and fork and leaned forward. "Do you have any brothers?"

Thankfully, an easy answer. "No."

"Then you're lucky. Because having five older brothers is a pain in the ass. Not only did they try to constantly ditch me when we were little, but all the ones still here when I tried dating in high school did their best to scare all the guys away." She glared at her brother. "They even tried it with my prom date."

Beck shrugged one shoulder. "I'd seen him in town, kissing another girl. I told him to leave you alone. If he didn't, I'd have to visit him again and make sure he listened."

Millie mimicked punching and rolled her eyes.

I blinked. "You were going to beat him up?"

Beck didn't hesitate. "Any man who tries to hurt my sister will pay. My brothers and I can tease her and make her life hell but not any other man. Ever."

I noticed Abby stiffen, a look of panic crossing her face. But it was gone before I could blink. I wondered if her body language had something to do with her earlier statement about being back in Starry Hills from who knew where.

Not your job, Sabrina. Leave it alone.

Abby seemed to recover. "I'm not sixteen any longer, Beck. I'll deal with my own mistakes, thank you very much."

Aunt Lori jumped in. "Listen to her, Beck. If Abby needs our help, she'll ask. We'll just have to trust her to know she's not alone."

Abby shifted in her seat.

Okay, yes, there was definitely something going on. But Abby had Millie, much like I had Taylor, and would probably be okay.

Talk turned to an upcoming wedding that Millie was planning, and I focused on eating my dinner. Soon, I ate my final piece of steak—I always left my favorite part for last—and finished off my wine. I was full, relaxed, and sleepy.

Alcohol loosened my tongue. If I didn't want to blurt out something—like ask Abby what was wrong or why Beck had taken over the winery at such a young age—then I needed to head upstairs.

Pushing my plate back, I stated, "Thanks for dinner. It was delicious."

Lori nodded. "Beck's a fabulous cook. If not for this place, he might've had his own restaurant somewhere."

Beck grunted. "That's a whole lot of stress I don't need." He pointed at me. "And you can't leave the table yet."

I blinked. Did I need to ask to be excused? I thought some families did that, didn't they?

Abby rubbed her hands together. "No, you can't. Dessert is the best part."

I patted my stomach. "I probably shouldn't."

Beck stood. "Just try one bite, and then I'll leave you alone."

He left the table without a word, and I stared after him.

I blurted, "Does anyone ever disobey him?"

As soon as I heard the words, I wanted to crawl into bed and hide. He was their beloved brother and nephew, and it was highly unprofessional of me. The wine had to be the culprit, meaning I'd have to be more careful in the future.

Millie nodded. "Yes. Even though he's the second oldest, Beck has been sort of the father stand-in for a long time and is used to being in charge. You just sort of learn when you can ignore him."

I murmured, "Maybe I should've asked for that family tree after all."

My face heated. I really, really needed to avoid drinking wine around this family.

Grinning, Abby winked. "I'll make one for you tonight."

I was about to say I'd been joking, but Beck charged in with a tray. On it were five small dishes.

He placed one in front of me, and the smell of apples, cinnamon, and warm sugar filled my nose. He explained, "An apple crumble, complete with homemade vanilla ice cream."

Really, who made their own ice cream? Maybe Lori had been right—in another life, Beck would've been a chef or had his own restaurant.

I stared and debated trying it. Ever since I'd overheard my ex talking with his friend about how I'd be a lot prettier if I were thinner, I'd battled with eating what I wanted and trying to lose weight.

My mother's voice filled my head. *No man wants a fat bitch in their bed.*

I stood abruptly and laid down my napkin. "I really can't. But thank you. I'll see you tomorrow morning."

Before I could leave, Beck asked, "What time do you want breakfast?"

"Seven, if that's not too early."

He snorted. "We may make wine, but it's still a farm. I'll be up long before you, city girl."

I merely nodded and fled the room.

After changing into pajamas and writing in my journal, I felt a lot better. My mother's voice was gone, and all I wanted to do was sleep.

I set my alarm, just in case. I was an early riser, but I wasn't about to oversleep and prove Beck right. I had probably upset him again by refusing dessert. Which meant I needed to be a hell of lot more careful going forward. I wouldn't waste the chance at this promotion. So even if it killed me, I needed to be nicer to Beckett Wolfe. My future depended on it.

Chapter Seven

Beckett

I watched Sabrina all but run out of the dining room and fought the urge to go after her.

She'd looked at the crumble like it was ambrosia, then shame had filled her gaze, and she'd fled. I wondered if some douchebag ex had made her feel bad about herself, feeding her bullshit to try to shape her into what he wanted instead of accepting her as she was.

The protective urge to find out who the asshole was, hunt him down, and tell him he needed to appreciate how beautiful Sabrina was rushed through me.

Wait, where the fuck had that come from?

Aunt Lori spoke, bringing me out of my head. "Don't march up there and demand she try it, Beck."

My gaze snapped to my aunt's. "Why the hell would I do that?"

She raised an eyebrow and sipped her wine—her way of saying, "I know what you're thinking, and it's a bad idea"—then motioned for me to sit down.

After passing out the dessert dishes to everyone, I plopped down in my chair and stabbed my ice cream with a spoon. "I won't."

Abby tossed a crumpled-up napkin at me, and I growled as it hit my head. "What the fuck? You're not five years old any longer."

But of course, my sister never backed down when it came to her brothers. "Why were you rude to Sabrina? I heard all your little muttered remarks, and she probably did too."

I grunted. After watching Sabrina eat her grilled cheese and make little moaning sounds earlier, it had taken me twenty minutes to get my dick back under control. I hadn't wanted the same thing to happen at dinner and had been proactive.

Although the more I watched Sabrina and noted her reactions, the more I sensed her background wasn't as happy as mine. And that was saying something, considering I'd lost both my parents by the age of twenty-six. "I was being myself. You know Zach's the charming one. I can't help it if the idiot thought climbing trees in the dark was a good idea."

Millie leaned forward. "I think something

happened, but he won't tell me, no matter how often I text him about it."

Abby replied, "You saw the group text—he was talking about spider aliens and probes. Do you really want him to go into more detail about legs up his ass?"

I snorted. "It wasn't his finest hour, and when I saw him earlier, he actually looked embarrassed for once."

I felt Aunt Lori's eyes on me, but I didn't look at her. Yes, it was cowardly as shit. But she could always see things no one else could, and I didn't need her to keep teasing me about my attraction to Sabrina O'Connor—an attraction that only seemed to get more intense with time.

Fuck. And I had to give her a one-on-one tour tomorrow? That was a bad idea.

An idea popped into my head, and I pinned Abby with a stare. "How about you and Millie give Sabrina the tour tomorrow? I know how you like your girl time so that you can talk shit about your brothers."

Millie rolled her eyes. "The Wolfe brothers aren't the center of the universe. The BFF Circle usually has more important things to discuss."

I knew the BFF Circle all too well. It included my sisters and two other girls from Starry Hills, and they were a force to be reckoned with.

Aunt Lori spoke again. "No, you'll give the tour, Beck. Then bring Sabrina to my office afterward."

"Why me?"

Finishing her wine, Aunt Lori stood. "Because you know more about every inch of this place than any of us. Plus, Sabrina sent me a text earlier and said she wanted to go over some of her basic suggestions with the pair of us."

I eyed my aunt. "Tell me you're not going to start a group-text chat with her."

She took out her phone, smiled deviously, and typed something. My phone vibrated in my pocket, and I sighed. Since I knew Aunt Lori would stand there until I checked, I pulled it out and read it:

Lori: This is Lori, Sabrina. And Beck. If you need anything, just send a message. <double heart emoji>

I glanced up. "That's pretty tame for you, Aunt Lori. And only one emoji. I'm almost impressed."

"Give it time, Beckie. Give it time." She waved. "Good night, girls. Maybe you can come over for dinner tomorrow. If we're lucky, Zach will be in his right mind again and can join us."

"Yeah, although I'll have to carry his ass down the stairs," I grumbled.

Aunt Lori patted my shoulder. "All that hard work you do that requires you to eat half a cow at dinner has prepared you well, then."

My sisters snickered, and I stood, pointing at them. "Since you're so into rules, you know it's your job to do the dishes."

They stood, and Abby replied, "No worries.

Loading a dishwasher isn't hard. And I want to check on Zach afterward."

"Let me do it first. He was bare-ass naked this morning, and I want to spare your eyes."

Abby scrunched her nose. "Maybe I should wait until tomorrow."

Aunt Lori said, "Yes, that's probably the better way to go. It's late, anyway, and I know Millie and you have an event meeting tomorrow morning."

It was still weird to hear about Abby and Millie working together. Until a few months ago, Abby had been a high school teacher in San Jose. She'd come home, moved in with Millie, and had only said the school hadn't been a good fit after all.

Which was bullshit. She'd gushed about it for months before that. Something had happened, but I knew my baby sister. She was as stubborn as her brothers and would only share when she was ready.

Abby went over and hugged Aunt Lori. "See you tomorrow, Aunt Lori. Love you."

She kissed Abby's cheek. "Love you too."

Millie hugged her next and whispered something I couldn't hear.

Aunt Lori chuckled. "We'll see, my dear. Love you."

"Love you too."

Once Aunt Lori left, my sisters picked up some dishes and were about to head into the kitchen when I growled, "Where the fuck are my hugs?"

Abby smirked. "I thought you were too old for that kind of thing."

I hugged her and then ruffled her hair. Abby squealed and pushed me away. "Stop that."

Millie laughed, then hugged me before letting go. "Some things never change."

As we all smiled at one another, my frustrations for the day faded away. At one time, being with any of my family would've done that. But in recent years, it only happened with either the women or Zach.

Not wanting to think of the three brothers I rarely talked to, I waved. "G'night."

My phone vibrated. As I headed up the stairs to check on Zach, I saw my aunt had contributed to the family group text:

Aunt Lori: <wine glass emoji> <steak emoji> <face with hearts around it emoji> Thanks for dinner, Beckie. I expect two hugs tomorrow since you forgot mine tonight.

Zach: Yeah, Beckie. Give her a big smooch too.

Abby: Maybe you should do the same, once you're done fucking the spider alien.

Millie: <laughing emoji>

Zach: Fuck off. I'm injured. Be nice to me.

Abby: <spider emoji> <heart-eyed emoji> <panting emoji>

Zach: <middle finger emoji> x 5

. . .

Shaking my head, I put my phone away. Leave it to technology to make our childhood squabbles and bickering possible, even when we weren't all in the same room.

Reaching Zach's door, I knocked. He grumbled for me to enter.

Covering my eyes, I opened the door. "Is it G-rated in here?"

A pillow bounced off me. "Yes, asshole."

Laughing, I opened my eyes. It was weird to see my brother in bed, being still. He loved to be constantly on the move as much as I did.

I pulled up the chair from his desk and turned it backward to straddle it. "Ready to tell me why the hell you fell out of that tree when you've been climbing them since you were five years old?"

He frowned. Zach had the same dark-brown hair I did but wore it shorter. And his eyes were blue, like our mother's, whereas mine were brown like our father's. "No, and stop asking about it."

"At least you're not talking about spider aliens anymore."

He grimaced. "Yeah, the medication made me really loopy. So I decided to stop taking it and just tough it out. Gives you all less fodder to use against me."

Silence fell, and I debated asking if he felt well enough to take over some of the meetings with Sabrina. But then Zach threw another pillow at me, and I caught it this time.

He said, "Abby sent me a picture of this Sabrina

O'Connor woman. Makes me fucking regret breaking my leg now. Smart and sexy? Damn. She could be my soul mate, and I missed my chance."

The thought of my brother holding Sabrina close, kissing her, and being the one to worship every inch of her skin made me clench my fingers into a fist and growl. "Stay the fuck away from her."

Zach smirked. "So Abby was right." I flipped him off, but it didn't deter him. However, Zach's face sobered, and it made me uneasy. "Just don't screw it up, Beck. All the preliminary shit she sent me was impressive. I really think she can help us save the winery and orchard, not to mention give Wolfe Family Farm and Winery a much-needed second wind."

"Why do you say that?"

We could joke and take the mickey out of each other one second and then be serious the next, as was the Wolfe family way. So it didn't surprise me when Zach replied, "I reached out to a handful of PR and marketing firms. Most had a lot of fancy talk that went over my head or only focused on numbers. Sabrina's pitch was more about using stories to sell our wines."

"Stories?"

"She'll explain it better than I can, but yes. And it just made fucking sense to me. I mean, we all love stories and root for characters and all that shit. She said something about making the customers the hero of the story and that our product could help them achieve things. It just sounds so much more interesting than the other people's responses."

I didn't know much about marketing and had never

claimed to. Our family hadn't done a lot of it, coasting on word of mouth and the festivals we attended. However, the bad harvest had really shown us how precarious that position was.

I muttered, "I hope it works."

"Give her what she needs, and it should—Edwina Jones and Associates are supposed to be miracle workers. But you're going to have to treat her more like an equal and not bark orders at her. And yes, you do that. Our family knows how to deal with it but not outsiders."

He was right, even if I didn't want to admit it.

Although my taking charge was what had saved us all back then, right after our father had died.

Zach threw another pillow at me.

I growled, "Why the fuck do you keep doing that?"

"Because sometimes you need something to hit you and snap you back to reality. You're far too introspective, and it weirds me out."

Feeling childish—in a way only Zach brought out of me—I stood, scooped up the three pillows he'd thrown, and headed toward the door. "Well, I'll take my reminders of reality with me, then. Good night. Hope you sleep well with just one pillow."

He cussed me out, and I smiled.

But once in my room again, I tossed his pillows aside and sighed. Tomorrow I'd make more of an effort to help Sabrina, actually ask more about her suggestions and ideas, and do what was the hardest thing in the world for me—lean on others and ask for help.

Chapter Eight

Sabrina

I woke up before my alarm—*win*—and spent a ridiculous amount of time doing my hair and makeup, which was silly, really. It wasn't as if someone like Beckett Wolfe would be interested in me beyond maybe a one-night hookup.

If that.

But for some reason, I wanted to look my best. Yes, I'd be with a hot guy all morning, but also, sometimes making sure every hair was in place and having my makeup on point was like wearing a type of armor. With them, I felt more badass, in charge of my life, and ready to tackle the unknown.

I'd just finished my hair when my phone vibrated with a message.

. . .

Taylor: Go get 'em! You're going to kick ass today. <heart emoji>
Taylor: PS—I get to knead some big buns this afternoon.

I burst out laughing. She was talking about the player on the team everyone dreamed of being able to play grab-ass with.

Me: Such a hard life you lead.
Taylor: I know, but I'll survive. You still need to send me a picture of your country boy hottie.
Me: Gotta go. Enjoy!
Taylor: Hm, later I'll repeat what I think…but work calls. Enjoy the <wolf emoji> <panting emoji>

Putting my phone away, I smiled. Before meeting Taylor, I'd thought I would never have someone to trust or laugh with or even break down with. But she'd refused to give up on me in college and had been the only one to get through my walls even a little.

I doubted I'd ever find a guy I could trust to that degree, but I had a best friend, and that was enough.

Glancing at the time, I cursed and grabbed my purse. Even if it was a bit fancy for a tour, it's all I had. If Beck made fun of it, so be it. I could grin and bear it, as long as I kept my goal in sight.

With my hand on the doorknob, I closed my eyes.

Today is going to be amazing, I'm going to wow the clients, and negative thoughts won't hold me back.

I waited for the inevitable, but my mother's voice remained silent. Probably because of my good mood, which always seemed to make it easier to lock away the past.

Not wanting to jinx myself, I opened my eyes and left my room. As I neared the dining area, music drifted from the kitchen—some kind of classic rock. And a deep voice started singing.

I inched toward the connecting door and peeked inside.

Beck was at the stove, flipping something in a pan so that it went into the air before landing again, and continued singing his heart out.

My lips curved upward as he danced a little too. I couldn't stop staring.

And for a moment, I wondered what it would be like to have a guy make breakfast for me, both of us singing in the kitchen, maybe even attempting to dance —attempt because I really couldn't—and feeling like I actually deserved it.

Then Beck turned, caught me staring, and cut off singing midsentence. His usual frown returned. "How long have you been standing there?"

Squaring my shoulders as if to do battle, I walked into the kitchen. "Not long. I wasn't sure if I should wait in the dining room or not."

He looked like he didn't believe my BS but merely shrugged. "We can eat in here. Aunt Lori isn't a big breakfast person, and my sisters won't be here until dinner." He gestured toward the island. "Sit."

His tone made it more of a request than an order, and it threw me off a bit. However, I sat and asked, "Where will we go today?"

"I thought you wanted the full tour."

"I do, but I also know you're busy."

He turned around, a teapot in one hand and a little bowl filled with tea bags in the other. He placed them in front of me, and I blinked. There were half a dozen types, and some were even caffeine free—he'd remembered my caffeine sensitivity. "You said you didn't have any tea."

"We didn't. I got some this morning."

I met his gaze. "It's barely seven in the morning."

The corner of his mouth ticked up. "I have my ways. And if I told you, I'd have to kill you."

He said it so deadpan that I couldn't help but laugh. "What? Are you part of some kind of underground winery mafia? Smuggler ring? Black market?"

He grinned, and my heart skipped a beat. Grumpy Beckett Wolfe was handsome, but a smiling version was beyond gorgeous, hot, and like a dream turned real. He even made the crinkles at the corners of his eyes look sexy.

Then the image of his head between my legs, those same eyes looking up at me as he devoured my pussy, made heat rush between my thighs.

Clearing my throat, I focused on the tea selection. "Thank you."

"No problem. But that's only the start. I made a little of everything for breakfast, since I didn't know what you wanted to eat. You'll need your energy if you're going to traipse across the property in your fancy city shoes. Just try not to break a leg. I already have one person to lug down the stairs tonight for dinner, and I don't need another."

And just like that, he was back to being a bit of a dick. I put a tea bag in the cup he'd given me, poured hot water, and replied, "For your information, I have tennis shoes on today. Well, more specifically, all-terrain shoes."

He grunted, clearly unimpressed, turned, and placed an enormous plate of food in front of me. Like, enough to feed three people.

It was on the tip of my tongue to say he needed to stop wasting food. But for all I knew, he fed leftovers to some farm animal or another.

I didn't know much about that part of his business, either, beyond the mention of horses in a review. Their website was sadly lacking in details beyond technical wine terms. I'd have to ask about that and added it to my mental list.

But then I noticed a mini cinnamon roll, my favorite. Even though I should eat something more substantial like eggs first, it smelled way too good. Lifting it to my nose, I sniffed, and the sugar-and-cinnamon smell was like pure heaven.

Beck grunted. "Stop sniffing, and just fucking eat it."

I eyed him and noticed a tick in his jaw. "Do you have rules for how we eat too?"

"No, but I'm considering them."

Tempted to stick my tongue out at him, I instead popped the cinnamon roll into my mouth and savored it. Much like the steak, it was the best I'd ever eaten.

Beck had his arms crossed over his chest. "Well?"

Was he serious? He expected me to review each thing? "It's good, of course."

"There's no of course about it. I tried a new recipe this morning, one I've been thinking about for weeks."

I blinked. "A new one? As in you made it up?"

"For the most part, yes. That comes easily to me." Before I could ask anything else, he gestured toward my food. "Keep eating."

I picked at my food and drank my tea as ideas bounced around inside my head. One, I couldn't hold back any longer. "Have you ever considered opening a restaurant here? Visitors could take the tour, do some tasting, and then enjoy wine with your amazing food."

He shook his head. "I don't have the time to run a restaurant."

"Can't you hire someone to do some of the outside work? In my research, I learned that many of the other winery owners don't work outside every day, like you seem to do."

"I'm not like the other fucking owners. I like being outside. I *need* to oversee everything. Just accept that. End of story."

His tone was final, and I didn't push.

Although as I chewed, I wondered if maybe he was

a control freak. To a degree, I understood that. I always needed to have a set amount of money in my savings, a balanced budget, and a certain amount of stocked food to ensure I always had something to eat.

Yes, it was extreme. I made decent money, and if I got my promotion, I would be even more secure. However, the little girl who'd worried about losing her home and getting dinner every night would always be there.

Which made me think there had to be some reason why Beck felt obligated to oversee jobs that he could easily delegate to the right people. The only question was whether it mattered to my end goal or not.

When I couldn't eat another bite, I finished my tea and took my dishes to the sink.

Beck jumped up and took them from me. "What the hell are you doing?"

Before I could stop myself—Beck always seemed to make me more reckless than usual—I blurted, "For a country boy, you're definitely not a morning person."

His gaze locked with mine. "I am a fucking morning person. But you're the guest, and guests don't do dishes."

"Another rule?"

"No, it's what we call good manners out here."

My cheeks burned. "People have manners in the city."

He raised his eyebrows. "The last time I visited, they didn't."

This man knew how to get under my skin in a way

no one else did. I wasn't a woman who lost her temper or verbally sparred with near strangers.

Yet with Beck, I couldn't hold back, no matter how unprofessional it might be. I poked his chest, ignoring the hard muscles under his shirt. "So by your logic, if one country boy fucks sheep, they all do? Which means you do too?"

Crap. I shouldn't have said that.

But Beck lightly grabbed my wrist, his warm touch nearly making me gasp. His thumb brushed once against my skin, making my nipples harden, before he growled, "I don't need sheep, sweetheart, when women are lining up to ride my dick."

I gasped and pulled back. He released me, and I narrowed my eyes. "There are things I want to say but won't. I'm going to my room."

I turned and grabbed my purse, and Beck asked, "What about the tour?"

Closing my eyes, I took a deep breath. I really needed to see the land, but it would mean spending more time with *him.*

Think of your promotion, think of your promotion, think of your promotion.

I wasn't off to a good start with Beckett Wolfe. But I needed to get my crap together and try to focus on my job. To do that, there had to be some sort of truce.

Yes, an agreement where we only talked about business. Maybe then I could finally get my temper and outbursts under control. Especially since I couldn't blame wine for my behavior this morning.

Even if Beck was being the bigger dick, I pasted a

smile on my face and turned toward him. "If we're to do the tour, then we need to establish some rules of our own."

He raised an eyebrow. "Like maybe not calling me a sheep fucker?"

I hid a wince. "Yes. And that we use civil tones and language with each other."

He eyed me, but unlike earlier when his gaze had been full of fire and something I didn't recognize, it was cool, calm, and collected. After a few beats, he nodded. "Truce, although I can't guarantee I'll keep my language clean. I'm used to saying what I want, and that won't change in a few days."

"Swearing doesn't bother me. I've…" I cleared my throat, realizing what I almost revealed, and steered the conversation back on track. "Curse all you want. But a truce sounds perfect."

I put out my hand to shake, and unlike with our first meeting, he wrapped his fingers around mine instantly. Having his warm, rough palm against mine made me wonder what it would feel like to have those hands over my breasts, ass, and thighs.

Quickly releasing his hand, I hitched my purse up higher on my shoulder. "I'll wait in my room until you're ready. Text me, and I'll meet you."

He nodded, and I instantly fled the kitchen, not exactly at a run but pretty dang close. I needed all the time I could get to calm my mind and banish any and all thoughts about Beck's hands or his touches.

We had a new start—officially—and I planned to take full advantage of it, no matter what.

Chapter Nine

Beckett

Aunt Lori: I heard shouting from the kitchen. What did you do now? <angry face emoji>
Me: How do you know it's my fault?
Aunt Lori: I just do.
Me: She tried to do the dishes.
Aunt Lori: So you yelled at her? <eye roll emoji>
Me: She's the guest.
Aunt Lori: And you yelled at her. I raised you better than that.
Me: I'm your nephew. You're supposed to be on my side.
Aunt Lori: It's because you are my nephew that I can call you out on your shit. Apologize and make nice. <man and woman holding hands emoji>

Me: Can you stop with the fucking emojis?
Aunt Lori: <eggplant emoji> <knife emoji> <happy demon emoji>
Me: Did you really just threaten to cut off my dick and be happy about it?
Aunt Lori: <angel emoji>

I tossed my phone aside and then finished loading the dishwasher and cleaning up the kitchen.

Yes, now that Sabrina was gone, I knew I'd been an asshole. I shouldn't have yelled at her or lied about women lining up to ride my cock. But something about the woman just got under my skin.

I mean, as soon as I'd woken up, all I could think about was making her breakfast and taking her on the best goddamn tour of her life. Probably to make up for all the naked dreams I had of her or something.

At first, I even thought I could be nice to her. But when I shared how I needed to oversee everything, I didn't like how she'd looked at me. It was almost as if she saw the part of me I kept hidden from most people—where I needed to do anything possible to help fulfill my father's dying wishes.

To give some of the responsibilities to anyone else just felt like…failure. So I'd retreated into being an asshole. The more distance I could put between us, the better. I definitely didn't want any more knowing looks. Fuck, next she'd pry out my secrets and be sympathetic.

But I'd taken it too far, and even if we'd formed a

truce, I would need to grovel a little. Not in some over-the-top romantic way, but I could help make her life easier while she was with us.

That meant calling in a favor. I texted my best friend, Kyle Evans, with a few requests. He helped run his family's dairy farm, but one of his sisters worked in a local shop, one that had what I needed.

After getting a thumbs-up, I took a deep breath and sent a message to Sabrina to meet me out front.

I exited the kitchen, grabbed my coat from my office, and arrived in the main lobby, where Sabrina waited, facing the front windows. Since I was coming from behind and she couldn't see me yet, I took a second to notice she was indeed wearing the tennis shoes. Not only that, but I could have sworn her hair was wound even tighter in a twisty thing at the back of her head than before.

I wondered what it looked like down, flowing around her shoulders.

Stop it. That kind of thinking is what got you into trouble in the first place.

Not wanting to remember how soft her wrist had been under my fingers, I slung on my coat and strode toward her. "Sorry to keep you waiting."

She turned, her expression unreadable.

Which I really fucking hated.

She's not yours, asshole. Stop thinking her eyes should light up when she sees you.

Hell, where was that romantic shit coming from?

She hitched her purse over her shoulder, even though she didn't need to. She'd done that earlier, and I wondered if it was a nervous or irritated tick. The thought of her being nervous around me made me hate myself.

I stepped around her and opened the door. "Ready to begin your tour, madam?"

She shook her head. "Madam makes me sound old."

Sabrina walked past me, her vanilla-and-woman scent making me want to lean down and nuzzle her neck.

Telling my dick to behave, I caught up to her and kept a respectable distance between us. "You look younger than my sister, which means I must be ancient."

Smiling, she said, "I'm twenty-seven. And since Abby sent me a family tree earlier, I know she's younger than me."

I sighed. "Of course she did. What did she say about me?"

She shrugged. "That you're thirty-four, overprotective, a workaholic, and a great cook."

I grunted, not knowing how to respond to that. Abby could've said much worse but hadn't. And I couldn't argue with her points.

Although realizing I was seven years older than Sabrina gave me another reason to stay away from her—I was probably an old man to her.

The ground crunched under our feet, and I noticed Sabrina rubbing her hands together. I took out a pair of gloves and handed them to her. "They're old and ratty—I use them for work—but they're better than nothing."

I nearly teased her about not getting her soft city hands chapped but bit my tongue. We'd made a truce, and I'd stick to it.

She took them. "Thank you."

Our gazes locked, and I noticed the flecks of gold among the green of her eyes—almost like a mixture of gold and emeralds.

Clearing her throat, she quickly looked away and put on the gloves. Her fingers drowned in them, and I pressed my lips together to keep from smiling.

She chuckled and waved her hands, making the fingertips of the gloves flop up and down. "Go ahead and laugh." She raised one finger and made it flop as she made a funny voice. "These are manly gloves for manly hands."

Laughing, I shook my head. "Are you going to draw eyes and a mouth on it next?"

Sabrina glanced at her hand. "As a child, I used to make dolls out of old socks." I studied her, noticing how she tensed. She quickly blurted, "Never mind. Sorry. I shouldn't mention personal stuff."

She picked up her pace, but I easily matched it. "You're getting to know my family quite well. Maybe sharing a bit of yourself will even the playing field."

"But it's my job to get to know you, your business, and your products."

I shrugged. "Maybe. I don't know how it works in the city, but out here, we like to get to know who we're working with. Loyalty is important to my family, but that requires some trust. And to trust you, I need to know you."

Part of that was bullshit, and I knew it. Talking about how she made dolls had nothing to do with forging a business relationship, let alone building trust about her job.

Yet I wanted to know. I sensed the story would reveal a little more of her true self. For the first time in my life, I actually wanted to know more about a woman and what made her who she was.

Sabrina sighed and put her hands inside her coat pockets. "I made dolls as a child because it was fun, and it was the only way to get one. Well, unless the thrift store had some in stock. But even then, we rarely got one, even for Christmas. So I started making my own." Her look turned bittersweet. "At one point, I made a whole family—a mom, a dad, and two sisters. The socks were the heads and the bodies, and I made clothes from the junk-mail sheets and hair from any string or yarn I could find. They got to go to Disneyland every weekend and to the beach in the summer and even visited the North Pole at Christmas."

She fell silent, took out her hand, and made the fingers flop again. "They were my favorite toys ever. As sad as it sounds, they were my friends."

Her voice was distant, almost as if talking about it was too difficult. Had she not had any friends growing up? I found that hard to believe, given how easily she'd fit in with my sisters and aunt.

Yet her eyes looked sad. Incredibly sad.

Not to mention lonely.

More than anything, Sabrina looked like she could use a hug.

Not your woman. I placed my hands in my coat pockets, knowing it was inappropriate to offer one. I should drop it, start the tour, and see if I could get her to smile again.

But I couldn't seem to let it drop. "What happened to them?"

She jerked as if she'd been lost in her memories. "My mother." Shaking her head as if to clear her head, she added, "But that's not important." She forced a smile onto her face and asked, "So, when does the tour start?"

Since it truly wasn't any of my fucking business to ask her to bare her soul, I nodded. *Time to focus on work and only work.* I'd already grown too comfortable and curious about Sabrina O'Connor. I couldn't allow myself to go further.

She had a job to do, and we needed her services. That was the extent of our relationship with each other. It had to be.

Clearing my throat, I guided her down the first row of vines we reached. Maybe if I showed her the grapevines and the wine-production areas, she'd forget about the orchard.

I hadn't set foot inside that place for sixteen years, and if I could avoid it for one more day, I would.

Chapter Ten

Sabrina

I didn't know why I'd told Beck about my pretend doll family. Not even Taylor knew about them or how I'd dreamed that I was part of the made-up, loving family who always laughed together.

One where the sisters stuck together, and the parents told them they loved their girls every day.

Where the mom didn't constantly tell her kids they were worthless and ugly and were lucky she hadn't tossed them onto the side of the road when they'd been babies.

At least I hadn't revealed how I'd broken down when my mom finally discovered them. Or how she threatened to destroy my dolls if I didn't do what she wanted. Which, of course, she carried out that threat later purely from spite, throwing my little pretend family away because she said it made me look like white trash.

And I'd been told if I made any more, I would have to stay out on the apartment porch all night without a blanket to learn my lesson. Given how she had made me stand outside in the cold for an hour with no coat or sweatshirt in winter, I'd known she wasn't joking.

I shivered at the memories, overly aware of Beck at my side.

So I did what I'd done as a child—put on a fake happy face and pretend my life had been just peachy. "So, when does the tour start?"

His gaze pierced mine, and for a second, I thought he could read my mind.

But then he gestured toward the first row of vines and thankfully didn't ask me any more personal questions. Instead, he reverently touched the plants as we walked and said, "These grapes will make the chardonnay. They're an early grape, meaning they get harvested first. The exact time frame changes every year, but it's either late August or early September."

Right now, they all looked dead to me. But even though I wasn't a whiz with plants, I knew many fell dormant in the winter. "How long has your family been growing grapes?"

He dropped his hand and gazed over the rows upon rows of posts and wires the grapes grew along. "Decades. Originally, my great-grandfather grew apples and raised cattle. But as things shifted and wine started being made in Napa, his son convinced him to try growing grapes and making wine." He lightly brushed a branch with his forefinger. "This was the first area they planted, in fact. By all accounts, it wasn't easy in the beginning, and they struggled. But since stubbornness runs in the family, they made it work."

I drawled, "I hadn't noticed about the stubbornness."

He grinned at me, and I laughed before Beck replied, "It has its uses. At any rate, as my grandfather became more skilled and got better at making amazing wine, he planted more and more grapes, even adding the variety needed to make the cabernet. My father was the one to really push for attracting more buyers and attending more festivals for exposure. He had a knack for selling our wine to anyone and everyone, even those who didn't usually drink it."

Beck stared into the distance, his smile turning sad. According to Abby's family tree, their dad had died sixteen years ago. The four youngest—Nolan, Zane, Zach, and Abby—had still been children.

And while I'd never known my father and didn't have feelings one way or the other about him, I already knew the Wolfe family was close. The death of Beck's father had probably devastated them.

I itched to reach out and take Beck's hand but instead balled my hands into fists inside my coat pockets. *Remember, this is business and only business. Getting your promotion is all that matters.*

Though that didn't sound as exciting as it had a few days ago.

Clearing my throat, I decided to change the subject.

"Maybe you could show me where the wine is made and packaged."

Nodding, Beck motioned toward the way we'd come. "It's a bit of a walk. I can get the truck, if you want."

I didn't usually go on long walks for fun, preferring to stay home and read. But something about the vineyard was magical. Maybe it was all the rolling hills in the distance, the way perspective made the rows look like some sort of artwork, or just the peaceful quiet, but I didn't want to leave this place yet. "No, let's walk."

He nodded and guided me toward a pathway. We walked in silence, but it oddly didn't feel strained. I sensed we both had a lot on our minds after our earlier conversation.

Although I refused to go back down memory lane. No, instead, I memorized everything around me, knowing it would become a sort of happy place for me if I needed it.

Because I had to remember that once the contract was signed, I might never be back.

Beck had been giving me the grand tour—showing me the giant metal containers where they made the wine before barreling it and storing them in a cellar—and we entered the bottling area.

We were approaching one of the workers who oversaw packing the bottles into boxes when a loud crash reverberated throughout the building, making everyone jump.

Beck shouted, "Shut it all off!" and raced toward the sound.

I wasn't sure what to do except follow him. Beck was faster, though, and rounded a corner before I reached it. When I did the same, I stopped in my tracks, stunned by the sight in front of me—smashed wine bottles littered the ground, the red wine a large pool that almost looked like blood.

A forklift had driven into stacked boxes and somehow overturned. Beck stood talking to a man in work clothes near the machine, gesticulating wildly. Beck didn't look angry, just annoyed and a little worried.

Eventually, he returned to me and stated, "There was an accident. I need to help with the cleanup and investigation. Can you get back to the house by yourself? Or if not, I can call my aunt to come get you."

"No, no, I can return on my own. Is there anything I can do to help?"

"No. And until I know what's going on, I need you out of here and safe at the house."

Lowering my voice, I asked, "Why are you worried about my safety?"

He hesitated before answering, "George doesn't know how the forklift crashed into the wine boxes. The keys should've been in the office, and no one was scheduled to work in this area until tonight."

Frowning, I replied, "That's weird."

"I don't know what the fuck it is. Sorry to cut the tour short and to probably miss the meeting with you and Aunt Lori, but you should still talk with my aunt."

I almost reached out to touch his arm to comfort him but resisted. "Okay. But I'll see you later today?"

He nodded. "I'll send a text."

With that, he left and went back to talking with George.

I exited the building and started the winding walk back to the main house. As I did, the hairs on the back of my neck stood up. Glancing around, I didn't see anyone beyond the three people pruning the vines, whom I'd been introduced to earlier.

Yet the feeling that I was being watched didn't go away until I was nearly to the house.

I was only a few feet from warmth and safety when my phone vibrated repeatedly, meaning it was a call and not an alert. After taking it out, I saw my boss's name on the screen.

The boss who hated talking on the phone. The one I'd sent text updates to the night before.

Frowning, I clicked Receive. "Hello, Edwina."

"Do you know what I discovered just a few minutes ago?"

Since my boss always jumped to the point, it didn't faze me. Although her tone sounded a little harsher than normal, which made me brace myself a little. "No. What did you hear?"

"That the client stormed out after your first meeting because you'd pissed him off."

The blood drained from my face. Had Beck called

my boss? After dinner and the tour, I thought we'd sort of started over. Unless he'd reported me yesterday?

This wasn't good. "Yes, but—"

"No buts. I should order you back to the city and hand over the job to Justin. Only because you've done some stellar work in the past am I giving you one last chance. However, I assure you that if you screw up again, you'll return to San Francisco. This client is an important step in my grand plans, and we need that contract."

Edwina was always ambitious, although she was more obsessed than usual—probably because her ex-husband's firm had secured Napa Valley.

And it was well-known in the city that no one should get between the two of them if at all possible. "Yes. I know, Edwina. And I plan to do whatever it takes to land it. I promise. I spoke to Mr. Beckett Wolfe yesterday and ironed everything out." I hoped. "They've never worked with any sort of advertising or marketing firm, and I think it was just overwhelming at first."

Edwina sniffed. "Well, see that they stay happy. If they ask you to kiss their shoes, do it, Sabrina. I want this foothold in Sonoma."

Then the line went dead. Sighing, I hung up and placed my phone back in my purse.

How the heck had she found out about the meeting and blowup with Beck so quickly? Did she have spies here?

Part of me was angry to think I was being watched. Yet I'd learned long ago that Edwina Jones did whatever it took to ensure she got what she wanted. Since I couldn't change her tactics, it just meant I'd have to be even more careful going forward. Anything and everything I did with the Wolfe family had to be related to securing the contract. No more sharing personal information or noticing how sexy Beck looked. No, work and only work was what mattered. There was no way in hell I'd let Justin get the promotion instead of me.

Since I had a little time before meeting with Lori to go over my initial suggestions, I headed back to my room. I spent the time reviewing all my documents and ideas and came up with a few more just in case.

I'd been reckless, letting myself relax and waste time doing things that wouldn't help either me or Wolfe Family Farm and Winery.

No longer.

I wouldn't let myself, Edwina, or our potential clients down, no matter what.

Chapter Eleven

Beckett

Aunt Lori: Sabrina told me what happened. Should I walk over to help you?
Me: No. I'm nearly done.
Aunt Lori: Was it an accident?
Me: I don't know.
Aunt Lori: You don't have enemies I don't know about, do you?
Me: No, there's no rivalry between me and some other winery. I rarely leave Starry Hills, and no one from town would do this, I don't think. Not even the newcomers.
Aunt Lori: Just be careful, Beckie. My Spidey senses are tingling. And you know I'm never wrong.
Me: Since when?

Aunt Lori: Since always.
Me: …
Aunt Lori: This is when you say, "Of course, Aunt Lori."
Me: Of course, Aunt Lori.

It had taken me hours to interview everyone inside the bottling facility and any workers in the surrounding area, but no one seemed to know what the hell had happened.

Only three of the staff were qualified to drive the forklift, and none of them had been scheduled until the evening. Not to mention the three of them were long-time, loyal employees I'd known most of my life. The keys had also been in the office, just like George said.

So who the fuck had driven the forklift and how? While we did have a few security cameras, I hadn't found anything useful in the footage beyond the fact we had a big fucking blind spot. That made me think the person involved had been to the bottling place before.

I clenched my fingers into fists as I walked back toward the house. I hated that someone could've hurt my workers or my family. Hell, what if I'd been showing Sabrina the stock and she'd been killed? The thought made my stomach churn.

No. I would find the culprit and hunt down the bastard. Even if I had to call in every favor from my friends and family, I wouldn't let anyone get hurt on my watch, not if I could help it.

The walk back to the house helped clear my head a little, allowing me to slowly control my anger. I'd have to explain things to my aunt—maybe even Zach, if he was clear-headed—and figure out what to do. Putting in more security cameras would be a stretch financially, especially with the fee we'd have to pay for Sabrina and her company after the contract was signed.

But I couldn't risk the lives of the people who worked for me and my family either. While I knew I could always ask my brother Nolan for a loan—he'd offered one in the past—I really didn't want to. I wanted Wolfe Family Farms and Winery to be self-sufficient, like when my father had run it. That meant I had to think of other ways to find the cash.

Sighing, I finally approached the front steps of the main house and smiled at our part-time delivery driver, Minnie. But when all she did was nod, I knew something was wrong. Minnie always asked after my family, and I did the same.

I stopped in front of her. "Hey, Minnie. Tell me what's up. Is it to do with the truck?"

She shook her head, her nearly shoulder-length black hair bouncing around her face. "No, no, the truck's fine. It's just that my little boy is sick, my husband is on the road, and I'm struggling to find someone to watch him for my entire shift."

Minnie's husband was a long-haul trucker and was away a lot. I'd always been flexible with her schedule, knowing that sometimes families' lives didn't fit into nine-to-five work weeks. "How many deliveries do you have today?"

"Just four—all in Starry Hills, near Main Street."

"Then go home and watch Teddy. I'll do the deliveries myself."

Minnie searched my eyes. "Are you sure, Beck? I met the PR lady, and I know you're busy."

I smiled wryly. "My aunt hired Max King to help with the pruning and other chores for a few days, so I have some time. Go home. Text me if he's still sick for your next shift."

Relief flooded her face. "Thanks, Beck. I'll get Teddy to make you a card when he feels better."

I'd learned long ago not to say that was unnecessary. The little boy loved drawing, and it would probably cheer him up. "I look forward to it. Now, go home. That's an order."

She gave a mock salute and dashed inside to grab her stuff from her locker.

I would've offered to do the deliveries even without Max's help. But it was like a fucking godsend today. After my upcoming meeting—Sabrina had moved it back at Aunt Lori's insistence—I could get some time away, be alone, and not have to worry about slipping up with Sabrina and being too personal.

Glancing at my phone, I noticed I had an hour before the meeting with Aunt Lori and the woman in question. So I dashed to my room, showered, and looked over what she'd sent to me via email. Because the less time I had to be with her in a small room, the easier it would be to keep my distance and not share things that didn't have anything to do with her job.

I'd tried my best to understand the materials Sabrina had sent. But understanding how a potential customer's mind worked wasn't my specialty. Unlike my dad, I didn't have the natural ability to sell things. That was probably why the winery wasn't doing as well as when my father had been in charge.

A small voice inside my head said, *Zach is good at it.*

Yes, my brother was good with people. But sometimes, he blurted the wrong thing and made things awkward. I'd even given Zach a trial period years ago, and it hadn't ended well.

Although a small part of me knew my brother was older, more mature, and had a hell of a lot more practice charming people at the local restaurants, bars, and hotels. It was why I'd given in to Zach's request to try this PR and marketing firm.

Maybe I should try giving my brother more responsibilities again.

But the thought of doing so and everything falling apart made me clench my jaw. No, I'd made the promise to Dad, and I would keep it. Maybe in a few more years, I could give Zach more to do. However, until we turned things around and could safeguard against another bad harvest, I needed to steer the ship.

Since it was time for my meeting, I picked up my phone and laptop. After walking down the hall, I turned the corner and knocked on the door to my aunt's office before entering.

Aunt Lori sat at her desk, with Sabrina on her right.

She'd changed into a black suit of some sort, and her hair looked even more tightly pulled back.

She barely spared me a glance before looking back at her computer.

That was the way it should be, I knew that. And yet part of me wanted her to ask me about what I'd found out and get her opinion.

Which was fucking ridiculous.

I sat in the chair across from my aunt. "Let's make this quick. Minnie's son is sick, and I need to take over her deliveries."

Aunt Lori's gaze turned concerned. "Is it anything serious?"

Shaking my head, I propped one ankle on my opposite thigh. "I don't think so. But Hal's away, so I thought it best she go home."

My aunt nodded. "Good lad. And you doing the deliveries is a stroke of good luck, actually. I was just telling Sabrina that she should go to Starry Hills and get to know the town a little. Since it's our community, full of our friends and business partners, I thought it might give her a bigger picture of what we're doing here."

I glanced at Sabrina, who still stared at her computer screen. "Did my aunt elaborate on the 'bigger picture?'"

Sabrina finally looked at me, her expression neutral. "Yes, about how the businesses have been working together to host bigger events—weddings, wine-and-cheese tastings, and special wine-pairing events with the local restaurants. Seeing these partners will help me better refine my ideas."

"But I thought our wine and winery were the focus."

"They are. But part of Starry Wolfe wine's story is tied to the community and the people of Starry Hills."

I heard the words, but her tone was distant. Almost as if dinner last night and the tour this morning had never happened.

While I should be fucking ecstatic at the turnaround—it would make my life easier—all I wanted to do was walk over to Sabrina, let down her too tightly wound hair, and ask for the warm, teasing woman to come back.

But I couldn't do that. Not only did I have no fucking right, but I also had no time for her or any woman.

I leaned back in my chair and looked at my aunt. "Maybe you could take Sabrina to town. I already informed our customers with deliveries today about the delay, and I won't push it back again to play babysitter."

The remark should've gotten a rise out of Sabrina, but she just continued typing on her computer, as if she hadn't heard the comment.

The woman who'd called me a sheep fucker would've reacted. Something must've happened. But what?

Not any of your fucking business, Beck.

Aunt Lori replied, "It's only four deliveries. Since

they're all close to one another, it should only take you an hour. Plus, Abby and Millie will be at Starry Eyes Bakery, visiting with Amber and Katie, so Sabrina can hang out with them until you're done." She glanced at Sabrina. "If you need to work, there's Wi-Fi at the bakery. And you really need to try Ellen King's blueberry scones—she's the owner—because they're to die for."

Sabrina smiled at my aunt. And for some reason, that made me clench my jaw.

She replied, "I didn't eat lunch, so it'd be great to try some local fare. Maybe I can learn what usually gets served at the wine-and-cheese tastings while I'm there too."

Before I could stop myself, I growled, "Why the fuck didn't you eat lunch?"

Shrugging, Sabrina still didn't look at me. "I had work to do."

This woman and her work. Hell, I admired her dedication, but I didn't like her not looking after herself.

Although why the fuck I should get angry about it, I had no clue.

Aunt Lori spoke, and I noticed a glint in her eyes. One that always spelled trouble. "You two should grab some dinner in Starry Hills, while you're there. I have a craving for frozen pizza, wine, and catching up with my soaps."

I made a face. "Frozen pizza is fucking awful and tastes like cardboard."

Aunt Lori shrugged. "I like it. So you two enjoy a night out on the town. Admittedly, it's not much compared to San Francisco, and things close early in the low tourist season, but it'll be good for Beck to get out for a change."

I glared at my aunt, and she smirked. She was fucking matchmaking. I knew it in my gut.

But she also knew I was a stubborn ass and could thwart her ploys. "I'll invite Kyle to join us." I moved my gaze to Sabrina. "He runs the Starry Evans Dairy Farm with his dad, and he can tell you more than you'd ever want to know about cheese."

I expected my aunt to frown, but she merely continued smirking.

What the fuck was she up to now?

Sabrina nodded. "The more I can get done in town today, the better. After all, I only have a week here."

Not wanting to think of Sabrina leaving and never coming back, I decided it was time to get this conversation back on topic. "I'll text Kyle after we're done here. Since it's a weeknight, he should be free. Now, I need to leave in a little over an hour, so let's get this meeting started already."

Not missing a beat, Sabrina said, "Well, most of my suggestions will probably need to be tweaked now that I have all these other elements to incorporate. However, the core focus will remain the same—family, tradition, history, and quality. These four things seem to be what matters most around here." When I bobbed my head, Sabrina continued. "I think the bigger dream we need to pitch is that with your wine—and these events—customers can become part of a community, a group, and have a place to belong. Even if it's only for a night or two during a visit or maybe for a wedding or even for a regular monthly subscription box, each time they sip Starry Wolfe wine, they feel a part of something. Comfort, family, friends, belonging—those are the vibes I get here, at least as an outsider, and I bet others would love to experience that too. Here's how we can do that with subscription boxes, to start."

And as Sabrina went into detail, outlining how to make customers feel special with simple things like collector pins, pictures, or other physical tokens showing they belonged to a group, I tried to focus on all the minutiae.

However, my mind kept focusing on her words about how she felt—comfort, family, friends, and belonging.

So she had liked her time at the winery. Now all I wanted to know was why the hell she was distant like when we'd first met. Maybe I'd have to provoke her again later and see if that cracked the cool facade.

No, that wasn't the smartest idea. Yet the thought of dealing with cold, rational Sabrina for the rest of the week didn't sit right with me.

She'd said it herself—she felt like she belonged and was part of the community. So I needed her to feel that way again.

For business reasons and research, of course. Not because I looked forward to poking the bear and seeing her fire again.

Most assuredly not.

Chapter Twelve

Sabrina

Taylor: While you're in town, you should find the fire station and look for a firefighter. <flame emoji>
Me: Um, no.
Taylor: Hm, what about a hot sheriff? <police car light>
Me: …
Taylor: I know! Maybe there's some burly ex-Marine wandering the streets, looking for the woman to heal his battered heart.
Me: This isn't going to turn into one of your mini romance stories again, is it?
Taylor: I mean, he could have a little boy at home, yearning for a mother. Oh, and a dog who only has three legs but will guard his family to the death. And…

Me: You're just going to keep going, aren't you?
Taylor: Once the guy learns about your love of reading, he gets your favorite book tattooed on his hip, where only he can see it.
Me: I'm going now.
Taylor: And then…

During the entire drive to Starry Hills, I stared out the window of the delivery truck and avoided looking at Beck.

Even though I needed to remain focused after my warning from Edwina, it had been pure torture not asking what he'd found out about the accident, who he thought might've done it, and so many other questions.

However, I'd merely gone through the motions of the meeting, moving us closer toward Beck signing the contract. After all, unless the accident prevented him from paying our company, it really wasn't my business. It wasn't like we were friends.

The vineyards, farms, and open pastures along the road slowly faded away until we passed a sign that read Welcome to Starry Hills. Houses zoomed past first, but soon, businesses popped up—grocery stores, antique shops, consignment stores, and even a farm equipment and rental place. But only when we hit the part proudly labeled Main Street did I sit up and take notice.

Shop after shop crowded next to one another, each business painted in one of a multitude of colors. Blues, greens, yellows, and even pinks dotted the streets. With unique planters and trellises in front of them as well, it was beyond charming, nothing like the beige strip malls I mostly saw in the suburbs of San Francisco.

The brightly colored buildings were so unique that I couldn't help but blurt, "Who decides which shops get what color?"

I kept my gaze on the shops as Beck parallel parked and answered, "Every five years, there's a town meeting where people can lobby to change the colors of their shops. Usually, the owners talk it out among themselves beforehand, though. The only real rule is that the same two colors can't be next to each other. Oh, and they have to be a solid color except for the trim, so no stripes or weird designs."

He expertly parked the truck, and I was a little jealous. Even living in San Francisco, I hated parallel parking with a passion. "It's beautiful. A picture of Main Street alone would get people up from the city for a weekend break."

After turning off the ignition, Beck grunted. "Once upon a time, it did. However, these days, people tend to head to Napa Valley and the towns over there."

"Because they have bigger tourism campaigns."

I knew that because you couldn't not see a billboard or hear an ad on the radio. Even with streaming music being more and more popular, Americans loved their cars and still often listened to the radio.

"Yes." He gestured toward the light-pink building beside us. "Here's the bakery. My sisters are inside with their friends, expecting you. I'll come back in about an hour. Then we can visit some businesses before heading to dinner with Kyle."

His tone was neutral, and I finally looked at Beck, who was staring at his phone.

Okay, so a part of me wished he'd look at me. But I'd given him the cool, distant treatment since the meeting with Lori, so I couldn't blame him.

It's better this way.

Clearing my throat, I put my hand on the door. "Well, I'll go now."

His head snapped up. "Stop."

I blinked, and the next thing I knew, he was out of the car and around the front to yank open my door.

"Um, what are you doing?"

"Opening the door."

"Why?"

His lips twitched, like they'd done this morning. "Because we have manners out here, city girl."

I shook my head and didn't bother hiding my smile. "Do you treat the sheep the same way? I mean, they deserve a little pampering before the big event."

He barked out a laugh and then rolled his eyes. "We don't even have sheep on the farm."

"Chased them all away, I bet."

We grinned at each other, the earlier ease and banter back in full force.

Although in the next beat, his gaze darted to my lips, lingering, and heat flooded my body. And despite all my efforts to keep things distant, I stared at his too. His lips were no doubt warm and soft, and the stubble on his face would feel delicious against my skin.

Clearing my throat, I grabbed my purse, then I hopped out of the car. "I'll see you in about an hour."

Without looking back, I hightailed it into the bakery. Yes, I was a coward. But if Beckett Wolfe ever leaned in to kiss me, I wasn't sure I could say no.

Someone called out my name, so I scanned the room until I found the table with Abby, Millie, and two women I didn't know sitting together.

I waved and headed toward them, noticing the cute decor of pink-and-white designs on the wall with some black accents. Pictures of various drool-worthy desserts dotted the place, and fake flowers—wisteria, maybe?—and leaves hung overhead. Combined with the cute round tables and scrollwork chairs, the atmosphere made me think of the pictures I'd seen of outdoor cafés in Europe.

Although the food here was American, for sure. I didn't think sprinkled donuts would be in a fancy European bakery. Or would they? I'd never left the US, so maybe I should look it up. Hell, maybe one day, I could finally travel.

I reached the table, and Abby gestured toward an empty chair. All four women looked about the same age and smiled warmly at me.

Abby motioned around the table. "Welcome to the best group of ladies in all of Sonoma." She winked. "We decided you could be a temporary member of the BFF Circle. Because after hanging around my grumpy brother so much, you definitely need a little bit of fun."

I smiled. "I'm here to work, so I don't mind.

Besides, your family has been extremely nice and hospitable."

Abby snorted. "No need to be polite." She gestured at a blond-haired, brown-eyed woman wearing a pink apron. "Say hello to Amber King. Her stepmom runs the bakery."

Amber waved, and I bobbed my head.

A woman with dark-auburn hair and blue eyes spoke up. "And I'm Katie Evans. Okay, so now that the intros are done, tell us—why did Beck race over to Millie's for tea at six o'clock this morning for you?" She leaned in and whispered dramatically, "Did you bark out an order like the high-powered women in movies? Or did he do it because he wuvy wuvs you?"

Blinking, I tried to process what she'd asked and not because she'd pronounced "lovely love" weirdly. Why would she even suggest something like that? I'd only met the man the day before.

Amber elbowed her. "Be nice, Katie. You know the Wolfe family always treats their guests well. It's no big deal."

Millie laughed and tucked her dark hair behind her ears. "Maybe. But I was sleeping when he arrived, and Beck rang the doorbell nonstop until I woke up. That seems like more than being a gracious host to me."

My cheeks burned. Beck had brushed off getting the tea, and I'd had no idea he'd made such a fuss. Part of me warmed at how far he'd gone to get it for me. But another part was annoyed.

And the irritated part won out. "I'm so sorry, Millie.

I could've just had water instead. I didn't demand it or anything. I promise."

Millie waved a hand in dismissal. "No worries. I would've gotten up in like fifteen minutes anyway."

Katie tapped her fingers on the table. "Then he likes you. I knew it. That man definitely needs to get laid. My brother Kyle was drunk one night and mentioned it's been a while."

"Katie!" Millie and Amber shouted.

Abby merely laughed.

And all I wanted to do was crawl under the table.

Smaller groups were easier for me to be myself around. But I didn't usually have a person sharing my hot client's sex life—or lack thereof—within minutes of meeting someone new.

The image of Beck naked above me as he pinned my hands above my head and fucked me hard flooded into my mind.

No, no, no. Not going there.

Amber lightly shoved Katie as she said, "Don't mind her. I swear Katie lives to get a rise out of people."

Katie shrugged. "I spend a lot of time with cows and cheese. So I take my kicks where I can get them."

I remembered her last name—Evans. Determined to steer the conversation far, far away from Beck's sex life, I asked, "Your family owns the Starry Evans Dairy Farm, right?"

Katie nodded. "Yep, that's us. And I know you want to talk business and all that jazz. But first, we're going to do two things: order some scones, and then you'll tell us the best places to visit in San Francisco. I haven't been since a school trip in high school, and I'm dying to see more than this small town."

Amber stood. "I'll go get some scones and hot chocolate. Unless you'd rather have something else, Sabrina?"

I didn't normally eat that much sugar at once. But what the heck. I needed to get to know this bakery, since it worked with the Wolfe family. And a girl had to taste things, right? "Scones and hot chocolate sound perfect."

Katie whispered, "Do you have any Bailey's to add to it, Amber?"

Amber rolled her eyes and walked away just as Abby said, "Nice try. But it's afternoon, and you know Amber is the rule follower out of us four. She'd never drink while working."

Katie sighed. "I know. And somehow, I still love her anyway."

Everyone laughed, including me. Even if I'd only just met the four women, I could tell they were close. Almost like sisters.

And it made me miss Taylor.

I'd call her later. If she and Katie ever teamed up, though, there would be a crap-ton of trouble to follow.

Katie leaned toward me. "While we wait—don't dish anything until Amber gets back, or we'll never hear the end of it—you're meeting my brother and Beck for dinner later, right?"

I rearranged my purse on the floor by my legs. "Yes. I want to learn more about the businesses that work with the Wolfe family. Plus, wine-and-cheese tastings would make great day trips or weekend getaways from San Francisco, Oakland, Sacramento, or even San Jose. There's a lot of potential there."

Scrunching her nose, Katie replied, "Just be prepared to die of boredom as Kyle talks about cheese. I know he's amazeballs at it, and he even won an international competition last year. But I'd rather hear about anything else. I don't want to work on the farm my whole life, and I would rather spend my time planning trips I want to take one day."

Wow, if Starry Evans Cheese had won awards, then I definitely needed to ask a lot of questions this evening.

Millie spoke up. "Remember your promise, Katie—to send us postcards and corny tourist T-shirts from every place you visit."

Katie gave a double thumbs-up. "Oh, I plan to find the tackiest shirts imaginable. But then you have to uphold your end of the bargain by wearing them and sending me pics."

As the three women discussed where Katie might go, I merely listened. When it came to my job, I would take charge and talk as much as needed. But in day-to-day life, I much preferred listening.

Well, that was true with most people. For some reason, I had no problem spilling long-ago memories about cheap sock dolls with Beck.

When Amber returned with our scones and hot chocolate, the conversation died down, and everyone stared at me, waiting.

Katie motioned for me to get going. "Try the hot chocolate and scones first, before us. It's been way too long since I've seen someone experience them for the first time." She rubbed her hands together.

That made me blink. "The scones aren't laced with weed, are they?"

Everyone laughed, and I smiled.

Abby caught her breath first and said, "No, although it would be a good plan. Because, well, people would get the munchies and keep eating. It would take the bakery to a whole other level."

Amber rolled her eyes. "We're not serving weed brownies or weed-laced anything else, for that matter."

Katie clapped her hands. "But just think of the killing you could make! I've tried to convince my brother to make some sort of weed cracker or bread to go with the cheese tastings, but he's against it." She sighed dramatically. "Why are there so many sticklers in my life?"

Amber tossed a small chunk of scone at Katie, and it landed inside her cleavage. When Amber put her hands up in success, Katie raised an eyebrow. "Really?"

Millie chuckled. "It's better than when she tries to throw peas or M&Ms."

Shaking her head, Katie retrieved the scone piece from her—yes, quite ample—cleavage and threw it back at Amber before turning to me. "This is what having big boobs is really like—your best friends use them for target practice. Oh, and add in guys staring without looking into your face and never finding clothes that fit, and voila, it's pure hell."

As the women started arguing for or against big boobs, I sipped the hot chocolate and closed my eyes in bliss. It was sweet yet had a slight kick, and I knew one cup wouldn't be enough.

The chatter died down, and Abby whispered, "See? Another one falls under your magical cocoa spell, Amber."

Opening my eyes, I took another sip—just to ensure it was as good as I thought, and it was better—and replied, "This definitely needs to be included in some campaign materials. I didn't see it at the Starry Hills Valentine's Festival, so maybe you should set up a booth for the next event."

Amber shrugged. "I've considered it but thought people would only want the free wine everywhere."

"Hm, well, some people probably visit the festival for the ambiance, date night, girls' night, or whatever, and would try it. And if you have sweet and savory breads that pair well with some of the popular regional wines, I think it'd go over extremely well." I sniffed the hot chocolate and added, "And I think I need to drink many, many more cups just to make sure I can describe it right."

As we chuckled, I couldn't help but relax. Even though the women were basically strangers, they'd somehow made me feel a part of their group.

And while I'd had Taylor since college, I'd never had an actual group of friends. When my sister and I were growing up, my mother hadn't let us go out to play, attend birthday parties, or even have people over.

No, she reveled in controlling everything so that we had to rely on her.

Had no choice but to give her our attention.

Over time, it'd damaged my social skills and made me a hermit. Heck, it had taken me a lot of years to even go out once a month with Taylor.

What I'd told Lori and Beck at our meeting earlier was becoming truer by the minute. Starry Hills was comforting, friends were easy to make, and the sense of belonging just felt right.

But then they'd asked me about San Francisco, and reality came crashing back. The city was my home, my career, and my entire life. One week away could be a nice break but nothing else. I needed to remember that.

So I shared with them where to go in the city, what to see, and some of the hidden gems most tourists overlooked. And even when the conversation drifted, which happened often, I didn't mind. I took mental notes, focusing on my job and how I could portray Starry Hills positively—which was becoming easier by the moment.

Chapter Thirteen

Beckett

I finished my deliveries a little early and went back to the Starry Eyes Bakery for Sabrina.

However, as soon as I entered and spotted her laughing with my sisters and the BFF Circle, I silently retreated to a corner table, sat down, and merely watched them.

It seemed as if she belonged without even trying. Hell, if she could win over Katie Evans, then she was definitely made of tougher stuff. That woman wasn't called the wild child of Starry Hills for nothing.

My phone vibrated. Since it could be Kyle, I checked it.

But it was from my sister:

Abby: I saw you slink in. Why are you being so creepy?
Me: I'm not being creepy. I didn't want to interrupt your good time.
Abby: Come over and join us. Amber's going to get some more hot chocolate.
Me: I can't.
Abby: Can't or won't? I didn't pin you as a chickenshit, brother. <chicken emoji>

Looking up, I met my sister's eyes and glared. She grinned and said something, and all the heads at the table swiveled in my direction.

Katie shouted, "Look who showed up! Come on. We promise we won't bite. This time."

The BFF Circle cackled, and I rolled my eyes.

Still, I could see Sabrina hunkering down in her chair, probably embarrassed, and I wanted to spare her any more unwanted attention. So I stood and walked over. When I could speak at a normal level, I said, "Anytime you're ready to leave, my chariot awaits, Sabrina."

Abby smirked. "Chariot, huh? Did you convince the Brown family to dust off their carriages for a tour?"

Sabrina's eyebrows came together. "Are there carriage tours here?"

I grunted. "Not usually. Sometimes for the big events, but nothing's happening right now." I jerked a thumb toward the door. "If you want to visit the shops, then you should get your hot chocolate to go. Things close early here in February."

Amber stood. "I'll get one for the road as well as some scones."

Before Sabrina could do more than open her mouth, Amber left.

I stood behind her chair. "Ready?"

"Yes," she said slowly. "But why are you standing behind me?"

"To pull the chair back as you get up."

From the corner of my eye, I saw Abby rolling her eyes. But I didn't care. I might not be able to kiss Sabrina O'Connor, let alone make her scream my name by having my mouth between her thighs, but I could treat her like she fucking deserved.

It was all part of the Wolfe family image, after all.

Fucking liar.

She looked back at me. "Um, how does that even work? Is there some sort of choreography I need to know?"

Katie snorted. "Well, seeing as most guys under the age of sixty don't pull out chairs around here, you'll have to ask Beck."

My father had always helped my mom sit or stand from a table. I ignored Katie. "Just stand, Sabrina, and I'll do the rest."

After grabbing her purse from the floor, she did, and I eased the chair back. Once done, she turned toward me and shook her head. "That seems unnecessary."

"You'll get used to it."

She frowned at me, and I couldn't blame her.

Sabrina would leave in a matter of days, which wasn't enough time to get used to anything.

Clearing my throat, I waited for Amber to come back and hand over her goodies to Sabrina before I placed a hand on her lower back.

The second I touched her, even through the fabric, a jolt shot through my body and straight to my cock.

Sabrina sucked in a breath and met my gaze. For a few beats, we stared at each other, as if the rest of the bakery didn't exist. I lightly stroked my fingers against her back, and she leaned toward me a fraction, her heat and scent surrounding me, and my eyes dropped to her mouth. She licked her lips, and my dick turned even harder.

Before I could do something stupid—like kiss Sabrina—Amber's return caught my eye, and I snapped back to reality. After dropping my hand, I put both into my pockets. I needed to add "Don't touch Sabrina" to my list of things to do while she was around. "Come on, let's go."

I headed for the door and waited until she said her goodbyes. Of course I opened it for her and followed her out.

Since it was late afternoon, when a lot of people were pulling out of parking spots and trying to get in, I moved to the outside of the sidewalk just in case someone drove up the curb.

At least she didn't think it weird or question me. No, she was too busy looking at the shop window next to the bakery. "What's this place?"

I moved closer, until I stood just behind her. The

scent of vanilla and woman drifted to my nose, and I nearly leaned down to smell her hair. Maybe it was her shampoo.

Or maybe it was just her.

Stop it. I backed up until I was about a foot behind her. "This is The All Things Shop."

"That's not exactly helpful."

I chuckled and pointed at items in the window. "But it's true. Dragon statues, pretty tea services, and even collector dolls—it's a treasure trove of things tourists love."

She glanced over her shoulder. "Just tourists, huh? Then there's nothing in this place, nothing at all, that you'd even look twice at?"

I grunted. "When my sister was little, I used to take her for her birthday. But it's been years since I've been inside, and I have no idea."

"Then let's find out if it's the same as you remember or not."

Smiling, she reached for the door.

With a curse, I stated, "I should open it."

She bit her lip as if to keep from laughing, and I frowned at her. After opening the door herself, she went inside and migrated to the collector doll section.

As she looked closely at the display, I remembered the story she'd shared with me earlier. Since her visit with the BFF Circle had wiped away her cool, distant facade, I decided to see if I could get the Sabrina from earlier back.

I stopped beside her and asked quietly, "Do you have any at home?"

Never taking her eyes from the rows of dolls displayed in a hutch, she replied, "No. Part of me wants to finally buy the doll I never had as a kid. However, I have a tiny apartment, and there's not really any room." She lightly ran a finger along the edge of the middle shelf, stopping in front of a doll with brown hair. She had a full figure and wore an evening gown that was probably from my grandparents' time. "Probably one like her."

I barely paid attention to the doll because all I could focus on was Sabrina's finger, which was so long and slender. Probably soft too.

And for a second, I was jealous of a fucking shelf.

Then I processed her words and found my voice again. "Why her?"

Her face took on a wistful expression. "Because one day, I'd like to have the confidence to wear something like that."

As soon as the words left her mouth, her cheeks turned red. "Never mind." She rushed to the next section, which had various fantasy statutes.

I stared at the doll for a moment. If Sabrina were mine, I'd buy her not only the doll but also a dress to match. Then when she wore it, I'd fucking convince her of how beautiful she was over and over again, until she never doubted it.

And if it took years of my worshiping her body with my tongue, hands, and dick, I'd do it.

The bell over the door chimed, cutting through my fucking dangerous thoughts. Sabrina wasn't mine and never would be. She'd find a guy to treat her right, but it wouldn't be me.

The rest of the time we were inside the store, Sabrina pretended she'd never even mentioned the doll. As she went through each section, she didn't give up trying to find something I'd like.

I'd just scoffed at a dainty mug with kittens on it when she found the corner I'd forgotten about—the collector sports card area.

I had no idea if people still collected baseball cards, but I'd done it when I was younger, usually with my older brother West. And as I scanned the signed cards mounted on special plaques, my eyes stopped at the last one. "Rickey Henderson."

Sabrina was instantly at my side. "Well, given how he's holding a bat, I know it's baseball. But who is he?"

"Who is he? Are you kidding me?"

Rolling her eyes, she hitched her purse higher on her shoulder. "I don't really follow sports much, unless it's something like a figure skating championship or going to a baseball game to support my friend. So who is he?"

"Only the best base stealer of all time. If that wasn't enough, he has the record for most runs scored. He's a legend. I even saw him once when I was a kid with my dad and older brother, back when he played for Oakland."

Back then, my worst worry had been that my brother would steal my baseball cards or that the toddler twins would try to follow me around. What I wouldn't give to go back to those days and have my dad back. Hell, my mother too.

"You should buy it."

I blinked and looked over at Sabrina. "What?"

"Those were good memories, right? Maybe you should get it to remember the good times whenever you see it."

Uncomfortable with how perceptive she was, I decided to lighten the mood. "You just want to prove there's something in this shop I like."

She searched my gaze, as if she could see straight inside my mind. The urge to turn around and walk away was strong.

But she smiled, and my uneasiness faded. "You caught me."

I grunted. "No, I'm not going to get it. And we should leave anyway. There are tons of other shops left on Main Street to visit."

She glanced around the place. "While logically I know you're right, my life has mostly been studying and working since I was a teenager. I've never really been anywhere that wasn't for my job, and I liked pretending to be a tourist in here for half an hour."

Before I could stop myself, I blurted, "You could come back to Starry Hills for a vacation. You're always welcome to stay with the Wolfe family."

With me.

And those intense green eyes stared at me again.

Fuck. I really shouldn't have said that.

But Sabrina's phone vibrated, and she looked away to fish it out of her purse. "Sorry, my boss texts a lot.

And if it's during work hours, I have to respond right away, or I'll get an earful."

She headed toward the door, and I followed. Only because I was watching her closely—I always seemed to be doing that—did I notice her shoulders tense.

As soon as we were outside, she stopped near a wall and stared at her phone. I should leave it alone. After all, unless her boss suddenly changed her mind about working with my family's winery, what happened between them was none of my fucking business.

Yet my feet had a mind of their own, and I stopped right next to her. When she still just stood there, staring at her phone, I asked quietly, "What is it?"

At first, I didn't think she'd answer. Then she took a deep breath and turned the phone toward me.

Displayed on the screen was a picture of her laughing with the BFF Circle, and below it the words "I'm watching you."

"What the fuck? Do you know who sent that?"

She shook her head, her hands trembling as she lowered her phone. Without thinking, I gently rubbed her upper arm to soothe her.

Sabrina relaxed a little after a few seconds and answered, "I have no idea. And it makes no sense. I'm nobody. Unless…"

"Unless what?"

Her gaze met mine, anger flaring in her eyes. "It could be Justin, that asshole."

Putting an arm around her shoulders, I guided her toward a small park at the end of Main Street, where we could sit on a bench with relative privacy. "Tell me who the fuck this Justin is."

She bit her lip, probably debating what to say. But no matter what she decided, I'd find out about the fucker who made her tense and freak out.

Because no one should be made to feel that way. Ever.

Once we finally sat on the bench at the edge of the park, away from the playground, she sighed. "A mistake."

"Be more specific."

She raised her eyebrows. "Are you ordering me around?"

"Not normally, no. But we're not leaving until I learn more about who this dickhole is."

"Dickhole fits. Or megadouche."

"Sabrina," I growled.

She patted my arm. I was so worked up over her being scared that I couldn't enjoy it. "Calm down, feral Wolfe." She chuckled at her own joke, and I almost smiled.

Before I could ask again, she sobered. "I work with him, and I made the mistake of agreeing to a date roughly a year ago. After dinner, he took me home and wanted to kiss me at the door. I said no, and he grew angry, saying he was owed something for paying for my meal, the dick. I'd made the mistake of opening my door, and he tried to push his way into my apartment." Her voice turned even quieter. "He nearly succeeded. Only because a neighbor came home and saw us did I manage to get inside and lock the door." She gave a wry smile. "He's made my life hell at work ever since. When I was given the first shot at this job and chance for promotion, he said I would fail." She looked down at her hands. "I'm not sure what he's capable of. Reporting him to HR did nothing. And I refuse to cower and simply give in because of his behavior." She clenched her fingers into fists. "I've worked too damn hard to get this far."

Anger roiled in my belly, and I jostled my right leg to keep from jumping up, finding out where this Justin lived, and ensuring he left Sabrina the fuck alone.

The Wolfe family protected their own. And even if only temporarily, Sabrina was one of us.

But as she clenched her fingers tighter, my anger faded. This woman needed me. The dickhole could wait.

Gently and slowly enough that she could tell me to stop, I moved a hand to lay over hers and squeezed lightly. Her gaze shot to mine. I didn't know what she saw in my eyes, but she relaxed. Pride rushed through me—Sabrina O'Connor didn't fear me and might even feel safe around me.

I squeezed her fist under mine again. "What can my family do to help you? Because I assure you if that fucker is the second choice to work with us, we'll flat-out refuse. Men like him need to be punched in the balls repeatedly, until they understand women owe them nothing just because they bought them dinner."

As she continued to look at me, I growled, "What?"

She whispered, "Who are you, Beckett Wolfe? And how are you real?"

I didn't know how to respond to the disbelief in her eyes. Had no man ever treated her right before?

Time stilled, like it had back in the café, and all I wanted to do was to be that man. First, I'd murmur how beautiful and smart she was before leaning closer and finally kissing her. Maybe caress her cheek and thread my fingers into her hair to tilt her head and take the kiss deeper, making her moan.

My gaze moved to her mouth, her parted lips, and when she licked them, blood rushed to my cock. Fuck, I'd never wanted to kiss a woman so badly before. It was almost like I couldn't resist her, no matter how much I wanted to.

Her purse buzzed, snapping me back to reality. Sabrina was here for a job, not for me. And even if she wanted to kiss me, too—which I thought she did—I wanted her to get the promotion. I couldn't let my dick ruin that for her.

She raised a hand as if to touch my face, and I knew I needed to break the spell. And fast.

Remembering her question, I cleared my throat and replied, "Who am I? Just a simple country boy. But there's more to us than working in the dirt and fucking sheep."

I waggled my eyebrows, and she burst out laughing. And even though the quip wasn't really *that* funny, she was probably leaning into the laughter to erase some of her stress.

That made me sit up a little taller. *This is how you treat a woman, you megadouche dickhole.*

When Sabrina could barely breathe, she stopped

laughing and took huge gulps of air. I congratulated myself on not staring at her boobs as she did it.

Although being a fucking gentleman sucked sometimes.

Once she caught her breath, she touched my arm. "Thank you, Beck. Both for relaxing me and finally admitting you have a thing for sheep."

I raised an eyebrow. "Really, you're going there? That's below the belt, missy."

She leaned toward me, her breast pressing against my arm.

You're. A. Fucking. Gentleman. Don't enjoy it when she's in distress.

She smiled. "Well, I have five or so more days here to learn about real country boys. Maybe by the end of it, I'll owe you an apology."

"And I look forward to that day." I rubbed my hands together. "Maybe I should make you a T-shirt that reads 'Country boys don't fuck sheep.'"

"Yes, because wearing that down the street wouldn't attract notice."

"You could always put a stick over the *U* in fuck and make it family friendly."

Rolling her eyes, she drawled, "Yes, because that word is the only reason people might take issue with it."

"Hey, you've got to become my ambassador."

"Only if you wear a shirt that reads 'Not everyone from San Fran is a gluten-free vegan.'"

"That's a bit wordy for a T-shirt."

She lightly swatted my arm. "I'll think of

something later. It's my job to think of taglines that resonate, after all."

"I sure hope so. Because if you use something like 'Starry Wolfe wine is amazing and awesome and the best ever,' I might have to rethink your services."

She narrowed her eyes, and I couldn't help but laugh. Her expression eased, and soon, we were smiling at each other. Had I ever felt so at ease with a woman I also wanted to kiss? *Fuck.* Thinking of kissing her only made me stare at her mouth again, and her smile died.

Just as I debated whether to say screw it and kiss her anyway, a dog barked, breaking the moment, and we both jumped. Sabrina quickly stood and hiked her purse higher on her shoulder. Then she did it again. Finally, she looked toward where we parked. "What time do we need to meet your friend? It must be getting close."

Realizing how close I'd been to kissing her and maybe messing up everything, I stood and checked my phone. I ignored the text from my sister and read Kyle's. "He's ready anytime. I thought it best to grab food at a place away from Main Street to give you a feel for what we locals like."

"Sounds good. Should we go now?"

I itched to throw my arm around her shoulders, letting everyone know she was under my protection.

But Sabrina was far from mine, so I kept my hands in my pockets. "Yeah. And I hope you like barbecue."

"I hadn't exactly pictured that for wine country, but I'm up for it."

"Hey, I love wine and fine cheeses as much as the

next person. But sometimes, nothing beats barbecue ribs and a cold beer."

Her eyes twinkled. "So you're going to wear one of those big bibs while you devour a heaping platter of meat?"

I smacked my lips. "Sounds like heaven."

She laughed again. "You have this silly, ridiculous side you hide super well. Whenever you're helping your aunt at an event, you should let it out more often. It'd probably mean fewer emojis from her too."

"Fewer emojis would be good. But I'm not like Zach, and I can't just turn it on. I only..."

Fuck, I'd nearly shared how I only revealed that side of me when I was comfortable with someone. And I didn't need Sabrina to know that.

Her phone buzzed again, and for once, I was fucking happy about it. Still concerned about the creepy-ass message from earlier, once she had a chance to read it, I asked, "Everything okay?"

Snorting, she looked up at me. "Yes, just my friend being her over-the-top self."

I raised my brows. "Do I want to know?"

"Probably not."

Sabrina looked like she was holding in laughter, and I narrowed my gaze. "Now I'm curious."

"Too bad. I'm not telling."

I itched to try and take her phone. Maybe she'd even let me chase her before I caught her and pulled her back up against my front, finally feeling her soft curves against me.

Nope. I needed to stop going there.

We reached the truck, and I said, "Well, maybe I'll encourage Aunt Lori to text you a few times. Then you'll beg me to get her to stop, and you'll have to tell me what this friend of yours said before I do it."

"Oh, I don't mind your aunt. Her texts are hilarious. I've never met someone her age who uses so many emojis."

"Hilarious? Are we both talking about Lori Wolfe?"

"Yes. Because I don't have any aunts or uncles, I've never had the chance to be exasperated or embarrassed like you. It's kind of… nice."

The second she finished, her lips pressed together, as if she regretted saying it.

First the sock dolls, and now no aunts or uncles? The more I learned, the more I thought Sabrina's life had been the opposite of mine.

I opened the truck door for her. "Then text as much as you want with Aunt Lori. She'll love having someone new to harass."

She nodded and fell quiet.

After racing to the other side of the truck, I slid inside and soon pulled onto the road. I kept peeking at Sabrina, who continued to stare out the window. I wanted to ask her so many questions but knew I couldn't. The silence helped remind me of who she was, what she wanted, and how easily I could fuck that all up.

Even so, there was one last piece of information I needed to help protect her. She might not be mine, but I wouldn't let her asshole coworker ruin things for her or worse. "What's Justin's last name?"

She whipped her head around. "Whitmore. Why?"

"I need to know who to tell to fuck off. Otherwise, I'll just have to assume every Justin I meet is the bastard who tried to hurt you."

She raised her eyebrows. "You're not going to round up the boys, grab your shotguns, and scare him off, are you?"

I chuckled. "You get all your ideas of country boys from movies, don't you?"

"Maybe."

Shaking my head, I replied, "I don't shoot people just because. Although there are some guys who need to be scared shitless and reminded how to treat other people. I did it plenty of times when Abby and Millie were in high school."

"Poor Abby and Millie. Growing up, I always wondered what it would be like to have brothers. Now I'm starting to wonder if I was lucky not to."

I nearly stuck my tongue out at her like a fucking child.

What was this woman doing to me?

Clearing my throat, I pulled into the parking lot for the bar. I risked asking, "You don't have any siblings?"

I parked and turned off the ignition.

When Sabrina spoke, it was barely a whisper. "I have a sister, but don't ask me about her."

With that, she opened the door before I could even get out of the car. She marched toward the entrance of the restaurant, and I dashed to catch up.

Not asking about her sister after that comment was

going to be hard. But Kyle waved at me as we entered the place, and I had to let the matter drop.

Kyle raised his eyebrows, clearly reading my mood, the bastard.

I approached him, murmuring, "Don't ask. Not now," and introduced him to Sabrina.

And as we ate—I even wore the fucking bib, just to get Sabrina to laugh—Sabrina retreated into her professional-yet-curious persona.

It stayed in place during the car ride home as well.

The only victory I managed was to open her fucking door before she could. But she barely said good night before fleeing to her room.

As I ascended the stairs, my phone buzzed, and I checked it:

Kyle: Tell me what you need, asshole. And don't say nothing.
Me: I want to know if any guy named Justin Whitmore shows up in town.
Kyle: Should I corner him and take him to my barn? Where he might fall headfirst into a pile of cow shit?
Me: Tempting. But I don't want your ass to end up in jail.
Kyle: My uncle's the sheriff. I doubt that'll happen, if the guy deserves it.
Me: Still, no. He's mine. Just tell me, okay?
Kyle: Of course. I'll start asking discreetly tonight.

Reaching my room, I tossed my phone onto the dresser. I knew I'd have to check whether my aunt had said good night via text or not—because if I ignored her, she'd whip out her emojis and harass the shit out of me tomorrow—but I needed a minute to calm down.

I most definitely didn't need extra worries on my plate. Yet there was no way I could ignore Sabrina's fear and anxiety from earlier.

If that dickhole showed up in town, Kyle would hear about it.

And then I might just have to pay him a visit and go all country on his ass.

Chapter Fourteen

Sabrina

Taylor: So, wait. <wolf emoji> is on the lookout for the douchebag dickhole? He's on the hunt? <laughing on the floor emoji>
Me: <eye roll emoji> Yes. Part of me hopes J shows up so he can kick his ass.
Taylor: My, my, someone is bloodthirsty.
Me: <tongue out emoji> Says the woman whose hubby tosses players across the room if they try to cop a feel during a session.
Taylor: Ben is rather amazing. I approve of your country boy.
Me: He's NOT mine.
Taylor: And who was front and center in your dreams last night? Or, maybe under or behind you?

Me: <middle finger emoji>
Taylor: Exactly what I thought.

The next morning, I tried my best to focus on work. But the words kept dancing across the screen, and my brain refused to cooperate. *Maybe a break would help.*

Sighing, I went to the sliding door that exited onto the wraparound balcony, put on my coat, and stepped outside.

Placing my hands on the railing and leaning against it, I took in the sky, which was painted in a multitude of colors. The mixture of the rolling hills and the pinks and oranges in the sky was breathtaking. It looked unreal, almost as if it were another world. Definitely a far cry from the busy streets I saw from my apartment window.

I couldn't even imagine waking up to this scene every day. Would I ever get tired of it? Used to it? Forget how amazing it was?

A door opened farther down the veranda, and I turned to see a man on crutches. He resembled Beck quite a lot—the same strong jaw, the same dark hair except a lot shorter, and he was also just as tall. When the guy saw me and flashed a grin, I had a feeling he was trouble.

He spoke first. "You must be the mysterious Sabrina O'Connor. We've talked via email, but we haven't met in person yet. I'm Zach Wolfe. The much smarter, more charming version of Beckett."

I nearly smiled but knew it would only encourage him. Still, he had a cast on his leg, so I walked over to save him the trouble before replying, "Nice to meet you. Sorry to hear about the leg."

He shrugged. "I was an idiot. But I'm sorry to switch out with my brother. He can be…a bit rough around the edges."

The need to defend Beck rushed through me. "He's been amazing so far. Well, after the first meeting. I've learned so much from him already about this place."

He studied me a second before chuckling. "Who knew my brother had it in him?"

"Excuse me?"

Zach cleared his throat. "Nothing. I'm still getting over my painkillers. Those things are trippy as hell."

Despite his friendly demeanor, I wasn't exactly sure what to say. Probably because I was exhausted from not sleeping much the night before—both because of Beck and because of Justin.

Leaning against the railing again, I looked over the Wolfes' land once more. The sun had just peeked over the hills, changing the colors and making the smattering of clouds almost purple. "It's beautiful here. We'll definitely have to take some pictures."

Zach cleared his throat. "I'm an amateur, but I dabble in photography. I'm sure I can get you some decent images, if you want."

I glanced over, but Zach was staring out at the vineyard below. It was hard to tell, but I would almost say he was embarrassed. Why?

But it wasn't my place to ask. So I merely replied, "That would be great. Send them to my email when you get a chance, and I'll look them over."

He nodded, took a deep breath, then faced me again, his smile back in place. "I should go back to my room. If my aunt discovers I'm outside when I should still be resting, I'll never hear the end of it. Nice to meet you, Sabrina. Hopefully I'll see you at a meal soon."

After waving goodbye to Zach, I stared at the land again. Sunrises in the city couldn't compare to this one, and I wanted to burn it into my memory.

A girl could get used to a view like this.

Once the sun was up, I rushed into the bathroom and finished getting ready. I needed to talk with Millie Mendoza about her wedding and event business since she worked the closest with the Wolfe family.

After my visit with her, I should be able to sit down and really nail my pitch. I might even be back in San Francisco within a day or two.

Although the thought of driving away, back to my tiny apartment and maneuvering the hilly, crowded streets of the city made me sigh.

At one time, the anonymity of the city had been exactly what I'd wanted. Unlike when I'd been younger and the butt of jokes about my secondhand clothes or taped-up shoes, the only people who really noticed me in a big city were at work. And even then, only people in a few departments. It'd been a kind of freedom from judgment, which allowed me time to heal from my childhood, grow more confident, and reinvent myself a little.

However, the more I was around the Wolfe family

—or even the BFF Circle—the more I wanted to be seen.

To have a real place to belong.

Be realistic, Sabrina. You're not going to move to Starry Hills and start over. Again.

I'd just about finished my hair when someone knocked, so I went over and opened the door. "Hi, Lori."

"You really should just call me Aunt Lori. Everyone does. Can I come in?"

I noticed the shopping bags in her hands as I motioned for her to come inside.

"Shut the door, dear."

I did, and she took out some clothes—jeans, flannel shirts, sweaters, and a set of sturdy boots.

"I hope you don't mind, but I snooped around a little to find out your size. I wanted to make sure everything fit."

I blinked. "Pardon?"

Lori held up a pair of skinny jeans and a sweater. "These are for you. And you'll need them, if you're going to ride a horse today."

"Horse?" I echoed.

What was she talking about?

"In early summer, before any of the grape harvests, there's a big festival in the area, with all kinds of events and activities. One of the things our family offers is horse riding for people who've never ridden, plus hay-wagon rides for the kids. To better understand everything we do, you should ride a horse too." She raised her eyebrows. "Because you haven't before, have you?"

"Er, no. But—"

She tossed the clothes at me, and I caught them. Lori turned back to the pile on the bed and rummaged some more. "Beck has breakfast waiting downstairs for you, and then he'll take you to the stables."

"But I have a meeting with Millie."

"I know. You'll ride over to Millie's place. That way, you get the full wedding experience of the bride riding up to the barn before the ceremony." A far-off look came to her eyes. "I wish I'd been a bride in cowboy boots. My Tim would've loved taking off everything but the boots for our wedding night." She smiled and sighed happily.

Er, was she going to go into detail about said night? As much as I liked Lori Wolfe, I really didn't want to hear about her bedtime romps with her late husband. For all I knew, she would ask me for stories, of which there weren't many.

Not that I'd tell a virtual stranger—a woman older than my own mother, at that—about my rather-lacking sexy times.

So I steered us back to the horse riding. "I'd rather not get on a horse if I can help it."

"What happened to needing to experience as much as possible?"

After glancing down at the clothes in my arms, I played with the hem of the sweater. How did I share my deep-seated need to be perfect at everything? Or at least not make a complete fool of myself in front of my clients?

Because despite everything, they might become my clients.

No matter how much I wished we could be friends.

Lori gently touched my arm, and I met her gaze. The warmth and empathy there confused me. "Look, we're not trying to make you look stupid on purpose or set you up to fall on your ass and laugh at you. Beck and Millie both love horses—Millie more than Beck—and they just wanted you to get a little taste of that. But if you absolutely don't want to do it, then just tell me, and I'll axe their plans."

Trust wasn't something I did easily. Yet for whatever reason, I believed Lori Wolfe. Unlike my mother, I didn't think she or her family would berate me and tell me how I was useless or stupid or any other number of negative criticisms.

My mother's voice blared inside my head: "*You're a clumsy, fat cow. Not only will you fall off, you'll look ridiculous stuffed into those pants.*"

Lori's voice halted my mother's words. "Either way, the clothes are yours to keep. I wish I had a rear like yours, dear. Pants just slide right off my ass."

She sighed dramatically, and I nearly smiled. Even though she couldn't mean it, I appreciated her trying to cheer me up.

And right then and there, I decided to take a chance. "I'll try riding a horse."

Lori patted my arm. "Good. Then let's get you

dressed and fed. Beck should have Snowbell ready for you when you're done."

As Lori went on about the horse and how she'd been Abby's until she moved away, I relaxed a little. Hearing about happy family memories was getting easier for me. Especially since with the Wolfes, there was always something ridiculous or hilarious to laugh at.

I knew it hadn't always been like that for the Wolfe family—both parents had died rather young—but they'd always had one another to help them pull through.

Not for the first time, jealousy reared its ugly head.

After pushing it away, I dressed and ate breakfast as I chatted with Lori, and then we went looking for Beck.

Chapter Fifteen

Beckett

I petted Blaze's neck as I finished my last check of the reins. The flash of white on his forehead—the rest of him was chestnut—was the reason for his name. It wasn't the most original, but I didn't care. It suited him, especially since he could gallop fast, like a fire racing through a dry forest.

He butted his nose against my shoulder, and I absently stroked him. "No, no apples until later. We're going to leave soon."

Blaze blew out a breath, as if he understood me. But then he lifted his head, and I knew someone was approaching.

Turning around, I saw Sabrina and Aunt Lori

walking toward us. But while I knew my aunt was there, I couldn't stop staring at Sabrina.

Gone were the work dresses, pants, and shirts. In their place, she wore formfitting jeans that hugged her legs like gloves, highlighting every curve. And I couldn't stop seeing an image of those lush thighs wrapped around me as I fucked her sweet pussy, making her cry out my name as she came.

On top of that, she had on a more formfitting coat, the kind that protected against the rain and wind. Though it wasn't overly tight, it still stretched across her belly and tits, making me imagine how she'd look with nothing on.

Luckily for me, my hips were turned mostly toward my horse, hiding my thickening cock.

I waved in greeting and did my best to get my erection under control. My jeans were tight enough to show my reaction to Sabrina's new clothes, and I didn't want either her or my aunt to notice. For reasons I didn't understand, the city girl made me feel like a teenager again, back when I couldn't control my dick.

Aunt Lori and Sabrina stopped next to me. After tugging down my coat a little, I turned more toward them. "So, you came."

Sabrina shrugged. "Well, I figured during the walk to the stables, I could check to see if I saw any sheep."

Happy that the teasing version of her was back, I played along. "There's a lot of land here you haven't seen yet. Riding Snowbell to the Mendoza place will give you plenty of time to continue your search. Maybe you'll even admit defeat after our ride."

Aunt Lori glanced between us. "Do I even want to know?"

Sabrina's cheeks reddened as she replied, "Er, no. It's not important."

My aunt smiled. "Well, I'll be off, then. Someone has to get some actual work done today."

I rolled my eyes, and Aunt Lori laughed. As she walked away, I gestured to the white horse saddled and waiting near the mounting block. "Ready to meet Snowbell?"

She bit her bottom lip, and I wished it were my teeth nibbling her plump flesh.

Get your shit together.

Easier said than done. But then my phone buzzed in my pocket. Even without looking at it, I knew it was probably Millie or Abby asking where I was.

Sabrina blurted, "Does she bite?"

Her question alone told me she didn't have experience with horses. "No. Snowbell is the mildest of all our horses." I paused and added, "I'd never let anything hurt you."

She searched my gaze, and I did my best not to fidget. When Sabrina nodded, I mentally let out a breath.

She replied, "Maybe it's weird, but I believe you."

I relaxed at her words. If nothing else, I wanted her to feel safe with me.

Snowbell shook her head, wanting attention again. Sabrina took a step backward.

I placed my hand on her lower back. Ignoring the flare of heat at the touch, I focused on Sabrina and the horse. "She's just saying hello. And if you give her this, she'll love you forever."

After taking an apple piece from the baggie in my pocket, I held it out. Blaze whinnied, and I knew I'd have to give him some, too, before our ride. "Put this in your palm, hold it out, and let her eat it. Do your best not to show fear, because she'll pick up on it." I glanced at Sabrina as something dawned on me. "You weren't hurt by a horse as a child, were you?"

Shaking her head, she replied, "No. I got a picture on a pony outside the grocery store when I was nine and lived to tell the tale."

My lips twitched, imagining little kids lined up in a parking lot to get photographed with a horse. "Then try giving Snowbell the apple piece. I'll be right here if you need me."

Sabrina took the apple slice and placed it on her palm, and I watched as she slowly approached Snowbell. Blaze pawed the ground, and I offered him an apple chunk, never taking my eyes from Sabrina.

She stopped near the horse and put out her hand. Snowbell sniffed, lowered her head, and ate it off Sabrina's palm.

She laughed. "It tickles."

After patting Blaze's neck, I went over to Sabrina's side. "Wait until she sniffs your neck. If you're not paying attention, it can scare the hell out of you."

She raised and lowered her hand as if debating whether to try petting the horse.

So I encouraged her. "Let her sniff you, and then slowly stroke her neck."

Without thinking, I put a hand on Sabrina's lower back again and lightly stroked. For a second, her breath hitched.

The urge to lean down and nuzzle her neck rushed through me. I'd lightly nip her, leaving a mark to tell others to fuck off.

Sabrina stepped away from me, and I focused back on the horse.

And as Snowbell sniffed and then allowed Sabrina to stroke her neck, I wondered what it would be like to have those fingers against my skin, lightly caressing, and driving me wild with only her touch.

My pants grew tight as blood rushed south.

Fuck. Yes, I was jealous of a horse.

Then Sabrina grinned at me in triumph, and I wanted to tug her into the barn, find a quiet spot, and kiss her before celebrating her joy with a few orgasms.

Clearing my throat, I merely nodded, careful to keep my expression mostly neutral. "Good. Now, let's get you in the saddle, and I can teach you the basics."

I strode over to Snowbell, took her reins, and guided her into place next to the mounting block.

Sabrina frowned before going back to her fake smile and polite persona. "Thank you. I don't want to be late for my meeting with Millie."

It didn't take long to get her in the saddle—and fuck, the view of her jeans pulling tightly against her sweet ass nearly had me groaning—then I went over the basic spiel I did during the Summer Star Festival, when people wanted to try riding for the first time.

The familiar words helped to get both of my heads

under control. Once I swung into Blaze's saddle, I gestured for us to go.

And since we were using a path where we could ride side by side, I could mostly focus straight ahead and not be drawn in by Sabrina swaying on a horse.

Which was good because the last thing I needed was to show up at my sister's place with a hard-on.

Not only would I never hear the end of it, but it would probably encourage Millie. She was as bad as Aunt Lori when it came to asking me why I hadn't at least tried dating.

Although, given how Millie's living revolved around planning weddings, I supposed I could excuse her. Mostly.

Chapter Sixteen

Sabrina

Beck's touch, combined with his hot breath on my neck, had made me wet and hot and aching. And sitting atop a horse, where my clit kept bumping against the leather saddle, only made it worse.

Glancing over at him, looking all confident and at ease atop his horse, didn't help either.

Stop it. Yes, he was sexy. And if Taylor had set me up on a blind date with him, I would've embraced my attraction and maybe seen where it ended up.

However, he wasn't some random man. No, Beck and his family were potential clients, ones who would help me reach my dream of becoming a brand manager.

Although why that didn't stoke as much excitement in me as it had before, I had no idea.

Or, at least, I didn't want to think about it because maybe I did know why.

Concentrating on the ride helped me to relax a little, as did the scenery. We'd left the vineyards and were going through a fence that separated the two properties. In the distance were fields of mostly dead-looking bushes.

Beck gestured ahead. "Those are Millie's lavender fields. They're not much to look at in the winter, but the field is purple and green in the late spring and summer."

I could just imagine it. If a breeze came, the movement would make it look like a rolling purple sea.

Although I'd probably never get the chance to see the lavender in bloom unless I came to visit on my own. Once the Wolfe family signed, there would be an initial flurry of activity, but then most of my work would be done in the office. There'd be no need to come out to Starry Hills, except for maybe special events.

And even then, a lower-level employee would probably be assigned. I'd be off to another business, getting to know them and forming a plan.

Over and over again. Just like I'd dreamed of for years.

A loud bang sounded nearby, and I jumped a little. The horse under me bolted, and all I could do was lean forward and wrap my arms around her neck, hoping I wouldn't fall off.

I'm going to die. I'm going to die. I'm going to die. As

Snowbell ran faster and faster, I clung harder because if she reared back, I'd fall off, no question, and probably break something.

Or worse.

I knew I shouldn't close my eyes, but I couldn't help it. I could still feel the horse flying across the ground, but not seeing the blurry scenery helped me to not completely lose my shit.

Please let me survive this. Please.

Thundering hooves approached, and Beck shouted, "I'm coming, Sabrina! Hold on!"

Part of me wanted to snap that of course I'd hold on.

But then the horse's movements changed, as if she were jumping, and I just squeezed my eyes tighter.

The pounding sound of hooves drew nearer, and Beck spoke again. "She'll tire soon. Hold on, and I'll try to get her to slow down."

He made some noises, but Snowbell ignored him. She ran and ran until eventually I felt her slow down.

I still didn't dare look. At this point, holding on was all I cared about.

So consumed with the fear and anxiety swirling about in my head, I jumped when a hand touched my leg. "You're not moving, Sabrina. Open your eyes, sweetheart."

I wanted to, but my body wasn't listening. But the more Beck stroked my thigh, the more my heart calmed, and reason returned to my brain.

"That's it. You're okay. You're safe. When you're ready, I'll help you down and get you inside."

His gentle tone washed over me, and I took a deep breath.

Slowly, I released my grip and blinked open my eyes. Not far away was a white stucco house but smaller than the Wolfe family's home.

"Look at me, Sabrina."

I slowly sat up and found Beck's brown eyes.

He rubbed my thigh, up and down, and the touch was more soothing than sexual. He nodded. "There you are. Now, let me help you down, and we'll go inside."

My entire body was stiff, as if I were still in shock. But somehow, Beck's gentle commands helped me swing my leg over. He put his hands on my waist and helped me down, sliding my body against his.

When my feet landed on the dirt, I looked up. He ran the back of his knuckles down my cheek, and I wanted to lean into it.

He asked softly, "Are you hurt anywhere?"

At the concern in his voice and gaze, emotion choked my throat. "N-No."

He searched my eyes, as if looking for something. But I also noticed the fear in his eyes, the fear for me.

It couldn't be real, of course. Yet for that brief moment, I allowed myself to wonder what it would be like to have this man care about me. To make me laugh, stoke my temper, and persuade me to try new things I might not try on my own.

To imagine what it would be like to have someone who wanted me, faults and all.

While nice, the image was a mere fantasy. One I couldn't allow myself to hope for.

He finally said, "Let's get you inside."

In the next instant, he scooped me into his arms, and I had to wrap mine around his neck to stay in place. "What are you doing?"

"Getting you inside, sweetheart."

He walked, carrying me like I weighed nothing.

Part of me liked it. A lot.

And another part knew it was ridiculous. Not only would he hurt himself, but being in his arms felt nice. Too nice.

Tired of fighting it, I laid my head against his shoulder, closed my eyes, and pretended that Beck was mine for a few minutes. Just a little fantasy to tuck away for later, to remind myself what it felt like to be pressed against a sexy, caring guy who wanted me.

Millie's voice filled the air. "What's wrong? Did something happen? Why are you carrying Sabrina?"

Embarrassment flooded my body. "Put me down, Beck."

For a beat, he merely tightened his grip on my body. But then he slowly set me on my feet, keeping his hands on my waist until I was steady.

Our eyes met, and his cool gaze—a sharp contrast to his earlier heated one—slapped me back to reality. My little fantasy was definitely over.

I stepped back and turned toward Millie, who stood next to us.

She searched my face, then Beck's, before asking again, "What happened?"

Beck grunted. "I'm going to find out."

Millie's brow furrowed with confusion, and Beck added, "There was a loud noise, almost like a car backfiring. But we were on the trail between our properties, far from any cars."

I didn't know if it had been a gun, a car, or some machinery. However, just thinking about it caused the memory of the initial moments of terror to return. The lack of control. The fear of dying. The regrets at not trying harder to live my life instead of hiding under a mountain of work.

My eyes heated, tears threatening to fall. Wrapping my arms around myself, I tried to hold it together. Beck and Millie weren't my friends. I needed to be professional and not burst into tears.

I am strong. I can conquer this and kick ass.

As I took a few calming breaths, Millie's expression turned serious. "You think it was done on purpose. Don't you, Beck?"

I blinked and glanced at him. "What?"

Beck's face turned grim, and he replied, "It's the only thing that makes sense. But I won't say more until I look into it and find out for sure." He gestured toward Millie. "Go with Millie for now. I'm going to head back to where the noise came from and investigate. When you're ready, she can drive you back to our place. Right, Millie?"

Millie nodded. "Of course. But if you find anything, you'd better tell us, Beck."

He grunted his assent, took the reins of both horses, and guided them away.

Once he faded from sight, my body started to shake. Hugging myself tighter, I tried to calm down. But the reality of how close I'd been to dying was strong.

Millie placed a hand on my shoulder. "Come on. Let's get you inside. You can help me taste some of the new cake samples I got from the bakery."

I probably couldn't eat anything if my life depended on it, but I nodded and followed her. I needed time to work on packing my feelings away until I could face the Wolfe family again and not lose my shit.

Once we were settled inside, I somehow forced down some cake, barely tasting it. No, my mind was too busy whirring with one question: If I died today, who would care? Taylor, her husband, and that was about it.

My sister would probably never even hear about it. And even if she did, would she be sad? Or would she be indifferent after viewing me as the enemy for so many years?

Although why I was wasting time thinking about Sydney's feelings after her betrayal, I didn't know.

Millie didn't let my mood bring her down. She overreacted to each sample, smacking her lips and sometimes closing her eyes in bliss. After a while, my worries started to fade. And as I ate the cakes she raved the most about, the combination of sugar and hot tea helped to calm me down and get my head on straight again.

If—and it was a big if—Beck was right, and someone had deliberately spooked the horses, then I would have a problem. Because while I didn't know for certain, my gut said that Justin hadn't been joking when he said he would do anything to get the promotion.

I'd known he was an asshole, but I didn't think he would try to kill me. I would have to be more careful from now on and constantly watch over my shoulder.

But right here, right now, in Millie's airy, homey kitchen, I was able to distract myself. And as Millie gave me the tour of her place and explained how her most popular wedding setups played out, I relaxed a little more.

The renovated barn, in particular, was beautiful—a bright red on the outside but natural wood inside. White string lights hung from the ceiling. And the showcase sample table, set up with a light-green tablecloth and decorated with flowers and some crystal rocks, was stunning.

If I ever got married, I would want it to be here.

Not that it'd ever happen. Some people just weren't meant to be loved that way. After all, I'd heard it enough as a child.

Needing to focus on my job—and what I could control, such as my promotion—I spent the next few hours snapping photos, taking notes, and learning as much as I could from Millie.

I stuck around longer than I was probably welcome. But I needed to pack away not only my attraction to Beck but also the emotions hiding just under the surface before I saw him again.

Chapter Seventeen

Beckett

I found a cheap Bluetooth speaker along the fence between the two properties, hidden by a post. Since people went along this path fairly often—both on foot and via horseback—I had no fucking clue when it'd been placed or by whom.

Scanning the surroundings, I didn't see anyone. Of course not. That would be too fucking easy.

Still, I took the speaker with me. I could look it up online and find the range. That would at least give me a better idea of the culprit's location when they'd played the sound.

I resisted growling about finding out so little when all I wanted to do was hunt down the person responsible and stop them from trying to hurt Sabrina again.

The image of her holding on for dear life, Snowbell bolting away, flashed into my mind, stirring my anger and fear all over again. For a few moments, I'd thought I would lose her and never see her again.

When I'd held Sabrina in my arms earlier, all I wanted to do was kiss her. Badly. Like I'd regret it forever if I never got the chance.

And while I shouldn't, I wanted that chance. Because for some reason, the woman knew how to bring out the lighter side of me I'd buried long ago, the side I'd had to ignore in order to focus on keeping the farm and vineyards running and my siblings taken care of.

And I missed being the person who liked to pull pranks on my older brother. Running through the orchard, we played hide-and-seek or saw who could climb the highest. We even set competitions about who could find the biggest apple.

But I hadn't really had fun in years. Apart from the scare this morning, I'd had more fun with Sabrina over the last few days than the last ten years combined. Just having an inside joke about sheep fucking made me smile.

As I drew nearer the stables, I maneuvered Snowbell in that direction. I had sent Blaze home on his own—I'd trained him to do that years ago—but Snowbell was still shaken from the noise earlier. She'd need extra care and brushing before I could return to the house.

I turned the corner and stopped at who I saw standing near Blaze, undoing the straps for the saddle.

It was my older brother West.

He must've noticed movement, because he stood tall and faced me. "Hello, Beck."

West looked the same and yet older since the last time I'd seen him. He had a little bit of gray at the temples of his dark-brown hair and frown lines around his mouth. My brother had never been smiley, even as a child. But I had a feeling his late wife had caused most —if not all—of the frown and worry lines etched onto his face.

Part of me wanted to run over and hug him. Because despite everything, I'd missed him. But the sting of West abandoning us when we'd needed him, of abandoning *me*, kept me in place. "West. When the fuck did you get here?"

West went back to removing the saddle. "This morning."

Succinct bastard, as always.

But if he was waiting for me to start chatting away, acting as if we were boys again with nothing between us, he would be in for a long fucking wait.

Ignoring him, I guided Snowbell to the area where I could rub her down. The actions of removing her saddle and tack before brushing her were familiar, almost therapeutic. For a short time, I could ignore my tall-ass brother standing not ten feet away from me.

However, when I finished with Snowbell, I looked around and noticed West had vanished.

We'd have to face each other eventually. But for now, protecting Sabrina was all that mattered.

I headed up to the house, stopping to question the workers pruning the vines and even the staff inside the winery. But no one had seen or heard anything.

Resisting a sigh, I headed home to look up more information about the speaker.

I hadn't found out much in the hours between the incident and when I had to make dinner.

Sabrina still hadn't returned home or replied to my texts. At least Millie had sent me an update about how Sabrina was going through everything to learn how she ran her Starry Dreams Ranch events. She would also eat dinner at Millie's tonight.

Was Sabrina afraid to come back here?

Pounding some chicken flat before breading it was a great way to work out some frustration. I kept imagining it was this mysterious Justin's face. I had no proof, but my gut said it was him.

The forklift incident, the threatening text to Sabrina, and the horse spooking—it was exactly the type of stuff a fucker wanting to get Sabrina's promotion would do.

I went through the motions of prepping the breaded baked chicken, roasted potatoes, and salad. When it was nearly done, Aunt Lori waltzed in, and I braced myself. No doubt she wanted me to patch things up with West.

Maybe I could eventually, but I still hadn't forgiven him yet.

She leaned against a counter, crossed her arms over her chest, and stated, "West and his kids will be at dinner tonight. I hope you've made enough."

Guilt at not going to see my niece and nephew rushed through me. They'd done nothing wrong, and I needed to remember that. "I figured."

"Avery is allergic to strawberries."

"Yes, I remember from her last visit. I have apple turnovers."

Silence fell again but not for long. Aunt Lori stood tall. "You should talk to your brother. And no, don't be a smartass and ask which one. West has gone through a lot, too, you know."

I focused on chopping cucumbers for the salad. "I'm sure he has. But I have a lot of my own shit to worry about right now, Aunt Lori. I already agreed to give West some stuff to do around here. But I said nothing about making nice and pretending the last however many years haven't happened."

Nearly sixteen, in fact.

Aunt Lori harrumphed. "Fine. Given the events of the day, I'll leave you alone for now. Speaking of which, have you learned anything new?"

I shook my head. "Not a fucking thing."

She patted my arm. "We both have our networks in town keeping an eye out. We'll find who did this, Beckie. I know we will."

"Thanks, Aunt Lori."

"Of course. And if Sabrina needs to talk later, let me know."

I mumbled my thanks, and Aunt Lori left to check on something.

After finishing the salad, I checked my phone to see if Zach was ready for me to carry his ass down the stairs. Yep, he'd sent a few messages:

Zach: I'm ready for you to be my noble steed. Come fetch the prince from his tower.
Zach: No, really, the prince is starving.
Zach: Where are you, asshole?
Zach: Okay, you've been demoted from noble steed to jackass.

My brother thought he was hilarious, but most of the time, he was just irritating as fuck.

Still, I understood how hard it was for him to remain in his room so long and not move about or work. The doctor had said he shouldn't take the stairs for at least a week.

So I trudged up to his room. Just as I turned the corner, two sets of eyes locked on me—one brown and the other blue. The pair of ten-year-olds blinked at me.

The girl spoke first. "Uncle Beck?"

The uncertainty in her voice shot straight to my heart. I hadn't seen Avery or her brother, Wyatt, in far too many years.

I opened my arms. "Come here, Tater Tot."

She'd earned the nickname during the summer West had asked us to watch his kids while he took care of some shit. And the whole time, she'd basically only eaten tater tots and chicken nuggets.

Avery rushed toward me, and I wrapped my arms around her. "Look at how tall you are. In a few more years, you might be taller than me!"

She pulled back and shook her head. "Stop being silly, Uncle Beck. I'm one of the shortest girls in my class. Or was."

Sadness flashed across her face, and I ruffled her hair to distract her. "Hm, maybe you're tired and need to rest. I'll just have to eat all the apple turnovers by myself."

Avery gasped. "That's not fair! You can't!"

I chuckled. "Well, maybe you're right." I glanced at my nephew, who'd always been the quieter of the two. "What do you say, Wyatt? Should I share them?"

He shrugged but said nothing else.

The apple didn't fall far from the tree. Wyatt was West's son. That was for sure.

My niece spoke again. "That means yes."

I raised an eyebrow. "A shrug means yes?"

"It does for Wyatt. We have our own twin language, you know? So don't try to understand it, because you'll never get it."

I laughed. "All right." I gestured downstairs. "If you want to help me set the table, I'll be down in a minute. I just need to get your uncle Zach. He broke his leg and can't really walk or even hobble down the stairs yet."

Avery nodded. "We saw him earlier. He thinks we're still babies, though. I mean, a hand puppet show? Really? I'm ten, not five."

I fake whispered, "Your uncle Zach will always be a child at heart, so just go with it." I walked over to Wyatt and gently patted his shoulder. "Help your sister set the table."

He nodded and went to Avery's side. After whispering to each other, they dashed down the stairs.

Not wanting to think of all the years I'd missed with them, I went to Zach's room.

In short order, I had him in my arms. Although when he brayed a few times, I was tempted to drop him on his ass.

But as everyone sat down for dinner, two people were missing—West and Sabrina.

Where the fuck were they?

Chapter Eighteen

Sabrina

Taylor: I just saw your texts! Are you okay?
Me: Mostly. I'm not sure I'll get on a horse anytime soon, though.
Taylor: Do you want me and Ben to go up to Starry Hills and be your security team?
Me: Neither of you has experience.
Taylor: Maybe. But I'm serious—do you want us to come?
Me: No, it should be fine. I'll just keep vigilant.
Taylor: Are you sure?
Me: Yes. I know Ben has an away game tomorrow.
Taylor: Call me anytime, I don't care. Promise?
Me: I promise.
Taylor: Good. Maybe you can get <wolf emoji> to

stand guard outside your door. Even better—sleep next to you, just in case.
Me: Bye, Taylor.

As Millie parked the car in the rear family section, I willed myself to smile.

On the inside, I was exhausted. I'd loved learning about Millie's business and touring her property, but I'd had a near-death experience and spent way too much time trying not to decipher Beck's cool look right before he left.

Just after I opened the door and exited the car, my phone vibrated. Checking the screen, I saw a text from my boss. I opened it, and a photo of me on a horse filled the screen. I blinked and then scrolled down to her words:

Edwina: Why the fuck are you riding a horse? Are you taking this job seriously? Call me immediately. If they aren't about to sign, you're done.

I raised a hand to my throat and swallowed. Edwina got angry sometimes but didn't threaten lightly. And if she was just as pissed on the call, then I could be heading home tomorrow.

The thought of leaving Starry Hills so soon combined with everything else that had happened today made a tear escape my eye.

I quickly brushed it off, drew in a breath, and tried to calm my racing heart.

Millie's concerned voice greeted my ears. "What's wrong, Sabrina? Tell me."

I wanted to, but I couldn't. As nice as it was to pretend the Wolfe family members were friends, they weren't.

So after repeating, *Pull it together, and get the job done,* inside my head a few times, I opened my eyes and faked a smile. "Just some work stuff I need to take care of. Tell Beck and Lori I'm sorry to miss dinner, but I need to go to my room and take care of this."

Millie placed a hand on my arm as she searched my gaze. "You can talk to me, Sabrina. If you need me to keep a secret, I can."

I longed to share everything. But I couldn't. The last thing I needed was for Edwina to get wind of my crying or breaking down in front of someone related to a potential client.

Shaking my head, I replied, "I'll be fine. I'm just tired. If someone could send up a sandwich, I'd appreciate it."

Millie nodded. "Of course. And you have my number. Text me anytime, Sabrina. I mean it. I know what it's like to be surrounded by the Wolfe boys. And sometimes, it's too much and makes you want to scream."

A gravelly male voice I didn't recognize spoke up. "And what, exactly, are we like, Emilia?"

Turning, I spotted a tall man with broad shoulders, slightly graying hair, and a familiar set of eyes—ones like Beck's.

Millie narrowed her eyes at the man. "Don't call me

that. And I never thought I'd see the day when Weston Wolfe showed his face around here again."

He grunted. "You haven't changed."

Ah, so this was West, the mysterious older brother.

Millie sniffed. "And how would you know that? I moved in with your family fifteen years ago, and you've only been back how many times? Oh, that's right —twice."

Folding his arms over his chest, West shrugged one shoulder. "You're still the little girl trying to get into everyone's business. Eight, twenty-five, doesn't matter."

After making a sound of frustration, Millie stuck her tongue out at him and gave him her middle finger. "Fuck you, Weston Wolfe. For so many reasons."

She rushed into the house, not giving West another glance.

I had no idea what was going on between the pair. But at least the drama and appearance of yet another Wolfe brother distracted me from my own problems.

I walked up to him and held out a hand. "Hello. I'm Sabrina O'Connor. I don't know how much you've been told, but I'm here to help with marketing, PR, and taking Wolfe Family Farm and Winery to the next level."

With yet another grunt—seriously, this guy loved them—he shook my hand quickly and dropped it. "I'll see you around."

Then he turned and left.

Well, he clearly wasn't the congenial brother.

A million questions raced through my head about Millie, West, and the Wolfe family in general. But my phone was still heavy in my hand, a solid reminder that their personal lives weren't my business. Nothing outside of their winery mattered.

Since I was alone, I hustled up to my room. The longer I put off calling my boss, the worse it would be.

I did take a second to splash water on my face and reinforce myself for the potential verbal beating to come. Once calm—as calm as I could be—I picked up my phone again. I saw a text from Lori but ignored it for the moment as I dialed Edwina.

She picked up on the third ring. "What were you thinking, wasting time by riding horses recklessly? If the horse had been injured and they had to put it down, there's no way they would've ever worked with us."

Frowning, I tried to make sense of her words. "The horse bolted at a noise. I just tried to keep from falling off."

"That's not what I heard. Seeing this picture and hearing about you pissing off the client is trying my patience. Maybe you weren't ready for this, and you should come back."

Even though I should've held back, I blurted, "No, I can do this."

"You say that, but why should I let you stay there? The smart, focused woman I hired years ago wouldn't have made so many damn mistakes, let alone waste time talking to people who have nothing to do with the Wolfes."

"I'm still that person, Edwina. And there was a reason I visited with the neighbors and rode a horse." I quickly explained my plan of including joint events, ones the Wolfe family provided the wine for, as part of my overall strategy and added, "I'm really close to making the final pitch. Part of this job is building trust with the clients. And how can someone from the city do that if they won't dip their toe into the local life and way of doing things?"

Edwina hummed before answering, "I can accept that to a point. But you now have most of the research you need, correct?"

"Yes."

"Good. Then no more days out or chatting with locals apart from the Wolfe family. Sweet-talk them into signing."

Without another word, she hung up.

With a sigh, I put down my phone and rubbed my face. I'd hoped to take the full week, maybe ten days, to truly get to know the family and their business.

Someone knocked on the door, and I nearly screamed. Couldn't a girl get a little peace and quiet when her career was about to fall off a cliff? "Who is it?"

"Beck. Open this door, Sabrina. Now."

His authoritative tone sparked my temper. Maybe if I weren't emotionally exhausted or hadn't just suffered through being chewed out by my boss, I could've smiled and been polite.

But the day had been crappy to the tenth power, and I couldn't stop myself from shouting, "No!"

"Damn it, Sabrina. Open this door."

The knob rattled, and I wondered if he would

break down the door. If it were just Beck's house, I'd say good. He deserved to deal with his temper's aftermath.

But Lori and the others didn't. So I yanked the door open and glowered. "What do you want?"

"Why aren't you coming to dinner?"

"I have work to do."

He leaned down until his face was mere inches from mine and growled, "You need to eat and take care of yourself."

I leaned forward an inch. "I'm not a child."

"No, you're not." Something flashed in his eyes, and it shot straight to my core.

No, no, no. Don't let his sexy look distract you.

Poking his chest, I bit out, "I have work to do. Not to mention today's been a really, really long day. So just leave me alone, okay?"

It was on the tip of my tongue to tell him to fuck off, but I managed to restrain myself, just barely. He wasn't my boyfriend or husband, and he had no reason to look after me or care about my welfare. It was probably just some sort of power game to show he was still in charge despite his older brother coming back.

Beck took a step forward, but I didn't retreat. The heat of his body, combined with his scent of pure male twined with something woodsy, made my belly flutter and heat rush between my thighs.

Beck's breath danced across my lips as he said, "What happened today was partly my fault, which means it's my job to look after you."

His words threw me. "What are you talking about?"

Beck's hand brushed mine, and I nearly shivered. "This is my land and my home, and I should be able to protect you. And since I didn't, I have to ensure you're looked after."

He brushed some hair off my cheek, and I sucked in a breath. My heart started to race, and a steady pulse began between my legs.

Holy hell, I was in trouble. Big trouble.

Which meant I desperately needed to put distance between us.

Just as I raised a foot to retreat, Beck said, "You're coming to dinner, Sabrina. Even if I have to tie you to a chair and feed you myself, I'm going to make sure you eat and take care of yourself."

And without another word, he promptly tossed me over his shoulder.

I squealed like a little girl. And for a second, I lay there stunned and distracted by his large hand on my ass. One that I should be slapping away. And yet I wanted him to move his fingers down, down until he finally touched me where I ached for him.

What the hell? No, I couldn't let him touch me, no matter how much I might want it. Too much was at stake.

With my head a little clearer, I pounded his back. "Put me down, Beck. Right now. This is ridiculous."

But all he did was pat my butt and grunt.

When had he become such a Neanderthal?

And why did I like it?

Because no one has ever cared about you so much that they'd literally carry you to dinner to look after you.

No, no, no. That was crazy talk. This wasn't like in books or movies. Guys simply didn't go around tossing women over their shoulders and expecting it to be okay. Maybe for a sex fantasy or something, but I was positive Beck didn't have the same dirty thoughts as me.

My mother's voice returned: "*No man wants a fat bitch in their beds.*"

For once, I welcomed the awful words and took a deep breath. I needed to get this situation under control, and quickly.

I growled. "Put me down, Beckett Wolfe. It's embarrassing and rude, and you'll only end up hurting yourself."

He just grunted and patted my ass again.

"Gah, you're so infuriating. Do you know that?"

As soon as the words left my mouth, I mentally cursed. Given my luck so far with this assignment, Edwina would somehow learn of this scenario too. And then I really would be back in the city, getting the most menial tasks ever, my future full of social media posts and nothing else.

We drew closer to the dining room, and I closed my eyes. *Forget Edwina—what will his family think if they see us? What would they say? Would they ever want to work with me?*

But Beck stopped a little before the doorway and slowly slid me down his body. Unlike with the horse, when I'd been scared witless and numb, I felt every hot, hard inch of him.

My nipples pressed against his hard chest, making me wonder if he had chest hair I could rub against.

Then his hands slid down my sides slowly, until they rested on my hips before moving to cup my butt possessively.

When he squeezed, I nearly moaned. And then he pulled me close, his hard cock pressed against my soft stomach, and I sucked in a breath.

Beck leaned over, his hot breath caressing my ear as he whispered, "Will you come to dinner quietly? Or do I need to carry you into the dining room? Because I'll do it if necessary."

When he leaned back, I searched his gaze. "Why are you doing all this? I don't understand. You could've just sent dinner to my room."

"Because you're good at keeping yourself alone. But right now, after today, you need to be around people who care and make you laugh."

His words threw me, and I tried to make sense of them. Because, well, he was kind of right. I was so used to being alone, fighting things by myself, and trying to bottle up my emotions and feelings to cope.

Whereas when I was growing up, all I'd wanted was a family. One that could support me and be there for me. One that I could laugh and make memories with. One that could love me.

I hadn't thought about wanting all that in a long, long time. Yet Beck had instinctively known I wanted company tonight, even if I'd said I didn't.

How the hell had Beckett Wolfe seen that? Seen *me*?

He motioned his head toward the dining room, his voice softer now as he said, "Come on. Everyone's waiting for us."

"You didn't mention how you were going to go all caveman on me, did you?"

His lips twitched. "Nope. It's up to you whether they see it in action or not."

I rolled my eyes. "Now you're giving me a choice?"

His fingers brushed mine again, and part of me wanted to grab his hand.

But I resisted, focusing on his reply.

"I give choices most of the time. But sometimes, we all need to be yanked back into the reality we try to ignore."

I raised my eyebrows. "First, you're all Tarzan-like, a beat away from pounding your chest. And now you're getting deep?"

Tilting his head, he replied, "There's a lot about me you don't know, sweetheart. Now, come on. Dinner's getting cold."

He took my hand and tugged. But as soon as I moved my feet, he released me.

And for some reason, I didn't like that. Not at all.

Chapter Nineteen

Beckett

Thank fuck I was wearing an untucked flannel shirt tonight. Because, damn, having Sabrina's curves pressed against me, with her heat and scent surrounding me, as I carried her had turned me hard.

The hardest I'd ever been in my life.

I hadn't planned to cart her down the stairs. But I'd needed a distraction to keep myself from doing something stupid—like pressing her against the wall and kissing her until she moaned. Our tongues tangling, her thigh around my waist as she ground against me, and her cheeks flushed when she finally called my name.

Fuck. I was getting tired of fighting my attraction to

her. If she were someone in town, I'd just have one night of sex and get it out of my system.

But Sabrina was different. Even putting aside how we might work together, from the bits and pieces she'd shared about her life, she hadn't had a comfy family full of people who loved her. I also had no idea what was up with the sister she didn't want to talk about.

And I wouldn't even get started on the dipshit coworker of hers.

What she needed was to not be alone forever. No, she deserved a guy who could give her a relationship, and maybe a future, and have enough time to treat her as the queen she was.

But I wasn't that man. The winery needed me. My family needed me. And while it was nice to have a few days off to be with Sabrina, it wasn't something I could do long term.

In other words, I couldn't be the man Sabrina needed.

And that meant no sex with her. Ever. Because I'd rather cut off my dick than hurt her. She'd been damaged enough and didn't need any more pain.

However, I could be the one to make her feel welcome while in my house. Hence the flinging her over my shoulder and bringing her downstairs.

After Sabrina moved to follow me, we finally entered the dining room, Sabrina on my heels.

I noticed West had joined us, but he merely glowered at Millie. Who, in turn, completely ignored him.

I didn't know what lay between them. Millie had

barely seen West since she was nine years old, when he'd married and moved away. But given all the shit I'd dealt with today, I wasn't going to touch yet another problem with a ten-foot pole if I could help it.

Aunt Lori spoke up. "There she is. We were worried about you, dear. You didn't reply to my texts."

I sighed. "If you'd had a scare on a horse, would you really be in the state of mind to reply to half-decipherable texts with too many fucking emojis?"

Sabrina spoke up. "Sorry, Lori. I was busy talking with my boss."

I whipped my head around and noticed the tightness around her mouth.

What the fuck had her boss said now?

I nearly spit out the question but didn't want to ruin the dinner. Especially since Avery and Wyatt were watching and listening to everything we said like it was some sort of TV show.

Aunt Lori waved a hand in dismissal. "No worries. And before I forget, I'd like you to meet my great-niece and great-nephew, Avery and Wyatt Wolfe. You met West earlier, and they're his kids. Twins, in fact."

I glanced at West, and he met my gaze for a beat before he went back to glaring at Millie.

West could be a rude son of a bitch, and I hoped he hadn't made Sabrina's day even worse.

Sabrina's voice was decidedly more upbeat than earlier as she addressed the kids. "Hello, Avery and Wyatt. I'm Sabrina. Nice to meet you. When did you get here?"

Avery bounced in her seat. "Today. But I heard

about your scare on the horse! Daddy first taught me to ride years ago and made me repeat over and over again what to do if one bolts. I can teach you, if you want. Since I heard today was your first time riding."

I watched Sabrina's face closely for any signs of distress, but she merely smiled at Avery. "That would be super helpful."

Avery patted the empty space next to her. "Uncle Beck was going to sit here, but you can do it instead. That way, I can give you some tips. Horses are amazing but can also be dangerous. Safety first, as Daddy always says."

West gave his daughter a small smile.

Well, well, the bastard softened sometimes. At least for his little girl. Something I'd never seen him do after our dad's death, not even with his wife.

Not wanting to go down that road, I moved behind Sabrina's chair and held it out. Her cheeks pinkened, but she allowed me to help her into the seat.

Once done, I ignored the looks around the table—thankfully Abby was out interviewing for a teaching job in another city for the next two days, or she would've said something—and sat next to my nephew. Bumping my shoulder with his, I whispered, "What happened in the latest soccer match you watched?"

Wyatt's eyes lit up. I was a baseball guy, but Wyatt loved soccer, especially since a famous striker in England was originally from Starry Hills. Even if we hadn't seen Millie's much-older brother in more than a decade, the town still took pride in their homegrown son.

My nephew said, "It was epic. Well, mostly. Rafe Mendoza was hurt pretty badly at the end, and they said he might not be able to recover and come back. Does that mean he'll return to Starry Hills, and he could sign my jersey?"

I shot my gaze to Millie to see if she'd heard. Given how she laid down her fork and stared at her plate, I suspected she had.

Part of the reason Millie had lived with us after her parents' unexpected deaths was because her brother had refused to take her in and raise her. My mother had been made her guardian—she'd been best friends with Kim Johnson Mendoza since elementary school—and it had worked out in the end.

Looking at Wyatt, I replied, "He was just injured, so who knows. At any rate, let's eat before everything gets cold. I even baked fancy chicken tenders just for you and Avery."

As the kids dug in—I'd even made some homemade fries for them—Aunt Lori didn't miss a beat. "So, West, are you planning on buying a home in Starry Hills?"

Zach snorted, clearly unconvinced West would stick around, but quieted down when West glared at him. He had only been eleven when West left, and he still didn't really know how to tread around him.

West shrugged. "I'm playing it by ear."

Aunt Lori tsked. "You're just using that phrase because I can't stand it when people say that."

West gave a small smile. "It's the truth."

Avery had finished her chicken already—almost as

if she needed to eat quickly to join the conversation—and said, "I told Daddy we should stay here forever. I can't wait until spring and summer, when we can play in the orchard and among the grapes. Me and Wyatt can have epic games of hide-and-seek here, unlike at the Grenville Ranch."

That was her maternal grandparents' place in the Central Valley.

Aunt Lori smiled at Avery. "You can stay as long as you like, Tater Tot. I love having you here." She fake whispered, "There are far too many boys around."

Zach chuckled. "And here I thought you had a soft spot for me, Aunt Lori." He placed a hand on his chest as if he'd been struck. "I'm hurt."

Aunt Lori rolled her eyes. "You're not ten, lad. So stop trying to get all the attention."

He grinned. "Never."

As Millie and Aunt Lori teased Zach, my gaze found Sabrina's. I glanced at her plate, her mouth, and back again.

Rolling her eyes, she picked up her fork, dramatically speared some chicken, and put it between her lips.

I should've looked away—maybe I should've tried to add to my nephew's one-sided conversation about today's soccer game—but I couldn't take my gaze from Sabrina's mouth.

As soon as she swallowed, she licked her lips.

Fuck. What would it feel like to slide my cock between those soft beauties, to feel her moan around my dick, and then brand her throat with my cum?

When I met her eyes again, I saw a flash of heat that she quickly hid. Sabrina then made a point of talking to Avery and ignored me for the rest of dinner.

That was probably for the best. I did want to learn about what her boss had said to upset her, but that was it.

I most definitely wouldn't corner her somewhere and kiss her.

Nope. Never going to happen.

Chapter Twenty

Sabrina

I somehow managed to leave after dinner and dash to my room without Beck catching up to me.

Yes, I'd fled. But considering the heated looks he'd given me during dinner, ones that had me pressing my thighs together to try to tame my arousal, I hadn't wanted to chance it.

His making me eat was one thing. Allowing him to kiss me was another.

Plus, if he'd cornered me and asked, I would have ended up admitting he'd been right about my needing to be around people for a little while. Watching Zach, Millie, and Aunt Lori tease one another—with Avery always trying to join in, even if what she said was unrelated—had greatly improved my mood. Not even the broody oldest Wolfe brother had brought the familial air down.

And yes, for a while, I'd pretended I belonged with their family.

But the next morning, I texted both Beck and Aunt Lori about eating in my room so that they knew to leave me alone—*take that, Beckett Wolfe. Two can play your silly games*—and I could do some work.

Because if I got one more strike against me, Edwina would yank me out and give Justin a chance. Even if I thought he was behind some of the stuff making me look inept and stupid, I had no proof. In fact, if Edwina talked with HR and heard about my complaint, she might think I was just being petty.

I'd always wondered *why* HR had ignored my complaint. But there wasn't much I could do about that now.

Not wanting Justin Whitmore to take up any more space in my head, I reviewed and tweaked my presentation.

I didn't know how long I'd been typing and editing stuff on the computer when my phone vibrated. I checked and saw a text from Taylor:

Taylor: I'm still waiting on an update about the <wolf emoji>.
Me: You do know that I'm here to do a job, right?
Taylor: You can do both. I mean, everyone has to take breaks to eat. And we already know he likes cooking for you.

Me: He cooks for everybody.
Taylor: Maybe. But he also offered to hunt down the person who sent the creepy text. You also haven't told me any details about the horse scare. Is it related?
Me: Um...

My phone rang, as I'd thought it would. I answered, "It's complicated, Taylor."

"Well, then explain before I come up with some scary, weird story and drive up with a baseball bat wrapped in barbed wire. Or maybe a propane flamethrower."

And she would do it too.

I quickly recounted the bang and how Beck had slowed the horse and carried me into Millie's place. "And then he left to investigate the noise. That's it."

"He thinks it's related. And so do you, don't you?"

"Maybe. But I have no proof, Taylor. And I won't let Justin scare me off, if it is him."

Taylor sniffed. "I should hope not. I'm still debating whether I'll get Ben and all his super-strong pro baseball friends to go scare him a little. I bet Justin would piss his pants."

"No, don't make it worse. Promise me you won't make it worse."

"I don't want to, but fine, I'll promise. For now. What is your wolf doing, then? Has he found out anything?"

"Not much, really. Although Millie mentioned how he asked his friends to keep an eye out for Justin."

"So wait. This random guy you work for has put out a call to his friends, looking for the guy who might be fucking you over? That doesn't sound like a completely professional relationship to me."

Maybe I should have kept my mouth shut, but I blurted, "He also tossed me over his shoulder and carried me down the stairs."

"Wait. Are you serious?"

I grumbled. "Yes."

Taylor laughed. "Did he also shout, 'Mine!' while he was at it?"

"No. Stop being ridiculous. And I really should be getting back to work."

"You know, I'm still waiting for a picture of this guy. After all this, I need it, stat."

I sighed. "I've been busy. You know, trying to finally push my career to the next level. That kind of thing."

Taylor harrumphed. "You can get as much work done in a day as it takes most people three. Take a moment today to covertly snap a pic. Maybe when he takes off his shirt and lugs heavy things around. He'll be sweaty and glistening, which will show off his six-pack."

I laughed. "Just what are you imagining Wolfe Family Farm and Winery is like? It's February. And any lugging would be in the storage part of the winery, inside. Where you don't take off your shirt."

"He might if you asked him to."

The image of Beck shirtless, carrying cases of wine to his truck for deliveries knocked up my temperature a few degrees. I cleared my throat. "Don't be ridiculous."

"Hm, then Ben and I might need to book a cute little bed-and-breakfast near… What was it? Starry Hills? Then I can see him for myself. Maybe offer him my massage services."

"You're not a masseuse."

"I can be."

"Right, while your husband just watches?"

"Oh, Ben knows he's the only man for me. He's seriously got the biggest dick, and—"

"Nope, that's enough. You enjoy your husband's penis. I've gotta go. I have stuff to do."

She sighed dramatically. "Spoilsport. But in all seriousness, we're coming up, Sabrina. I need to validate theories."

"Fine. Whatever. But just don't expect a bunch of free stuff."

"You're not going to charge me for your time, are you?"

I snorted. "Bye, Taylor."

"Okay, from your tone I can tell you're getting irritated. So talk to you later, Sabrina."

She ended the call, and I checked the time. *Damn.* It was nearly noon already. And I'd already promised Lori I would meet with her for lunch and visit the last place on the farm I hadn't seen—the orchard.

After throwing on a pair of black pants and a sweater, I grabbed my purse and dashed out of the room.

And I instantly bumped into a tall, hard lump of man—West.

He steadied me, but unlike with his brother, his touch did nothing to my lady bits.

He grunted. "Are you okay?"

"Er, yes."

"Good."

With a nod, he went down the hall and into what I assumed was his room.

I blinked. Weston Wolfe was probably the least verbose man I'd ever met.

Pushing that thought aside, I hurried down the stairs and found Lori, Avery, and Abby in the kitchen. I blinked since Abby wasn't due back from Santa Rosa until later today.

Abby noticed me and smiled. "Once I learned West and his kids were here, I came home straight away."

Avery blurted, "Auntie Abby didn't get the job, so we're baking cookies to cheer her up."

I joined their group at the large kitchen island. "Oh, I'm so sorry, Abby. I'm sure you'll find something."

She shrugged. "Maybe it's a sign that teaching isn't for me. Millie has been asking me to work full-time with her, and maybe I will."

Avery stopped stirring the cookie dough. "Can I work with you guys too? I want some girl time."

Lori hugged Avery with one arm. "You can have all the girl time you need with us, even if I'm a million years old."

Avery shook her head. "You're not a million, Auntie Lori. Maybe a hundred but not a million."

We all laughed. And just like that, Avery Wolfe had made my day better—just like her uncle often did.

Nope, not going there. "Is there anything I can do to help?"

Avery blurted, "You should marry one of my uncles, and then you can stay here forever!"

I froze, and the room fell quiet.

Eventually, Lori patted Avery's shoulder and said, "Friends are always welcome here. You don't have to marry someone to be invited to visit. Sabrina's our friend." Her gaze met mine. "And she's welcome here. Always."

The sincerity in her voice caused emotion to choke my throat. Even if it wasn't really true, it meant a lot to me.

The oven beeped, and Abby tapped the empty cookie sheet. "The oven's hot, so let's get the cookies in. That way we can have hot, fresh ones right after lunch."

Avery scrunched her nose. "Do we really have to eat sandwiches first? Cookies would be a much better lunch."

Booping her niece's nose, Abby said, "Cookies afterward or not at all."

Avery sighed. "Fine. But I might accidentally get some batter on my fingers, and then I'll have to lick it off."

The adults all shared amused glances.

And so the time went quickly as I ate lunch and cookies with the three Wolfe ladies.

Although somewhere along the line, I started to

wish I could do this with my sister again. We'd made cookies every Christmas—it had been a special treat to buy chocolate chips—and had also tasted the cookie dough, even though we shouldn't have.

I hadn't thought about my sister recently, and pain stabbed my heart. We'd had some good times, despite our shitty mother. I'd thought we would always be close.

Yet in the end, Sydney had turned her back on me.

Not wanting to waste what little time I had in Starry Hills, I pushed aside the pain and memories and ate another cookie, focusing on the present.

Chapter Twenty-One

Beckett

Aunt Lori: I have something urgent to discuss. Come to the kitchen. <siren emoji>
Me: Is anything on fire? Do I need to bring a fire extinguisher?
Aunt Lori: You want to be a firefighter now? Yes, then you could start a <fire emoji> calendar for charity. Shirtless guys + kittens = <money bag emoji>
Me: So no then.

Since it wasn't an emergency, I finished going over the inventory with George—including what was lost in the accident—before heading toward the main house.

I had a feeling I knew why my aunt was calling me back. Today was my dad's birthday, and while the day wasn't as hard as the anniversary of his death, it still put me in a shitty mood.

As I walked through the vines, I remembered his teaching me to prune, how to check for disease, how to cull the least-productive grapes, and so many other things.

West had always treated it like a chore, but I'd loved it.

But it had been a struggle to keep loving it all once my dad died. I'd mostly gone on autopilot out of necessity to provide for my four younger siblings and my mother.

However, the joy had returned slowly. Though it was a fucking lot more stressful being in charge, I wouldn't want any other job in the world. Just imagining myself behind a desk for five days a week, eight hours a day made me itch to run the other way.

And it was because I loved this place so much that I struggled with what jobs to give to West. While the harvest last year had been fucking awful, we were a few rough years away from being destitute—and working with Sabrina should help turn things around. In other words, I could afford to let my brother work here and provide for his kids.

The problem was that giving away some of my responsibilities felt like I would break the promise I'd made to my dad.

My aunt's words came back to me: *"You don't have to do everything, Beck. Your father had a solid team to help him. He would want you to do the same and be free to live your life a little."*

For the first time ever, I started to wonder if she was right.

I reached the back entrance to the main house and went inside. As I approached the kitchen, I heard a lot of feminine laughter. Slowly, I moved to the doorway and peeked inside.

Sabrina laughed along with Abby and Aunt Lori as my niece had her hands held out, her eyes puppy-dog big, as she said, "Pretty please, Aunt Lori. You know cookies taste the best when they're still warm."

When Avery's eyes grew even bigger, Aunt Lori sighed. "One more, but that's it. Then you promise to go play outside with your brother?"

Avery nodded. "I will. Wyatt won't like it, but I'll drag him outside. I'm good at getting him to do what I want."

I didn't doubt it. Avery would be trouble when she was older. I just knew it.

Then Abby spotted me. "Man sighting at ten o'clock."

All heads swiveled toward me, and I walked into the room. I swiped a cookie and took a bite, the chocolate still warm and soft. "Fuck, that's good."

Avery waggled her finger. "That's a bad word, Uncle Beck."

"It's so delicious that I couldn't help it, sorry. Did you make it?"

Avery bobbed her head. "Yep. Auntie Lori and Auntie Abby helped. They're to make everyone feel better."

Sabrina gave me a subtle shake of her head before motioning toward Abby.

I met my sister's gaze, but it was guarded. "What happened?"

Abby shrugged one shoulder. "Nothing big. I just didn't get the job. Maybe it's a sign to give up teaching."

Her entire life, my sister had wanted to be a teacher. She'd played school with Zach and Zane—the twins were the closest to her in age—and hadn't wavered a second when picking her major in college.

Whatever had happened in San Jose at her last job had to be the reason for her about-face. "I'm sorry, Abby. You can always live here if you need to."

"Thank you, but no. Living with Millie is like when I was at college and had fun with my roommate. I like being close enough to visit you all often but in a different building so that I can have some peace and keep my sanity."

Needing to lighten the mood, I said, "You could live as far away as Australia, but if I got wind of some guy not treating you right, we'd all fly out and kick his ass. No one messes with our baby sister."

Abby rolled her eyes. "There's no guy at present. And in my current mood, maybe never."

I raised my eyebrows, and Abby did the same.

Nope, she wasn't going to talk about it.

So I turned toward my aunt. "What did you need me for?"

Aunt Lori gestured toward Sabrina. "You need to give her a tour of the orchard."

"Why?"

The word had come out harsh, but my aunt knew I didn't go to the orchard. Ever.

Aunt Lori shrugged. "I have invoices to pay, and I'm a little behind with the bookkeeping. Since Max King is still working for us, you should have the time to spare."

I narrowed my eyes at her.

She smiled. "I can waste time showing you my backlog, or you can just be a good host and take Sabrina on a private tour of the orchard."

Abby jumped in, "And no, I can't do it. I'm taking Avery to Starry Hills for some new clothes. She needs something awesome to wear to make her feel like she can conquer the world for her first day at her new school next week."

Zach couldn't give the tour in a cast, and West would probably grunt, say, "These are apple trees," and leave it at that.

No doubt my aunt had orchestrated the plan, but whatever.

I finally turned to Sabrina. And my eyes instantly zeroed in on the little dab of melted chocolate at the corner of her mouth. The urge to lean forward, lick it off, and taste her sweet lips rushed through me.

Putting my hands in my pockets to keep myself in check, I said, "You have some chocolate on your mouth."

Her hand flew up, and she ran her thumb across her bottom lip, and I itched to replace her finger with my own.

When she asked, "Did I get it?" I shook my head. "Is it here?"

Her tongue dabbed at the wrong corner.

The peek of her pink flesh made my dick harder. Fuck, what would it feel like to have her lick up my cock, until she reached the tip and made a show of licking off my precum? Her eyes trained on mine as she moaned and teased and all around tortured me sweetly with her mouth.

Sabrina tried the other side but still didn't get it. My restraint snapped, and I lifted a hand to her lips. Slowly, oh so slowly, I rubbed the corner of her mouth and removed the chocolate. Her gaze met mine as I sucked the chocolate off my thumb.

Her cheeks flushed, and her pupils dilated. And damn, she then had to go and lick her lips again.

Then Avery said, "It's gone!"

Clearing my throat, I moved my gaze and frowned at the smile on my aunt's face. For all that was holy, she was going to meddle.

Well, good thing I knew most of her tricks. Not to mention I was a stubborn bastard. The Wolfe family motto should read All as Stubborn as Mules.

Grunting, I turned toward the door. "Come on, then. Let's get this over with."

Despite how much I needed to put distance between us, I still waited by the door until she caught up. Then I opened it and followed her outside.

We walked in silence at first, which gave me a chance to get my cock under control. The cold air helped too.

Sabrina spoke first. "Thank you."

"For the chocolate or giving you a tour?"

She cleared her throat. "The tour. I know you're busy and all. But while the main focus is the winery, I also know you allow Millie to hold events in the orchard from time to time. And you sell the apples too."

I kicked a rock along the pathway. "I know it's not the most financially lucrative part of our business here. But my mom loved the orchard. It's also where a special tradition for the Wolfes takes place."

Fuck. Why had I let that slip?

"What tradition?"

I blew out a breath, knowing she wouldn't let it go. "Well, my dad proposed to my mom there, as did my grandfather and great-grandfather. Even my uncle Tim brought Aunt Lori here to do the same." I shrugged one shoulder. "Plus, I know Zach and Nolan want to propose in the orchard one day, and I can't tear it out to plant grapes and deny them that bit of history."

"That sounds so romantic and exactly the kind of thing that would help people feel closer to you and your family."

"What? We should tell strangers about it?"

"Maybe. Only if you're comfortable with it, of course. But people love romantic stories. And who knows? People might want to try doing the same thing. Especially if you have the orchard open for a set number of hours each week."

"I don't know. I'll have to talk to my family about it first."

"Of course. Especially if Zach and Nolan have partners right now, and they're just waiting for the right moment."

I shook my head. "Not that I know of. My brother Nolan—better known as Nolan Drake—never seems to keep a girlfriend for long."

Sabrina gasped. "Wait. Nolan Drake is your brother? As in the superstar who's in all the big movies?"

Glancing over, I smiled at her dropped jaw. "Yep, that's him. I'm surprised your research didn't dig that up."

She bristled. "I'm not a private investigator and never claimed to be."

"And yet, you know about stereotypes of country boys and sheep."

Sabrina stuck out her tongue, making me laugh.

Damn, it felt good to laugh again with someone other than my niece. "As for my brother, Nolan is super busy and rarely comes home. And probably only his superfans know his true name. Some of them used to book tours and ask questions, but we don't say much about him on purpose. Word of mouth spread about our being close-lipped, and the starry-eyed men and women stopped coming, for the most part."

"You wanted to help respect his privacy."

"Yes. I thought you'd want to start Nolan Drake tours or something like that."

"Sometimes people want to hide their personal lives and usually for a good reason."

I could tell her words were loaded. "Do you want to hide yours?"

For a long while—probably only a minute, in reality—she said nothing. Then she swung her arms and replied, "Yes, to a degree."

I wanted her to elaborate. However, glancing at her faraway look and furrowed brow—like she was trapped in a memory she didn't want—I restrained myself. Instead, I returned to her original question about my brothers. "And no, Zach doesn't have anyone."

True, his best friend had been in love with him for years. But I doubted he would ever notice Amber King in that way.

Sabrina readjusted her purse strap on her shoulder. "Well, getting back to your family tradition. If your family gives the okay, then mentioning it on tours might make couples reminisce. And if you have temporary wine stands in the orchard on weekends or special days, they may want to enjoy some wine and talk about those memories."

"You're really good at that."

"At what?"

"Finding angles to appear heartwarming while having an ulterior motive for people to buy or drink wine."

"Well, that's kind of what I do. If you just tell people to buy something, it means nothing. Maybe with millions and millions of advertising dollars, it could work. But most small or family businesses don't have that kind of cash. So you have to come up with more creative ways to advertise, to find a way for your brand to stay with a person or maybe resonate on a deeper level, making them want to try your product or service."

For the first time in my life, I was interested in advertising. "Is this related to that story stuff you sent Zach initially?"

"Yep. A lot of levels go into a fantastic ad campaign. If you can paint the customer as the hero looking to achieve a goal, and your company is the guide to help them along the way, it usually has a great outcome—and generates income. Appeal to the customer and their problems while saying you can help them, and it's a win-win scenario."

At times, Sabrina looked uncomfortable or uneasy. But when she talked about her work, she was confident and authoritative, and damn if I didn't find that sexy.

Who knew talking about ad campaigns could make me want to toss a woman over my shoulder, find the nearest empty room, and make her come with my tongue?

Fucking hell. There I went, thinking of Sabrina's pussy again.

Needing to run far away from those thoughts, I asked, "You love your job, don't you?"

She ran a hand over a shrub, her fingers trailing over the small leaves. "Well, most of the time. I hate the grunt work I've had to do over the last few years. But my goal is to work with clients, help them figure out their brand identities, and develop marketing campaigns. This assignment is how I'll achieve it." She bit her bottom lip and then added, "I hope, anyway."

Stopping, I gently put a hand on her shoulder. "Why wouldn't you? You've worked so fucking hard since you've arrived. You even got up on a damn horse despite being afraid, all to get to know us. It's far better than what I imagined working with you would be like."

She tilted her head. "And how did you imagine it? I'm curious."

I chuckled. "Working with some middle-aged guy who went on about percentages, reaching out to social media people, and who we'd pay a shitload of money to create ads."

"Well, I'm definitely not middle-aged or a man. But you are getting a discount, you know. My boss wants a foothold in Sonoma."

Zach had never mentioned that. "Why?"

"Because her ex-husband handles most of Napa Valley, and she's determined to take over Sonoma, even if it temporarily means a lower bottom line."

I whistled slowly. "Well, I guess I should be grateful she has such a huge fucking grudge against her ex. Otherwise, I might never have met you."

Shit. I probably shouldn't have said that.

Sabrina smiled as she met my gaze. "I'm glad I met you too."

For a few beats, we stared at each other. Her being outside, among the vines, a smile lighting up her face and eyes, made her so fucking beautiful.

So much so that I ached to pull her close, say fuck the world, and kiss her.

Her phone buzzed, and she said, "Sorry. It's probably my boss again."

I should be grateful for her cockblocking boss keeping me from doing something stupid.

She frowned, typed something, and then put it away.

"What is it?"

She waved a hand in dismissal. "Nothing. Just usual boss stuff." Pointing, she asked, "That's it, isn't it?"

I tore my gaze from her face and looked over. The large orchard of apple trees, the branches still bare and not yet showing the first signs of spring, lay just ahead.

Memories related to that day rushed back—listening to my dad's advice about which trees to cull and where to plant new ones and his suddenly clutching his chest before dropping to the ground.

My holding him, trying to figure out what happened, and the wail of the ambulance as I kept doing CPR. Later, my mother's pale face and tears when she returned from the hospital. My younger siblings asking why Dad couldn't tell them good night.

My walking through the vines for the first time by myself, feeling overwhelmed and uncertain.

I wanted to run in the opposite direction. Yet after so many years, part of me wanted to finally face the place where my father had died. Today being his birthday almost seemed fitting too.

Glancing at Sabrina and noting her excited expression, I had another reason to conquer my past. I wanted to be the one to show her the orchard, tell her some family stories and make her laugh, and finally revisit one of the most magical places from my childhood and see it as the treasured place it had been once upon a time.

Maybe with Sabrina at my side, I wouldn't dwell as much on the past.

Keeping my eyes on the trees, I replied, "Yep, that's the orchard. Come on. I want to get started before your boss bothers you again."

Without thinking, I grabbed her hand and lightly tugged. Sabrina followed and didn't try to pull her hand away.

And even though I should have, I didn't let go.

Chapter Twenty-Two

Sabrina

Edwina: Have they signed? I better hear yes today. I'm done being patient.
Me: Not yet, but I'll do it. I'm with the owner now.
Edwina: Update me in an hour. Do whatever it takes.

Not even Edwina's terse check-in comment could ruin my mood. Something about being outside, talking to Beck, and learning more about him and his family felt right and perfect and almost like I belonged.

Which wasn't true, of course. And yet it was nice to pretend.

I kept pretending when he wrapped his fingers around mine, trying my best not to notice how warm and big and deliciously rough his hand was.

But more than my wanting to pretend he was my guy for a little while, I'd seen his expression earlier, one of hurt and wariness and sadness. Something had happened in the orchard, but I wasn't sure what. For all that he was grumpy and strong, carrying the weight of his family and their business, he could be vulnerable too. It took everything I had not to ask him what was wrong.

However, I was already on thin ice with my boss. I needed to focus on nabbing the contract instead of anything else.

Although I couldn't resist squeezing his fingers in mine, and he did it back, which made me want to pull him close and never let go.

No, he's not for you, Sabrina. Remember that.

We were nearly to the large group of trees when we reached a big wooden sign that read The Wishing Tree Orchard.

Before I could ask, Beck explained, "Yes, we have another tradition here—the oldest tree, in the center near a bench, is called the Wishing Tree. Supposedly, if you place a hand on it and make a wish, it'll come true. Although if you really want to make it happen, you climb up until the tree surrounds you, where the magic is supposed to be stronger, before making your wish."

I almost wanted to dash ahead to find the tree, climb it, and see if it worked for me. Instead, I settled on asking Beck, "Have you made wishes with it before?"

He nodded. "When I was a kid."

"And they came true?"

He laughed. "The only one that came true was that I got a sister instead of yet another little brother. Although in retrospect, the sister ended up being more trouble."

I lightly shoved his arm. "Stop it. Abby's lovely. I like her."

Laughter danced in his eyes, and I stopped breathing. Happy, playful Beck was beyond handsome —he was almost god-level sexy. It took everything I had to focus on his words.

"I love my sister. But as her older brother, it's my right to complain about her sometimes. To be fair, I was spared the worst of her attentions, since there's a nine-year age gap between us. Zach and Zane are only two years older than Abby, so she became their constant shadow."

Before I could stop myself, I murmured, "It must be nice to have so many siblings."

"Most of the time. Although it was fucking difficult having that many strong personalities in one household. Thankfully my mom knew how to handle us. Even though we're all so different and required different types of attention and encouragement, she somehow just knew what we needed." He paused then added, "I miss her."

According to the family tree Abby had made me, their mom had died eight years ago.

My own mother had died nearly five years ago, but I didn't miss her. If only I could make her voice and criticisms leave me alone, life would be so much easier.

Although as I glanced over at Beck, I had to admit that around him, she was mostly quiet.

"I'm sorry, Beck. But I know your mom would be proud of how hard you've worked, both for keeping the winery going and for looking after your siblings. More than merely looking after them. It's as clear as day that you love your family, and they couldn't have asked for a better brother."

He raised his eyebrows. "Was that a compliment? From you?"

I stuck out my tongue, uncaring that it wasn't exactly professional. "Maybe I shouldn't be nice to you again."

"It's happening more and more. By the time you leave, I'm sure I'll be your favorite person." He winked.

I couldn't help but laugh. "Don't count on it."

When he leaned forward, his scent and heat surrounded me, making it hard to concentrate on his words. "Are you sure about that, sweetheart?"

It was on the tip of my tongue to say I already liked him far too much. However, that was a line I couldn't risk crossing. There was something else I could ask, though, and change the topic, put distance between us, and have less temptation. "What happened here that makes you sad?"

Beck frowned and moved his face away from mine. "What the fuck are you talking about?"

"No need to get all bristly. You're good at hiding your thoughts most of the time, but you let a few emotions show as we got closer to this place."

He grunted and looked away, and I thought he'd refuse to answer.

After tugging my hand and getting us going again, he asked, "Did you know that my father died in this orchard?"

I stumbled. Only because Beck quickly tugged to keep me upright did I not fall over. "What?"

Once he was sure I was standing on solid ground again, he nodded. "He died of a heart attack when I was eighteen. He and I were out here, checking to see if the apples were ready to harvest, and he fell to the ground." Beck swallowed before continuing, "I freaked out, unable to believe my strong and solid father could be dying. I barely understood his last few sentences before he stilled in my arms. Shock made me freeze, and I could do nothing but stare, precious seconds wasted. I don't know how long it took before I started doing CPR. I yelled at him to stay with me, to think of Mom and the family. I said he couldn't go. But no matter how loud I was, he didn't respond. He never woke up or breathed again, and by the time the paramedics arrived, it was too late. They said he was gone."

I placed a hand on my throat, willing myself not to cry. To have a parent you loved, one you wanted to save, and then couldn't was unfathomable to me. "Oh, Beck."

He smiled grimly. "For a long time, I thought that if I'd just tried harder, hadn't hesitated before starting CPR, I could've saved him, even if everyone told me that a few seconds wouldn't have made a difference.

Eventually I had to accept that sometimes people die, and there's nothing you can do about it." His gaze swept the orchard, and he pulled me along again. "But one thing I never forgot was the promise I made to him right before he died—that I would keep this place going, thriving, and be able to pass it on to the next generation. I was barely an adult and had hoped my older brother would help me."

But even I knew West had left not long after the father of the Wolfe family had died. "That's why you and your brother don't get along. Because he left Starry Hills. More than that, he left you alone to deal with everything."

Beck nodded. "Yes. After our father's death, West went on a wild streak of fucking one woman after another for a while and ended up getting one of them pregnant. He married her and ran as fast as he could to her family's farm. I didn't even know he planned to leave Starry Hills until the day of the wedding."

My eyes heated with tears. Despite how happy the Wolfe family seemed most of the time, they had their own ghosts and demons and pain.

Raising a hand, Beck followed along one of the branches with his finger as we passed. "West abandoned the family when we needed him the most. Even worse, he stayed away." He looked over at me. "That's what's between him and me."

Beck's eyes were sad and tired, and I could see how heavily everything weighed on him.

It also made me realize that though my family had been fucked up, it was far from the only one. That was the only reason I whispered, "My sister turned her back on me, too, so I understand."

We'd stopped walking, and he faced me. As he gently brushed a few escaped strands of hair off my face, I leaned into his touch. He felt so warm, solid, and almost familiar.

"What happened?" he asked.

As his gaze bored into mine, as if he could see straight to my soul, I debated blurting it all out. Not even Taylor knew the whole of it, only the abridged version.

Although I sensed if I told Beck about what had happened to my sister, I'd cross a line.

A line I might not be able to come back from.

Would I dare?

My lips parted, and I had no idea if I would've shared everything or not because suddenly, Abby dashed into the orchard and shouted, "Beck! Beck! There's a fire in the bottling house!"

Instantly, he dropped my hand and ran toward his sister. I followed close on his heels.

Abby leaned over, huffing, as she said, "West is there with everyone who can help. The fire department is on the way, but it still might be fifteen or twenty minutes before they get here."

Beck nodded. "Take Sabrina back to the house and then see if any of the people from the Evans' farm can help. Just in case it takes the fire department longer to get here."

Abby stood up. "I already called. Kyle and his dad are coming with some of their workers."

Beck grunted. "Good. Watch over Sabrina."

And with that, Beck ran down the road toward the billowing dark smoke in the distance. Hearing there was a fire and seeing how big it was were two different things.

My stomach churned with worry and fear. "How bad is it?"

Abby's expression turned grim. "Bad. I don't know if they can save the building, to be honest. It started out of nowhere and blazed to life quickly, from what the employees say."

"No one saw what caused it?"

Abby shook her head. "But given the explosion, I'm guessing it hit the wine almost right away."

I didn't think it was a coincidence that yet another accident had happened so quickly after the others. I didn't have proof, but my gut said it was my fault.

Chapter Twenty-Three

Beckett

Everyone tried their best, but in the end, the only thing we could do was keep the fire from spreading to the wine-making house, which was in a separate building.

But the bottling and packing building, complete with all bottles that had been stored but not yet moved to the warehouse, had been lost.

I stood next to West as we watched the fire crew drive away. They'd battled it for hours—the blaze had been fucking intense because of the alcohol—and had done everything they could. It was too early to tell the cause, but given all the other accidents and incidents, I suspected it had been arson.

And I bet Justin fucking Whitmore played a part in it somehow.

West placed a hand on my shoulder, and I glanced at him. My older brother's face was streaked with soot, his clothes were just as sweat-drenched as mine, and he looked as worn out as I felt. "The insurance means we can rebuild, Beck. At least no one was hurt."

That in and of itself had been a miracle.

Still, I walked away from my brother and ran my hands through my hair. "This never would've happened if I hadn't gone gallivanting around the property with that woman. I never should've taken my eyes off the place, stopped my daily checks, or allowed Aunt Lori to hire someone like Max King to take care of my duties."

West crossed his arms. "I highly doubt that even you could've stopped this, Beck, if turns out to be arson like the fire chief suspects. You're not a god and can't predict what people will do."

I growled, "How the fuck would you know this wouldn't have happened if I'd been more vigilant? You haven't been here in years, asshole."

My brother didn't even bat an eyelash. "Maybe not. But I've learned the fucking hard way that sometimes, you can't take care of or fix everything. Shit happens, and you just have to make the best of it."

I shook my head. "No, what I need to do is tell Sabrina to leave. After this mess…" I gestured toward the smoldering remains of the building. "There's no point in hiring her company. And without her to distract me, I can focus solely on making sure nothing else goes wrong."

Before I could turn around, West grabbed my wrist. "You're not fucking doing that."

"Let me the fuck go."

"No. Because if I do, you're going to make an ass out of yourself and possibly make a mistake you can't undo."

"What the hell are you talking about?"

West didn't bother to answer me. "What you're going to do is take a shower and put on some clean clothes, and then we're going to The Watering Hole."

I tugged, but damn West, he was too fucking strong. "I'm not going out. I have a shit-ton of work to do."

West leaned forward. "You. Are. Going. Out. Until you calm the hell down, I'm not letting you anywhere near that sweet woman."

Narrowing my eyes, I spit out, "Sweet woman? What does that mean? Are you looking for a new mother for your kids?"

He rolled his eyes. "Believe me, I have zero desire to be in a relationship ever again. But Sabrina is nice, and best of all, she makes you less of a prickly asshole."

"Only because I have to be nice to her. We wanted —and still need—her help."

"Tell yourself that."

"Fuck you, West. Now—"

"No. If I have to drop you into one of the horse troughs to shock some sense into you, I will. But we're following my plan for the night."

I tugged my hand free and tried to run.

But West grabbed me from behind, wrapped his arms around my waist, lifted me, and carried me as if I weighed nothing.

"Put me down, motherfucker."

"No."

I tried to kick his knee or balls but couldn't manage it.

And the bastard did indeed find the nearest horse trough and dumped me into it.

I sputtered, trying to sit up. "You are so fucking dead, West."

He crossed his arms. "Now, you're going to stay in there until you chill the fuck out. I don't care if your balls shrivel and turn blue either."

Glaring at him, I gave him the double-bird. When we were kids, West had always acted the part of the big brother, usually getting whatever he wanted because he was older and stronger. It had always been a battle between us. But right here, right now, it was about more than his wanting me to keep my temper under control.

This was years of pent-up anger about to burst free.

I jumped up and launched myself at my brother. West hadn't expected it, and he fell backward. I tried to punch him, but he caught my arm.

We tumbled, each trying to punch the other but never quite succeeding.

I had no idea how long we rolled around on the ground before Aunt Lori bellowed, "Enough!"

We both froze. Hers was probably the only voice, apart from our mother's, that could do that.

She walked up to us and tugged on each of our ears, seeming not to care that we were grown men. Once we stood, she released us and shoved West's arm and then mine. "What the hell are you two doing out here?" She pointed at West. "Your kids are worried sick, waiting to see that you're okay." She turned to me. "And you—Sabrina's locked herself in her room and won't come out." Looking between us, she said, "So tell me why the fuck you're out here fighting like children."

Oh shit. If Aunt Lori was swearing without drinking several glasses of wine, she was pissed.

And with the anger haze all but gone, I realized how we looked. West and I were wet and covered in filth and had been acting like we were ten and not men in our thirties.

Although I couldn't resist muttering, "West started it."

My brother rolled his eyes as Aunt Lori placed her hands on her hips. And even though she was at least a foot shorter than either of us, I still felt like we were looking up at her. "I get that boys—yes, boys, not men—like to punch one another then make up or something like that. I've never understood it. But now is not the time. You need to get back, clean up, and eat something. Tomorrow, we can face all the shit that happened today and form a new plan. But only once your emotions have settled down."

West leaned over and whispered in Aunt Lori's ear, and she nodded. "I agree with West. You should go out with him and drink yourself into oblivion, and Abby will get you when you're ready."

I grunted. "No, I'm not going out."

Aunt Lori pinned me with a take-no-shit stare. "I know your temper, Beckett Wolfe, and how much trouble it causes. Calm the fuck down before you do more than get clean inside my house."

While it was technically my house, I wasn't about to argue.

Glaring at West, I replied, "I can't promise he'll come back with that pretty face intact."

Aunt Lori sighed. "If you two need to hit each other to start loving each other again, then by all means, do that. Just not in my house or in my sight. However, don't expect any sympathy from me after the fact." She pointed toward the house. "Go. And don't even think of trying to talk with Sabrina tonight, Beckett. She doesn't deserve your temper."

As the adrenaline in my body waned, exhaustion weighed me down. "The last thing I want to do is talk to anyone rationally right now."

"Good. Then talk in grunts with your brother. You used to do that." She clapped once. "Now, march. Or I'll find a branch to prod you along like cattle."

Under any other circumstance, I might've laughed at the image of tiny Aunt Lori poking us. But today had been shitty, I was tired, and getting drunk sounded more and more enticing.

After all, it wasn't as if anything else could go to shit before the morning.

Later, after Abby dropped us off at The Watering Hole, West and I remained silent. I hadn't talked to him, or vice versa, since Aunt Lori scolded us.

And if I had my way, I wouldn't do anything but drink a shit-ton of beer and eat hot wings for the rest of the night.

Once we entered the familiar bar, a few people murmured how sorry they were about the fire. I did my best to smile but could only manage to nod.

Luckily, Kyle was nowhere to be seen. Though I could ignore West easily, ignoring my best friend would be harder.

The bar's interior was weathered wood, the walls had road signs and old pictures, and a few worn leather couches sat in the back. After ordering a pitcher of beer, we sat on one of the couches. I chugged the first glass, wanting to numb my mind. Because if I thought too hard, I'd dwell on how I'd failed my father in a massive way.

West sipped his beer, though, and bounced his leg on the floor.

I glared. "Can you stop that?"

His leg stilled. "Someone's tetchy."

I poured more beer into my glass and drank some more. "Of course I'm motherfucking tetchy. I know you haven't been around, but last year, the harvest was really bad. And now with the fire? It's going to be fucking tough."

He sipped and then said, "Just rent a facility from one of the closed-down wineries in the area. It'll work until we rebuild."

I frowned at him. "What?"

West shrugged. "It'll be a pain in the ass to

transport the aged wine barrels, but it's better than halting production altogether."

I drank another gulp of beer, the alcohol starting to ease my nerves a little. "Since when do you care about wine?"

His gaze was unreadable. "Just because I've been tending cattle for over a decade doesn't mean I've forgotten everything Dad taught me." He paused, sipped his beer, and looked forward. "And what I hope you'll teach me."

"Why now?"

West didn't try to misunderstand. "The Grenvilles wanted to send Avery and Wyatt to a fancy private boarding school, saying I didn't have time for them. Not that they ever offered to help take care of their grandkids." His grip tightened on his glass, and I half expected it to shatter. "And all while I was working my ass off to keep their ranch going. Fuck them. They have no legal right to Avery and Wyatt, and I wanted to take them away from that toxic-ass family. So I came home."

Since I'd met his late wife, I understood a little about what it must've been like to live with her. "Why now, though?" I asked again. "You stayed away for a long time, brother."

West sighed. "I was trying to make my family work. And it took Andrea's death for me to realize that sometimes you can't save a person if they don't give a fuck about anyone but themselves."

We both drank our beers and fell into an almost-comfortable silence. Knowing my brother had been hurting for so long made most of my resentment fade.

Most but not all.

"If you fucking run away again, West, then you won't be welcomed back."

He shook his head. "I have no intention of running. Wolfe Family Farm and Winery is where Avery and Wyatt belong." He paused and added, "Where I think I belong."

And just like that, I couldn't stay too mad at my brother. Hell, for West to admit any of that shit was monumental.

Which meant he really wanted to be back with his family again. "Don't dump me in a horse trough again. Ever. Because I will kick your ass next time, no matter what Aunt Lori says."

West's lips twitched. "More like I'd kick yours. You've gone all soft from working with grapes, whereas I've been wrestling fucking cattle for years."

"I'm still taller."

"And I'm stronger."

We looked at each other, an understanding passing between us. While not perfect, we were much, much better.

And with a little more time, we might be friends again, like we'd been as kids—well, when we hadn't been trying to kill each other.

The pitcher was empty, so I went to the bar to get another one. As the bartender filled it, the front door opened, and a flashy guy wearing a suit with his hair perfectly styled and a big gold watch on his arm walked in. I didn't recognize him or the three men with him, only that they weren't local.

Sure, Starry Hills had its fair share of tourists. Wine tastings were in high swing in the summer, but a few still ran in February.

But tourists didn't usually find The Watering Hole, which was off a side street, toward the edge of town, and was a haven for locals to gather.

The bartender returned with my pitcher. After I paid, I headed back toward the couch just as the outsider's voice carried. "Not much longer, guys. As soon as I sign the Wolfe account, I'll treat you all, and we'll celebrate. By now, that bitch should be packing her bags and leaving with her tail between her legs. Maybe now she's learned her lesson not to fuck with me."

Stilling, I looked over at the man. My last name had caught my attention, and suspicions bounced around in my head.

Then he said, "First the Wolfe family and then all of Sonoma County. I'll be the king of wine advertising, and you helped make it happen. I won't forget that."

Son of a bitch. The bastard had to be Justin Whitmore.

Before I beat his ass, I needed to be sure. So I kept my anger as bottled up as I could manage, went to the table, and asked, "Wolfe family? You mean their winery?"

The guy sat taller, clearly not recognizing me. "I shouldn't say, but yes. They're going to be my clients very soon. Maybe even by tomorrow. Are you another winemaker in the area?" He reached into his suit jacket and pulled out a business card. "Take it. The name's Justin Whitmore, and I'm with a very exclusive marketing-and-PR firm in San Francisco."

Red descended over my gaze, and I balled up the card and threw it at him. This motherfucker had been causing hell and scaring Sabrina.

Fuck, he'd nearly killed her with the horse stint. Because yes, I knew in my gut it had been him.

I tossed my pitcher of beer at Justin. It distracted him long enough for me to reach over, grab his fancy shirt, and yank him across the table until his face was mere inches from mine. Fear filled his eyes.

Good.

I pulled him even closer, until he tried to struggle. "Listen, dipshit. I'm Beckett Wolfe, and you're not going to fucking work with my family. Not now, not ever. And if you ever try to mess with my family or anyone under my roof again, I will hunt you down and ensure you get the message." I tightened my grip on his shirt. "But first, I'm going to kick your ass like you deserve, you little dickwad."

"Stop, or I'll—"

Before I could reply, West put a hand on my shoulder. "Let him go, Beck."

Justin squirmed, and the urge to punch the motherfucker coursed through me. "No. This is the guy responsible for all the accidents. For nearly getting Sabrina killed."

West was still cool and collected as he replied, "He's not worth it, Beck."

Until you have proof was left unsaid.

As I stared into Justin's smarmy face, the urge to acquaint him with my fist—repeatedly—grew stronger. He deserved to have his ass kicked and to realize there were consequences to his actions.

Yet a small part of my brain knew that if I beat him up, his company would want nothing to do with us, which would hurt Sabrina more than it would hurt this asshole.

And she deserved better. Earlier, I'd been blaming her but it was actually this bastard's fault. The entitled jerk with a tiny dick, whose ego had been hurt, was looking for ways to punish the person who didn't think he walked on water.

After one last shake, I tossed him back. "Thank my brother, or you'd probably be in a hospital within the hour."

Justin didn't say anything, just scrambled away and ran out the door.

When I glanced at the bartender, we nodded at each other. I'd known John Thompson my whole life, and he trusted that if I'd been about to kick someone's ass, I had a reason.

I shared a glance with my brother, and we headed out the door. As we waited for our sister to arrive, I told him about all the incidents and a vague version of how Justin was looking to punish Sabrina.

In the end, he agreed to help me keep an eye out for any more trouble. West would also help with setting up some more security cameras and even offered to visit some bottling facilities to find the best one for us to rent.

It felt weird to discuss things with my big brother after so many years apart. While we were far from being best friends, at least we could talk and make decisions about the business.

Although he was leaving the PR and marketing aspect to me, provided Sabrina's company still wanted to work with us. I would have to make the case that production would be up and running again soon, and the fire shouldn't affect our output too much.

Yes, in the morning, I'd seek her out and try to get things in motion.

Except once I finally woke up and went to her room, it was empty.

Sabrina was gone.

Chapter Twenty-Four

Sabrina

As I closed the door of my apartment behind me, my eyes swept around the place—the couch, the small table that served as my desk, and the tiny kitchen had been my refuge for so long. But as I tossed my keys into the bowl near the door and shrugged off my coat, my home seemed emptier than normal.

Even with the constant hum of traffic below, it was quiet—no family squabbles, laughter, or even the constant vibrations from Lori's texts.

In less than a week, I'd become addicted to life with the Wolfes. It had been nice pretending I belonged with them too. But that time was over, and now I needed to get back to work and reality.

I'd let my boss know about the fire, and she asked

me to return to the city. I would have a meeting with her later today to plead my case about how we shouldn't give up on the Wolfe family. Yes, the fire had devastated their bottling facility. But knowing Beck, I was sure he'd find a way to bounce back and keep going.

After all, he'd been doing it since he was not much older than a child.

Beck. I'd wanted to see him one last time. But I knew he was probably angry with me and for good reason—no doubt Justin had caused the fire, even if I didn't have proof.

My presence had only ever caused that family problems, and I couldn't stay and hurt them further.

My mother's voice rang in my head: *"You ruined my life. You're worthless and unwanted, and you should never have been born."*

I tried to muster the strength to fight back but couldn't.

Sighing, I rolled my suitcase into my tiny bedroom, unpacked, and then took a short nap. I did everything I could to avoid looking at my phone or my computer.

But as lunch came and went, I knew I couldn't put it off much longer. And when I finally unlocked my phone, I found a crap-ton of texts waiting. I almost deleted Lori's string of messages to me without reading them. But I wanted—no, needed—one more experience with her. Just one. And then I could go back to my old life.

So I read:

Lori: I hope you'll come to breakfast.
Lori: I mean it. I think you need a hug.
Lori: Why did you leave?
Lori: You know what, I'm mad that you didn't say goodbye.
Lori: Avery wants you to come back, and I think it's a good idea. When are you coming to visit?
Lori: Sabrina? Don't shut us out, dear. Text me back.

The words blurred as I held back tears. She hadn't even used emojis, showing how serious she was.

But no, leaving was for the best. If Justin could set an entire building on fire, what else would he do to get the promotion instead of me? Would Avery or Wyatt be his victims next time? What if Beck ended up having an accident and maybe dying?

I couldn't have that on my conscience.

After deleting Lori's messages, I skimmed Taylor's. I'd call her later.

As for Beck, there was nothing from him, which I should've expected, yet it still stung.

Since it was nearly one o'clock and I had a meeting at four, I decided I'd better check my email and do some work. The best way to handle Edwina was to be prepared to kick ass and take names.

I'd barely opened my email when someone knocked on the door, making me jump. *Who the heck could it be?* Taylor would be at work, and my boss would never waste time visiting an employee at home. It was probably one of those religious people wanting to give me a pamphlet or something like that.

Looking through the peephole, my heart skipped a beat.

Because standing on the other side of my door was Beckett Wolfe.

"Sabrina?" He knocked again. "Open up. We need to talk."

I froze. How did he know where I lived?

More than that, what would I say to him? What did he need to say to me?

He probably just wanted to chew me out for the fire and to officially let me know he wanted nothing to do with me. Maybe my employer had given him my address, or he'd found it online.

Stop stalling and get this over with. After taking a deep breath, I undid the chain lock and the bolt before opening the door. I peeked out and did my best to ignore his sexy dark scruff, flannel shirt, and jeans that ended inside a pair of dark-brown cowboy boots.

After clearing my throat, I asked, "Yes?"

"May I come in?"

No shoving in or demanding to see me. Was it because he remembered the story about Justin?

More likely, it was just the good manners he always had with me.

Stepping back, I gestured inside. "Come in."

He waited until I'd shut the door and turned around before asking, "Why did you leave without saying goodbye?"

His prickly tone rubbed me the wrong way. Any guilt I felt fled as I said, "It's none of your business."

Beck stepped forward, forcing me to retreat, until my back hit the door. As his large, warm body crowded mine, my heart rate kicked up. His breath tickled my cheek, and I itched to close the distance between us. To feel his hard body under my fingers, to feel his lips against my skin, and then to rub against him to ease the ache pounding between my thighs.

Stop it. I clearly needed to put some distance between us if I was to survive this conversation. I placed a hand on his chest, intending to push him away. But as soon as I felt his hard muscles through his shirt, I looked up into his eyes.

Eyes that were filled with a combination of anger and heat.

I blinked, confused.

He leaned forward, his breath dancing across my lips as he asked, "I repeat—why did you leave without saying goodbye?"

Doing my best to act as if his nearness didn't affect me, I said, "I thought it was obvious."

Beck leaned in another inch, his scent invading my senses, tempting me again.

"Did you give up on my business? Was that all the last few days have meant to you? You were just schmoozing a client and then walking away when it looked like there was nothing to gain for your job?"

Narrowing my eyes, I spit out, "Of course not! I'm the cause of all your problems! That's why I had to leave. I couldn't let anyone else get hurt because of me."

Tears pricked my eyes, and I willed them to stay back.

Which became exponentially harder when Beck's gaze softened. He slowly raised a hand to my face, waited a moment to see if I'd tell him no, and then cupped my cheek. Having his warm fingers against my skin made me suck in a breath.

As he stroked my face, each pass sending more heat throughout my body, he murmured, "You were worried about me. About my family."

A tear slipped out. "Of course I was worried. I still am. You all have been so nice and welcoming, and for a short while, I could pretend—"

I stopped before I embarrassed myself.

Beck wiped away my tear with his thumb, so gentle and tender, which only made more slip down my cheeks.

"Shh. Don't cry, sweetheart."

I struggled to get myself together. All the while, Beck continued to stroke my cheek as he searched my eyes. Each caress of his warm, rough finger helped calm me a fraction.

Well, calm me while also setting my body on fire.

He was so close, his scent everywhere, and combined with his touch, I wanted to cross the line—the one between being colleagues and maybe becoming something more.

Beck asked, "Pretend what, sweetheart? Tell me."

His words were soft and coaxing, and I couldn't

resist him any longer. "I could pretend to have a family." Something flashed in his gaze, something I couldn't read, and I quickly looked away. "I know. It's pathetic. I'm an adult, not a child."

"Look at me, Sabrina."

I resisted, but when he gently tried to turn my face, I complied. But instead of pity or derision in his eyes, I saw warmth, understanding, and something I couldn't identify.

He said, "It's not pathetic to want something you've never had. From what I've gathered, your family wasn't like mine."

I shook my head, not ready to reveal just how much.

He continued, "Well, it's a good thing you like my family so much because Avery and Aunt Lori have all but ordered me to convince you to visit. Even if there's no contract, no working relationship, they want to see you again."

"And what about you?"

Damn. I shouldn't have asked that. I sounded so needy.

But Beck's gaze flared with wanting. "Do you want the truth, sweetheart?"

He'd called me that a few times now. My heart soared, but I still refused to hope.

Beck added, "Well, I'm going to give it to you straight—yes, I want you to come back. But no, not just as a business associate."

"As what?"

"As mine." He nuzzled my cheek, and I almost

moaned at the feel of his rough stubble against my skin. "When I found your room empty, all I could think about was heading to the city and finding you."

"Why?"

After leaning back, he replied, "So I could finally do this."

Beck pressed his mouth to mine. Desire, wanting, and heat rushed through my body. He was gentle at first, barely brushing his mouth against mine, teasing me. But it wasn't enough, not nearly enough.

I dared to run a hand up his chest to the back of his neck.

He smiled against my lips before tugging my bottom lip between his teeth. "Open for me, sweetheart."

Yes. I didn't hesitate. And as his tongue invaded my mouth, claiming me, I dug my fingers into his long hair. That made him growl and take the kiss deeper, harder, and more desperate, our tongues tangling. I wrapped my other arm around his back and rubbed against him, needing the combined feel of his mouth on mine and his hard body against my hard nipples.

I moaned, lost to the feel of him, the taste of him, even the smell of him. My pussy ached, and my clit throbbed. I wanted more, so much more.

Beck ran his hands down my sides, to my hips, and moved them around to grip my ass. He rocked me against his hard cock, and I sucked in a breath, breaking the kiss. As I stared into his heated gaze, he did it again, making me whimper. "Beck."

He pressed me even closer against his body as he

took my mouth once more. I moved my hand, threading my fingers into his long hair, and tugged lightly. His growl made me shiver, sending even more wetness between my thighs. We became a blur of tongues and teeth, trying to get as close as we could with our clothes still on.

He finally tore his mouth away to kiss down my neck, licking me, then nibbled where my neck met my shoulder before soothing it with his tongue.

Between his cock pressing against my clit and his sweet torture with his tongue and teeth, I moaned, clinging to him. "Beck. Please."

His eyes found mine again. "Are you close?" When I nodded, he rocked me against him. "I want to hear you scream, sweetheart. Ride my dick, and come for me."

Beck placed his hands at the bottom of my butt and lifted, and I wrapped my legs around his waist. As I arched against his hard cock, he groaned. "Fuck, you're going to kill me."

Pride rushed through me at the thought that I could do this to him.

He took my mouth again, squeezing my ass like a command. I moved, rubbing harder, faster, lost to sensation and desire and pleasure. I was close. So close. When Beck bit my bottom lip and dug his fingers harder into my ass cheeks, it was the final push I needed.

Pleasure coursed through my body as my pussy convulsed. I cried out as it went on and on, Beck moving my hips to prolong it, to the point that I thought I might cry from how damn intense it was.

Finally, he stilled, and I came down from the high oh so slowly, until I laid my head on his shoulder and wrapped my arms around his torso, too sated to do anything else. The sound of his heavy breathing was soothing, his musky male scent comforting.

It was like a dream I never wanted to wake up from.

But as my heart calmed down and the seconds ticked by, my brain started to work again, and it dawned on me what I'd just done.

As if sensing my panic, Beck slowly rubbed circles on my back. "Not yet, Sabrina. I need to hold you close for at least another minute, sweetheart."

His words made me tighten my arms around him. I had no idea what would happen after the next minute, but for now, I could do what I did best—pretend.

Pretend Beck was mine.

Pretend he couldn't wait to strip me and fulfill my fantasy about being fucked in cowboy boots.

Pretend I'd finally found a guy I connected with, who wasn't an asshole, and who wouldn't mind how screwed up I was, thanks to my mother.

I memorized how his hard body felt against me, how his warmth made me sleepy, and how he held me as if he wanted me forever.

It couldn't last. I knew it couldn't. But right here, right now, I had Beck all to myself. And I'd make the most of it until he was gone.

Chapter Twenty-Five

Beckett

I hadn't planned on making Sabrina come by riding my cock so soon after knocking on her door. Yet as I held her afterward, her soft, warm body wrapped around me, I wanted more. So much more.

I wanted to strip her naked, caress every inch of her skin, and explore her curves with my tongue. Only when she bucked and squirmed would I finally thrust into her and make her fall apart around my dick. Then I'd start all over again, claiming her every which way I could imagine, until we were both too exhausted to do anything but fall asleep in each other's arms.

And I'd do the same every day, making her mine bit by bit, until she was my girl for good.

Finding Sabrina's room empty back at my house

had sent a rush of panic through me, and it'd been so fucking strong. The thought of never seeing her, never getting the chance to kiss her, and never knowing if she felt this pull as much as I did had kicked me into motion.

So here I was in San Francisco, her sweet body in my arms, her cries of pleasure still ringing in my ears.

But as she stiffened, I wondered if she regretted what had just happened. We hadn't really talked beforehand, and I couldn't put it off any longer.

"Put me down, Beck."

I helped her slide down my body, barely resisting the urge to taste her lips again.

However, as soon as she was on her feet again, I hated how she wouldn't look at me. After placing a finger under her chin, I gently lifted it and forced her eyes to mine. The uncertainty in her gaze shot straight to my heart, almost as if she was waiting for me to reject her, push her away, or some shit like that.

I wouldn't. Even if the pull toward her was as inconvenient as fuck, I couldn't seem to resist it. "Tell me what's going on inside that head of yours, Sabrina."

She gave a bitter laugh. "You really, really don't want to know that."

Leaning forward, I placed a gentle kiss on her lips and whispered, "But I do. I really do. Even if I need to make you come again—maybe this time with my tongue—to relax you enough to talk, I'm up for the challenge, sweetheart."

Her brow furrowed as she searched my eyes, her

own full of confusion. "I don't understand. I thought men didn't like that kind of thing."

Well, the dickheads before me clearly didn't know how to treat their women. I growled, "I could eat your pussy for hours and still crave more."

Her cheeks turned red. "Don't tease me."

"I'm not fucking teasing you. You felt how hard my dick is. I want you, Sabrina. But I can also be patient. Something has clearly spooked you, and I want to know what it is."

She glanced to the side, and I waited.

If I pressed her too hard, she might close down and push me away.

She finally spoke, her voice quiet. "Why are you really here, Beck? Don't lie to me."

"I'm here because finding you gone made me crazy. The thought of never seeing you again? Fuck, I couldn't live with it. I know it hasn't been long, but we have a connection, Sabrina. One I'm not ready to give up. Haven't you felt it too?"

Her gaze finally found mine, and the tears in her eyes surprised me. "I do. But I can't act on it, Beck."

Fuck it, I couldn't let her suffer and not comfort her. I took her hand in mine and squeezed gently. "Why?"

"Oh, I don't know—my boss wouldn't like it, you might not get the contract at the discounted rate you can afford, and what if Justin doesn't give up and keeps causing trouble? I couldn't put your family or business through that."

"That's something we all decide together, not you alone."

She shook her head. "I won't let your family get hurt because of me, Beck. Not after how kind they've been to me."

Damn, she worried and cared about my family after such a short time, and it did something strange to my heart. "Justin shouldn't be a problem again, so don't worry about him."

At my confident tone, she frowned. "Why do you say that?"

"He and I met in a bar, and let's just say I scared the shit out of him."

"What did you do?"

"Well, my beer may have accidentally ended up in his face, and my hand might have accidentally yanked him across a table to make a few threats."

She blinked. "What?"

"It was fun watching that dickhead squirm. My brother West snapped a picture of him, too, so now everyone in our circle knows his face. If that jackass shows up again, he'll probably trip and fall into a pile of cow shit before hightailing it out of town."

"Wait. Are you saying you're going to round up the boys and chase him out of town with shotguns?"

I grinned. "If need be. I bet he'd piss his pants, maybe even scream too. We can take a video so you can enjoy it as well."

Sabrina rolled her eyes, but her smile betrayed her true feelings.

"Oh, come on. You'd love it. Being honest is the best policy, after all."

"I've been honest with you, Beck. Being around me will only cause you trouble."

I raised an eyebrow. "Yes, but not for the reasons you think."

She huffed. "Why are you being so stubborn about this? I'm not worth putting your family in danger."

I risked cupping her cheek and nearly hummed when she leaned into my touch. "We know a lot more about the threats now. Plus, our friends and neighbors and others in town will help protect my family too. Aunt Lori hates bullies, and she wants Justin's head nearly as much as I do."

Her lips curved upward. "Did she tell you that via emojis?"

"No, but don't give her any ideas."

As we smiled at each other, it made me want Sabrina all the more—the teasing, the easy conversation, the ability to discuss anything with her and knowing she'd listen.

She sighed. "You *are* like a dog with a bone, aren't you?"

"Not the most flattering comparison, but yes." Stepping closer to her, I caressed her cheek with my thumb. "Does that mean I can kiss you again?"

"Focus, Beck. What about if my boss finds out about us and cuts all ties with your family? You know your business needs the help."

I shrugged. "I would find a way to make it work.

Maybe I could hire a freelancer, such as a city girl who looks sexy in skinny jeans and a sweater that brings out her eyes, one who already knows my family." She opened her mouth, but I placed my forefinger on her lips. "I had the entire drive here to think this over, to think of the consequences, to debate the pros and cons. But you know what? I've never felt this kind of connection with a woman before." After removing my finger, I tugged her toward me. "I want to give us a try, Sabrina. So what do you say? Will you go on a date with me?"

"Are you sure?"

"Really, really sure."

After searching my eyes for a few moments, Sabrina sighed. "I don't know if I can say no to you."

"So that's a yes?"

"Well, that depends. Will it be a real date? Or just some tumble in a barn, where we have to keep quiet and not scare the horses? Or cows? Or whatever you have?"

Placing my hand on her hip, I replied solemnly, "The barn fucking isn't until a few dates in. I have to make sure you're worth the straw that'll poke my ass and balls and sting like a motherfucker."

She laughed. "Maybe the barn could wait until I'm better used to your farm-boy ways."

"Farm boy, huh? Is that better than a sheep-fucking country boy?"

Her lips twitched. "If I switch to calling you a farm boy, does that mean I don't have to apologize and wear that stupid T-shirt?"

I grinned. "Oh, no way. I'm getting that shirt made for you. It'll be part of your apology."

Arching an eyebrow, she moved a hand to the back of my neck. I struggled to breathe as she caressed my skin slowly. "There are other things I could do, you know. Much more enjoyable things than wearing an offensive T-shirt."

"We'll see, sweetheart." I nuzzled her cheek. "But you still haven't answered my question—will you give this a try and go on a date with me?"

"I want to say yes, but my boss…"

"If she still wants to work with my family, I doubt she'll do much until the bottling facility is rebuilt, and that gives us a little time to get to know each other without her any the wiser."

"And what about your family? What will we do about them?

"I'm pretty sure my family has already guessed what's going on."

"And what's that?"

I trailed my knuckles down her cheek. When she shivered, blood rushed to my cock, making me want her all over again. "That I have the hots for a certain city girl."

"The hots, huh? What are you? Like, sixty?"

Amusement danced in her eyes, and I couldn't help but lean forward and nip her bottom lip. "Fine, I'll be more explicit." I moved my mouth to her ear, tugged her lobe for a second, then added, "I'm constantly hard for you, Sabrina. I'm dying to feel your hot, wet pussy, especially when you come around me and scream my name." I licked the outer edge of her ear. "How was that?"

Her entire face was pink. "Er, better."

"Good. So? Will you go on a date with me, then?"

"I know I shouldn't, but—"

"But you can't resist me?"

Shaking her head, she replied, "I wouldn't go that far. But despite your sudden ego, yes, I'll go on a date with you, Beck.

Triumph surged through me. "That deserves a little celebration, don't you think?"

"What? Wine and cheese?"

"No." I nuzzled her cheek, loving how she dug her nails into my neck in response. "I want dessert first." I moved so that I could see her eyes again. "I want to taste you."

Her cheeks turned red. "W-Why?"

At the confusion in her gaze, something dawned on me. "Has no one ever made you come with their mouth?"

She shook her head. "Not really. My exes didn't like it."

How some guy could call this woman his and not want to explore every inch of her with his tongue was beyond me. "Well, I've been dreaming of your pussy since that night we met at the festival." Stroking her cheek, I murmured, "You'll be sweet and tart and fucking perfect. Tell me I can taste you now, Sabrina. I bet you're wet just thinking of my mouth on your cunt, teasing that hard little clit of yours, while you hold my head in place, ensuring you come before letting me up for air."

She sucked in a breath. "Beck."

I stroked her cheek with the backs of my fingers. "Is that Beck, yes, or Beck, no?"

Searching my gaze, she whispered, "Beck, yes."

Fuck yes. "Where's the bedroom?"

She blinked. "To the right."

Without another word, I tossed her over my shoulder and lightly slapped her ass.

Sabrina giggled. "This again. Really?"

"Yes, really. I'm in a hurry."

Within seconds, I entered her bedroom. I barely paid attention to the small, sparse room, my gaze zeroing on the bed—one with a floral-design blanket.

Gently, I laid her down on the bed and drank in her body. All of her lovely softness, the curves of her breasts, her generous hips, and lush thighs I couldn't wait to feel wrapped around me, skin-to-skin.

The hard part was deciding where to start first.

Chapter Twenty-Six

Sabrina

I still couldn't believe I was awake and not dreaming. I had the sexiest guy in the world standing above me, his eyes caressing my body as he took me in, licking his lips as if I were his favorite dessert.

No man had ever looked at me that way before.

The longer he stared, the wetter I became, until I pressed my legs together, impatient for him to do something. *Just ask him.* If only it were that easy. Still, I tried to gather up the courage to reach for him or ask for a kiss or for him to hurry up and touch me before I burst into flames.

When his eyes finally met mine again, he murmured, "I need to touch you."

"Please."

Beck sat on the edge of the bed and lightly brushed my taut nipple through my sweater, and I arched toward his touch. He smiled as he did the same to the other. "So fucking responsive. I can't wait to suck your hard nipples into my mouth, nibble them, and make you beg for more."

Normally, I would scold him for being so damn cocky. But as he toyed with me, pinching one nipple and then the other, all rational thought left my mind. I moaned, desperate to feel his rough fingers against my skin.

Then I felt cold air hit my stomach as he lifted my sweater inch by agonizing inch and stopped just under my breasts. When he finally ran his hand across my stomach and back again, I moaned at the roughness of his callouses against my skin. "Why are you taking so long?"

Beck smiled, leaned down, and kissed my belly. "I need to make sure you're nice and wet for me, sweetheart."

"But I am!"

I bit my lip, surprised I'd shouted like that.

He chuckled, nuzzling my stomach with his stubbled jaw, which felt way too good. "But I'm having too much fun unwrapping you."

After reaching up, I threaded my fingers through his hair and lightly tugged until his face came to mine, and he kissed me.

Beck leaned over me, the feel of his flannel shirt

against my stomach reminding me we both still had on too many clothes. Finding the strength to pull away, I said, "Take off your clothes."

A mixture of humor and heat danced in his eyes. "Why? To ensure I don't have an 'I love sheep' tattoo somewhere?"

I rolled my eyes. "Silly man." He laughed, but I said screw it and went to work on the buttons of his shirt.

The action must have snapped something inside Beck, because he stood and quickly divested himself of his shirt and tossed it behind him.

As I took in his leanly muscled chest dusted with dark hair, my heart raced, and my fingers itched to feel his hot skin.

His voice was deeper as he said, "Take off your top, Sabrina. Or I might rip it off."

Maybe I should tease him about going all caveman again, but I was too impatient. I tugged my shirt over my head and tossed it to the floor. Beck's gaze trailed over me, and only because of the desire burning in his gaze did I not feel self-conscious.

"So fucking beautiful." I was about to tell him not to be ridiculous and just get on with it. However, he came over, took my hands in his, and maneuvered until he was over me, my hands pinned above my head, his hips between my thighs. He pressed his hard cock against me, and I arched into him.

"That's right. Feel how much I want you, sweetheart. And while I'm tempted to tease you for at least an hour, I'm fucking impatient. After so many dreams of you, and days of me coming to images of you exactly like this, slow and torturous will have to wait."

He kissed me, his hot stomach pressing against mine, and I wrapped my legs around him. I burned to explore his shoulders, his back, his ass.

With a groan, Beck broke the kiss. "Fuck, I want you, Sabrina."

"Then have me."

He tugged my bottom lip with his teeth before releasing my hands and moving back to pull off my socks and leggings. I expected my panties to follow, but he merely traced the crease where my hip met my torso, back and forth, the barely there touch driving me crazy.

"Beck, that is not hurrying."

He chuckled, leaned down, and kissed one inner thigh and then the other, taking his time to pause and breathe me in as if he were addicted. "As my girl wants."

After moving a finger underneath the material, he ran it through my center, and all thoughts left my head. He toyed with me, never touching my clit or thrusting into my pussy, and I moved my hips in frustration.

"Beck."

He removed his finger. "How attached are you to this underwear?"

"Not much."

"Good."

And he ripped them down one side and then the other, until he could tug them off and toss them over his shoulder, adding to the ever-growing pile of clothes.

Before I could do more than note he'd actually ripped clothes off me, Beck pushed my legs even farther apart, his gaze intent on my pussy. "Fuck, you're dripping for me." He looked into my eyes again. "Tell me who made you this way."

With anyone else, I'd be beyond embarrassed. But with Beck, it felt natural to reply, "You did."

"Good girl." He moved his head until I could feel his warm breath against me.

I could still see his eyes, just barely, and Beck's gaze turned hot and appreciative, and any lingering hesitations I had faded away.

He inhaled deeply. "Fuck, you smell so good. And now, I need to taste this perfect pussy."

His hot, wet tongue ran through my center, and I jumped, but Beck had his hands wrapped around my thighs and kept me in place as he licked and lapped, making me burn even hotter. I threaded my fingers through his hair to keep him from leaving, and he growled before finally teasing my clit with his tongue. A light flick here and a slow stroke there. Over and over again, bringing me close but not close enough.

I whispered, "Please, Beck. Stop teasing me."

Lifting his head, he licked his glistening lips. "Tell me what you want, sweetheart."

My cheeks had to be burning, but I whispered, "Touch me faster, Beck. Don't hold back."

Squeezing my thighs, he nodded before suckling my clit between his teeth. He licked and teased, and soon, I fell over the edge, pleasure rushing through my body as my pussy pulsed, and I screamed.

When he thrust a finger into me and curled it upward, hitting just the right spot, the orgasm became more intense, to the point that I thought I might cry. Eventually, my body relaxed, and I melted into the bed with a contented sigh.

Raising his head, Beck removed his finger and placed it in his mouth, sucking it clean. I imagined my mouth around his cock, tasting him as he'd tasted me.

He pulled his hand away before kissing one inner thigh and then the other. His lips moved to my belly, my neck, and then he took my lips in a brutal kiss.

The taste of myself on his lips was oddly arousing, and even though I'd come twice already, I wanted to feel his cock inside me as it happened again.

Beck pulled away, kissing my nose, my forehead, and my cheek before moving to my ear. "Fuck, I can't wait to do that again."

As I stroked his jaw, I said, "Next time, it's my turn to tease you with my mouth."

He growled, leaned back, and met my gaze. "You want to suck my dick?" When I nodded, he caressed my cheek. "Let me hear it."

"I want to suck your cock."

His fingers traced my jaw as he murmured, "Good girl."

Every time he said it, warmth bloomed inside my chest.

Running my hand over his hard chest, I played with the dark hair there. Doing something I'd never done before, I leaned up and licked his nipple before biting it gently.

Beck groaned. "Fuck, I want to be inside you so bad. Tell me I can."

I wanted to scream, "Yes! Hurry up and do it!" But when my eyes flicked to the clock on the nightstand, I sighed. "I wish I could, but I need to go into work soon. And since it's a meeting with my boss, I can't really call in sick."

He grunted, almost pouting, and I reached a hand up to ease away the scowl on his face. "We haven't gone on that date yet, Beck. So you'll see me again."

"Tell me you'll come to Starry Hills this weekend and stay with me. As much as I want to stay in the city and take you out tonight, I need to meet with a construction company early tomorrow morning about rebuilding the bottling facility."

Still stroking his chest, I replied, "Of course. I might have to use some of my favorite toys to help keep the edge off until then, but I'll find a way to survive."

He raised his eyebrows. "Toys? Care to share them with me?"

I smiled. "Later. You'll just have to remember to ask me about them. I really do need to get ready for work."

He grunted. "Fine. Then come up Friday night."

"I'll try. If not Friday, then definitely Saturday. But…"

"But what, sweetheart?"

"Well, um, I'm not sure how I feel about doing

anything under the same roof as your aunt or your niece and nephew."

The corner of his mouth kicked up. "If today was a preview, you won't be quiet. That's for sure." He kissed me quickly. "Don't worry. There are some guesthouses on the property, ones we let out in the summer for the busy season. I'll have one ready for us. Although…"

"What?"

"We won't be able to stay in bed the whole time, no matter how much I want that. Aunt Lori will expect you at dinner. And breakfast. And probably most of the day. Otherwise, we'll have a never-ending stream of ridiculous messages with emojis that don't always make sense."

I remembered Lori's serious messages from earlier. "I'll have to apologize to your aunt first, though."

"Why?"

I brushed some of the hair from his cheek. "She sent me some texts, worried about me, and I ignored them. It was just too painful to reply when I thought I'd never see you or any of your family again."

He nuzzled my cheek. "Don't worry, sweetheart. She'll forgive you, in this case. Just bring her some Ghirardelli's chocolates, and she'll be happy."

Ghirardelli's was based in San Francisco, and visitors could explore their landmark-designated building.

"It's sold everywhere these days, so it's not that special."

"But she can brag that it came from the source. She'll love that. Trust me."

"And are there any other city-food requests? Gluten-free vegan cookies, perhaps?"

He laughed, and I couldn't help but smile.

"I'm sure they're great, but Avery has been baking up a storm, and we definitely don't need more sugar in the house."

"Yet you want me to bring chocolate."

He kissed my nose. "That's different."

We smiled at each other, and I nearly pinched myself. It all felt like a dream.

However, my phone beeped with the warning alarm that I had to leave in fifteen minutes, and I sighed. "I really need to get ready, which means you need to go."

Nuzzling my neck, he murmured, "I could stay to watch you get dressed first."

"Which would only distract me. The weekend is almost here, anyway, so it won't be long until I get to see you again."

He kissed the side of my neck, my jaw, my lips, lingering to push his tongue into my mouth and slowly caress mine with his own.

I somehow found the strength to pull away. "You have to go, Beck. I'll text you, and we can finalize the details. It'll probably be early Saturday instead of Friday, though, since I have stuff to catch up with at work."

He grunted. "Arriving at eight a.m. on Saturday morning isn't too early."

I laughed, shook my head, and replied, "We'll see."

As we gazed into each other's eyes, I wished he didn't have to leave.

But after a few more lingering kisses, he did. And after a few fortifying breaths, I got ready and went to work. Who knew what would happen with my boss, but somehow, having a weekend with Beck to look forward to made it a little less daunting.

Chapter Twenty-Seven

Beckett

Aunt Lori: Well, did you find and kiss her? <smiling face with heart eyes emoji>
Me: I'm heading home now.
Aunt Lori: Don't keep me in suspense, Beckie. <angry face emoji>
Me: She'll be in Starry Hills on Saturday.
Aunt Lori: <party cracker emoji> <fireworks emoji> <dancing woman emoji> Good job, Beck.
Me: …
Aunt Lori: I was worried you didn't have it in you.
Me: …
Aunt Lori: I'm tempted to bring out <eggplant emoji>
Me: You just did.

Aunt Lori: But it could be a lot worse. <demon emoji>

The time between my driving down to San Francisco to see Sabrina and the arrival of the weekend flew by, mainly because the local community had really pulled together to help my family after the fire.

West had easily found a place to rent for bottling our wine, thanks to a neighbor's tip. Tony Wilson, the father of Zane's best friend, ran the biggest construction company in the area and assured us he would make rebuilding a top priority, no matter what it took. And even more neighbors volunteered to clear out the rubble, once the arson investigation concluded.

About the only thing that dragged on and on was my aunt's constant teasing about how she might have her first wedding to plan if I didn't fuck it up. Considering she'd been saying shit like that since my twenties, I didn't get too upset.

Yes, I wanted to know Sabrina and was open to the idea. However, I wanted what my parents had shared—a loving partnership that endured decades. It was too early for me to think of proposals and happily ever after.

But early Saturday morning, as West and I watched the fire investigator go through the ruins of the bottling facility, my brother said out of nowhere, "Be careful with Sabrina, and don't think with your dick."

I frowned at him. "What the fuck are you talking about now?"

"Relationships. In the beginning, it's lots of sex and

walking around with your head in the clouds, thinking everything is perfect. But the rosy times will end, brother, and she'll show her true colors."

West hadn't talked about his late wife since coming back, and we all just kind of tiptoed around the subject, both for his sake and his kids'.

But if he was going to bring it up, I was done ignoring such a huge fucking part of his life. "Not everyone is like Andrea, West. I'm not sure Sabrina has a deceptive bone in her body. Besides, I don't plan on knocking her up and marrying her out of some sense of duty."

West crossed his arms and stared straight ahead, silent.

So I pushed. "Why did you do it? Why did you marry her? You could've been involved without a wedding."

After what seemed like years, he replied, "I had no way of knowing she'd lose the baby. And I wasn't about to let any child of mine grow up without a father."

"In a way, I get that. But you married her and moved away, as if you couldn't get away from us fast enough. Why? You've never told me the reason."

At first, I thought he'd ignore me and not answer. However, West finally said quietly, "Everything reminded me of Dad. Mom was upset, and nothing we said helped. And since I was supposed to be there that day with you two, I felt guilty. Because with the two of us, maybe we could've found a way to help Dad sooner."

"Nothing would've helped, West. Believe me. It

took me years to accept that. But unless he'd been within five minutes of a hospital, no one could've saved him."

West grunted, looking unconvinced.

Knowing my brother and that he wouldn't say more until he was ready, I changed the subject. "And now? How long will you stay in Starry Hills?"

"As long as you need me. A small parcel of land was set aside for each of us, in case any of us wanted to build homes." He finally met my gaze. "And if I prove I'm an asset to you and can help you run the winery, then I want to stay nearby. Both for me and my children."

My aunt's words about my always taking on too much ran through my mind. Could I trust West to shoulder some of the burden?

A resounding yes went through my head. Trusting my gut, I nodded. "I want that too."

West grunted, and I did the same. Zach would probably have given me a one-armed bro hug, but West wasn't that way. His grunt was as good as a hug.

The fire investigator, Charlie, emerged and removed his hard hat.

As soon as he was close enough, I blurted, "Well? Was it arson?"

He nodded grimly. "Yes. I have samples to send in, but based on all my years of experience, I think someone poured some gasoline in the storage area, near the boxes of wine, and it spread quickly. Once the bottles exploded, throwing more fuel onto the fire, there was little hope of saving the place."

I tamped down the anger coursing through me. "And has the sheriff's office finished going through the security feeds?"

Even if the cameras had melted, they backed up periodically to the cloud. I had no idea when the last recorded footage had done so, but the authorities were looking into it.

Charlie shook his head. "Not yet. But we should know more next week, so you can file your insurance claim." He put out a hand, and we shook. He nodded at me and then West. "I need to get back, boys. But you have my number, if you find anything else or have any questions."

After thanking Charlie and saying goodbye, I turned to West. "If we're lucky, it'll show that asshole starting the fire. And then he can go away for a while."

West agreed with me that Justin or one of the guys who'd been with him at the bar was the most likely culprit.

Just as I was about to suggest we head back toward the main house, my phone beeped with a message from my aunt.

Aunt Lori: <bride emoji> is here! Get some <rose emoji> and <wine emoji> to romance her. <double heart emoji>.
Me: I'm on my way.
Aunt Lori: <celebration cracker emoji>

Rolling my eyes, I said to my brother, "Sabrina's

here. Just be grateful Aunt Lori has given up trying to provoke you with useless emojis."

West gave a small smile. "My children have emoji-shaped pillows. I'm pretty immune at this point."

Grinning, I slapped him on the shoulder. "And I'm sure you have pillow fights with them on a regular basis. Maybe I should buy a poop one to throw at you."

West rolled his eyes, and I laughed before getting serious again. "Can you swing by the cellars and talk with Jose about transportation logistics?"

Jose was in charge of getting the wine from fermentation to the barrels then to the bottling facility. Thank fuck the man had taken the latest disaster as a challenge instead of running away screaming.

West nodded. "Sure. Just remember what I told you, and don't let your dick make all your decisions."

With a wave, I resisted making a quip and headed back toward the main house, picking up my pace.

It was going to be hard enough not to instantly sweep Sabrina into the guesthouse and strip her naked. But my aunt had a few things planned for the morning. And as much as she'd want to see me, I knew Sabrina would love spending time with my family as well.

But come late afternoon, she would be mine. All mine. And my dick hardened at what exactly I had in mind for her.

Chapter Twenty-Eight

Sabrina

Beck: Are you here yet?
Me: It's only six in the morning.
Beck: You're awake.
Me: <laughing emoji> Someone's impatient.
Beck: Damn straight. My hand's getting tired.
Me: I told you to get a toy to help with that. Should I bring one for you?
Beck: Just get up here already.
Me: I can hear you grumbling from those words.
Beck: Grumble. Grumble. Grumble.
Me: <laughing emoji> Okay, let me grab my breakfast and I'll head up. I have news to share with you from work anyway.
Beck: Tell me.

Me: Later. Go take another shower while you wait.

I pulled my car into the back parking lot used for the family section of the big house and turned off the ignition. Taking a few deep breaths, I pulled the visor down and looked into the small mirror. "Don't be nervous. It won't be weird. It won't."

As I stared into my green eyes, I willed myself to believe the words. Beck had been texting with me when he could, flirting outrageously, but I knew from past experience that how people acted behind a keyboard wasn't always the same as in real life.

Stop it. I'd spent days with him, almost constantly, and this wasn't some blind date where I'd meet a guy from the internet for the first time, unsure of how things would go.

Taking a few deep breaths, I remembered all the conversations I'd had with Beck, the teasing and even flares of temper, and slowly, my nerves calmed down. Beck wasn't a complete stranger.

My phone vibrated, and I checked it. Even though it was the weekend, my boss might still contact me. She didn't know I was in Starry Hills, and that was on purpose. Edwina had temporarily suspended activity with the Wolfes until she could assess whether they were worth pursuing, given the latest catastrophe. I'd been shuffled back to my old duties for the time being.

However, it was just Lori:

Lori: I see you in your <car emoji>! I have <cookie

emoji> and we need to chat. Hurry. <dashing person emoji>

Smiling, I put my phone in my purse, took one last fortifying breath, and exited the car. I'd barely climbed the steps to the porch when little Avery opened the door.

"You're here!"

Her enthusiasm was infectious, and I grinned. "I am. Can I come in?"

"Of course." She took my hand and tugged me inside. "Dad and Uncle Beck will be back soon. But first, I want you to try my latest cookie invention. Everyone else said they've eaten too many cookies and won't try it. But I think it's going to be my best ever."

We entered the kitchen, and Lori waved. "You made it! I was about to bring out tea and cookies to the car if you didn't come in soon." Then she walked over and engulfed me in a hug.

For a second, I froze. Then I tentatively patted her back with one hand. Displays of affection hadn't been a part of my childhood, and it took some getting used to, for sure.

Lori released me and looked up—she made me feel tall, and I was only five foot six—before nodding. "I'm glad you came for the weekend, Sabrina."

At the honesty in her voice, my heart squeezed. And to think I'd ignored her concern about me. She didn't deserve that. "I'm so sorry, Lori. For not replying to your messages."

"Well, that's easy enough to remedy. Call me Aunt Lori from now on, and all is forgiven."

"Um, okay?"

She raised her eyebrows.

I smiled. "Aunt Lori."

She patted my cheek. "Perfect. Now, let's sit down until my nephew gets here." She winked. "And save those thoughts for later. You're spending some time with me first."

Avery frowned. "What thoughts?"

Aunt Lori shook her head. "Never you mind. You'll understand when you're older."

Sighing, Avery placed a plate of cookies in front of me. "Everyone keeps telling me to wait until I'm older. But I'm ten, nearly eleven. I'm not a baby."

Aunt Lori shook her head. "True. You could always ask your dad. Maybe he'll answer you. Actually, I should bring it up at dinner one night. I'm sure West would love that."

I bit back a smile, imagining the stoic, grumpy brother trying to explain it to his daughter.

Picking up one of the cookies, I decided to change the subject. "What kind did you make this time, Avery?"

She shook her head. "Nope, it's a blind taste test. I'll tell you after."

I glanced at Aunt Lori, who shrugged. "She's a pretty good baker, and none of us have gotten sick from any of her cookies. Yet."

"Aunt Lori!"

She winked at her great-niece. "Okay, never. I wish

they weren't so good. At the rate I've been eating them, I'll need new pants soon."

I paused with the cookie halfway to my mouth, expecting my mother's criticisms and harsh words to surface again. But they didn't. So I took a bite and savored the sweet, chocolatey texture with a hint of peanut butter. "They're good, Avery. Really good."

She clapped excitedly. "They're kind of like if a chocolate chocolate chip cookie and a peanut butter cookie had a baby."

After I finished it, I gave a thumbs-up. "You'd better write down the recipe because if no one else ever eats these again, it'll be a sad, sad world."

As Avery rattled off the ingredients, I wondered what it would be like to have a daughter of my own. One I could encourage instead of constantly put down.

One I could love and let her know how she was forever wanted.

Before I could think too much about it, Beck strode into the room, walked up to me, and took my hand. After he kissed the back of it, he murmured, "You'll get a hell of a lot more than that later."

The wicked glint in his eyes spoke volumes, and my heart raced at my eagerness to see what he had planned.

Aunt Lori cleared her throat. "And you wondered why I knew you'd go to San Francisco to find her. It's been written all over your face for a while, Beckie."

He didn't let go of my hand or look away and asked me, "Did you have a good drive up?"

"Er, it was okay." I burned to talk to him, both

about what my boss had shared and what was going on between us. So I turned to Aunt Lori. "I know you said we have stuff planned, but can I talk with Beck alone for just a little bit?"

She clicked her tongue. "I suppose. But you two had better not show up all rumpled, or the whole town will know what you've been up to."

Beck tugged me to my feet and put an arm around my waist. It felt weird that he was so open about us in front of his family. Yet a small part of me squealed and jumped for joy that he was.

He replied, "We'll be decent. What time's the tea party?"

"Tea party?" I echoed.

Aunt Lori answered, "Yes. Later, you and I will meet Millie and Abby for tea at the bakery." She whispered loudly, "They want to share some embarrassing stories about Beck."

Beck hugged me tighter against his side and sighed. "Save the worst ones for later, okay?"

His aunt winked. "We'll see."

Back in the city, I'd thought I might've romanticized how his family acted with one another. However, it was as good as I remembered. Maybe even better because the guarded, asshole version of Beck had disappeared.

With that, he guided me out of the kitchen and down the hall, into a room that looked like an office. After he closed the door, he pressed me against it and kissed me.

Moaning, I parted my lips, and his tongue met mine stroke for stroke as I dug my fingers into his hair and pressed my front against his. Each lick and lap and nibble only reminded me of the last time he'd had his mouth on me.

When he finally broke the kiss, we both breathed heavily. The look in his eyes was predatory in a good way, and I pressed my thighs together.

His deep voice rolled over me. "Hi."

I laughed. "Hi yourself."

Beck took my bottom lip between his teeth and tugged gently before releasing it. "It's felt like months since the last time I kissed you, not days."

I traced his jaw with my finger, loving how even in the morning, he had a faint stubble. "I'm just glad you still wanted to kiss me again. I thought maybe you would change your mind."

Beck took my face in his hands, stroking my cheeks with his thumbs, and gazed into my eyes. "Not only have I dreamed of it every night, but I also came hard in the shower this morning, thinking of having these sweet lips against mine. Of their brushing my chest and heading lower. As they became swollen from sucking my cock."

"So you've thought of me a little, then, huh?"

"More than a little." He nipped my bottom lip. "I've also dreamed of bending you over a fence, a desk, and hell, even my truck, before fucking you hard and making you scream."

It took everything I had not to squirm. Because I'd been dreaming of him too. "That's a lot of screaming. Someone's pretty cocky about his abilities."

He moved his mouth to my ear, his hot breath

dancing against my skin as he said, "Oh, it's not cocky if it's true. I can prove it to you now, sweetheart. Just lock the door, and I'll get started."

I fumbled behind me and locked the door.

With a growl, he took my lips in a demanding kiss. I didn't hesitate to let him in, meeting each stroke of his tongue with my own, pressing my body against his, reveling in his heat and hardness.

Never breaking the kiss, Beck moved his hand down to my breast and tweaked my nipple. I cried out in pleasure, and he did it again. I didn't know how long he tweaked and tugged and drove me out of my mind. Eventually, he stopped kissing me and met my gaze, his eyes heated, his hand on my boob possessive.

"Fuck, what I wouldn't give to have enough time to undress you and explore your body again, driving you wild until I was finally inside you." He ran his hand down my stomach and stopped just above my clit. "But my family will look for you soon enough, and we should stop."

"They can wait."

He laughed. "I'd rather not have them listening to you moan and scream my name." His fingers moved south, finally brushing my clit through my jeans.

I sucked in a breath and arched into his touch.

His voice was deeper as he said, "But I'll still make you come, sweetheart. And you won't have time to change your panties, so you'll be reminded of me and what I can do to you the whole time you're at tea."

I croaked, "That's not fair. I'll have to suffer, and you won't."

"My dick will be as hard as a rock until I get you naked, Sabrina. I'll suffer plenty."

Emboldened by Beck's touching me, I placed a hand on his jean-clad cock. When I lightly squeezed, he sucked in a breath.

Never in my life had I been so turned on yet still wanted to tease like I did with him. "Maybe you're just hiding a tiny penis, delaying the inevitable, until I finally see it."

Quickly, he pushed my hand away and then undid his fly and unzipped his pants before pulling out his cock. He stepped away, and I nearly cried out. But then he stroked himself, and my eyes zeroed in on his erection—his very long, very thick erection.

He growled. "Judging by how you're licking your lips, sweetheart, I know you're pleased."

"Maybe," I teased.

He moved in front of me and kissed me, his hard cock pressing against my belly, his touch almost burning me through the layers of my clothes.

After breaking the kiss, Beck asked, "Are you drenched for me?"

"Yes."

He growled in appreciation. "Remind me the next time you come up to stay to meet you in secret first. Then I can fuck you before you hang out with my family."

My lips curved upward. "Is there a former sheep barn or whatever it's called we can use?"

He snorted. "You never stop with that, do you?"

"Nope."

His gaze turned molten. "I know of a way to get you to forget all about the sheep."

"Oh?"

In the next second, his fingers were pressing against my clit, and I had to grab his arms to keep myself upright.

"I think it's working too."

I opened my mouth, but he shut me up with a kiss.

Between his skilled fingers against my clit and his tongue claiming my mouth, I forgot about anything but Beck—his taste and scent and touch.

The pressure built, and with a few more rough strokes, lights danced before my eyes as I cried out, my pussy clenching and releasing as pleasure shot through my body. I stared into Beck's hot, possessive gaze, which only made my orgasm even more intense.

When I finally came down and slumped against the wood at my back, Beck kissed me again. This time it was sweet, slow, and tender—such a contrast to his earlier demanding ones.

Eventually, he pulled away, his eyes meeting mine again, his gaze still intense as he cupped my cheek. "Look at how flushed you are, your lips swollen, and your expression that of the cat who got the cream."

"Cocky man."

"Just telling the truth."

Shaking my head, I tried to make my brain work again. How I was supposed to take tea with Aunt Lori and the others soon without them guessing what I'd been up to, I had no idea.

Beck put an arm around my waist and guided me

toward the chair behind the desk. "Come on. You look like you're about to fall down."

"What? No tossing me over your shoulder this time?"

"My dick is out and unprotected. I won't risk you reaching for it and taking your revenge."

My gaze drifted down to his cock straining upward. "Maybe I should torture you a little."

"Later, sweetheart. We don't have long, and I want you to explain your text earlier, the one about work. Is everything all right? You didn't get into trouble, did you?"

He sat and pulled me into his lap. I laid my head on his shoulder, grateful when he wrapped his arms around me. The contact eased some of my worries, and I replied, "No. But I saw Justin. And he wasn't happy."

Chapter Twenty-Nine

Beckett

I'd thought only a long, cold shower would be able to deflate my dick. However, as soon as Sabrina mentioned her asshole coworker and tensed in my arms, my body cooled.

I forced myself to ask calmly, "What happened?"

Sighing, she snuggled more against me, and I gently squeezed my arms around her. "He said I'd never get the promotion, and we'd never work with your family. He'd make sure of it."

My protective instinct wanted to tell Sabrina to stay with my family while I went to find the dickhead and ensure he left her alone for good.

But being here for Sabrina was more important than my hunting for assholes. Besides, I was still trying to gather evidence against that Justin douchebag. Once I had it, I'd take him down. "Did he threaten you further? Act hostile? Violent?"

"No." She scrunched her nose. "He did that creepy thing where he smiles as if we're getting along but his words are malicious. And it was in the break room, so it wasn't as if I could ask him why he'd been here in Starry Hills, let alone ask about the picture I'm sure he sent me."

Of course he'd only talk to Sabrina in public, so she couldn't slap him or shut the door in his face.

I growled, "Well, I'll never fucking work with him. And somehow, I'll make sure he pays for what he's done to you and my family."

She lifted her head and met my gaze. "Don't round up the boys or anything like that. I don't want you to get in trouble over him."

I traced her cheek with my forefinger. "I won't pounce unless I have proof. Although if he trespasses on my property, I have the right to kick his ass off it, maybe a little roughly."

"Beck."

"I won't do anything stupid. I promise. Just keep me updated, okay? I hate the thought of you dealing with him alone in the city."

She took one of my hands and threaded her fingers through mine, her touch easing my anger a little.

"I'll be fine. I had to grow up fast and moved out when I was twenty, so I know how to take care of myself." She shrugged. "And Justin might've lost his mind out here, but San Francisco is his home. Not to mention he's determined to rise up the ranks of the company. If nothing else, he'll protect his own interests and ass."

I kissed her. "I want to learn everything about you. But I know my aunt will interrupt us soon. So you'll have to tell me later how you thrived on your own from such a young age."

"Really? But you were only eighteen when your—" She placed a hand over her mouth. "I'm so sorry, Beck. I didn't mean to bring that up."

For so long, just the mention of my dad had fucking hurt. However, after so many years of not really talking about my father, I wanted to—because of Sabrina.

After clearing my throat, I replied, "It's fine." When she raised her eyebrows, I added, "I mean it. Between talking to you about my dad and sort of mending things with West, I'm starting to heal from old wounds, I think."

Fuck, the fact I'd just admitted that was huge.

However, as Sabrina caressed my jaw, nodding at me, peace washed over me. I wanted her to know me, know about my family. I didn't want to keep secrets.

Needing to be closer to her, I kissed her slowly, savoring her. When I finally pulled back, I laid my forehead against hers. "I'm so fucking happy you came back to stay with me, Sabrina."

"Me too. And not just because I wanted to tell you in person that my company hasn't completely abandoned you, just delayed things."

Rubbing my nose against hers, I replied, "As much

as I hate the fire, at least it means I have more time with you."

I didn't know her company's policy about fraternizing with clients, but it probably wasn't good. And she'd worked so hard and was so fucking smart that I didn't want her to lose it all because of me.

But I wasn't about to give her up any time soon. Somehow, some way, I wanted to find a path where I could still have her.

Stroking her hip, I murmured, "I want to make you dinner tonight. Tell me one of your favorites."

"Even if it means running over to Millie's again and banging on her door at odd hours to get what you need?"

I nipped her bottom lip. "Even if I have to do that again. Although I'm stocked up on tea, so no more early-morning runs for that. If you go through all twenty boxes in a weekend, you might have a problem."

She snorted. "And I'd always have to pee."

"So? Tell me your dream meal, Sabrina. Then I can make it come true."

Leaning back and furrowing her brow, she studied me. "Are you real? Because right now, this feels like a dream."

"Why? Because I want to cook for you? Has no one ever done that for you before?"

"Er, not really. My best friend is the worst cook ever, and I had to do the cooking growing up, from the age of ten or so."

"Why?"

She hesitated and looked away. Like talking about my dad had been fucking excruciating, talking about her childhood was probably the same way.

I wished I could simply wave a hand to take away those memories and give her new ones. But since magic wasn't real, I'd just have to work on treating her like she deserved and giving her new memories to replace the old.

Sabrina's reply garnered my attention. "Because it was either learn to cook or eat canned soup or ramen every day. My mother didn't cook anything not in a can for us, only for herself."

"What?" I growled. She flinched, and I stroked her side, trying to calm down. "Your mother would make stuff for herself but only give you canned soup or ramen?"

"Or I could make a peanut butter and jelly sandwich. But yes, that was how it was. At least during the school year, I had school breakfasts and lunches. But any other time, it was either quick food, or I had to cook it. And after getting tired of watching my mom eat spaghetti, tacos, or even just chicken and potatoes, I decided to learn how to do it myself."

With only a few short sentences, Sabrina had painted a clear picture of her childhood. No wonder she'd pretended my family was hers.

It was hard for me to even imagine a mother doing that kind of stuff. My mom might have died too young, but she'd loved me and my siblings fiercely, never letting us forget it with kisses, hugs, and even little notes in our lunches.

I couldn't help but kiss Sabrina's forehead. "Well, while you're here, I'm going to be your personal chef. Tell me whatever you want, and I'll make it."

She paused, playing with the material of my shirt, before asking softly, "Can you make lasagna and garlic bread? It's one of my favorites."

"Done."

Blinking, she asked, "But isn't that a lot of work?"

I kissed her nose. "Not for you."

Her eyes turned watery, and fuck, I was afraid she'd cry.

Then she sniffed, kissed me, and leaned over to my ear to whisper, "Later, you'll have to tell me what you like too."

And I knew she wasn't talking about food.

With a growl, I moved her head and took her lips in a hard kiss. She opened easily, and I devoured her slowly, leaving no inch unexplored, until someone knocked on the door.

After breaking the kiss with a sigh, I whispered, "I don't want to leave this room just yet."

Sabrina smiled and brushed some stray hairs from my face. "I don't think we have a choice. Your aunt can be really determined. Although I think we might need a minute to tidy up. I'm sure I look a mess."

"You look beautiful." She looked uncertain, and yet again I hated everyone who'd made her doubt herself. "But yes, a little like I made you come apart with your clothes still on."

As if on cue, my aunt's voice came through the door. "Sabrina and I need to leave in the next ten minutes, Beckie. So finish up and get your ass out here."

Aunt Lori's footsteps grew fainter as she walked away, and I shook my head. "I love her. But sometimes, I wish she'd be a little more reserved."

Sabrina snorted. "No, you don't. You love her just as she is."

"For reasons I'll never understand, I do, random emojis and all."

We chuckled, and as I stared into Sabrina's eyes, full of happiness and amusement, something shifted inside me. I wanted to make her laugh every day, to see her smile, and to wake up with her in my arms.

After such a short time together, it was fucking crazy. But I didn't care. I wanted a chance with her.

Not that I'd say that right now, the timing wasn't right. So I merely kissed Sabrina one last time before whispering, "Keep the panties on," and finally exited the room with my arm around my girl.

Chapter Thirty

Sabrina

As I sat with Aunt Lori, Millie, and Abby inside the Starry Eyes Bakery, I did my best to ignore my panties. I wanted to be mad at Beck. Yet it sort of turned me on to have a constant reminder of what he'd done to me inside that office.

But since I was in the presence of his family, I did my best to hide any blushes or stupid grins about what had happened. Luckily, I had a lot of practice concealing my emotions as a child, so I thought I was doing a pretty good job in the present.

Once the tea and scones arrived, Abby didn't beat around the bush and asked, "So you've hooked up with my brother, haven't you?"

Before I could answer, Millie jumped in. "I mean, it

was bound to happen. As soon as Beck pounded on my door at the ass crack of dawn to get Sabrina some tea, I knew something was up. Especially after so many years of barely paying attention to women beyond one-night stands."

Aunt Lori shook her head. "I don't want to hear about any of Beck's one-night stands, thank you very much. And considering he's your brother, you shouldn't want to even think about that."

One-night stands? The revelation only reminded me that I didn't know Beck as well as I wanted to. I didn't even know if he'd had a ton of girlfriends or not. And I shouldn't care—the past was in the past, as I often reminded myself.

Not that I always listened to my own advice. And despite my best efforts to not care, as customers milled about, I wondered if any of the women here had been with Beck. Even though it was irrational, the thought of any of them being naked with him made me rub my hand against my thighs in irritation.

I must've let something show, because as soon as Amber King walked away to take another order, Abby laughed. "No, Amber would never want to be with Beck like that. Zach, maybe. But definitely not Beck."

I did my best to sound nonchalant. "It's none of my business anyway."

Millie snorted. "Liar. But in all seriousness, my brother needs someone like you."

After sipping my tea, I asked cautiously, "What are you talking about?"

"Well, for one thing, you don't let him walk all over

you or intimidate you with his temper. Hell, it's like you're the Beck whisperer or something. It's been a long-ass time since he's whistled first thing in the morning."

I tried not to smile at the image of Beck whistling as he made breakfast or as he helped prune the grapevines or performed any other task around the farm and winery.

Aunt Lori spoke up. "We can talk more about Beck later. The reason I wanted us to have tea—apart from just getting to know you, Sabrina—is because I wanted to invite you to our annual Easter egg hunt next month. And no, it's not just for children. We have a hunt specifically for the kiddos, of course. But years ago, we started having an adults-only event where it's hard to find the eggs, and the ones containing the greatest prizes are hidden in a sort of obstacle course."

Millie scrunched her nose. "One filled with mud pits, bars you have to make it across or fall into cow crap, or where you just get wet falling in the stream."

Abby bumped her shoulder against Millie's. "Since when did you turn into such a spoilsport? You used to be the champ of that course."

"Well, not this year. I'll help set it up, but I have an event the next day and can't spare the time."

Abby stared at Millie as if trying to read her mind but finally said, "Fine. That means maybe I can win this year."

I'd never heard of an intense adults-only Easter egg hunt before. "Is it only locals who participate? Or do people come from out of town too?"

Aunt Lori replied, "It's mostly held for the town, but in recent years, word has spread a little on social media. If it keeps up, we'll have to limit the entries."

"Do you charge a fee to participate?"

Aunt Lori shook her head. "I didn't invite you to the Easter egg hunt to try and get free work from you, Sabrina. I just wanted you to have fun."

"I know. But I can't switch off that part of my brain —it's like a constant puzzle I want to solve. Besides, if it's another way you can bring in some income, all the better."

Aunt Lori patted my hand. "Thank you, dear. I'll keep that in mind. But this year, I just want you to have fun. Will you come? It's on the Saturday before Easter, and you could stay with us again."

Easter was nearly a month away. My past relationships had never lasted very long, and I was worried this one would be the same.

No. Everything about Beck was different. Maybe it wouldn't work out, but I was going to give it my best shot. "Yes, I'll come."

Abby clapped. "Awesome. With most of my brothers coming too, it should be a lot of fun this year. Maybe next year Zane will finally have some leave and join the hunt too."

Zane was Zach's identical twin brother and a navy SEAL. "That has to be hard for your brother to be away so much. When was the last time you saw him?"

"Almost a year ago. But Nolan's coming this year, which is exciting! We'll have to be his bodyguards and security team, though, in case any of his fans show up."

I couldn't help but have a little fangirl moment. "Nolan Drake will be there? I can meet him?"

Millie nodded. "He's just wrapping up his latest movie. And yes, just ask him for an autograph, if you want. But don't get too cozy with him. The last thing we need is for Beck and Nolan to go at it again."

Again implied there'd been trouble before.

Just as I was about to ask what had happened, Aunt Lori waved a hand in dismissal. "When the cameras are off, Nolan's the shyest one of us all. You won't have to worry about him flirting and driving Beck crazy."

Interesting. I'd just assumed all actors were charming since they almost always smiled and joked when in front of a camera or microphone.

Abby jumped in. "Nolan will be more outgoing when we're alone at dinner, though. Still, I won't poke the bear and place him next to Sabrina at the table, not for a million dollars."

I rolled my eyes. "I'm sitting right here. And I doubt he'll dive under the table and try getting into my pants in front of everyone, if he's as shy as you say."

I slapped my hand over my mouth. What had gotten into me? I was used to saying whatever came to mind with my bestie but not with near strangers.

After winking at me, Aunt Lori poured some more tea for us all. "Say whatever comes to mind, Sabrina. Between my late navy husband and my spending so many years around the Wolfe boys, there's not much you could say that would shock me."

Abby huffed. "Hey, what about me?"

Raising an eyebrow, Aunt Lori asked, "You have some work to do in that department, dear."

Abby stuck out her tongue, and I laughed.

Even though I hadn't known them long, it felt right being with these women, teasing, laughing, and simply having fun.

Millie jumped in. "Oh, but Katie sometimes surprises you, Aunt Lori." She turned to me. "You remember her from the last time we were in the bakery?" When I nodded, she continued, "Well, Katie's actually banned from the Easter egg hunt."

"Do I want to know?"

Abby snorted. "A few years ago, she set traps for her siblings, who also participated in the event. It slowed them down, for sure, but one also ended up getting stitches. She did feel bad about it, but her parents forbade any of them from ever participating again."

Aunt Lori sighed. "It's probably for the best, as entertaining as the Evans family is. And don't worry. We'll tell you what to look out for. Since most of the locals have done the hunt for years, they have little tells and tricks."

I blinked. "This all sounds really serious."

Abby crossed her arms. "Oh, it is. The winner gets bragging rights for the entire year. Some even go as far as to put the little plastic trophy on their dashboard."

The thought of any of my coworkers getting so amped up over a fun event, let alone wanting bragging rights over it, was foreign to me.

Yet I definitely wanted to participate. I doubted I

could win, but still, it would probably help me understand Beck and his family a little better.

Thinking of Beck, I tried my best not to keep checking the time. Because as much as I loved hanging out with these women, I was eager to be alone with him again.

Chapter Thirty-One

Beckett

Me: Aren't you back yet?
Sabrina: Nearly. I'm learning a lot about this Easter egg hunt thing.
Me: It's vicious.
Sabrina: Will you help me?
Me: I wish, but I put it together. So, nope.
Sabrina: <pleading eyes emoji> Not even a little?
Me: Hm. Maybe if you bribe me.
Sabrina: <eye roll emoji> I'm not that into it.
Me: Then just watch your back.
Sabrina: Okay, now I'm scared.
Me: You should be. Wait until you learn what some have done in the past to win…
Sabrina: No dead bodies, I hope.

Me: <smirking emoji> Well…

The lasagna and garlic bread were in the oven of the guesthouse I'd picked for me and Sabrina and were nearly ready. Now, freshly showered, I paced the kitchen, waiting for her to show up.

After tea, my aunt had taken Sabrina around the town to introduce her to some of her friends. I wasn't sure if Sabrina wanted to meet the other fifty-to-sixty-year-olds of Starry Hills, but she'd probably been too nice to say no. Not that I was worried—most of the locals were nice. Or at least the ones who were friends with my aunt.

Still, I couldn't resist checking my phone again to see if Sabrina had sent an SOS message. I saw that my aunt had texted again:

Aunt Lori: She's heading over, lover boy. <kissy face emoji> I expect both of you to be at lunch tomorrow. Or <angry demon emoji> I won't play nice.
Me: <thumbs-up emoji>

Since I rarely used emojis, when I did, it usually quieted my aunt for a while as she tried to figure out what was wrong. Nothing was wrong, but I wanted her to leave me the hell alone for a bit.

At the sound of the doorbell, I rushed to the front door and opened it, and my jaw dropped.

Sabrina wore a dress that hugged her breasts before flaring out around her middle and to just above her knees. The bright green and gold dress made her eyes pop, and her hair was in a twist atop her head, which only highlighted her gorgeous face.

Leaning down, I placed a kiss on the upper swells of her breasts, and she laughed. "Are you a boob guy, then?"

Lifting my gaze, I murmured, "I'm just a Sabrina O'Connor guy."

At her stunned expression, I pulled her inside. After shutting the door, I kissed her gently and said, "You're stunning tonight."

"It's just a dress. I've worn one before."

I was starting to understand that she didn't take compliments well. But it didn't stop me. "This one makes you glow and teases me with just enough skin and curves. I'm going to be hard and aching all throughout dinner."

Heat flared in her green eyes, and the look shot straight to my cock. She murmured, "Maybe we could have a late dinner."

Pulling her against me, I nuzzled her cheek. "After the appetizer?"

"Which is?"

"You."

She hooked her arms behind my neck and leaned against me. The dress was thinner than anything she'd worn before, and her body heat seeping through the material made me groan.

She murmured, "Don't tease me for too long, Beck. I had all day to think about you and your cock."

I loved how she was getting bolder with me. "Is that so? Did you imagine me fucking you from behind as you arched your back, moaning as I rubbed that perfect spot inside you?" I kissed the side of her neck. "Or maybe how it felt as those perfect, plump lips of yours sucked me deep, to the back of your throat?" I kissed where her neck met her shoulder. "Or maybe as I held your hands above your head and tortured you slowly, never quite bringing you over the edge until you were so needy you squirmed and begged?"

She sucked in a breath, and my dick grew even harder.

I fucking loved making her hot with words. "I bet you're soaking wet for me already, aren't you, sweetheart?"

"Yes."

I ran a hand down until I found the hem of her dress, lightly brushed the skin of her thighs, back and forth, and she leaned her head back. "Beck."

"Did you change your panties?"

"No."

I moved my fingers up slowly, taking my time to caress her skin, until I could feel where her leg met her hip. But all I found was bare skin. Fuck, she didn't have on any underwear at all.

I couldn't resist moving my fingers and lightly skimming them through her pussy lips. I grunted in approval. "So wet and swollen and hot for me, sweetheart." I slid a finger into her, and she cried out.

"Fuck, you're so tight."

After pulling my finger out, I thrust it back in, making sure the heel of my palm hit her clit.

"Beck."

"I think you're right. We're going to have a late dinner."

Removing my hand from her pussy, I quickly threw her over my shoulder and raced to the kitchen. It was hard to concentrate on anything but her soft body pressing into mine, or how hot her ass was through her dress.

But I managed to turn the oven to warming mode before dashing to the bedroom. She didn't protest me manhandling her again but she did wiggle her hips, as if to tease me.

I lightly slapped her ass. "Impatient, aren't you?"

"Do you really need to ask me that?"

Chuckling, I maneuvered her to the bed, and she squealed as she landed softly on her back. "Is throwing me over your shoulder going to become a regular thing?"

I crawled over her until my face was level with hers. After nipping her bottom lip, I replied, "That depends."

"On what?"

"On whether you try to leave this bed before I've begun to tame my appetite, at least enough not to constantly crave you." I kissed her. "Oh, and I need to torture you a little for finding the panty loophole."

"Hey, it's not my fault you didn't think things through."

I ran a hand down to her breast and tweaked her already-hard nipple. "You definitely keep me on my toes."

"Good. Someone needs to."

From the start, this woman had stood up to me. And fuck if it didn't charm the hell out of me.

I kissed her, taking her lips harder and rougher than earlier, needing to devour and claim her mouth, letting her know she was mine.

Her hands tangled in my hair, tugging me closer, and I growled, lowering myself. But we both still had clothes on, and I wanted more. Much more.

"I need to feel your skin against mine, sweetheart. Either you take that dress off, or I try to rip it off."

"Really? Again with the clothes ripping?"

"I'm not joking."

She must have noticed something in my expression, because she sighed in acceptance. "Fine. But you need to get up first."

I kissed her once more before moving to the side. I waited, watching her, and somehow restrained myself from taking out my dick and stroking it.

Sabrina merely smiled and moved to her knees, toying with the skirt of her dress. Just as I was about to reach out and follow through on my threat, she held up a hand. "Okay, okay. I'll get undressed."

I watched as she took the hem and lifted.

Chapter Thirty-Two

Sabrina

I had never gone commando before. But something about Beck brought out my playful side, one I only usually shared with my best friend.

His surprise at finding me bare under my dress had been priceless. And not even his tossing me over his shoulder yet again could erase how my skin felt too tight, how I burned to feel his weight on me, and how desperate I was to finally have his cock inside me.

Now he waited for me to undress. I hesitated at first—damn my childhood insecurities—but when he reached as if to tear it off, my nervousness faded away. After all, this man was desperate enough to tear my dress into pieces in order to see me naked.

So I slowly pulled up the skirt, revealing my thighs, and stopped short of my pussy.

Beck growled. "Either keep going or touch yourself."

My heart pounded, and my face heated. Never had a guy wanted to watch me.

However, I wanted to do it—for him.

Slowly, I moved my fingers between my thighs and lightly ran them through my center. I sucked in a breath at how good it felt and covered my fingers in my wetness before stroking my clit.

Even though Beck was still fully dressed, the desire in his eyes made me moan a little as I continued to rub slowly.

His gravelly voice rolled over me. "Are you close?"

"Yes."

"Then stop." When I whimpered, he added, "I want to taste you again, sweetheart, and watch you come apart against my tongue."

His words only made me hotter, and I had to fight against rubbing harder. Because it wouldn't take much more.

"Sabrina."

I finally moved my hand away. Impatient, I tugged my dress over my head and tossed it aside, leaving me only in my lacy black bra.

"The bra too."

I did the little moving-the-bra-straps-down-and-twisting-it-to-remove-it dance. Not exactly sexy, but as soon as I also tossed it away, Beck all but tackled me to my back, pinning my hands to the side of my head. He kissed me, his tongue claiming my mouth, and as he lowered his body, I arched my hips.

He nipped my bottom lip. "I want that too. But first, I need to taste you again."

"Yes, please."

He smiled smugly and kissed my jaw, the side of my neck, then my shoulder. "So soft and warm." His lips traveled down, stopping to suckle my nipple.

I couldn't help but hold his head close, loving how he nibbled and licked and even tugged, bringing me to the border between pleasure and pain.

I tried to rub my lower body against him, but his weight pinned me down.

"Soon, sweetheart. But first, I need to give your other hard, tight nipple the same treatment."

And he did, but my body was already on fire, aching for more of his touch and kisses.

"Beck, please. Stop teasing me."

He released my nipple and met my gaze. "As you wish."

After trailing his lips down my stomach, he stopped to trace my belly button with his tongue and then went ever farther south. Once he reached between my thighs, he pressed them wide. "Fuck, I'll never tire of your pretty pussy."

Before I could reply, he teased my clit with his tongue, and I dug my fingers into the bedspread underneath me. My moans and groans quickly told him what I liked, and soon, I was sweating, desperate for the orgasm just out of reach. Then he suckled my clit between his teeth, and I screamed, pleasure shooting through me. Beck never stopped, drawing it out, until I finally relaxed against the bed.

He kissed one inner thigh and then the other before leaning back. I nearly cried out and reached for him, but as he undid his shirt, I relaxed and watched as his hard, muscled chest came into view. I hadn't had the time before, but I wanted to kiss and lick my way across it, learning how to drive him wild.

His jeans went next, revealing no underwear, and I laughed. "It seems I wasn't the only one planning ahead."

As he stroked his cock, he moved closer to me again. "I've been dreaming of you every day since I left San Francisco."

I couldn't take my eyes from his dick, wanting to taste the drop of wetness at the tip. "So have I."

"Oh? And what is it you want to do right now?"

Being bold in the bedroom wasn't usually me. But with Beck, I kept surprising myself. "I want to suck your cock and taste you too."

He growled and moved to the side of me, putting his cock a few inches from my face. "Then do it."

Meeting his eyes again, I swallowed and reached out a hand. His dick was hot and hard, and I tentatively stroked it. Beck's moan made me bolder, and I squeezed him gently.

"Fuck, you're killing me. Either take me into your mouth, or let me finally feel how hot and wet your pussy is."

I wanted both but leaned over and licked the tip, lapping up his musky precum, and then licked my lips.

I needed more, much more, and I took him into my mouth.

He was big, though, and it took a second for me to breathe through my nose. But once I managed it, I gripped and stroked the bottom part of his cock with my hand as I moved my head with it in tandem, loving how he arched into my touch, moaning and murmuring dirty words until he said, "Don't be gentle. Grip me harder. Yes, just like that. Good girl."

His praise rolled through me, and I moved my head, twirling my tongue and trying to take him deeper each time. When I finally stopped, keeping him in as far as I could go, he stroked my head and said, "Yeah, just like that, sweetheart. I fucking love your hot, wet mouth. And seeing those pretty lips around my dick? I'm going to be hard for days."

Each time he complimented me, I grew bolder and hesitated less. I was so focused on pleasing him that when he put a hand on my forehead to stop me, I jumped a little.

Stroking my hair, he murmured, "I can't take much more, sweetheart, or I'm going to come in your pretty little mouth. And while I want nothing more than to coat your throat with my cum, I want to be inside you the first time." He lightly tugged my hair, telling me to let him go.

After giving one last swirl of my tongue around him, I pulled away and wiped my face. Beck gently touched my cheek, and I leaned into the touch.

"Now let's make sure you're nice and wet before I finally feel your tight little pussy around my dick."

I was tempted to take his hand and show him how much I wanted him already. But before I could, Beck guided me onto my back and then followed, until he was kneeling between my legs, his cock in hand.

As he lightly slapped the head of his dick against my clit, I moaned and arched my hips. "Don't make me wait any longer, Beck. Please."

His hand moved down my belly, over to my hip, and finally between my thighs. He lightly stroked me before thrusting two fingers into me. "You're so fucking wet. You liked sucking my dick, didn't you?"

I nodded.

"Tell me."

"I loved it. Loved driving you crazy too."

He smiled. "Good girl." Then he removed his hand and pulled away.

I was about to protest when I saw him reach for the condom packet on the nightstand. He quickly ripped it open, rolled it on, and positioned himself back between my legs.

"You're fast at that."

"I'm impatient, sweetheart."

He kissed me quickly before leaning back and watching as he pushed into me. I gasped as he entered me slowly, until he was finally to the hilt.

I reached up and took hold of his arms. "Move."

I expected him to tease me, but instead his eyes turned molten. "Promise me you won't close your eyes. I want to watch you as you come on my cock." The damn man remained still.

"Fine, I promise."

"Good girl."

Then he started to move, rocking his hips slowly at first then building the intensity. Digging my nails into his forearms, I never broke eye contact. The heat and possessiveness and determination there only kicked me into action, and I moved my hips to meet his. Soon, the sounds of flesh hitting flesh filled the room, but I barely noticed, too far gone with the way he thrust into me.

When I dug my nails in even harder, trying to find the orgasm hovering so close, he growled, "Yes, hold on to me, sweetheart. Leave a mark so that every time I see it, I can remember how fucking greedy your pussy is for me. Weeping and gripping, desperate to be claimed."

I'd never wanted to scratch a guy before, but I gave in to temptation.

"Fuck, yes, just like that."

He increased his pace, his pelvis hitting my clit with nearly every thrust, and I wrapped my legs around him. Digging my heels in his fine, tight ass cheeks, I struggled to keep my eyes open as my orgasm built.

I'd never actually come with a guy inside me before, but I wanted it to happen. Badly. "Don't stop. Please. Faster. Go faster."

With another growl, he increased his pace and snaked a hand between us. He caressed just above my clit, which made me arch my hips, wanting—no, needing—his rough touch to set me off.

"Come for me, sweetheart. Let me see you fall apart."

He firmly rubbed my clit, and everything inside me shattered. Lights danced in front of my eyes as my pussy clenched and released, feeling so damn good with Beck's thick cock still inside me.

Only when I finally relaxed into the bed did Beck groan and still. I had just enough energy to watch his face as he came, a mixture of relief and wonder that I didn't quite understand.

Then he collapsed on top of me for a few seconds, his weight not stifling but rather comforting.

Rolling to his side, Beck brought me with him and settled me half on his chest until my cheek rested over his pounding heart. Nuzzling the hair under my skin, I inhaled the slightly musky scent of Beck and sex and sighed in contentment. Sex had never been like that for me before.

We lay silent for a while, Beck stroking down my back and up again as we both caught our breath. The quiet wasn't strained, just peaceful. And for a second, I wished I could lie like this against him every day. Because here, skin-to-skin, the rest of the world melted away.

Not just the world but also my past, my insecurities, and my worries.

As he played with my hair—such a simple thing that made the moment that much more intimate—I whispered, "Thank you."

His hand stilled. "For what?"

"Not making it so I had to fake it."

He resumed stroking my head and running his fingers through my hair. "If you have to fake it, then the asshole in your bed clearly doesn't know what he's doing. Always tell me if I'm doing it wrong or you want to try something different or even new. Don't hold back with me, Sabrina. Ever."

"I'll try." I ran my fingers through some of his chest hair and tugged. When he grunted, I smiled. "You make me bold, Mr. Wolfe. So who knows what I might ask for next."

His chuckle reverberated under my ear. "As long as I don't have to share you, then ask for any fantasy, any position, any location—I'm up for all of it."

"Like over a desk, against a tree, or in a barn?"

"I'm telling you, sex in a barn isn't all it's cracked up to be. Straw is the fucking devil."

I laughed. "I'll take your word for it."

He put a finger under my chin and lifted my head to kiss me again. "Are you hungry?"

"I thought guys were supposed to pass out after sex."

"Well, if the woman's worth it, I'll get my ass up and take care of her. And you're definitely worth it, Sabrina. You're mine now."

"I knew you were going to go all caveman again."

"You fucking love it, though."

I couldn't help but grin. "I'm going to regret this, but heaven help me, I do."

He took my lips in a slow, tender kiss. "Now I'm tempted to make you a T-shirt that reads Beck's Woman."

I rolled my eyes. "You and the T-shirts."

"Hey, I can't help it. You helped me discover a new passion."

"One I hope to kill at some point."

"Naw. I'm sure you'll find your own ways to get back at me."

"Damn straight. But I'll be sneaky, waiting for when you least expect it."

"Now I'm shaking in my boots."

He made an exaggerated, horror-filled face, and I giggled. I loved it when Beck was like this—relaxed, teasing, and so very different from the grumpy asshole who hid his true self from strangers.

I kissed him, and we took our time, reveling in the simple feel of lips and skin and the coziness of the bed.

At some point, Beck pulled away and cupped my cheek. "Are you hungry yet?"

"Starving."

"Good."

"You don't have, like, a pasta sauce fetish, do you? Because I'm hungry and am not wasting any of your lasagna."

"No. Although at some point, I wouldn't mind feeding you cheese, caressing your lips, and playing with you before giving you some wine."

My lips tingled as I imagined it. "Food, Beck. More sex later. But if I don't eat, I'm going to be super cranky soon."

He sat up, taking me with him. "I'm tempted to see that."

"Beck."

"Fine, fine. As you wish."

He stood and turned, and I blinked in surprise.

"You have a tattoo."

"Oh, that. Yeah, West and I got drunk one night and each ended up with one."

After standing, I reached out and traced the wolf howling at the moon. "Are they in the same place?"

"No. West has his on his upper arm."

"And your other brothers?"

"Yes, they thought it'd be hilarious for all of the Wolfe brothers to have wolf tattoos in different places." His tone was grumpy, but his gaze was warm.

"I think it's fun. It bonds you together, like a pack, even if you're far apart."

He turned and cupped my cheek. "This is getting far too deep for a man on an empty stomach. Let's clean up and eat. I'm especially eager to see if my world-famous lasagna will make you moan as loudly as when you came around my dick."

My lips twitched. "Do you have a decibel-detector thing to make sure?"

He pulled me close until I was pressed against him, and I squealed.

"Maybe I need to make you come one more time before dinner, just so I have a good frame of reference."

Stroking his firm, toned back—all while thinking of how I'd like to scratch down it in the throes of an orgasm—I replied, "Make it quick. Unless you want Grumpy Sabrina to come out and ruin the mood."

Beck took my lips in a rough kiss and didn't waste time making me scream his name even louder.

Chapter Thirty-Three

Beckett

Later, as I placed a plate in front of Sabrina, I couldn't tear my gaze from her lips on the wineglass. It was as if having her mouth around my dick and then my cock inside her pussy hadn't eased my hunger at all. If anything, I craved her even more.

She lowered the glass and raised an eyebrow. "Are you just going to stare and make me wait?"

"Wait for what?"

"I can't eat if you're not sitting down."

Needing to distract myself from thoughts of whisking Sabrina back to bed, I teased, "Ah, so city folk do have some manners after all." When she stuck out her tongue, I chuckled. "Still being polite, I see. My sisters would've given me the bird."

"Well, I'll save that for later. I like to keep you guessing."

Amusement danced in her green eyes, and it made her even more irresistible. "Then that means you'll just have to come back up to Starry Hills every weekend, to keep me constantly in suspense."

The words had just slipped out, but I didn't regret them. I wasn't being selfish by not offering to go to the city—I would if she asked me to. But Sabrina just seemed more at peace here, more relaxed, as if she could leave her burdens behind in San Francisco for a while and be more herself.

It was almost as if she belonged in Starry Hills.

Sabrina shrugged before picking up her silverware and cutting into her lasagna. "Well, your aunt invited me to the Easter egg hunt thing, so I'll be here for that. As for any other weekends, I guess it depends on how good your food is."

"My cock and mouth aren't enough, huh?"

"Well, your cock is passable." When I growled, she laughed. "What? Do I need to tell you it's amazing? Nice and thick? Feels good in my mouth?"

The breath whooshed out of my body. I'd liked the slightly teasing version of Sabrina from before. But the one who could also joke about my cock in her mouth over dinner?

Damn, I could fall for her.

Clearing my throat, I gestured toward her plate. "Hurry up and eat, or I'm tempted to toss you over my shoulder again."

She took a bite, and after a second, she sighed.

"How is it fair that you can be so sexy and also such a great cook?" Sabrina placed a hand over her mouth and muttered through her fingers, "I can't believe I said that."

Grinning, I sat up a little taller. "So I'm sexy, huh?"

She glared. "You know you are."

"Does that mean you've been checking me out when I wasn't looking? Taking inventory of the goods?"

"I plead the fifth."

Leaning over, I mock-whispered, "I don't need to plead anything. I've been checking out your ass since the first day."

"Beck!"

I shrugged. "Hey, we all do it. So why hide it?"

"Maybe. But usually, it's a baseball player as he bends over on the field." Mischief danced in her eyes as she added, "Or inside the locker room, when he has a towel wrapped around him and nothing else."

As she sighed dreamily, jealousy churned inside me. "When did you see a half-naked baseball player?"

She took another bite and, after swallowing, said, "My best friend is a physical therapist for a major league team. Her job definitely comes with perks, ones she often shares with me."

I finally started eating. "Which team does she work for?"

"It's a secret."

"Why?"

"Well, because Taylor learned the hard way that when she mentions it, people hound her for free tickets or to meet players or something like that, and then they get pissed off when she says she can't give them what they want."

I grunted. "I've never met this Taylor, so it's not like I could ask for anything. Not that I would anyway. It'd be like if some acquaintance just walked up and demanded a free case of wine—irritating as fuck and poor manners."

"Does that happen to you?"

"Not often. Starry Hills is a close-knit community, and while we don't mind pitching in for events or gatherings, we would never expect our neighbors to just give us free stuff because we're friends. Favors and presents should be offered, not demanded."

As she sipped her wine, I watched her throat as she swallowed, wanting to nuzzle her there again, breathe in her scent, and trace her pulse with my tongue.

Her voice nearly made me jump, gaining my attention again. "So, what kind of events and gatherings do you guys have around here where you all pitch in? Do you mean like the Valentine's Day festival and the Easter event?"

I raised an eyebrow. "Still not going to tell me the name of the baseball team?"

"Maybe later. I want to know more about you first."

Though I wanted to know more about her, too, I couldn't deny her and answered, "Yes, the Easter egg hunt is one example. We all donate things so the kids can do their hunt for free—we provide the place, others help with donating eggs, and the rest give some plastic eggs with prizes and surprises inside them. Adults have to pay a fee for the extreme version, but it all goes toward the cost of prizes, refreshments, and supplies."

She nodded. "If the adult one gets any more popular, then you should think about doing it over several weekends before Easter. That way you can offer it to more people and start earning a small profit. If it's even possible to host it so many times in a row. I'm still somewhat ignorant of grape-growing cycles and the like."

"It's a good idea. However, the only problem is that Easter changes year to year, which makes the planning a problem."

"True. But if that's the case, then what if instead of more egg hunts, you create a scavenger hunt for the fall, after the harvest? Kind of the same thing but different. There are so many ways you could add revenue streams to help stabilize your family's business. Especially given how beautiful it is here. Once word of mouth spreads, people will be flocking to come here."

Watching her face light up as she talked about her ideas, I smiled. I could never do what she did—I'd go crazy, being inside so much, let alone working on a computer for hours on end—but she was so fucking smart, inventive, and creative. If her boss didn't give her the promotion, she was an idiot.

When she finally finished going over her last idea, she looked sheepish. "Sorry. I just get carried away sometimes. After so many years of doing grunt work and almost-mindless tasks, I've built up a lot of ideas."

"Never apologize for talking about something you're passionate about."

She frowned. "Really?"

The doubt in her voice didn't sit well with me. "Of course. I could go on and on about all the possible diseases for grapes. It might bore some people, but others are just as interested in the topic as I am. You just have to find your people."

The corner of her mouth ticked up. "Is there some sort of secret grape-grower cabal you belong to?"

I leaned over, put a hand to the side of my mouth, and whispered, "Since they watch my every move, I can't tell you. Because if I do, I'd have to kill you."

Sabrina laughed, the sound echoing in the room. Pride coursed through me at knowing I'd done that.

I liked making her happy.

Before I could worry about where that thought had come from, I asked, "What about you? Are there giant online groups for marketing? Or advertising? Whichever you like best?"

"There are, but I usually like the in-person conventions better. I've never been able to travel much apart from business trips. So I kind of look forward to them."

"And you'd be able to go on even more trips if you got the promotion."

"Yes. I'd have to meet clients, and not all of them would be in San Francisco or even California."

I was starting to see how the promotion meant more to Sabrina than just a pay raise or advancement. No, she'd finally be able to use some of her ideas, travel more, and really be able to shine.

I'd already decided to sign the contract with her

company, but I wanted to help speed things along. "Maybe I should meet with your boss—well, me and my brother—and we can sing your praises before signing. Provided your boss still wants to work with us, of course."

She frowned. "I didn't tell you about my ideas to pressure you."

"I know."

Tilting her head, she studied me. "How?"

"You've not once tried to sweet-talk or manipulate me into getting what you wanted. You could easily have kissed my ass from the first day. Or talked with my aunt and scared her about our circumstances to such a degree that she'd put pressure on me to sign with you. But you didn't. Instead, you tried to win us over with your ideas and interest in our business."

She opened her mouth and then closed it again. After a second, she said, "You're unexpected, Beckett Wolfe."

"In a good way, I hope."

"The very best way."

As we stared at each other, the urge to pull her across the table and kiss her coursed through me. Sabrina O'Connor was fast becoming an addiction, one I didn't want to fight. But she hadn't finished eating yet, and if she let me have my way with her again later, she'd need her strength.

Reaching across the table, I took her free hand and squeezed her fingers. "Finish eating so we can clean up and go to bed."

"To sleep?" she asked innocently.

"Not until you've come at least two more times, maybe three."

Her cheeks reddened as she licked her lips, which shot straight to my dick. "Now I'm torn—this is super delicious, and yet so is your cock."

How was I supposed to resist a statement like that? I couldn't.

So I dropped my fork, and it clinked against my plate. "We can have the cake I made as a snack later." I rushed to her side and put out a hand. "Come with me, sweetheart. Because I want you for the next course."

She didn't hesitate to put her hand in mine, and I tugged her toward the bedroom.

Where I made good on my promise and even managed an orgasm of my own before lying with Sabrina's soft, warm body in my arms—and falling into the deepest slumber I'd had in years.

Chapter Thirty-Four

Sabrina

Beck: I miss you in my bed.
Me: It's only been a week.
Beck: I almost used an emoji there. Hurtful, Sabrina. Hurtful.
Me: I'll have to try harder.
Me: Oh, I have an idea! You're getting an emoji T-shirt.
Beck: It'll be a cold day in hell before I wear it.
Me: Not if I promise you'll be rewarded afterward. <winking emoji> <overheated emoji>
Beck: Grumble. Not fair.
Me: <laughing emoji> Hey, you do this to me all the time. It could be worse.
Beck: How?

Me: I could snap a picture of you wearing it and send it to your brothers.
Beck: Do that, and it's war.
Me: You say that as if it's a bad thing.

Three weeks after lasagna in the guesthouse, I'd plucked at my skirt and rearranged the vase on the dining room table for the fifteenth time when Taylor said, "It's fine, Sabrina. It's not like Beck is going to take one look at a slightly off-center vase and run the other way."

"Is it off-center?"

Taylor sighed. "No. But calm down, okay? From everything I've heard, I'll like him."

I met her gaze. Taylor was my only real friend, and if she and Beck didn't get along, it would kill me. "I hope so."

She raised her dark-red eyebrows. "You keep saying it's just laughs and sex, but you're falling for this guy, aren't you?"

Biting my bottom lip, I adjusted the vase again. "I don't know. Romantic love is sort of a mystery to me. Besides, it hasn't been that long."

"If you can't stop waking up and wishing he was there or feel like home is wherever he is or want to run to him with news before anyone else, it's definitely a sign. If you also feel like the best version of yourself around him and feel comfortable in your own skin, then you might be falling for him, my friend."

For too many years, I'd learned not to hope for things—or at least anything I couldn't control. And while I could study hard to get good grades, I couldn't control how Beck felt about me.

I murmured, "It's too soon."

Her voice softened. "Don't let your mother win in this, Sabrina. I swear, if that bitch were still alive, I'd go kick her ass myself."

Taylor didn't know everything about my childhood, but she knew enough. And my bestie was a very determined person when she wanted to be, and I could totally see her carrying out her threat.

I shrugged one shoulder. "I've been doing pretty well lately when it comes to blocking out her words. Ever since..."

"Ever since when?"

"I first went to Starry Hills."

Taylor smiled. "It's Beck and his family. And no, don't look at me like that. I love you like a sister, but I know I haven't been around quite as much since I married. It wasn't deliberate, I promise. Which is why it makes me so happy you've found Beck and his family. They help you forget about your shitty childhood and instead help you make memories to erase the past."

"Maybe."

"It's true. And I also call bullshit on the too-soon thing. After all, I met and married Ben within two months. That was almost five years ago, and we still can't get enough of each other."

"But your story is like some sort of movie or book or something. It doesn't usually happen in real life that you literally get hit in the head with a baseball and fall for the guy who sent you to the hospital."

Ben was a retired baseball player. When she'd been scouting the team and attending a game, thinking of working for them, Ben's foul ball had hit her. Two months later, Taylor and her baseball player had been madly in love and got married.

Smiling, Taylor replied, "It does happen, though." She tapped her chin. "Don't they grow apples at the Wolfe farm? Maybe one will fall and hit you on the head, doing the same as the baseball did to me. Better yet—he could keep you at his place and be your nurse. All that alone time… just imagine what could happen." She waggled her eyebrows.

I huffed out a laugh. "Don't hold your breath."

A knock on the door made me jump. That had to be Beck. Since Taylor's husband was a coach and had an away game, it would just be the three of us.

Please let it go well. Please.

After taking a deep breath, I went to the door and opened it, and Beck looked as sexy as always. But instead of a flannel top or T-shirt and jeans, he wore an untucked button-up shirt and some slightly nicer dark jeans. His brown cowboy boots were still there, though.

My face flushed at the memory of Beck presenting me with my own boots and then fulfilling my fantasy of fucking me with nothing but them on.

His lips twitched as he clearly read my mind. "Calm down, sweetheart. Unless you're suddenly into having sex in front of other people?"

Taylor's voice rang out. "I love you, Sabrina, but I don't need to see your lady bits."

Beck chuckled, and I motioned for him to come

inside. From behind his back, he brought forward a small potted plant.

I whispered, "You remembered."

After kissing me, he nodded. "You don't like cut flowers because they die so quickly. I'm not sure if this is easy to take care of or not, but Millie suggested it."

The plant was a miniature rose bush with lots of little red flowers. "It's perfect."

As we smiled at each other, it took everything I had not to throw myself into Beck's arms and kiss him. It still felt weird to have a boyfriend who not only listened and supported me but also fulfilled every sexual fantasy I asked for. The first time had been the hardest—the cowboy boots—but after that, it had gotten easier.

Beck just made everything easier—well, most of the time. He could be stubborn, and so could I. But it wasn't a deal breaker, not even close.

Taylor appeared at my side. "So here's the sexy country boy, finally in the flesh. You clean up nice." She put out her hand. "My name's Taylor Adams." After they shook, she leaned in to add, "And if you ever hurt my friend, I will cut off your balls and shove them so far down your throat that you'll choke."

Beck raised an eyebrow. "Noted."

I sighed, but Taylor ignored it. "Let's eat. I'm starving, and since I hate sweets, you two can enjoy dessert alone." She winked.

Beck chuckled. "Sabrina shared a few of your texts, and I have to say you're exactly the same in person."

Taylor shrugged. "I try."

I took Beck's hand, and he threaded his fingers

through mine. Even though he'd done it hundreds of times, it still sent a little thrill through me. The affection-starved child inside me couldn't get enough.

Beck leaned over to nuzzle my cheek. "I missed you."

Though it wasn't the first time he'd said it, it still amazed me.

Before I could reply, Taylor moved to the kitchen. "Come on, you two. The sooner we eat, the sooner I can leave, and you can go at it like rabbits."

My cheeks heated. "Taylor!"

She grinned. "Hey, I remember the early days. Don't get me wrong—my Ben still has quite the sexual appetite—but when it's all new, it's just something else entirely." Taylor sighed wistfully.

Beck jumped in. "Before I forget—will you tell me which team you work for? Sabrina won't say, and I can't stop thinking about it."

"We'll see, lover boy. First, we eat."

I grumbled, "You're being bossy today."

My friend shrugged. "Because I'm hungry. If I had to wait for you two to stop making eyes at each other, I'd be here all day."

Squeezing my hand, Beck said, "Tell me about your team, and you'll have my full attention."

I could tell he was teasing—even just being able to recognize that was weird for me—but I still said, "Stop asking already. Please?"

He sighed. "Fine." When he moved his mouth to my ear, his breath danced over my skin as he added,

"But only if you say please later in that desperate voice of yours, right before you come."

Heat flooded my body. "Maybe."

He nipped my earlobe. "I look forward to it, sweetheart."

Taylor dished out the food and set the plates on the table. "Come on, you two. It's dinnertime."

As we sat, Taylor spoke first, asking the question I knew she'd ask. "Is your brother really Nolan Drake?"

Considering her husband had been a famous baseball player—and still was, even in retirement—I thought it was cute how she got excited over a movie star.

Beck nodded. "Yes. He'll be at the Easter egg hunt event in Starry Hills. Are you coming?"

Taylor shook her head. "Sadly, no. I already promised my husband we'd visit his family in Colorado for a long Easter weekend."

I teased, "I'll take a few selfies with Nolan Drake and send them to you. You can live vicariously through me for once."

Taylor gave me the finger. "Screw you, Buttercup."

She and I burst into laughter, and Beck looked at us as if we were crazy.

Once I caught my breath, I explained, "I had trouble saying I loved her for years. So we came up with a system—whenever we say, 'Screw you,' along with a silly nickname, it means I love you."

Beck's lips twitched. "I'm sure that goes over well in public."

"Actually, it's pretty funny to see people's faces. It's not swearing but just weird, and it's great."

I could see another question, about why I'd had a hard time expressing my feelings, burning in Beck's eyes, and I shook my head slightly and mouthed, "Later."

He nodded, his gaze determined, meaning he wouldn't forget.

Taylor gestured between us. "You two can already have an entire conversation without words. How cute."

"Screw you, Twinkle Toes."

Taylor grinned. "Good. Now, while we eat, I want you to tell me all about your siblings, Beck, and how I can meet Nolan Drake one day."

As Beck talked about his family, he slipped a hand under the table onto my thigh. He squeezed, I placed my hand on top of his, and he threaded his fingers through mine.

We both ate with one hand—we were eating stir-fry, so it wasn't that bad—and I kept sneaking glances at him.

I could deny it to my friend but not to myself. I was falling for Beck and hoped that for once in my life, everything wouldn't soon turn to crap.

Chapter Thirty-Five

Beckett

Later, as Sabrina lay against my chest and I stroked her back, I wished I could have this every night. Not just the sex—which was amazing—but I loved the simple things like talking about my day or cuddling on the couch or arguing over the best movies as I finished making dinner.

After so many years of sacrificing almost everything for the family and work, it felt strange and yet nice to slow down a little, just like my family had been trying to tell me to do for years.

I hugged Sabrina tighter to me and kissed the top of her head. If I wanted to keep trying with her, then I needed to ask her questions about her past. I understood not wanting to bring up painful memories, but I also suspected bottling everything up held her back.

The woman in question slid a leg up and over mine, running her foot against my calf, and my dick took notice.

However, I was determined and asked, "Why did you have trouble saying you loved Taylor?"

She stilled her fingers, which had been tracing shapes on my chest, before resuming. "My mother didn't give me any affection growing up. I didn't really know any other family apart from my mom and sister either. And if you've never had someone say they care for you or love you or anything like that, it feels weird and uncomfortable to have to show or admit affection. Does that make sense?"

The thought of Sabrina as a child, never having a mother say she loved her or hug her, made my chest tighten. I'd been so fucking lucky and had taken it for granted for so long.

I hugged her tighter against my side. "It makes sense." I stroked her back again a few times before asking the question I'd held back for weeks. "What about your sister?"

Sabrina remained silent for so long that I thought she wouldn't answer.

But as she sighed, her breath dancing across my skin, I felt her relax a little. "I thought we were close. Once. But I was wrong."

"What happened?"

She sat up, pulling the blanket over her chest, and

plucked at it with her fingers. "She picked our mother over me."

I moved to sit behind her, wrapping my body around hers with my legs on either side of her hips. When she leaned back against me, a sense of rightness coursed through me. I liked being her rock, the one she could take strength from.

Her voice was so quiet that I almost didn't hear it when she said, "Sydney is seven years younger than me. We have different dads, although it doesn't really matter, since I don't remember mine and barely remember hers. They both left before we were born, according to my mother.

"At any rate, my mom thought I was old enough to be a full-time nanny to my sister from the age of seven. I had to learn to take care of her because my mom would just leave her to cry, not change her diapers, and barely remembered to feed her."

Sabrina swallowed, and I wrapped my arms around her middle, placing my chin on her shoulder. Telling the story was hard for her, but I hoped she kept going because sometimes, talking about something helped with healing—much like when Sabrina had asked about my dad during our visit to the orchard.

She placed a hand over mine before continuing. "I loved my little sister. I took care of her, chased off anyone who made fun of our secondhand clothes or taped-up tennis shoes, and did what I could so that my mom focused her rants and put-downs on me and never on Sydney. When she was older, Syd always said she loved me and we at least had each other." She took a deep breath, as if needing strength, and added, "Then the day came when it all fell apart.

"But I need to back up a bit. I had no choice but to leave her when I finished community college and needed to go to university to get my bachelor's degree. Getting that degree was the way out of the life we'd led, and I wanted better for us both. I was twenty, and she was thirteen. I cried when I left, let her know she could call or text or email me any time, and promised her I'd come as soon as I could to visit. My going away was to help us both, and it'd only be for two years.

"At first, we kept in touch. Lots of texts and emails, and I called her nearly every day. However, as the months went on, Sydney's messages came less and less often, to the point that I basically only got them for holidays. She wouldn't even meet me when I had breaks from college and could visit her, saying she was too busy. Eventually, I said I wanted to see her to give her a birthday present, and my sister sent a long email full of accusations and mean words. All about how our mother was sick and that I'd been selfish to leave for school. And worst of all, that I'd abandoned her and must not love her after all."

Her voice broke on the last word, and I tightened my arms around her. I sensed words would only make her break down, and I knew how Sabrina hated that, so I held her close, letting her know I was there, and hoped it was enough.

After taking a few deep breaths, she squeezed my fingers before speaking again. "My sister's words were echoes of what my mother had said to me right before

I left. She wasn't sick yet—although I wonder if she'd really been that sick at all, knowing how she liked to guilt-trip us to get what she wanted—but my mother hadn't wanted me to go to college. Not because she'd miss me but because she couldn't have me as a maid to cook and clean and run errands. Not to mention she'd have to assume some parenting responsibilities for Sydney for the first time in her life.

"I was so upset over my sister's words that I even went home to try and see her. But Sydney opened the door, told me she hated me and never wanted to see me again, and slammed it in my face. That was the last time she spoke to me, apart from when I had to sign my mother's death certificate. And even then, it was only through email and all about business." She choked out a sob. "And I lost the only person in the world I loved and who loved me."

She started crying. I moved until she could sit on my lap and put her head on my shoulder, stroking her back to try to soothe her.

Fuck, I'd known her childhood was shitty, but her story revealed so much more.

I couldn't even imagine my siblings turning on me like that, for false reasons. At least with my squabbles with Nolan—and until recently, West—we'd had concrete reasons for them.

Not to mention that all of us had more family than we knew what to do with to support us. Unlike Sabrina, who'd had no one back then.

I held the strong-yet-fragile woman in my arms,

offering soothing murmurs and gentle strokes, hoping she could cry it all out and still talk to me afterward.

However, when Sabrina finally quieted, leaning heavily against my chest, she whispered, "I'm so damn tired, Beck. I know you came all this way, but I really just want to go to bed now."

"Of course, sweetheart." I kissed her forehead. "But I'm staying with you."

She lifted her head, and her puffy eyes made my heart squeeze. "I thought you had to drive back tonight."

"There's no fucking way I'm leaving you alone. Now, I'm going to lay you down and get you a warm washcloth. Okay?"

Sabrina was so fucking fragile right now, and I didn't want her thinking I'd be gone for long. Whether she'd admit it or not, she needed someone tonight.

No, not someone—she needed me.

She nodded. "Okay."

Once she settled on the bed, I kissed her lips gently and went to the bathroom. I returned with a warm, wet washcloth and gently wiped her eyes, cheeks, and nose. Then I folded it over to the other side and cleaned up between her thighs too.

She watched me the whole time, as if waiting to wake up from a dream and have me disappear.

After tossing the washcloth into the bathtub until tomorrow, I settled next to her, kissed her gently, and lay on my back. Opening my arms, I said, "Come here."

Without complaint, Sabrina melted against my chest and, emotionally exhausted, quickly fell asleep.

I didn't follow for a long, long time, though, lost in my thoughts.

Little by little, Sabrina had wormed her way into my life and my heart. But after her revelations tonight, one thing had become clear—I wanted her forever. Somehow, some way, I needed to find out how to make it work between us despite all the obstacles that stood in our way.

Even if I had to ask my family for help, I'd find a way.

And soon, I fell asleep with the woman I wanted to be my future in my arms.

Chapter Thirty-Six

Sabrina

Abby: Ready to kick ass at the Easter egg hunt?
Me: Maybe.
Aunt Lori: Where's your enthusiasm? <sad face emoji>
Me: Um, yes! I'll do great.
Millie: I still didn't learn anything to help you guys. I swear, whenever I try to sneak into Beck's office, West is there to grunt and piss me off.
Abby: Losing your temper only encourages him.
Millie: I can't help it if he has zero manners. <angry face emoji> So I'm totally on your guys' team. If I can slow down the others, I'll do it.
Aunt Lori: Oooh, you're getting devious and sneaky. I love it! <heart-eyed emoji> <smiling demon emoji>

Me: Um, I don't want anyone to get hurt or banned.
Abby: That won't happen. Probably.
Me: It's the "probably" that worries me.

The next few weeks flew by in a blur.

The morning after my breakdown, I'd felt somewhat lighter. For so many years, I'd worried about appearing weak and living up to my mother's words and kept most of the past with my sister secret, even from Taylor. However, with Beck, it had been almost too easy to bare my soul to him. Not once had he made me feel less for being open, either.

And just remembering him cleaning up my tears and snotty face after sobbing warmed my heart. No one had really cared for me like that before, apart from when I'd been super sick and Taylor had brought me some food and medicine.

However, I could almost imagine relying on Beck without worry, wanting to help take care of him in return, almost as if we could be true partners.

Well, partners who had mind-blowing sex too.

As I drove up the road leading to Wolfe Family Farm and Winery, I was excited to see Beck's family and experience the infamous Easter egg hunt. I'd spent nearly every weekend in Starry Hills, and I sometimes wished I could live there permanently.

That was ridiculous, of course. It hadn't yet been two months since I'd started dating Beck, and with my track record, it might not last much longer.

Stop it. Beck is different.

He was, on so many levels, but optimism was still difficult for me.

Not wanting to think about the future, I took in the early buds on the trees, the almost-past-their-prime tulips, and other little signs of spring. In addition to nature, there were a lot of colorful decorations with bunnies, flowers, eggs, and baskets tied to the fence posts.

Beck hadn't shown me the location of either the kid or adult versions of the egg hunt, saying he wanted to surprise me. I smiled as I remembered his teasing me about what might be in the adult course. I mean, shark pits? Really? I wasn't five.

I pulled into the back lot of the Wolfe place. There were more cars than usual, as everyone from the Wolfe family except Zane would be here this weekend.

Flipping down the visor, I looked into the small mirror and brushed my hair with my fingers. Though it was mostly for Beck, I felt a little giddy about meeting Nolan Drake. I would never pick him over Beck, but it was still fun to tease my boyfriend about it.

Boyfriend. It was still weird to call Beck that, yet it felt right.

After saying, "Don't drool, and try to be charming, Sabrina. You can do this," I exited the car.

I'd barely set foot on the ground before Beck strode toward me. When he reached me, he pulled me close and kissed me.

I didn't know how long we stood there, lips locked, until Aunt Lori's voice filled the air. "Let her up for air, Beckie!"

I smiled, and Beck groaned.

"We should go inside," I murmured.

"Why? They can wait a little longer." He kissed my neck. "I missed you."

His words made my heart warm. "I missed you too."

Beck took my mouth again, and I melted even more against him.

Then I felt my phone vibrate in my purse at my side. After a short pause, it happened again.

Laughing, I broke the kiss. "I think your aunt might be texting me. Do I even want to know what she said?"

Beck laid his forehead against mine. "Did you want to adopt a meddling aunt, by chance?"

A few months ago, the words would probably have made me clam up or brought back my lack of family.

But it didn't now. Because I wasn't alone any longer—I had Beck and, to a lesser degree, his family too.

Smiling, I replied, "She already said she's my adopted aunt."

With a sigh, Beck released me and took my hand. "Maybe you should rethink that. Hell, she's been using sex emojis about you and me lately, and it's fucking mortifying."

Laughing, I squeezed his hand. "Well, it could be worse. I mean, she's not a blood aunt, so it's not technically incestual."

"Gee, thanks. That makes me feel so much better."

I grinned at Beck, and his lips twitched.

"You know me—always looking for an alternate angle."

After bringing my hand up to his mouth, he kissed the back of it. "Just like I'm always looking for new angles and positions too." He waggled his eyebrows, hinting at how he'd managed to bend me over a fence rail and fuck me in an isolated part of his land the previous weekend. And then there was the time he'd sat in the bathtub with me on top, and we'd sloshed most of the water out of the tub.

I lightly hit his side. "Behave. I don't want to have red cheeks when I meet Nolan Drake for the first time."

Rolling his eyes, Beck tugged me along. "Do you have to use his full name every time?"

"Definitely yes. Nolan could be anyone. But Nolan Drake? He's nearly as handsome as my boyfriend."

"Nearly, huh?"

"Yep. Although I'll soon find out if that's true in person or not."

He growled. "Do you want me to toss you over my shoulder and keep you to myself in the guest house? Because it's looking more and more appealing."

I laughed.

Aunt Lori asked, "What's so funny?"

Shaking my head, I replied, "Nothing. How're you, Aunt Lori?"

She walked up to me and tugged me away from Beck to give me a hug. "Great now that you're here. I have a surprise for you."

As soon as she released me, I glanced over at Beck and raised my eyebrows in question. He knew I didn't like surprises.

He mouthed, "You'll like it."

And I trusted him.

As Aunt Lori guided me inside, she asked, "Are you tired, dear? I know you had to work this morning."

Since it was Friday, I'd taken a half day. "It's fine. I don't know what's in the air, but something about Starry Hills gives me energy."

"It's definitely an amazing place to live, maybe the best in the world."

That wasn't the first time she'd hinted about my living here instead of in the city.

Beck growled in warning, "Aunt Lori."

Aunt Lori put her hands up in surrender. "Fine, fine. I'll drop it. For now." She stopped a few feet from the living room. "Close your eyes, Sabrina."

At the excitement in her dark-brown eyes, I complied and allowed her to maneuver me.

Finally, Aunt Lori said, "Okay, stop here, and open your eyes."

I did and gasped.

The room was filled with potted miniature roses and balloons, and a three-tier cake sat on the table. Surrounding it were nearly all of Beck's siblings, including Nolan Drake.

"Happy early birthday!" they all shouted.

Tears filled my eyes as Beck placed an arm around my shoulders. "I know it's not until next week, but I figured having my movie-star brother here would make your surprise party even more special."

I turned toward him and took his face in my hands. "Having you here for it is special enough, Beckett Wolfe."

Though it was on the tip of my tongue to say I might love him, uncertainty kept me from doing so. The last thing I wanted was to send him running away in panic.

He kissed me, and I wrapped my arms around his neck. Not even the whistles coming from his family embarrassed me as Beck devoured my mouth.

When he finally let me up for air, he rubbed his nose against mine. “Happy early birthday, Sabrina O’Connor. I’ll give you your presents later, when we’re alone.”

At the heat in his gaze, I knew it had to be something for us to enjoy while naked.

Abby rushed up and managed to get me away from Beck to hug me. “Happy birthday, Sabrina.” She leaned back. “Amber made the cake. I didn’t know what was your favorite, but Beck suggested lemon cake with raspberry curd. If nothing else, it’s pretty.”

Turning to the cake, I smiled. Each tier had beautiful flowers and swirls, and it was probably the most elegant thing I’d ever seen. “It’s beautiful. I’ll have to tell Amber so the next time I see her.”

Zach was sitting in a nearby chair, the leg in a cast propped up, and he added, “I tasted the prototype, so I know it’s good. I’m secretly hoping you’ll leave the leftovers for us. After all, nothing beats having cake for breakfast.”

West rolled his eyes. “Do you have any manners?”

Zach winked at me. “Never.”

I laughed but was soon distracted by little Avery running up to me. She held out a small, lumpy wrapped package. "I have a present for you! I made it myself."

Touched, I gave her a one-armed hug. "Thank you."

"Open it now!"

I unwrapped it, revealing a scarf. Even though it was a motley of blues, greens, and yellows—not to mention that it was uneven and probably missing some stitches somewhere—it touched me. "Thank you, Avery. It's lovely."

She beamed. "My brother helped to make it, although he'll deny it."

Wyatt was sitting on the sofa, beside his dad, quiet like usual. I smiled at him and said, "Thanks, Wyatt. It looks so warm and comfy."

The little boy shrugged and remained silent.

A tall man with black hair and blue eyes walked up to me, smiling shyly. "Hello."

Clutching the scarf to my chest, I whispered, "Nolan Drake!"

"Nice to meet you. I would give you a hug, but Beck said he'd cut off my dick if I touched you, so I won't."

I narrowed my eyes at Beck. "Seriously?"

Beck grunted. "Yep."

Rolling my eyes, I said, "He's just a little jealous. I'd heard of you long before meeting Beck, and he doesn't like that reminder." I lowered my voice to a mock whisper. "Which is why I remind him of it often."

Nolan chuckled. "I like you."

Beck moved to wrap his arm around my waist. "She's mine."

Aunt Lori clapped. "Enough teasing. That cake has been calling my name all day, and it's high time we sang 'Happy Birthday' and ate it."

Millie sidled up to me. "I think Aunt Lori tasted some from the back of it earlier but keeps denying it."

Aunt Lori clicked her tongue. "How would you know that?"

Millie raised a dark eyebrow. "Even if I hadn't gone and pulled the cake forward to see the damage, I know the main flower on the top faced the front before but is now to the side. A dead giveaway for when a kid finds a cake at one of my events and we have to turn it around to cover up the missing frosting."

Aunt Lori waved the long lighter she held in the air. "I will neither confirm nor deny it. Now, give me a second to add the final touch."

I watched as Aunt Lori lit the candles, and Beck kissed my cheek. I bit back a laugh, wondering how many more times he was going to claim me in front of Nolan. It might be a little caveman-like, but deep down, I kind of liked it.

Soon, they were singing "Happy Birthday," and my eyes filled with tears. I'd only met these people in February, and already in April, they were throwing me a party and getting me a fancy cake.

Once they finished the song, Beck whispered, "Make a wish."

I did before blowing out the candles.

"What did you wish for?" he asked.

I smiled up at him. "I can't say, or it won't come true."

And I desperately wanted it to come true.

Soon, we all sat around the dining room table with our cake and ice cream, and Avery asked, "Are you going to watch me and Wyatt do the kids' Easter egg hunt, Sabrina? Everyone's going to cheer us on, Daddy especially, and we want you there too."

"I'd love to, as long as there's enough time between the events."

Beck answered, "Yes. We do that deliberately and have people here to watch the kids in case their parents want to participate in the adult one."

"Then yes, I'll be there."

Avery nodded. "Good. I suppose you don't have enough time to make a sign, but you can share Daddy's."

I glanced at West, who cleared his throat. "You have enough signs, Avery."

"But Daddy, the kids at school have a competition about how many signs they get."

"Then they're focusing on the wrong thing, love. You should just have fun."

Avery sighed. "I guess."

West smiled at his daughter, transforming his face and making it less intimidating. He was the sibling living in Starry Hills I'd talked with the least, but I'd have to work on that in the future.

Discussion then turned to Nolan's latest project, how long he could stay, and when he'd be back. I did my best not to fangirl over him, and by the end of the evening, I saw him a little more as one of the Wolfe family than some actor put on a pedestal.

Once it grew late, Beck didn't waste time in getting me out of the house and walking toward what I'd come to think of as our guesthouse.

We strolled hand in hand, the sky already dark and full of stars. When I looked up, the sight of so many pinpricks of light took my breath away. "It's almost unfair how pretty it is here."

"I'll admit I didn't appreciate it growing up. I think a lot of kids who grow up in Starry Hills dream of leaving and going to the city one day."

"But you didn't?"

"No. I didn't really have the choice, anyway, since my family relied on me after my dad's death and later after my mom's."

Beck had shared that his mom had died of cancer eight years ago, making him even more duty bound to look after his family.

"I still think you take on too much."

He grunted. "I've given West some of my responsibilities. It's a start."

A question that had been lingering at the back of my mind rushed forth. "Wait a second. Nolan Drake has been a super-famous movie star for years. Didn't he try to help you?"

"He did, but I refused."

"Why?"

Beck studied the stars a few seconds before answering, "Because I made the promise to my father that I'd keep the winery going. And taking Nolan's money meant I would've failed."

I wanted to say that was ridiculous, but I knew how seriously Beck took that vow to his dad.

"And now? Would you feel the same way about accepting Nolan's help?"

He blew out a breath. "Honestly? I don't know. I want to ensure this place is self-sufficient, and taking Nolan's money still feels wrong."

I suspected he would always think that. However, an idea that might help the two brothers patch things up a little hit me. "Then how about having your brother do some ads for the winery? Or for any of the events you have here? Maybe he could even make some videos about how this place runs. That way, he's helping you and driving customers here without handing over any cash. It seems like a win-win to me."

He stopped, yanked me close, and lowered his lips to an inch away from mine. "Have I told you lately how fucking smart you are?"

Smiling, I wrapped my arms around him. "Just don't ask me how to make wine."

He laughed, the sound deep and melodic.

"I'll talk to Nolan. I'm sure he'll agree to smile at the camera to help the winery."

"Good. Now the only male siblings I have left to help are Zach and Zane."

Beck shook his head. "I don't know when we'll hear from Zane again. But I'll have to warn him."

"Why?"

"Because you might suggest a shirtless navy SEAL calendar or something."

Wanting to tease him, I asked, "Oh, so is he super muscled? Does he have an eight-pack? Ten-pack? Should I volunteer to oil him up before the photoshoot?"

Beck growled and said, "The only Wolfe-brother chest you'll be touching is mine."

With that, he tossed me over his shoulder, and I couldn't stop laughing. "Beck, don't you dare cart me off to the bedroom yet. I want to see what your present is first."

"Part of it requires you to be naked, sweetheart. So it's my job to make sure you're ready."

He lightly slapped my butt a few times, as possessive as always, before stroking down my thigh and squeezing, the touch a promise of what was to come.

After opening the door to the guesthouse, Beck stepped inside and gently put me back down. He traced my jaw and then took my chin between his thumb and forefinger. "I plan to take my time with you tonight and give the birthday girl one of her fantasies. But first, I want to give you the two other presents I got you."

He dashed to the hall closet and removed two packages wrapped in shiny, striped paper and ribbon—one was large and rectangular, and the other was small and soft. "Happy birthday, sweetheart."

After taking the smaller one first, I ripped it open and laughed. I held up the dark blue T-shirt which read "Country Boys Don't F*ck Sheep."

"You actually made me one."

He grinned. "Yep. Now I just need to think of a time for you to wear it."

"Hey, I never agreed to this bargain."

"It was implied. Don't worry. It won't be for the Easter egg hunt. Although it would definitely distract your fellow participants if you wore it."

I stuck out my tongue at him. "I'll keep it, but I'm *not* wearing it."

"We'll see, sweetheart." He offered the bigger gift. "Open this one now."

After tossing the shirt at Beck, I opened the bigger one and gasped. The doll from the All Things Shop in town stared back at me, the dress-wearing curvy one who looked as if she was about to take on the world. "Beck."

He cleared his throat, and I looked up to see him rubbing the back of his neck. "I know you're not a little kid or anything. But I saw how you looked at it in the shop and wanted to get it for you."

After gently placing the box on the ground, I jumped and wrapped my arms around his neck as I buried my face into his chest. "I love it. Thank you."

Hugging me, he said, "You're welcome. I know your apartment is small, but you deserved to have a brand-new doll for once in your life."

Tears filled my eyes. "Seriously, Beck, it's one of the best presents I've ever received." Taking a deep breath, I leaned back. "Almost the best."

He raised an eyebrow. "Almost?"

"I'm still partial to the cowboy boots."

"Then you're going to love the next present."

"What is it?"

He kissed me quickly. "Get naked, and wait for me on the bed. Then I'll give you your last present."

I'd previously hated surprises, but with Beck, I actually looked forward to them. After giving him one last, long kiss, I walked away from him, holding my shoulders back and swaying my hips, wanting to torture him just a little.

Once I reached the bedroom, I stripped, got ready in the attached bathroom, and sat on the bed, waiting to see what he'd do next.

Chapter Thirty-Seven

Sabrina

My heart pounded as I tried not to squirm on the bed, impatient to see what Beck had planned. Just as I debated checking on him, the man appeared in the doorway bare chested, wearing jeans, cowboy boots, and a cowboy hat.

Then he removed a hand from behind his back, pulling forward a lasso, and he grinned.

I clapped in excitement. "You remembered!"

He swung it in front of him, making it go in a circle, showing off a little. "I haven't done this since I was a teenager, but I'm going to try tying up my girl like she asked and driving her wild."

Beck had told me that as a kid and teen he'd sometimes stayed with a great-uncle who owned a ranch, and during the visits had learned how to rustle cattle and even lasso them.

When he'd told me some stories of his time there, I blurted that I'd like to have him lasso me and tie me up too.

And he'd remembered.

I pressed my thighs together in anticipation and licked my lips. His eyes followed the action, and my nipples tightened.

As Beck walked toward me, he continued moving the lasso in a circle. "It looks like we have an escaped city girl here, and I need to make sure she doesn't run off." He moved closer. "Then I'll need to inspect every inch of her, just to make sure there aren't any injuries."

I put my arms out, holding my wrists together. "I'm ready for you to take me back. I don't like it out here after all."

Beck didn't even blink at the role play. After twirling the rope, he flicked his wrist, and it went around my wrists. As he tugged it tighter—but not too tight—the pounding between my legs increased. Once the rope was snug, he yanked it. "Come here."

I stood and let him rope me in. His eyes never left mine, his gaze burning and full of promise. By the time he took hold of my bound wrists, my heart raced and my pussy throbbed.

Taking my chin, Beck kissed me. He took his time, nipping my bottom lip before exploring my mouth, each lick and suckle making me moan and arch toward him. It was both frustrating and thrilling that I couldn't reach out and touch him like I wanted.

Breaking the kiss, Beck met my eyes. Slowly, oh so slowly, he ran a hand down my back, up my hip, and then traced around my breast. With each pass, he drew closer and closer to my nipple, until he was just shy of touching it. And still he teased me, avoiding where I ached. "Beck. Please."

He rolled my hard peak, and I groaned, loving how he then pinched me hard, not quite enough to be painful but enough to send a rush of wetness between my thighs.

His deep voice rolled over me as he said, "I've only just started my inspection of you, city girl. I'd best take you home for the night so I can finish the job."

He maneuvered so he could heft me over his shoulder, making me laugh. This man would never stop being ridiculous, and I loved him for it.

He nipped my butt cheek, and I squeaked. But as he laved the spot with his tongue, soothing the sting, I sighed.

"No injuries right here. But I've barely begun, sweetheart. The night is young."

In the next second, he laid me on my back and tugged the rope until my wrists were above my head. As he hitched the other end around the wooden bedpost, my heart pounded harder. My skin was on fire, I ached between my thighs, and only Beck could give me the release I so desperately needed.

Once the rope was tied to the bed, Beck ran a finger along the sensitive skin of my inner forearm. Each brush of his rough, warm fingers made me arch my hips, wanting him to touch me lower, much lower.

"Beck."

He tossed away his hat before placing his palms on my inner thighs and pushing them open. "I'm going to start here. Keep your eyes on me, sweetheart. I want you to see how much I fucking love eating this perfect pussy."

I growled in frustration. "Stop teasing, and get started."

His thumbs brushed against my inner thighs. "That's right. Don't be afraid to tell me what you want." He moved one hand to caress the crease where my leg met my pelvis, and I jumped. I'd never realized that spot could be so sensitive.

He asked, "Understand?"

"Yes."

As soon as I said the word, he lowered his head and licked my slit, stopping just short of my clit, before going back again. Over and over, he teased me, lapping, lightly nipping, and making me desperate for more. Much more. "My clit. Please, my clit."

After thrusting a finger into me, he murmured, "As you wish," and twirled his tongue around my bundle of nerves, not quite touching but near enough for me to get closer and closer to the edge.

I tugged at my restraints. "You're still teasing me."

He suckled my clit and flicked his tongue in a steady rhythm, and finally, lights danced behind my eyes as I screamed, pleasure coursing through me, intense, hot, and almost painful.

When it eventually calmed down, I relaxed into the bed, trying to catch my breath.

Beck's hand rubbed up my legs and over my belly, and he finally cupped my breasts and fondled them. "I'm still not done with my inspection, ma'am."

Smiling, I raised my eyebrows. "Oh?"

His mouth closed over my nipple, and any thought of role-playing left my head as he suckled. His hand rolled my other nipple, the dual sensations making me hot and achy all over again.

"I want you inside me."

After lifting his head, Beck smiled slowly. "Not yet."

In the next second, he'd flipped me onto my belly. My arms were still tied, but he'd left enough slack that I could rest my forearms on the bed without issues. "Beckett Wolfe!"

He slapped my ass, and I bit the inside of my cheek to keep from moaning. It was a small act of rebellion, but his grunt afterward made it all worth it.

As he ran his hands over my hips, my ass, and then my back, I sucked in a breath. "You're taking too long."

His fingers brushed through my slit. "Nearly there, sweetheart. I want you dripping for me first."

Considering I'd already orgasmed once, I couldn't imagine being any wetter.

However, he brushed his lips over the backs of my thighs, my calves, and even the bottom of my feet before moving to my lower back. I tried widening my legs and lifting my hips, inviting him. But he merely took his time licking my skin, nipping parts of my back, then his mouth lingered on my right shoulder.

He whispered, "Maybe one day, you can get a wolf here to match mine."

I blinked, taking a second to process his words, and realized he meant get a tattoo to match his.

"Why?"

Beck kissed my shoulder again. "To be the mate of mine."

As I tried to process his words, he removed his mouth, and his heat vanished. I strained my head to see him shuck his jeans and boots before taking a condom packet from the nightstand drawer. He was about to tear it when I said, "Wait."

He raised his eyebrows in question.

"I'm on the pill now, and I'm clean."

Beck walked to the bed and lightly traced the curve of my cheek. "I'm clean as well. Are you sure?"

"Yes. Consider it another birthday present you could give me—nothing between us when you're inside me."

After leaning down until he was eye level, he kissed me. "It'll be more of a gift for me to feel your tight, wet pussy gripping my dick. But as my lady wishes."

Just the thought of feeling Beck without anything between us made even more wetness rush between my thighs. I'd never had sex without a condom before, but I desperately wanted to experience that with Beck.

He moved behind me, his warm hands rubbing circles on my butt, and he leaned down to kiss the back of my neck. "Happy birthday, sweetheart. Time to make you come harder than ever before."

I wanted to roll my eyes, but then I felt the tip of his cock at my entrance. As he eased inside, he felt hotter than with a condom and, though it was ridiculous, thicker too. By the time he was inside me to the hilt, I had my forehead on the mattress and my hips arched against him, until my butt was pressed against his hips and abdomen.

He lightly smacked my ass, and to get back at him, I clenched my inner muscles.

"Fuck, Sabrina. Do that again."

I did, loving how he moaned and gripped my hips, as if he was afraid I'd move away.

"You're so fucking tight and wet and hot, sweetheart. It's pure heaven." He caressed my hips before adding, "And I can't wait until I can brand you with my cum and then watch it drip out of your pussy."

His words were crass. Yet to feel his release inside me and to know he wanted to see his cum drip out of my pussy, as if to reinforce that I belonged to him and only him, made me squirm. "Then don't make me wait any longer, Beck."

That snapped him into action. He never stopped caressing my back as he moved his hips slowly at first, with long, deep strokes that hit that special spot inside me, driving me wilder and making me hotter. I didn't even care that I whimpered and soon started matching his rhythm.

As he increased his pace, the erotic sound of flesh slapping against flesh filled the room, making my clit throb for attention. But since my hands were tied, I couldn't touch myself. "Beck. Please, touch me."

He didn't even need clarification. His hand brushed my clit, and I jumped. Then he moved his fingers in slow, deliberate strokes, just as I liked.

Panting, I focused on the hot feel of Beck's dick inside me, the way he stroked me, and how he continued caressing my skin.

"Fuck, Sabrina. I love feeling you this way. I never want to leave. You're so fucking perfect."

Perfect. Beck's words sent me over the edge, and pleasure exploded as my pussy milked his cock.

He never stopped thrusting, the motion extending my orgasm to the point that I thought I might cry.

Then he stilled and groaned, releasing inside me. I loved having him bare, feeling the subtle pulses of his cock, his warmth filling me up.

Beck slumped over me and kissed the back of my neck. He was slightly out of breath as he said, "Damn, I don't have words for that, sweetheart." He kissed my shoulder. "I wish I could just stay inside you forever."

Though it was on the tip of my tongue to tease him, I wished he could stay too.

But I knew he was still coming down from an orgasm high and couldn't mean what he said, especially since our living together in Starry Hills would be a huge step.

I tugged at the rope. "Can you let me go now?"

"Just a second." Beck paused a beat before pulling out. Then his hands were between my legs, and he spread me wide. He growled. "Mine, Sabrina. You're mine."

I shivered at his words, loving how husky and possessive they sounded.

Beck finally released me to remove the rope from the bedpost and loosened it enough to slide it from my hands. He kissed one of my inner wrists and then the other. "Glad I didn't hurt you."

"You never would."

We stared at each other, the atmosphere charged with heat and unspoken words, ones I couldn't quite bring myself to say.

Beck finally cleared his throat. "Stay here, and I'll get a cloth to clean you up."

I watched as he walked away, my eyes zeroing in on the wolf tattoo on his shoulder. Beck's words came back. *"Maybe one day, you can get a wolf here to match mine."*

He returned, gently wiped between my legs with a warm washcloth before kissing me. After rushing to put the cloth in the bathroom, he came back, jumped over me to his side of the bed, and pulled me against him.

I yawned before saying, "This was the best birthday ever, and that was the best present ever."

As he stroked my hair, he asked, "Better than the cowboy boots?"

"Oh yes. Although imagine if you lassoed me while I wore them."

He chuckled, the sound rumbling in his chest and making me smile. "We'll see. I should save that for a special occasion. Otherwise, we'll run out of fantasies far too soon."

After lifting my head, I propped my chin on his chest. "That's not possible, you know."

"What?"

"Running out of fantasies. Because any type of sex with you would be one."

"I feel the same way, sweetheart. Now, kiss me so that we can go to sleep. Tomorrow's the big day."

I kissed him quickly. "Yes, because it's the day I win the Easter egg hunt."

Amusement danced in his eyes. "That confident, huh? Even without knowing what's to come?"

"I've seen some pictures from past years. I may not be a private investigator, but I can use Google like anyone else."

Chuckling, he moved his hand to thread his fingers through my hair. "Prepared, as always, sweetheart. And I can't wait to see how you do."

I ran my hand through his chest hair, loving how his heart still raced a little. "If I win, consider hosting scavenger hunts at different times of the year, as a trial to see if it helps to bring awareness not only to your farm but to your wine as well."

"And here I thought you'd say I had to wear the emoji T-shirt you mentioned."

I grinned. "I'll get you in it yet. Just wait and see."

He chuckled. "And if you lose?"

"Then we'll do one of your fantasies."

"The one where you put on a bathing suit and run slowly to me so that I can watch your tits bounce?"

Even three months ago, the thought of doing a *Baywatch*-style run for my boyfriend would've turned me beet red. However, this was Beck, the man who loved to kiss every inch of my body, told me how beautiful I was, and didn't mind dusting off his lasso skills to make me happy.

Smiling, I said, "Deal."

"Let's seal it with a kiss."

And we did, savoring each other's mouths, as if we had all the time in the world, with years ahead of us.

I only hoped that turned out to be true. I wanted him more than I'd wanted anything in my life. I might even love him, if the constant need to be around him, talk to him, and simply enjoy his comforting presence was any indication.

But as I fell asleep in his arms, my gut wasn't so sure of the future. So many times before, my life had turned to crap out of nowhere. But I hoped for once my gut was wrong, and I could keep this man forever.

Chapter Thirty-Eight

Beckett

Abby: You'd better not make Sabrina late to cheer on Avery and Wyatt.
Me: We'll be there.
Abby: And don't even think of taking a "nap" later. Sabrina can't miss the adult Easter egg hunt.
Me: You're taking this year very seriously.
Abby: Well, I have a bet with Zach, and I won't lose.
Me: Betting with Zach is a bad idea. He loves dares.
Abby: <eye roll emoji> I have lived with the guy before. For nearly two decades.
Me: Just checking. You've been distracted lately.
Abby: Don't even go there. Just make sure Sabrina isn't late. Or else.
Me: Or else, what?

Abby: You might accidentally get gum stuck in your hair, and I'll let Avery cut it out.
Me: Now who's being mean?

Getting out of bed the next morning was one of the hardest things I'd done in a long, long time. Having Sabrina's warm body next to me, her leg resting across mine and her soft breasts pressed to my side, was pure heaven.

And being inside her without a condom the night before had been a fucking dream. I'd never been bare with a woman before, and it had felt so much hotter and wetter, to the point that I'd had to hold back to keep from coming too soon.

I would have stayed in bed all day with her, too, but we couldn't disappoint my niece and nephew. After the kids' Easter egg hunt had finished—Avery had gotten second place—we walked hand in hand toward the main house. There was a little time before the adult event started, and I wanted to ensure Sabrina got something to eat for lunch.

Sabrina's voice garnered my attention. "You should talk to Nolan today."

"What?"

"Ask him about the ads, videos, and stuff we talked about. You mentioned he sometimes goes silent when really into a role or on a job, and often, you don't hear from him for weeks. Better to hash it all out now, right?"

The corner of my mouth kicked up. "You're not going to let me put it off until later, are you?"

"Nope." Her expression softened. "Besides, I've noticed how much happier you've been since mending things with West. If you patch things up with another brother, you'll probably walk around with a constant grin on your face."

I stopped and tugged her to me. "You're forgetting a very important piece of the puzzle to my recent happiness."

"Oh?"

"You, sweetheart. If not for you, I'd probably still be the grumpy asshole who refused to talk with my brother, let alone delegate tasks to him."

"I think you give me too much credit."

"No, I don't. If I have to tell you how amazing you are every day, I will, until you finally believe it." She opened her mouth, but I placed a finger over her lips. "No excuses. You're beautiful, smart, and creative. And mine. You can't forget that part."

And I loved her too. But I didn't think she was quite ready to hear that yet. Not to mention there was the tricky problem of Sabrina loving her job, which was in San Francisco, and I couldn't leave Starry Hills. There had to be a solution somewhere, but I hadn't found it yet.

As she talked, I removed my finger. "Yours, huh? You seem to be saying that a lot lately."

"Because it's true. I'm definitely getting a shirt that reads Beck's Woman for you to wear for your next visit."

"I'm not a piece of property."

"No." I leaned down and tugged her earlobe with

my teeth. "But if we belong to each other, it's fair and pretty romantic, don't you think? And feel free to get me a T-shirt if you want to stake your claim. I'll wear it proudly."

"Even if it has emojis on it?"

Chuckling, I leaned back and shook my head. "It depends which ones. I'm a respectable member of the community, so I draw the line at scandalous ones."

"But it'd be the talk of the town, and you know what they say—any press is good press."

I pulled her close and possessively gripped her ass. "So your professional opinion is to start a scandal?"

Amusement danced in her eyes. "Maybe."

"Well, maybe I should start one right now and take you to the barn. Then you'd show up to the Easter egg hunt with flushed cheeks and straw in your hair, and everyone will know what you've been up to."

After wrapping her arms around my neck, she leaned fully against me. "I think—"

Abby interrupted Sabrina. "There you are, Beck! Zach sent me to say he needs your help ASAP. Or the mud pit is going to turn into a pool."

I sighed. Having a lot of siblings was a pain in the ass. Good thing I loved them, or I would've committed murder years ago.

After kissing Sabrina, I released her and faced my sister. "Fine. But take Sabrina to the main house and get her some lunch before the next event starts."

Abby nodded. "Of course. Text me if you or Zach need me to get anyone else to help you."

I kissed Sabrina. "I'll see you soon."

I jogged past all the grapevines, past where they were rebuilding the bottling facility, until I reached a remote area of my land where the soil was poor, unable to grow grapes. As I drew closer, I saw a tall figure bent over in the mud—Nolan.

It was unusual to see him outside, getting his hands dirty—he'd never liked working with the vines like I had. Most of his teenage years, I'd been too busy running the winery, and his love of acting had taken me by surprise. In retrospect, I regretted not getting to know him better.

But I'd promised Sabrina I would talk to him. I approached my younger brother and asked, "What's wrong, and how can I help?"

Nolan growled in frustration and stood. "I can't find the shutoff for this water line. It's somewhere in the mud, but I don't remember where."

I walked about ten feet away to slightly higher ground. "You wouldn't know, Nolan. It was installed in the last few years." I crouched and lifted the lid to the concealed valve. Taking the small tool I left here for the purpose, I shut off the water. "Did it stop?"

"Yes!"

After shutting the lid, I stood and walked back to my brother. He was covered in mud up to his knees, and remembering all the years we'd lost, I decided to treat him as the brother I should have.

So naturally, I charged at him, tackling him to the ground.

"What the fuck, Beck?"

I leaned up and grinned. "I've always wanted to do

that to you. But when you were younger, I was told you were too young. But now? You're fair game."

Nolan narrowed his eyes, crouched to his feet, and jumped at me.

We rolled over and over in the mud, trying to pin each other. The mud wasn't deep enough to drown in, but it felt satisfying when I managed to get the upper hand on my brother. "Forfeit."

"Fine. I forfeit. Just let me out of this fucking mud."

Laughing, I stood and offered my hand. Nolan took it and then yanked me to the ground.

He stood, smiling. "Payback's a bitch, asshole."

Then as we took in each other, covered in mud and our hair sticking up every which way, we burst out laughing.

Nolan managed to help me to my feet, and I slapped him on the back.

"That felt good. Nearly four years between us doesn't matter now like when I was eleven and you were seven."

As he wiped mud from his face, Nolan said, "No. Especially since I'm stronger than you now."

I raised an eyebrow. "Care to prove it?"

"Maybe later. If we don't finish getting things set up for this afternoon, I don't even want to imagine Aunt Lori's scolding. I'll probably have to run back to my place in Malibu just to nurse my ears." Nolan sobered and added, "I'd still like you to visit someday, Beck. The offer's always open."

Damn, I felt like a dick. My brother had invited me multiple times, and I'd always refused, mostly because I didn't want to argue about taking his money. However, I had a new plan, and it might solve that problem once and for all. "I'd like that. Maybe in the winter, when there's less to do here. It'll also be a hell of a lot warmer in SoCal than here."

"Southern California does have its benefits—just not fresh air like in Starry Hills." Nolan's gaze roamed the landscape. "I miss this place sometimes."

"But I thought you loved your job."

"I do most of the time. When I'm on a shoot, playing a character, I fucking love it. It's all the people and press and events that I can't stand."

Even as a child, Nolan had been socially awkward in large groups. When he'd started taking acting classes, it had puzzled me at first. Later he explained how he liked the escape of being someone else for a little while, and when he did that, the crowds melted away and didn't bother him.

I squeezed my brother's shoulder. "Well, you're welcome to stay here anytime."

"Thanks, Beck." He cleared his throat. "We should probably head back now."

He turned as if to leave, and I blurted, "I also have a favor to ask you."

Nolan turned back around. "Anything, Beck."

"Anything?"

"Well, within reason. I'm not going to dress us in spandex and do somersaults, for example."

I made a face. "I don't need to see my brother in spandex, thank you very much."

"Good. Then what is it?"

After taking a deep breath, I said, "Sabrina suggested that maybe if you did some ads or videos about the winery, it could help us. That way, you could help the family, and we'd stop fucking arguing over the money."

"I'd be happy to help. I just need to look over my schedule first."

The corner of my mouth kicked up. "Do I need an appointment to make an appointment?"

He punched my shoulder. "Shut up, asshole."

As we laughed, a little more weight lifted off my shoulders. I kind of regretted going so many years without fixing things with my brothers.

However, I couldn't change the past and could only focus on the future. And for the moment, that meant the adult Easter egg hunt. "Now, tell me what's left to do. I have to live here, and I shudder to think what Aunt Lori might start doing if we fuck up today."

So my brother and I went to work setting up the rest of the adult Easter egg hunt. It felt good to tease my younger brother and for him to do it right back. The age difference wasn't annoying like when we'd been kids.

I had my little brother back, all because of Sabrina.

That woman was the best thing to happen to me in a long time, maybe ever. Now I just needed to think of how I could win her over for good.

Chapter Thirty-Nine

Sabrina

Taylor: Good luck! Represent San Fran today.
Me: Um, it's not the World Series or anything.
Taylor: Still, I can't be married to a pro baseball coach and not want to win. Ben says he can give you a last-minute pep talk, if you want.
Me: <laughing emoji> No, thank you. I've gotten a lot of it from Abby and Aunt Lori.
Taylor: I wish I could've been there. I could've worn my cheerleading Halloween costume and come up with some cheers.
Me: Save that for your hubby.
Taylor: He does love that costume…
Me: And they're calling my name. I'll let you know what happens.

Taylor: Goooooo, Sabrina! <clapping hands emoji>

The last leg of the adult Easter egg hunt was no joke. I'd found the required half-dozen different colors and just needed one more, a golden one. And it was hidden somewhere in the mud-filled area, which had triggers that would set off random sprinklers.

As I accidentally set off another one, I cursed.

Only five other adult participants were in this area, a few I'd seen during the earlier stages but didn't know personally. Regardless, I paid them little heed, trying to figure out where the hell I'd hide an egg if I were trying to trip someone up.

And to think early on in the course, I'd laughed at how easy it was. Eggs had been hidden behind apple trees and under flowerpots, just like during the children's event.

The strategy was sound—get someone to underestimate the situation and then frustrate the hell out of them later.

As I trudged through a few inches of mud and tried not to lose my shoes, I cursed Beck and his brothers for their devious streaks.

I moved to a section empty of other people, which was in the corner of where the mud met the dry ground. Hiding the egg in the mud was too obvious. If I were being particularly evil, I'd put all kinds of gold-colored stuff in the mud to mislead everyone. And considering I'd found some gold balls and even a few gold-painted rocks, I sensed the actual find would be outside of it.

When I was nearly to the edge of the mud, someone shoved me, and I fell facedown. I tried to push myself upright, but a weight held me in place.

Panic rushed through me, and no matter how hard I tried to get up, I couldn't. I struggled harder, not wanting to drown in a few inches of mud. But no matter how hard I pushed, kicked, or tried to grab at the person behind me, I couldn't get free. Dark spots started to dot my vision. Just as my lungs burned to the point that I wouldn't be able to hold my breath any longer, my head was yanked up by my hair.

I gasped as an unfamiliar male voice whispered, "Watch your fucking back, Sabrina."

Then something hit me, and the world went black.

Slowly, I opened my eyes, my skull pounding, and blinked to adjust to the light in the room. Beck came into focus, sitting in a chair next to a bed.

I croaked, "Beck."

He jumped up and sat next to me. As he took my hand, he used his other one to caress my forehead. "Sabrina. Are you okay? Are you hurt anywhere?"

At his frantic expression, I squeezed his hand. "I'm fine. My head hurts a little, but that's it."

For a few moments, he said nothing, merely took in my face as if to reassure himself I was alive. Then he finally said, "I'm trying to find out who did this to you. We have his profile on the security cameras, but I didn't recognize the guy. Thankfully, one of the other participants found you passed out and called for help." He cupped my cheek. "I'm just glad you're okay, sweetheart. You scared me half to death."

I swallowed, trying not to remember being held in the mud, and managed to say, "Me too."

He raised our clasped hands to his lips and kissed the back of mine. "I want to let you rest, but the sheriff said to ask if you remember anything. The more information he has, the better chance we have of catching the bastard who hurt you."

I hesitated. I knew they needed my help, yet I also didn't want to relive almost dying.

As if reading my thoughts, Beck said softly, "If you need more time, just tell me. You went through hell today, and I don't want you to go through it again."

"Help me sit up and hold me, Beck."

He did as I asked. As soon as I snuggled into his warm chest, some of my fear and anxiety eased. Did I want to think about earlier? No. But with Beck's strong arms around me and his heartbeat a reminder that I wasn't alone, I thought maybe I could try.

I racked my brain, trying to recall anything useful. For a second, I remembered my lungs burning. Then Beck held me tighter, and the memory faded. Finally, I managed to sift through to the end. "I just recall being held down by someone strong and a male voice warning me to watch my back. He even knew my name."

"Did you recognize the voice?"

"No."

"Son of a bitch. It was probably someone hired by that dickhead, Justin."

"Maybe. But we don't know for sure." At the fury blazing in his eyes, I worried he'd take matters into his own hands and ask questions later. "Promise me you won't do anything stupid, Beck."

He clenched his jaw before finally letting out a breath. "You're more important to me than seeking justice." He caressed my cheek, and I leaned into his touch. "I'm just glad you're okay, sweetheart. You scared me."

Tears pricked my eyes, but I willed them away. If I started crying, I didn't think I'd be able to stop. And I wanted to find the person or persons responsible before finally letting it all out. "I'm here, Beck. And I'll be fine."

He brushed hair off my face, his touch so tender that my throat tightened with emotion. "I want to make sure. One of the adult participants today is a doctor, and she's waiting downstairs. I'll just go get her."

I clung to him, not wanting to be alone.

He said, "That's exactly how I feel. Here, let me just take out my phone, and I'll get Aunt Lori to send her."

One-handed, Beck managed to call his aunt. Once he was done, he tossed his phone aside and pulled me close before kissing the top of my head. "I should've been there to protect you, and I wasn't."

"Stop it. You can't watch me every moment of every day. Besides, I'm still here. And I won't let this ruin what has been a fantastic weekend."

Leaning down, Beck murmured, "You're an amazing woman, sweetheart." He kissed me until someone knocked on the door. "Can I come in?"

Beck broke the kiss, looked at me, and I nodded. He replied, "Yes, come in."

The door opened, revealing a woman I assumed to be the doctor. She had curly black hair and dark skin and was probably in her thirties. "Hello, Sabrina. How are you feeling?"

Her voice was soothing yet confident, exactly the type to help me relax. "My head hurts a little, but that's it."

She smiled as she took a few steps into the room. "That's definitely a good sign. Although I need to examine you just to be safe. I'm Dr. Washington, by the way."

"Nice to meet you. I'm Sabrina O'Connor."

Dr. Washington walked toward the bed and looked at Beck. "I know you want to stay with her, but it's easier if you wait just outside."

Beck grumbled and tightened his hold on me.

I stroked his cheek. "It's okay, Beck. It might be embarrassing if you stay."

"Why? I've seen you naked before."

Dr. Washington bit her bottom lip as if to keep from laughing.

I sighed. "Please, Beck?"

"Fine. But I'll be just outside the door. Shout if you need me."

"I will." I kissed him, and Beck left, grumbling the whole way.

The doctor smiled. "Let's get started, shall we?" She sat on the edge of my bed and opened her large purse. After putting on a pair of disposable gloves, she extracted a pen light and clicked it on. "Look straight ahead."

I did, and she shined the light in my eyes.

"Now, follow my finger."

I did that too, and she nodded.

"I just need to feel the back of your head, if that's okay."

"Of course."

I flinched a little when the doctor touched the sore spot, and she withdrew her hands.

After she asked me a few questions about the day's date and my current location, she finished with "I don't think you have a concussion. And earlier, I listened to your breathing, and I didn't hear anything abnormal in your lungs. Do you feel as if you inhaled any mud?"

"I don't think so. I tried not to open my mouth or breathe it in."

She nodded. "If you have any trouble breathing in the next few hours, if the pain increases, or you notice any other changes to your vision or memory, come see me." After pulling a business card from her purse, the doctor handed it to me. "I'm in Starry Hills, in the town itself. I do house calls, but it's best if you can come into my clinic so that I have all my resources available."

I didn't know how much longer I'd be in Starry Hills, but I still replied, "I'll try. I live in San Francisco, though."

"Well, any doctor will do. Although if you're ever here and need help, come see me." She hesitated a second before adding, "Now that I've finished as your doctor, can I ask you something on a more personal level?"

"Um, sure."

She took off her gloves. "I heard about what you have planned for Beck and this place. Do you do branding work for clinics as well? I recently bought mine from an older doctor who retired, and it desperately needs a new look and update. I can tell you just about anything to do with the human body, but when it comes to marketing and that kind of stuff, I'm nearly clueless."

I blinked and tried to process Dr. Washington's words. "You want to hire me?"

"I think so. We'd need to chat and go over some ideas first, of course. But if Beck, Zach, and Lori Wolfe love you and sing your praises, it's at least worth a meeting to see if we fit."

I nearly blurted, "Yes!" but remembered my boss's policy on small businesses. Edwina would never bother with a small-town clinic. It wasn't profitable enough.

Yet the thought of turning down the doctor didn't sit right with me. Her offer was what I'd always wanted to do—make a difference in people's lives. Not just for giant companies with the big bucks but smaller businesses as well.

The one snag was that the paperwork I'd signed for Edwina Jones & Associates didn't allow me to do my own consulting work on the side.

But then an idea of having my own company in Starry Hills formed.

The thrill of living here permanently rushed through me. I already knew so many people, wouldn't have to deal with big-city traffic, and of course, Beck and his family were here as well.

However, I wasn't sure I had enough courage to uproot myself and start over. I could fail and lose everything—both professionally and with Beck. Edwina wouldn't like my leaving her, and she was an enemy no one wanted. She had too much sway.

As for Beck, there was no guarantee things would work out long-term. It would take a giant leap of faith on my part. Could I do it?

Since I needed time to think, I finally replied, "Let me see what I can do, Dr. Washington. If I can't fit you into my schedule, I'll let you know by next week."

She nodded. "Sounds good. And please, call me Nichelle. If we're to work together, Dr. Washington will feel strange." She put out a hand, and we shook. "I look forward to hearing from you, Sabrina."

The doctor gave a few last-minute instructions and exited the room. I stared down at her business card, thinking about all the paths I could take.

Before long, Beck was back and sitting on the bed beside me, his arm around my shoulders. "What did the doctor say?"

I closed my fingers around the business card and looked up at him. "She doesn't think I have a concussion, and everything seems fine. I just need to make sure that if I feel weird or things change or get worse, I see a doctor again."

He kissed my cheek. "I'm glad, sweetheart." Gently turning my head, he said, "I did have another surprise for you tonight, but I guess it'll have to wait."

"You can't just bring that up and not tell me what it is, Beck."

He smiled for the first time since I'd woken up. "I could if I wanted to."

"Are you really going to be mean to an injured lady?"

Concern filled his gaze. "Do you need anything?"

Sighing, I shook my head. "No. I was just teasing you." I took his hand and threaded my fingers through his. "Tell me what you had planned, Beck. Maybe I can still do it."

"You need to rest, sweetheart."

"Just tell me. I'd tickle you to get it out, but I don't want to jerk my head around right now."

"I never should've let you know I'm ticklish." When I wiggled my fingers in warning, he sighed. "Fine. My siblings and I wanted to take you out tonight to celebrate."

"Celebrate what?"

"Our signing the contract with your boss so that you can officially work with us."

At first, joy rushed through me. Then a sense of something not being right came next. Why hadn't Edwina told me about this? "When did you sign it?"

"Earlier in the week. I asked your boss to let me be the one to tell you."

Okay, Edwina would never bow down to that level with a client—at least, not unless she had an ulterior motive.

I tried to focus on the good news, though, and not ruin the moment with Beck. "It's great she still wanted to do business with your family despite the fire and subsequent rebuilding."

He shrugged. "Zach and I sent a detailed plan about our production schedule while we rebuild what was lost in the fire. True, it's an extra expense to rent another bottling facility temporarily, but it's not too bad. In general, we said politely that we were fucking amazing and could kick some ass with a little help from her agency."

"Oh, Beck. I'm so happy for you!"

Beck cupped my cheek. "And me for you, sweetheart. I'm sure you'll get the promotion now, right? That's not the main reason we signed, not by a long shot. Your ideas won us over. Still, it wouldn't be a bad bonus."

I hope so. Edwina had said that whoever snagged the contract would be promoted, but I hadn't heard anything about it.

Once I was back in the city, I would find my boss and ask her about it.

For now, all I wanted to do was share in Beck's joy. "Fingers crossed. Kiss me for luck."

He pressed his lips to mine for a second before pulling away. I tried to follow, but he shook his head. "No, sweetheart. As much as I want to strip you bare and celebrate that way, we need to wait. I want to make certain you're okay."

"That would be the sensible thing to do."

His lips twitched. "Yes, that's me, Mr. Sensible."

I snorted. "Right, because you were totally sensible when you all but yelled at me during our first meeting."

"That was my temper, which has nothing to do with my good sense."

I was tired, and my head hurt, so unable to come up with a witty reply, I stuck my tongue out at him.

Beck chuckled. His phone beeped, and he quickly checked it, frowning.

"What is it?"

"My siblings and I were going to celebrate with you tonight at The Watering Hole—they have a colorful Easter cocktail tradition—and Abby is wondering if we're still going. I just need to tell her no."

"Don't!"

He met my eyes again. "You nearly died today, Sabrina. You're not going out for drinks."

"I'll ask the doctor. If she says no, then I won't. But, Beck, I really could do with something fun after the day I've had."

"I want to lock you in here and say you're not going anywhere. But my good sense is telling me you'd probably contact my siblings to help bust you out."

"Maybe."

Sighing, he hugged me harder. "We'll listen to the doctor. If she says no, you'll stay here. Okay?"

"Yes, Beck."

"Then I need to see if Dr. Washington is still

downstairs. Aunt Lori invited her for tea and scones, but I don't know if she stayed."

"Then hurry up and check." He looked torn, so I added, "As long as you rush right back to me, I'll be fine."

He caressed my cheek with the backs of his fingers. "I'll always come back to you, sweetheart."

After giving me a gentle kiss, Beck went to find Dr. Washington.

And I lay on the bed, wondering if he truly meant his words.

Chapter Forty

Beckett

Abby: I can't believe you ruined our big surprise.
Me: I didn't even want her going out.
Millie: But the doctor said it was okay for one drink.
Me: You do realize she's my girlfriend, right? Not yours?
Millie: <tongue sticking out emoji>
Abby: <middle finger emoji> She's my friend.
Zach: I just want to watch you make calf eyes at her.
Me: WTF? Since when has Zach been in the group text?
Zach: Since always. I like being in stalker mode and pouncing when you least expect it.
Me: Now you're a stalker. Great.

Abby: <laughing emoji> He'd fail, big time. Zach doesn't like to be in the shadows. He likes attention.
Zach: Fuck you, sister. I thought you were on my side.
Abby: I am. This is how I show my love.
Me: You all are crazy.
Abby: <blowing a kiss emoji> Love you too.

In the end, the doctor had okayed Sabrina going out.

But I was going to watch her like a hawk. At the first sign of fatigue or weakness, I'd carry her out of the bar if it came to it.

We settled down on the couches at the back. Since the group consisted of all six of my siblings, my best friend, Kyle, and Sabrina, we barely fit. As it was, my girlfriend had to sit in my lap, which wasn't a hardship.

As I held her snugly in my lap, it was getting harder and harder to imagine my life without her. Just the sight of her unconscious and covered in mud earlier had nearly given me a heart attack.

Though it had made some things pretty fucking clear. I needed to not only tell her I loved her but also find a way for us to be together, no matter what it took.

Our drinks arrived, and Sabrina laughed. "You weren't joking—it's like a rainbow of cocktails."

I took the Rainbow Paradise—it went from blue to green to orange and finally to red. Sabrina took the bright-pink one with sprinkles around the rim, a birthday cake martini.

"For a place that usually serves beer and whiskey, it's definitely weird. But since it only happens once a year, the regulars and some of their friends always come for the spectacle. Although I think it's more of an excuse to drink before Easter and help them get ready to face family visiting or kids high on sugar."

She sipped her drink and sighed. "It's like a cake in a glass."

"You only get the one, per doctor's orders."

Even if the doctor had okayed Sabrina going out, I still didn't like how her attacker could be anywhere, maybe even at the bar.

Abby snorted. "Beck, you've said that a million times already. We all know, so just relax."

I glared at her. "Excuse me for wanting to take care of my woman."

Millie raised her eyebrows. "Your woman, huh?"

Sabrina laid her head on my shoulder. "Well, he did say I could make a shirt saying he's mine. So I don't get too upset about it."

Kyle smirked at me, and I flipped him the bird.

Zach—who could now hobble on crutches—interrupted everyone by raising his purple-and-green concoction. "To Sabrina and her finding a way to mellow out my brother!"

He waggled his eyebrows, and I gave him the middle finger.

Abby also raised her blue-colored glass. "To Sabrina! Maybe one day, we'll finally even the numbers, and I won't have so many damn men about."

Nolan chuckled, and West grunted as he frowned.

Millie elbowed Abby. "Hear, hear! To Sabrina!"

Sabrina's cheeks were turning pinker and pinker. I

kissed one and murmured, "You're amazing, sweetheart. Embrace it."

She whispered for my ears only, "What for? Having a magical vagina?"

I nipped her earlobe, and she giggled.

Everyone took a drink, and we fell into some banter and regular chatting. Sabrina jumped in easily, and I could see that Abby and Millie really liked her. When it came to West, who the fuck knew, but that was normal. Zach teased her, which was his sign of approval. And even Nolan offered to invite her to a movie set if she wanted to see him work.

Aunt Lori had stayed home, saying she was too old to go out to a bar, but I knew she loved Sabrina as well.

It felt as if she belonged in our family.

As she relaxed against me and laughed at something Zach said, the front door opened so quickly that it smacked against the wall. We all turned our heads, and I growled.

Justin Whitmore. The asshole's shirt was untucked, he looked as if he hadn't shaved in days, and his eyes were wild.

I maneuvered Sabrina onto the couch and stood, putting myself between them. "Get the fuck out of here."

He looked around me and sneered at Sabrina. "Look at the whore who fucks the clients. Edwina said she doesn't like that."

Without thinking, I punched the asshole in the face. He dropped and covered his nose. "What the hell?"

Leaning down, I grabbed his tie and yanked him up

to his feet. "Apologize to her, and then get your sorry ass out that door."

"Apologize? No fucking way. And you should be careful—she led me on and used me long before meeting you. Now that the contract is signed, she's done with you and will ditch you. Just wait and see."

"Shut up, dickhead, and apologize."

He laughed. "No."

I narrowed my eyes and pulled my arm back as if to punch him again, but West grabbed my wrist. He said quietly, "Don't."

John, the owner, was already walking over, his son right behind him. Neither of them looked pleased.

Fuck. I'd broken the no-fighting rule and was about to get my ass booted out the door.

After dropping Justin, I sneered, "Leave us the hell alone. Because if you don't, you'll slip up, and then we'll have you, fucker."

Justin stood. "I'd be nice to me, if I were you. Because you'll be working with me from now on."

With that, he exited the bar.

What the fuck was he talking about?

Sabrina touched my arm. "Let's go, Beck."

At the worry in her eyes, I knew something was wrong. But I'd wait until we were alone to discuss it.

I apologized to John, and he said I had to leave for the night. Everyone came with us, and we made our way to our cars.

Before we divided up, I said, "I'm sorry but not sorry. That asshole needed to be punched."

West scowled. "Not in front of everyone."

Millie jumped in. "I think it was great. Beck stood up for his girl, as he should."

Kyle slapped my shoulder. "I'll find out if he leaves town or not. He must've driven straight in, or someone would've told me he was here."

I murmured my thanks and opened my truck's door and helped Sabrina inside.

The cab was silent as I pulled out of the parking lot and headed back home. When I glanced at Sabrina, she was frowning at her phone. "What's wrong?"

"I don't know yet." She bit her lip and finally added, "I sent a text to my boss about the contract, but I still haven't heard back. That was hours ago."

"Maybe she's celebrating the weekend with family."

"No. Edwina is a workaholic and almost always answers her text messages. Combined with what Justin just said, I have a bad feeling in my stomach."

I gently touched her knee. "Tell me."

She sighed. "Edwina should've told me about the contract being signed at the very least. And given Justin's reminder about how she doesn't like her employees sleeping with any of the clients, I'm worried she knows about us and won't promote me. Or in the worst-case scenario…"

"What?"

"She'll fire me."

"What the fuck? No. If not for the fact that we'd be working with you, I would never have signed the contract."

"And that's the point. Edwina would do anything to get a foothold in Sonoma. She might act as if I would be working with you but have hidden language in the contract about the assigned manager being at her discretion."

"I had my lawyer look over the contract, but she didn't find any red flags."

"It might not seem like a red flag."

She looked out the window and fell silent. I wanted to tell her it would be all right, that her boss couldn't be that bad or that I'd back out if that were the case.

However, the only way to back out of the contract was if there was some sort of criminal activity related to her firm or if they didn't follow through on their promises. And the more I thought about it, the more I couldn't remember the contract stating explicitly that Sabrina would be our brand manager.

Fuck.

We arrived home, and I guided Sabrina into our guesthouse. Once inside, I pulled her against me and kissed the top of her head. "We'll find a way to make it work, Sabrina. There has to be a way."

"I wish I could be that optimistic."

She sounded so defeated. The very thought of her losing everything she'd worked so fucking hard for and it going to an asshole who didn't care about hurting anyone if it meant getting what he wanted pissed me off.

However, anger wouldn't help her right now. So I helped her to bed, held her against my side, and willed things to work out. I'd only just realized I loved her, and I couldn't bear to think of losing her so soon.

Because if she were fired because of being involved with me, she might never forgive me.

But no matter what happened, I would fight for her —for us.

Hugging Sabrina tighter to my side, I took strength from her warm, soft presence. In the morning, we'd discuss what to do if her boss fired her and tried to get Justin to work with my business.

For now, I just held the woman I loved and fell asleep to dreams of the future I wanted.

Chapter Forty-One

Sabrina

The next morning, I was a coward. I snuck out of the guesthouse early and drove back to San Francisco.

I knew Beck would want to talk to me more about the future, and I didn't know what that entailed. And if Edwina wouldn't answer her texts, I needed to go to the office to see if she was there. I hoped so because I desperately needed answers. My life had seemed almost perfect twenty-four hours ago. But now? I felt like I was about to drive off a cliff.

Arriving at the office, I parked in my designated spot and went upstairs. I nodded to the security guards and tapped my badge to unlock the front office door. The room was dark, but the lights came on as I walked because of the motion sensors. It didn't bode well for

Edwina being here, and sure enough, her office was dark.

I could go home. I'd worry and pace and bite my nails, thinking through every little thing and how it could go wrong. Or I could stay, try to do some work, and wait for her.

The second option was more productive. Although it was difficult to concentrate on my laptop, let alone do much on my current list of projects. Still, I knocked out as many menial tasks as I could, only stopping to make some tea and eat some candy I had stashed in my top drawer.

If I'd stayed in Starry Hills, I would soon be having a huge Easter lunch complete with ham, mashed potatoes, and a multitude of side dishes. We'd each been told to bring one, and I'd even worried over what to bring and had left the ingredients for an asparagus salad back on the farm.

Soon. You can go back soon enough. But not until you find out what's going on.

Trying my best to ignore the uneasiness of my gut, I sent emails, created social media posts for clients, and even wrote out some directions for one of our graphic designers. It was after noon when a text arrived from my boss:

Come to my office. Now.

Edwina had arrived. Since our offices were on opposite sides of the space, I hadn't seen her come in.

Taking a moment to look in the mirror, I said, "This will turn out fine. Justin is full of shit and just wanted to scare you. Be strong."

The words sounded less than convincing. Regardless, I straightened my shoulders and headed for Edwina's office. Once I arrived, I knocked, and she told me to enter.

She gestured to the chair in front of her desk. "Sit down."

I complied, crossed my legs at the ankles, and waited. It was always best to let Edwina be the first to speak.

Like usual, she focused on her computer for nearly a minute before she met my gaze. "The Wolfe family signed the contract."

"I heard. That's good news."

She leaned back. "Yes. But going forward, I have my reputation to consider."

I resisted rubbing my hands on my skirt. "What do you mean?"

"Edwina Jones & Associates is one of the most sought-after PR companies in the Bay Area. If word were to get out that we slept with clients to get contracts, that would be disastrous."

Damn, she knew about Beck and me.

"It's not what you think."

She raised an eyebrow. "Are you or are you not fucking Beckett Wolfe, one of the owners of Wolfe Family Farm and Winery?"

"Yes, but—"

"On one level, I understand. I saw the pictures, and he's attractive. However, it's a line we can't cross, Sabrina. And you know it. Per the contract you signed when you were hired, it's grounds for termination."

My heart pounded, but I tried to keep it together. Edwina hated displays of strong emotions of any sort. “I didn’t do it to get him to sign.” I paused but decided it was too important to hold back and added, “I love him. I didn’t plan for it to happen, but it did. This isn’t something I’d do again.”

As she smiled slowly, I could tell I’d screwed up. I’d revealed a weakness, and she would use it against me.

Her next words only confirmed my suspicions. “If you care for this man, then walk away. You’re fired. That won’t change. But if you’re thinking of going back to him and helping him in any way, let alone try to get him to end his relationship with my company, I’ll destroy him and his family. A few well-placed calls will ensure that no one buys his wine. Rumors and social media can damage a brand quickly, and I know enough people to make that happen. If you really do love him, then you’ll never see him again.”

My stomach dropped. I couldn’t be hearing Edwina right. “What? Why would you do that? No one in Sonoma will work with you if you hurt the Wolfe family.”

She raised her eyebrows. “How will anyone know it’s me? They won’t. It’ll be your word against mine, and you’re a nobody, Sabrina O’Connor.” She flicked her hand as if I were a piece of dust in her way. “Besides, getting a foothold in Sonoma will be even easier when I offer a one-year free contract to the winner of a wine-tasting event I’ll host soon. Who would pass that up? Who would side with you over what I can do to increase their profits? No one.” She looked back at her computer screen. "Pack your things and leave within fifteen minutes. Otherwise, I'll have you thrown out." Her fingers flew over the keyboard as she ignored me.

A million thoughts rushed through my mind, my emotions were a jumbled mess, and I honestly didn't know what to say or do.

Edwina didn't bluff. I'd worked for her long enough to know what she was capable of. And if she said she'd ruin Beck and his family, she would. Period.

She also liked loopholes. I needed a confirmation before making a decision, so I blurted, "If I agree to never see them again, you'll leave him and his family alone?"

Edwina glanced up. "Yes. I'll hold up my end of the bargain as long as you hold up yours."

It was only her word, but what else could I do? Beck had worked so hard to keep his winery afloat, to fulfill his vow to his father, and to provide for his family.

Even if I didn't know what he felt for me, I loved him. I could never destroy his family legacy. And giving in to Edwina was the only way I could protect him.

Pain squeezed my heart and tears pricked my eyes, but I forced myself to keep it together. I wouldn't break down in front of Edwina. "Then I'll stay away."

"Good. Now, go."

She stood, walked across the room, and entered her attached bathroom, a clear dismissal.

The next little while went by in a blur. Somehow, I managed to clear out my desk and drive home without breaking down. But as soon as I got inside my apartment and shut the door, I slid to the floor, rested my head on my knees, and cried.

Because the first man I'd ever loved—the only one I wanted—I couldn't have. To protect him, I had to push him away.

I would never see him, kiss him, or tease him again.

I would never watch his eyes light up as he talked about the winery or see him roll his eyes when his siblings teased him.

I would never hold him close, feel him inside me, or fall asleep against his chest.

And worse, by pushing him away, it felt as if I'd lost a piece of myself that I'd only just found.

I sobbed harder, letting it all out, with hopes that somehow, some way, he'd forgive me one day.

Chapter Forty-Two

Beckett

Something was wrong.

Sabrina had left before I woke up, no note, no text, nothing. Then no matter how many times I tried to call or text her, she didn't reply.

Though I recognized that she might not answer me during her drive back, the hours stretched and stretched. I barely made it through Easter lunch. By the time the sun set behind the hills, I was ready to drive to the city and find her.

Just as I'd packed a bag and was about to head down the stairs, my phone buzzed. Sabrina had sent a message:

Sabrina: Justin was right. I used you to get the promotion. Don't contact me again.

I stared at the message and read it five times before replying:

Me: I call bullshit. What's really going on? Talk to me, Sabrina. Please.
Sabrina: Don't message me again. I'm going to block your number.

I tried sending more messages and called several times, but she didn't answer.

Just as I finished leaving yet another voice mail, someone knocked on my door. I was in no mood to talk to anyone and said, "Go away."

Aunt Lori's voice came through the door. "You'd better be decent, because I'm coming in."

Since I hadn't locked my door, she turned the knob and walked in. One look at my face, and concern filled her eyes. "What's going on?"

Part of me wanted to spill everything. My aunt was like a second mother to me, and she always seemed to have answers, even when I didn't want to hear them.

Yet sharing my feelings about Sabrina and then having my aunt say I was wrong and had just imagined everything was fucking terrifying.

You're a grown-ass man. Act like it.

"Something's not right with Sabrina."

"I knew she left early this morning without a word and wasn't at lunch. Was it an emergency?"

"I don't know. She only contacted me about an hour ago."

When I didn't elaborate, Aunt Lori tilted her head and asked, "What aren't you telling me, Beckie?"

Her ridiculous nickname for me was what finally pushed me to reply, "She said everything between me and her was fake." I ran a hand through my hair. "I think she's lying, but why?"

"I have no idea. But if the way she gazed at you was just an act, then I'd eat a whole pineapple pizza. Not even Nolan could do that good of a job."

Aunt Lori hated pineapple pizza more than anything in the world, which meant she was deadly serious. "Are you sure you aren't just saying that because I'm your nephew?"

"Do I tiptoe around things? Have I ever mollycoddled you before?" I shook my head, and she continued, "That girl had stars in her eyes for you. And you're even worse, like a lovesick puppy anytime she's with you." When I grunted, she chuckled. "It's adorable, really." Her face sobered. "The bigger question is what are you going to do about it?"

Done trying to tiptoe around it, I answered, "Fight for her."

"Good lad. Now, go get the girl."

Picking up my packed bag, I said, "I'm going to the city. I'm not sure how long I'll be away."

Aunt Lori waved a hand in dismissal. "We've got you covered, Beckie. The place will be fine with me, Zach, and West while you're away. I hope you believe me."

A few months ago, I would've balked at handing over so much responsibility. I'd truly thought no one could run the farm and winery as well as I could.

But Zach was able to get around again, handling the winery side of things. And West had picked up everything about the grapevines rather quickly.

Between them and the employees I'd had for years, everything would be fine. If anything, my father would've been proud of that. It had taken me a long-ass time to realize he'd relied on his staff and family to help around the place. He'd never tried to do it alone. My dad would've wanted me to do the same.

Once I kissed Aunt Lori's cheek, I rushed out of the room, down the stairs, and into my truck. The whole way to the city, I tried to come up with what to say to Sabrina. And the simplest idea seemed to be the best—to let her know I loved her and wanted a future with her.

Because I didn't even want to imagine what my life would look like if she really had tricked me and wanted nothing more to do with me.

No. My gut said it had been real. Something else had to be going on, and I was determined to find out what the fuck it was.

Chapter Forty-Three

Sabrina

The longer I lay on the couch, clutching a pillow to my stomach, the louder my mother's voice became:

You'll never amount to anything. You're too fucking stupid.

You little shit, you don't deserve love. I wish I'd abandoned you by the side of the road.

You think you're so smart, but you're not. I can't wait to see you fall on your ass so I can laugh.

You drag everyone down. The world is better off without you.

I hugged the pillow tighter to my chest and tried to block out her voice. Even if I had to make Beck believe everything had been fake, I knew it had been real.

Beck had cared for me, made me feel beautiful, and supported me in a way I'd never had as a child. Hell, Beck might've even been a bigger cheerleader for me than my best friend, which was hard to believe. He'd remembered the doll and bought her for me. And he'd given me exactly what I'd wanted for my birthday.

Had it really only been two days since he walked in with a lasso and tied me up? Sighing, I curled more around the pillow and willed myself not to cry anymore.

But my eyes watered, and a silent sob escaped my throat. Maybe my mother had been right—I didn't deserve for good things to happen to me. I only ever brought people down. And that would happen to Beck and his family if I was selfish and rushed back into his arms.

I must've fallen asleep at some point, because I jumped awake when someone pounded on my door.

I wasn't expecting any visitors. Even Taylor was out of town, which was why I hadn't bothered texting her with anything that had happened. I didn't want to ruin her vacation.

The pounding didn't cease, and eventually, a familiar voice came through the door—Beck's. "Sabrina, are you in there?"

I hugged the pillow tighter. Why was he here? Just hearing his voice made tears slip down my cheeks all over again.

"Sabrina, please, if you're there, open the door and talk to me. Because I call bullshit on your texts. If you were faking everything, I'll eat my hat."

I still didn't respond.

"I'm going to wait out here for a while and then come back tomorrow. And the day after. I'm not going to stop until we talk about this. If you can look me in the eye and say it was all a lie, that you were using me to get what you wanted, then I'll leave you alone. But until then, I'm going to keep coming back."

Minutes ticked by, but I stayed in place—just barely.

All I wanted to do was throw open the door and jump into his arms, where I could feel safe, protected, and wanted, like before my meeting with Edwina.

Yet I somehow found the strength to resist moving from the couch. I couldn't be the reason he lost everything, lost his father's legacy, and ruined his family. I just couldn't. I loved him too much to hurt him like that.

Eventually, something slipped under the door, and I heard his footsteps retreating. After a few minutes, I slowly went to the door and picked up the piece of paper. When I unfolded it, I read:

You're stubborn, but so am I. Game on.

—Beck

The words blurred, and I crumpled the paper in my fingers. My heart soared at his wanting to keep pursuing me until he found out the truth. Yet the rational part of my brain knew that could never happen.

So I went to my bedroom, hid under the covers, and cried.

Cried for losing the man who made me feel special and cared for.

Cried at losing his family, who made me feel like one of their own.

And cried at the glimpse of happiness I'd experienced and would probably never feel again.

I cried myself to sleep and dreamed about the man I loved with every part of my being but could never have.

Chapter Forty-Four

Beckett

Only because some of the neighbors had poked their heads out of their doors and asked me to be quiet did I eventually leave Sabrina's place. If I'd kept trying to get her to open the door, they might've called the cops. And I couldn't find out what the fuck was going on if I was inside a jail cell.

I spent the night in a cheap hotel and looked up where Edwina Jones & Associates was located because I planned to drop by for a visit. Even if I was still waiting for word from my lawyer about other ways to get out of the contract, I could at least let Sabrina's boss know about fucking Justin Whitmore's behavior.

The night was long, and I barely slept.

The next morning, at 9:05 a.m., I stood at the

reception desk of the PR firm.

The young man at the desk smiled. "May I help you, sir?"

The "sir" part was generous, since I hadn't shaved and I didn't even have on a tie, let alone a suit jacket. But the button-down shirt, jeans, and cowboy boots I was wearing were the best I'd packed. "My name is Beckett Wolfe, and I want to speak to Edwina Jones."

"Do you have an appointment?"

"No. But I'm a new client, and I want to see her."

The young man's eyebrows came together. "Let me see if she's available."

As he placed a call, I waited. Beyond the reception area was a sea of desks in an open space, and people rushed about. The sight of the overhead lights, dress clothes, and plethora of computers made me itch to go back outside and work with the vines.

It was hard to imagine Sabrina here day after day, stuck behind a computer.

The reception guy cleared his throat and said, "Right this way, Mr. Wolfe."

I followed him, trying to organize my thoughts as we walked. Something wasn't right, and my gut said this place was a part of why Sabrina was ignoring me.

We stopped in front of a set of glass double doors, which showed the conference room inside, and the man opened one of the doors. "Ms. Jones will arrive shortly. Please, sit down and wait."

Since taking out my mood on the employee wouldn't help anyone, I merely nodded and sat in one of the chairs.

I didn't know how long I'd tapped my fingers on the table until a woman—probably in her fifties—walked in. She wore a black skirt, a matching blazer, and a light-blue shirt. Her makeup was heavy and her hair perfectly pulled back from her face.

She sat and raised her blond eyebrows. "What can I do for you, Mr. Wolfe?"

My mom and aunt had always said it was easier to attract flies with honey than with vinegar. Even though it was tough, I managed to get out, "I want to discuss my contract."

Edwina Jones gave the fakest smile I'd ever seen. "Yes, we're so happy to be working with you, Mr. Wolfe. Mr. Justin Whitmore will be handling your account and will contact you shortly."

"No."

She blinked. "Pardon?"

"He's been rude to me and my family. Plus, I think he's destroyed some of my property. If he ever sets foot on my land, we'll shoot him for trespassing."

The woman didn't bat an eyelash. "I assure you Mr. Whitmore would never do such a thing. Unless you have proof?"

I didn't have any concrete proof to match my suspicions, so I focused on his behavior. "What of his attitude? He insulted one of my friends."

"By friends, do you mean Sabrina?" She didn't wait for me to answer. "She no longer works here, because she violated her contract. Besides, there was always a rivalry between her and Whitmore. Harsh words are to be expected. Competition is good for business, after all."

My temper slipped. "And what about her reports to HR regarding his behavior?"

"His record is clean. Clearly, Sabrina lied to you about that too." She stood. "I'd suggest forgetting that woman. We have a bright future together, Mr. Wolfe." Her gaze turned threatening. "And I suggest you don't try to break the contract. Legal battles can be costly, and you won't last long against me. I'd much rather work together. Wouldn't you?" She put out her hand to shake.

Ignoring it, I stood and said, "You'll hear from me again."

I left before I did something stupid. Yelling at that woman wouldn't help anything.

No, I needed to find a way to not only talk to Sabrina but also take Edwina Jones down a few notches. Preferably by exposing Whitmore for the unstable fucker he was.

As soon as I slid into my truck and shut the door, I closed my eyes and tried to think of what to do next. Sabrina might be pissed at me for being fired. But I had to show her there was more for her out there, that she could soar on her own. Even if she still pushed me aside, I'd do that for her.

Turning over the ignition, I knew I couldn't solve this on my own. I needed my family's help.

So even though it felt wrong to leave the city with stuff unfinished, I did. After all, I'd be back. And next time, I'd have reinforcements.

Chapter Forty-Five

Sabrina

Taylor: How did the Easter egg hunt go? Did you win?
Taylor: Are you busy celebrating? Enjoy, but let me know!
Taylor: Maybe you're hung over, but that's unlike you. Please text me back.
Taylor: Something is wrong. If you don't reply, I'll have to resort to drastic measures as soon as I return to SF.
Taylor: Drastic measures it is.

Despite Beck's note, he didn't come back. Not that I'd expected him to, but it still stung.

It had been two days of my barely eating or sleeping, let alone showering and looking human.

Most of the time, I stared at nothing or turned on the TV for background noise. While it had hurt when my sister sided with my mom, being without Beck was worse. Way worse. I'd loved my sister—and on some level, still did—but Beck hadn't been someone I'd taken care of and raised. He'd become a good friend, a confidant, and the person I felt most comfortable around.

One who made me feel beautiful and desired and cherished.

One I had thought was maybe my future.

Having that ripped away was painful. Not to mention his family had become a found family, one I missed too, which made the pain even worse.

I must've fallen asleep at some point, because someone shook my shoulder, and I jumped. Blinking, I saw Taylor standing over me, frowning.

"What happened, Sabrina? And don't you dare say nothing."

"What are you doing here?"

She held up the spare key I'd given her years ago. "For emergencies and watering your plants when away. I thought your not texting me or calling me back for days constituted an emergency." She knelt on the floor and asked again, "What happened, Sabrina?"

I tried to keep it together but couldn't, and I burst into tears. Taylor sat next to me on the couch and pulled me into a hug.

Only once I calmed down did Taylor ask, "Is this to do with Beck?"

"Yes, but not how you probably think."

And I proceeded to tell her everything—about Edwina's threats to Beck and his family, all the incidents, and even Justin's words at the bar.

When I finally finished, Taylor hugged me tighter. "I know you're trying to protect Beck. But he seems strong enough to face anything. Maybe you should just talk to him about this. He might have an idea of how to make everything work out."

I shook my head. "Beck and his family have suffered so much already. I don't want to cause them any more trouble." My voice turned to a whisper. "I'm not worth it."

Taylor sat up and pulled away until she could see my face. Her eyes blazed with anger. "Don't you dare let your fucking mother win in this, too, Sabrina. You are kind, smart, and one of the most loyal people I know. When I was in the hospital after being hit by that foul ball, you were there. And you stood guard, even yelling at Ben when he came to see me, uncaring that he was a famous baseball player who was stronger and taller than you." She squeezed my hand. "Let me just ask you this—which is more important: listening to your mother's voice and believing her vile words or fighting for a man who could give you happiness?"

"It's not that simple."

"Isn't it? She's dead, Sabrina. And I know she hurt you, and you can't just turn off or push aside years of her abuse. But you've mentioned that when you're with

Beck, in Starry Hills with his family, you rarely have to give yourself pep talks in the mirror. If that doesn't prove he's good for you, then I don't know what does."

It was true that my mother's voice had all but disappeared after meeting Beck and family, only returning when I had pushed him away.

And my mother *was* dead and gone. Her words had hurt as I was growing up, had left lasting damage, but I didn't want her to make me give up before I even tried.

I'd spent years building my reputation at Edwina's firm and had done whatever was necessary to accomplish it. Maybe, just maybe, I could try to do the same thing but for myself, on my own terms.

Edwina had threatened Beck and his family, but I had contacts as well. And if there was a way to prove Justin had done those things to Beck's family, it would be the leverage I needed. With that, I might have a chance of success.

And even without proving Justin's actions, maybe there was another way to win against Edwina. I wasn't used to relying on people to help me. But Taylor was right—I should talk to Beck first. Otherwise, I would spend my life wondering what might have been.

Taylor's voice snapped me out of my head. "I can see something's going on inside that head of yours. So do you have a plan?"

"Not fully, but I'm working on it."

She grinned. "Does that mean you're going to win back your sexy country boy?"

Tossing aside my pillow, I stood. "Yes. But first, I need a shower."

Taylor pinched her nose. "I wasn't going to say anything..."

I stuck out my tongue at her, and we both laughed. It was exactly what I needed to give me a shot of energy.

As soon as Taylor stood, I hugged her. "Here's a stinky hug full of love."

"My hugs are always full of love for my bestie, even when she smells like rotten eggs."

I eventually went to take a shower and started going through ideas, contacts I could reach out to, and what I'd say to Beck.

I'd let my mother win for too many years, but I sure as hell wouldn't let Edwina do the same. For once, I would take a stand and not let the bully win.

Beck had said, "Game on." And it was.

Chapter Forty-Six

Beckett

Kyle: Everything's set and ready to go. Are you sure about this?
Me: Yes. I want to make sure this bastard goes away.
Kyle: Just don't be a hero and ask for help if you need it.
Me: Maybe.
Kyle: Beck, I'm serious. If this guy is related to arson, intimidation, and maybe even attempted murder, he's dangerous.
Me: I know. And I'll be careful. But just give me this chance first.
Kyle: You've got it. My family and the sheriff's department will be waiting for when you're done. Now, trick the bastard and let him make his own noose.

I stood next to West and stared out the window overlooking the parking lot. "Where the fuck is he?"

West grunted. "He'll be here. The bigger question is whether you can keep from killing him or not."

Playing nice and inviting Justin to my land had been one of the most difficult things I'd ever done. "I have no choice. But if he happens to get a flat tire on his way out of here and the local garage can't tow him—their truck will, of course, be broken—then he'll be a sitting duck and shit out of luck."

"You and Kyle and your games."

I shrugged. "While it sucks to have everyone know your business in a small town, it works to your advantage when you want to fuck with an enemy." A small car—some sort of midlife-crisis convertible despite Justin being no older than thirty—drove into the lot and parked. Out he stepped in a dark suit, carrying a briefcase.

"You know your part?"

West rolled his eyes. "I'm supposed to be mad at you for fucking this all up and to play the good cop."

My older brother couldn't act for shit most of the time, so it was a risk, but Nolan had left and was too well-known. Zach was the worst liar and would never be able to keep a straight face. And since Justin didn't seem to treat women well, I couldn't use Aunt Lori either. So I hoped West could pull it off.

Right before the door opened, I turned on the digital recorder under the table. Maggie gestured Justin inside, and we all sat down.

Justin didn't waste any time. "Did you see the light and realize that bitch isn't worth losing this deal?"

I dug my fingers into my thighs to keep from jumping across the table and punching the asshole again.

West spoke up, allowing me a little more time to get myself under control. "I talked some sense into him. He knows he fucked up, and we need your help. But there are a few things we want cleared up first, if that's okay."

Justin leaned back and tapped one hand against the table. "Such as?"

West replied, "A man named Rocky recently claimed you paid him to attack Sabrina O'Connor during the Easter egg hunt. Is that true?"

The sheriff's office had caught a drunk man speeding on the outskirts of town, and a search of his car revealed a signed check from Justin Whitmore.

Rocky's confession had been part of a plea deal. Kyle's uncle was the sheriff and had agreed to let West and me talk to Justin before he was taken in for questioning.

And I had to admit it was pure magic seeing the fucker squirm.

Justin paled for a second but recovered quickly. "Absolutely not."

"That's what I thought. But then he also said you hired his brother to set the fire inside the bottling facility."

Justin paled further. He was less cocky as he replied, "Also not true."

West continued, "And that he helped you set up the speaker and remote so that you could spook the horse. You didn't do that, either, right?"

That West could even sound somewhat nice right now was goddamn impressive. The years he'd been away had definitely calmed him down.

Justin looked at each of us in turn. "What the fuck is going on here?"

I put up a hand to let West know it was my turn. "Just laying out the reasons why we won't ever work with you."

Justin bolted to his feet. "They're all fucking lies. And if you try to spread them, I'll make you pay."

I learned forward. "How? By trying to hurt someone in my family? One of my friends?" I leaned more. "Do you think I'll allow that to happen?"

His face was red, and he shouted, "You couldn't fucking stop me before, and you won't now."

I wasn't sure how long he'd keep speaking without a filter—the more he confessed, the better the case was against him. So I pushed. "What? You'll use paid goons to do your dirty work again? I bet you couldn't hurt someone to really get what you want, could you? You're a fucking spineless coward. You wouldn't have the balls to prove yourself, to prove you're dedicated to your job."

Fury blazed in his eyes. "I'll do whatever it takes to rise up. And when there's a fucking loose end? I take care of it."

Justin pulled a handgun from his briefcase, undid

the safety, and pointed it at us. "Which includes you two."

Holy shit, he had a gun.

If that weren't enough of a surprise, a second later, the door opened, and Sabrina strode in.

Before I could warn her, all hell broke loose.

Chapter Forty-Seven

Sabrina

The drive up to Starry Hills was nerve-racking, partly because I was anxious about seeing Beck again. But I also had a meeting with Dr. Nichelle Washington the next day to discuss taking her as my first client for my new company.

I'd only just picked a name—Starry PR and Marketing Solutions—and registered it. But ever since I'd made the decision to start my own business, I was eager to get started. Not only because I could take on the clients I wanted and be in complete control but also because I could base my company in Starry Hills.

Even if Beck somehow didn't forgive me for pushing him away, I didn't want to be anonymous in the city any longer. I'd needed that when I broke free of my mother and her narcissistic bullshit. But I was no longer a shy girl who wondered if anything she did was good enough.

Thanks to first Taylor and even more to Beck, I knew I could run my own business and kick ass. I'd worked super hard under Edwina, so I could do the same for myself.

As I finally drove up the gravel road to the Wolfe place, my heart raced. Why I'd ever thought I should flee instead of staying and fighting for my boyfriend and his family, I had no idea. I was eager to do whatever it took to go after the life I wanted with the man I loved.

I pulled into the parking lot and noticed the little convertible Justin sometimes drove to work. Since the license plate was the same—Da Man, although Douche would've been a better fit—I knew it was him.

Frowning, I exited the car and headed for the entrance. I waved to Maggie at the front desk. "Where's Beck?"

He must've not said anything about our breakup, because she gestured down the hallway. "In the meeting room. But he has someone in there with him and West right now."

No doubt it was Justin. I decided to fib a little. "I know. They're expecting me."

Maggie nodded. "Let me know if you need anything."

After smiling at her, I headed down the hallway. I had no idea what Justin was doing here, but I doubted

—no, knew—Beck would never work with him. So something else had to be afoot.

Justin hated surprises, and I wanted to catch him off guard, so I decided not to knock. I turned the knob and walked in but stopped in my tracks.

Justin had a gun pointed at Beck.

Noticing me, Justin sneered and lunged for me. Since he had a gun, I tried to move out of the way. However, he grabbed my arm and tugged me close. "Game over, bitch. I win."

Just as Beck tackled Justin to the ground, a loud bang echoed.

At first, numbness washed over me. Then pain radiated from my arm, and I started to feel woozy, like I might faint. Looking down, I saw my shirt was soaked with blood. So much blood.

I barely felt Beck caress my forehead and heard him say something unintelligible before I blacked out.

Chapter Forty-Eight

Beckett

Justin's lunge for Sabrina played out in slow motion. Getting to her felt as if I were wading through quicksand, everything trying to keep me from saving her.

I managed to jump at Justin just as he pulled the trigger. Sabrina screamed, but I focused on getting the gun out the fucker's hands. As soon as Justin hit the ground, he dropped the firearm. West kicked it away and took the asshole from me. "Go to her."

Not wasting a minute, I rushed over to where Sabrina had fallen. Blood soaked one sleeve, and she was clearly in shock.

I touched her forehead. "I'm here, sweetheart. I'm here."

Her eyes fluttered shut as her body went slack, and I cursed. But I pushed my panic aside and tore her shirtsleeve and then took off my own shirt. Part of it, I used to dab the blood away to see her wound. The bullet had hit her upper arm, and the bleeding was bad.

I tore off some fabric to tie off above the wound to slow the blood flow.

So focused on Sabrina, I didn't realize right away that Aunt Lori and Zach had entered the room. Even as their voices echoed in the background and I thought I heard someone on the phone with Sheriff Evans, I brushed Sabrina's hair from her face, never taking my gaze away. I kissed her cheek and whispered, "Hold on, Sabrina. Don't you dare die and let that asshole win. I need you alive so that I can tell you how much I love you. Stay with me, sweetheart. Stay with me."

I wouldn't have yet another person die in my arms. I might not have been able to do anything for my dad, but Sabrina could still be saved. I refused to believe otherwise.

After I spent a while murmuring words of encouragement and ordering her to fight, eventually the EMTs arrived and tried to push me aside.

"No, I can't leave her."

One of the EMTs was already at work, but the other one, a woman I'd gone to high school with named Gemma, said, "Let us help her, Beck. Two of us can work faster than one. As soon as possible, I'll let you hold her hand again. Okay?"

Her firm yet gentle tone worked. After telling

Sabrina one more time that I loved her, I released her hand and scooted backward, giving the EMTs enough room to work.

West sat next to me on the floor. "You saved her, you know."

I ran my hands through my hair. "You don't know that. She's lost so much blood, West. So much."

My brother squeezed my shoulder. "If you hadn't pushed Justin right when you did, the bullet would've struck her chest."

"She could still die." My voice cracked on the last word.

West squeezed my shoulder again. "If she loves your stubborn ass, then she's made of stronger stuff."

"I hope so," I whispered. "This is all my fault."

I should never have asked to talk to Justin before the sheriff's office took him in. I'd merely wanted to play the hero, and Sabrina was hurt, maybe even dying.

"Stop that bullshit right now," West said. "Sheriff Evans said a confession would ensure he went away for a long, long time. And maybe they could've gotten it out of him, too, or maybe not. But we had no way of knowing the bastard carried a gun."

Before I could think of another reason it was my fault, Gemma helped move Sabrina onto a stretcher and said over her shoulder, "Come with us, Beck, if you want to ride in the ambulance."

I stood and followed the EMTs. After climbing into the vehicle, I took the hand on Sabrina's uninjured side and asked, "Will she be okay?"

"We've stanched the bleeding and will continue to

do whatever's necessary. If she's taking any medications, now's the time to let us know."

In that, at least, I could help. "Just birth control pills and multivitamins."

"Okay. Now, let me focus on monitoring her vitals. We'll be at the county hospital in fifteen minutes if my partner drives as fast as usual. He's a speed demon."

If Gemma was trying to lighten the mood, it didn't work. For the remainder of the ambulance ride, I watched Sabrina's chest rise and fall, a reassuring sign she was still alive. Her face was pale, an oxygen mask covered her mouth and nose, and her arm was tightly bandaged.

And despite all that, she was still so fucking beautiful to me. I just needed her to wake up so that I could tell her that every day for the rest of our lives.

Chapter Forty-Nine

Sabrina

The sounds of buzzing machines filled my ears, and I slowly blinked my eyes open. Above me were LED lights and the ceiling squares that were always in hospitals or office spaces.

I tried to remember where I was or what had happened, but my mind was fuzzy, as if I'd drunk too much.

Turning my head, I checked out the rest of the room. But I barely paid attention to the framed art print or the soothing beige color of the walls. I only saw Beck asleep in a chair next to my bed, his head at a weird angle as he snored softly.

His hair was mussed, as if he'd run his fingers through it a million times, and his scruff was dark enough to signal that he hadn't shaved in at least a day.

At first, I merely stared at him, trying to work out why he was here—or, for that matter, why I was.

Then it all came rushing back—Justin holding a gun, Beck tackling him, and the gun going off.

Tearing my gaze from Beck, I noticed how my upper arm was bandaged. I was also hooked up to a bunch of machines and an IV drip.

Beck's scratchy, just-woken-up voice filled the room. "You're awake."

I turned my head toward his voice, expecting him to be at my bedside. But he remained in the chair, gripping the armrests as if his life depended on it. Maybe he was still pissed off at the way I'd dismissed him.

I wanted to explain it all, but my tongue was thick in my mouth, and I desperately needed a drink of water. I croaked, "Water."

He rose, picked up a small cup with a straw, and put it at my lips. Since I was propped up, I drank a little, and then some more. As soon as I released the straw, Beck returned it to the little side table and sat back down.

The action stung, making me wonder if it was too late to win him back.

Then Beck stood again and moved next to my bed. He wiped a tear off my cheek and whispered, "Don't cry, sweetheart. You're safe."

At his term of endearment, more tears streamed down my face. "You're not still mad at me?"

He frowned. “Of course not. Why would you think that?”

When he cupped my cheek, I leaned into his comforting touch. “You didn’t get up from the chair and looked like you could barely stand to be in the same room as me.”

“No, that wasn’t it.” He paused, searching my eyes before continuing, “I wasn’t sure if you wanted me here.”

I covered his hand on my cheek with mine. “Of course I do. That's why I came back to Starry Hills.”

He caressed my face with his thumb. “Shh. You don’t have to explain anything right now. You must be exhausted and need to rest, sweetheart.”

Even though I wanted to talk and figure it all out, he was right. I was struggling to stay awake. “For now, just tell me what happened and what the doctors had to do to me.”

He grimaced. “I pushed Justin too far, and he pulled a gun. When you walked in, I think he snapped completely.” Beck explained his questioning Justin and pushing him to reveal answers before saying, “I was being a fucking idiot, poking the bear. And the fact you were hurt because of my stupidity? It fucking kills me, Sabrina.”

“You had no idea I’d be there. If anything, I should’ve let you know I was coming.”

“No, this is my fault. Don’t try to take any of the blame.”

Damn, it was getting harder and harder to make my brain focus, but somehow, I managed to say, “We’ll argue about this later. Just tell me what the doctors did." I yawned. "I'm getting sleepy already."

Beck sat next to me on the bed, removing his hand from my face and threading his fingers through mine. "The bullet was still lodged in your arm, so they had to take it out. You're stitched up, and provided everything looks good tomorrow, you should be discharged then, as long as you agree to take it easy. Oh, and they said you'll have a scar."

Despite my sleepy brain, an idea struck. "Maybe that's where I can get my wolf tattoo, the mate to yours."

As soon as I said it, I mentally cursed. Tattoos were permanent, barring expensive laser treatments, and we hadn't even officially become a couple again.

Closing my eyes, I murmured, "Forget I said that. I'm tired, Beck. I just want to sleep."

When his lips brushed my forehead, I sighed.

His breath danced across my skin as he replied, "We'll talk more when you wake up, sweetheart. I'll be here waiting to take you home."

As I wondered where home might be, sleep finally won, and I slipped into darkness.

Chapter Fifty

Beckett

Sabrina's comment about getting a wolf tattoo to match mine gave me hope. And after an entire night of wondering if she'd even want to see me, it was what I'd needed to hear.

But we hadn't been alone to talk again since. My family kept rotating through to visit, though the hospital staff kept everyone from crowding inside at once.

West, Avery, and Millie were the latest visitors and were chatting with Sabrina.

Avery held out a handmade card to Sabrina. "Everyone signed it. Well, not everyone in Starry Hills. But all the family and Auntie Millie and Abby's BFF

Circle. The Evanses too. There are so many signatures that there's not any room left!"

Sabrina smiled and took the card. "Thank you, Avery. That was sweet of you."

"I wanted to bring a kitten to make you feel better, but they said I couldn't."

Sabrina blinked. "A kitten?"

Millie laughed. "I found a stray cat and a litter of kittens inside my barn the other day. Until they're old enough to be weaned and I can find homes for them, I'm taking care of the mama and babies. Avery is convinced we should keep them all, but I'm not having six cats inside my house."

Avery looked up at her dad. "We can have two, can't we, Daddy? Then me and Wyatt can have new best friends."

Only because I knew my brother so well did I see him flinch a little. She hadn't said it to be mean, but it killed West to cause his children any pain—like when he'd uprooted them from everything they knew to move back to Starry Hills.

Sabrina spoke up. "I love kittens. Maybe I can take a pair."

Millie frowned. "Will your apartment allow it? I know they can be strict about pets in the city."

Sabrina smiled, glanced at me, and then turned back to Millie. "I'm planning to move to Starry Hills soon."

My heart soared, and I wanted to ask her if she meant with me. Our eyes met, and I could have sworn I saw her nod slightly.

Millie cleared her throat. "I think Sabrina needs to rest again." She gestured toward the door. "Come on, Avery. I'll buy you a hot chocolate before we drive home."

"But I wanted to stay longer."

West grunted. "We'll see her again. And your brother is waiting for us at home. Say goodbye, and let's go."

As if knowing her dad wouldn't budge, Avery turned toward Sabrina. "I would hug you, but I know you're hurt right now. Come see me as soon as you're back in Starry Hills, and I'll show you the kittens!"

Sabrina smiled. "I can't wait."

After Millie, West, and Avery finished their goodbyes and the door clicked closed behind them, I moved to sit beside Sabrina on the bed. "Tell me more about your moving to Starry Hills."

"Caught that, did you?"

As I tucked some stray strands of hair behind her ear, I nodded. "I'm glad, but is it really what you want?"

"Yes. I'd decided before driving up here and the whole Justin thing." She placed a hand on my thigh. "I think I should tell you the reason I pushed you away, what it could mean if we stay together, and then talk more about my living in Starry Hills."

She told me about Edwina's threats and the bargain to protect my family, as well as the consequences if we defied her. She had ideas of how to maybe avoid being destroyed by her former boss but couldn't guarantee anything.

When she finished, she asked, "So are you still happy about me moving to town?"

I kissed her cheek. "First, I'm beyond happy about your moving closer to me." I brushed my lips over her brow next. "In fact, I want to wake up next to you every day, if you'll let me." Her breath hitched, but I kissed her lips and then met her gaze to add, "I love you, Sabrina O'Connor. Which means I want you whenever and wherever I can get you."

"D-Do you mean it?"

"I do. You can be fierce and stand up to me one minute and then be caring and gentle the next. And when I have you naked and alone?" I growled. "It's even better." I nuzzled her cheek. "I love you, sweetheart. And even if we have to fucking stand up to an entire army of angry marketing people, waving their smartphones as they shout at us, I'll do it."

She laughed. "It's not like they'd congregate in a mob outside your house."

I leaned back until I could meet her lovely green eyes again. "However they try to attack us, we'll face it together. Between your smarts and my charm, they don't stand a chance." I waggled my eyebrows, and she snorted.

"Your charm isn't obvious to most, so maybe we'll have to call Nolan to play the part. Have him put on a smolder and—"

I nipped her jaw. "If you weren't injured right now, I'd tickle you for that comment, until you begged for me to stop."

"I'm just teasing you. I much prefer the more rugged, leaner variety of Wolfe brother."

"Hm, is that so? Tell me more."

Sabrina cupped my cheek. "I love you, too, Beckett Wolfe. No other man has made me feel so special, encouraged me, or made me believe I'm beautiful like you have. And let's not forget you know how to lasso a city girl and make her come hard. That's a bonus, for sure."

I growled and leaned closer, until her lips were an inch from mine. "Say it again."

"I love you, Beck. So kiss me already."

Even though I couldn't kiss her and celebrate the way I wanted to—by worshiping her body and making her scream my name—I couldn't resist her sweet, soft mouth. Her lips parted instantly, and I took my time licking, stroking, and nipping her bottom lip until it was nice and swollen from my attentions.

When I finally broke the kiss, I laid my forehead against hers. "Move in with me."

For a second, she searched my eyes, and I wondered if I had jumped the gun. Then she replied, "Maybe. Are we going to have to live with your aunt and brother?"

It wasn't quite a yes, but it gave me hope. "We can use the guesthouse for now. One day, I want to build a house on my piece of land at the edge of the property—each of us received a lot from our parents upon turning eighteen. I can't afford to do that now, but someday, I'd love to build a house there for us."

"You seem so certain of everything."

"Because I'm certain of you. Of us. We just fit together, Sabrina. And not just in bed." As I stroked her cheek with my thumb, I continued, "I know you're afraid of my giving up on you like your sister did, but I won't. You're my future, sweetheart. Won't you give us a chance?"

She finally smiled. "Okay. On one condition."

I raised an eyebrow. "Which is?"

"You do all the cooking, and I'll do the dishes. Deal?"

I chuckled, kissed her, and murmured, "I think I can handle that." I kissed her again. "I can't wait until you're healed enough for me to show you just how much I truly love you, Sabrina."

She traced my jaw with her finger. "Me too. And since I didn't win the Easter egg hunt, it means you get a fantasy. But it's still too cold to wear a bathing suit outside."

I smiled slowly. "Oh, I have plenty of other fantasies we can do inside."

"Like what?"

"Hm, like covering your nipples in whipped cream and lapping it off slowly. Maybe even writing 'Beck's' in chocolate syrup on your belly before I lick that off too."

She shivered. "I'm not sure why I'm so turned on by that, but now I'm impatient."

"It's because you like when I go all caveman-like."

"Maybe."

"So yes."

She stuck her tongue at me, and I laughed. I loved this woman so hard.

Sabrina yawned, and I said, "You should get some more sleep."

She moved over and patted the bed. "Only if you sleep next to me, Beck."

I hesitated, not wanting to hurt her.

"This is my uninjured side. And I know you're not a restless sleeper. I could probably use a bullhorn, and you wouldn't wake up, let alone move."

Careful not to jostle the bed too much, I lay next to her. "Good thing, since you snore sometimes."

"I do not."

"You do." When she opened her mouth, I kissed her nose. "And it's adorable."

She sighed and snuggled more against me. "I'm too tired to argue right now. Hold me, Beck. That's all I want."

"Forever, sweetheart. I want you in my arms forever."

I held her close, drank in her warmth and scent, and fell asleep with her in my arms, right where she belonged.

Chapter Fifty-One

Sabrina

Me: I can't believe they did it in less than two months.
Beck: Your boyfriend has an in with the Wilson construction company. You can reward me later.
Me: <tongue out emoji> You know your family helped with the painting and decorating too.
Beck: Maybe. But I'm the only one who'll ask for a reward.
Me: You need a cookie?
Beck: Yes, lots and lots of naked Sabrina cookies. In many different places.
Me: <laughing emoji> Maybe I should bake me-shaped cookies and make you suffer.
Beck: I may need to bring out the puppy-dog eyes. Wait.

Beck: <sends a cute puppy picture>
Me: You're ridiculous sometimes.
Beck: Yet you still love me.

Nearly two months later, I stood outside a little bright-blue building and couldn't stop staring at the sign that read Starry PR and Marketing Solutions.

After I'd taken on Dr. Washington as my second client—my first being the Wolfe family, once they'd been freed from their contract with Edwina—word had spread around town. Especially once some of my suggestions for the winery had been implemented and Dr. Washington had reopened her clinic after a much-needed remodeling and redecorating. I had a growing list of clients from both Starry Hills and other parts of Sonoma County, to the point that working from Beck's and my small guesthouse was no longer feasible.

Since Edwina was too busy dealing with the fallout of what her employee had done to try to get a promotion, I assumed she wouldn't make good on her threat to me and the Wolfe family.

So I'd taken a chance and rented the space in front of me. While my new office was just off Main Street, I wanted to keep it in the same spirit and had gotten permission to paint the building bright blue. Millie and Abby had even gifted me two planters to put out front.

Beck exited the building and walked up to me. Turning, he glanced at the sign and put an arm around my waist, pulling me to his side. "You were right—that would've looked tacky on the front of our little home."

"I can't believe you suggested I put a giant sign on

the guesthouse. There's barely room for us and the two kittens, let alone any of my clients."

"And I still can't believe you talked me into adopting two cats."

I laid my head on his shoulder. "You love them just as much as I do. And cat guys are all the rage now anyway. Gone are the days when people made fun of crazy cat ladies."

He sighed. "I wish you'd stop showing me the videos of that one guy with a bunch of cats. He's a chisel-jawed actor, and it's just not fair."

"Oh, stop it. There's only one man who catches my fancy."

"Catches your fancy? What year is this?"

I playfully swatted his chest. "Says the guy who pulls out my chair every single time I sit down."

He grunted. "That's just me being a gentleman."

I smiled and hugged him tighter. "And I love you all the more for it."

Aunt Lori poked her head through the door. "Did you get lost on your way to bringing Sabrina inside, Beckie? Do you need a map?"

I bit my lip to keep from laughing as Beck grunted.

"Can't a guy get some time alone with his girlfriend?"

"You live together and hardly ever bring her over anymore. I miss seeing Sabrina."

"But I saw you last night at dinner."

Aunt Lori waggled a finger at me. "Just don't forget about tea this week, Sabrina. Now that your business is officially open, you can spare a little time to chat with this old lady."

Beck took out his phone and typed something, and Aunt Lori frowned.

After taking her phone out, she blinked then grinned. "You're getting better, Beckie."

He muttered, "Clearly, my message was lost on you."

I buried my face against his side to keep from laughing. Beck had slowly been including more and more emojis to please his aunt. Usually, when he used them, she stopped texting sooner—except for the group text chat, which I was permanently a part of.

After composing myself—these two could make me laugh for an hour if I didn't intervene—I stood up straight and said, "Let's head inside. Visitors should start arriving soon for the grand opening, and I'd like to thank all of you privately first."

"There's no need to do that, Sabrina," Aunt Lori said.

"Yes, there is." I pushed Beck from behind. "Let's go."

He wrapped his fingers around mine, and we walked inside hand in hand. Even though we'd lived together for months, his touch sent heat throughout my body and butterflies to my stomach.

Inside, all the Wolfe family was there, apart from Zane. Even Nolan had made the trip to be at my grand opening. Taylor met my gaze and winked at me before answering something her husband asked. It would be interesting to see if Nolan Drake or Ben Adams would get the bigger reaction from visitors, since I hadn't announced they would be here today.

Although I knew Beck would always get more excited over Ben Adams. When Taylor first revealed she and her husband worked for the San Francisco team, he'd been speechless and tried not to fanboy over Ben. Now, however, they were friends.

Avery rushed up to me and took my hand. "Come on, Auntie Sabrina. I have a surprise for you."

The little girl tugged, and we went to my desk. Next to the miniature rose bush Beck had first bought me was something new—a picture frame that read Meow at the top. It contained an adorable picture of my two kittens, Jack the tabby and Sparrow the calico.

Revealing my previous obsession with a certain fictional pirate had been mortifying, but Beck had let me name them whatever I wanted after that.

Avery said, "I know you can't bring Jack and Sparrow to the office, so I thought you'd like a picture so you can always see them. I always carry one of my two kitties."

I hugged her. "Thank you, Avery. It's perfect."

She beamed up at me before dashing over to Millie. While caring for the kittens, Avery had become rather attached to her, much to West's irritation. The pair still hadn't worked out their issues, although I hoped they would one day.

Zach—finally out of his cast and relegated to a walking boot—raised his glass of wine and gently tapped it with a pen. The room fell quiet, and he gestured toward me. "Come on, Sabrina. Say a few words for us."

With strangers, I might've blushed. But the Wolfes were my family now, and I didn't hesitate to smile and say, "Thank you all for helping me get this place ready in time. I couldn't have done it without you or your support. And no matter how many new clients I sign on, you all will be my most important. Because it's more than just business—it's family too." I raised my glass. "To making Starry Wolfe Wine the most popular and desired wine in all of Sonoma!"

Everyone echoed the sentiment and drank from their cups.

As soon as everyone finished, Aunt Lori came up to me and took one of my hands. "I'm so proud of you, Sabrina. I hope you know that."

"Yes, but I couldn't have done it without your help in spreading the word, Aunt Lori."

She waved a hand in dismissal. "Crowing about your abilities to my friends was no big deal. The monthly wine boxes are already doing pretty well. And after what you have planned for the Summer Star Festival this year, I imagine we'll be getting more orders than we know what to do with."

I was teasing the event on various social media videos and posts, and it had gained some traction. By coming to our booth and mentioning the hashtag phrase I'd created, customers would be entered into a contest. "I hope so."

Aunt Lori squeezed my hand. "I know so." She released me. "I see Avery and Wyatt found the cookies.

I'd better make sure they don't eat them all. Especially since Avery tasted more than enough when she helped make them."

She left, and Beck hugged my back against his front, putting his strong arms around me, and whispered, "I'm the proudest of you, sweetheart."

I placed one of my hands on his and stroked his warm skin. "Are you turning this into a contest?"

"Maybe. I want to be the one who holds you in the highest regard." He nipped my earlobe. "I love you."

I turned in his arms until I could place my hands on his chest. The emotion in his eyes never failed to amaze me. "I love you too."

Beck lowered his head, but a throat clearing behind us stopped him. Beck growled, "What the fuck do you want?"

Nolan sounded amused when he replied, "I see people lining up outside. Unless you want to give them a free show, you should probably save the kissing for later."

While Nolan would never be outgoing or grumble like his brothers, his quiet teasing had become more and more apparent the longer I'd known him. It was still weird for me to accept that he was a mega movie star who hated any sort of attention when not playing a role.

I turned and smiled at Nolan. "Thanks. Give me two minutes before letting them in, please?"

"Of course." Nolan smiled and walked toward the door.

Beck kissed me quickly and released me. "We'll

celebrate your grand opening later, at home." He moved his mouth to my ear, and his hot breath dancing across my skin made me shiver. "Then we can celebrate a whole other type of opening."

"Beck!"

He chuckled, nipped my earlobe, and straightened. "I couldn't resist, sweetheart. Now, go impress them all with your brilliance and let them see what I get to see every day."

His words made my heart squeeze a little. "You're too good to be true, Beckett Wolfe."

"No, I'm only this way because a stubborn city girl captured my heart and helped me heal. You're the one who's too good to be true, sweetheart."

Uncaring who saw, I rushed over and brought his mouth down to mine. Beck instantly wrapped his arms around me and devoured my mouth. Every lick, swipe, and suckle was a hint of what would come later.

By the time he finally let me up for air, I was panting.

He kissed my forehead. "Go get 'em, Sabrina O'Connor. They have no idea what's in store for them."

After smiling another few seconds at the man I loved, I took a deep breath, smoothed my dress, and went to the door, my lucky black heels clacking against the floor.

Nolan let them in, and a mixture of friends, acquaintances, and a few new faces swarmed inside. Some were there out of curiosity, some were truly interested in my help, and others were merely there to support me.

I was soon lost in doing what I did best, and by the end, I had new people interested in my services and others who'd suggested I stop by anytime to chat. It was such a far cry from when I'd been a little girl, lonely and unwanted, and made a sock-doll family to love me.

But as Beck hugged me to his side and his family and my bestie helped me clean up for the night, I was far from alone. I had a man I loved, a family that had unofficially adopted me, a friend who would always have my back, and a place to finally belong.

After so many years, I was well and truly wanted.

And later, after Beck made good on his promise to celebrate, he held me in his arms, and I fell asleep smiling and dreaming of what else our future might bring.

Epilogue

Sabrina

One Year and One Month Later

As Beck led me by the shoulders down the pathway, I nearly stumbled. "Are you sure I have to wear this blindfold?"

"Yes." In the next instant, he swept me into his arms, and I instinctively wrapped mine around his neck. "And I'm being a gentleman, not even tossing you over my shoulder tonight."

I laughed. "This might be the first time you've restrained yourself."

"Try to deny it, but you get nice and wet whenever I cart you off and have my way with you."

I tried not to think about the last time he'd done it, when he'd taken me against a tree, hidden away from prying eyes. "As much as I love your tongue, cock, and hands, the festival is tomorrow, and I have a ton of things left on my to-do list."

It would be my second Summer Star Festival, and I couldn't wait. Especially since I'd been able to sponsor the pony rides and picture booths for the kids, thanks to my thriving business.

"This is more important than the festival."

He didn't elaborate, and I knew interrogating him wouldn't work. Beck was good when it came to surprising me. His last big one had made me cry happy tears when he'd shown me the building plans to open a small restaurant on the property. It wouldn't open for months yet, but he'd delegated enough work from the winery to try to pursue his dream of running his own place.

And I would be running the best marketing campaign ever to help his restaurant—Starry Night—hit the ground running.

"You're not bringing me to a giant display of ridiculous T-shirts, are you?"

"No, but thanks for the idea."

"Don't you dare."

"Oh, come on. You only have what? Ten now?"

"Which is nine too many."

"Well, I have twelve, so you have some catching up to do."

I smiled, remembering the last one I'd given him—I

<heart emoji> <sheep emoji>. His brothers still made fun of him for it.

I felt the brush of leaves against my arm, where I'd gotten the wolf tattoo to match Beck's. "Are we there yet?"

"Nearly."

After a few more strides, he gently set me down and turned me until my back was against his front. He removed the blindfold, and I had to blink a few times to take in the scene.

We were in the center of the orchard, near the stone bench and wishing tree. White string lights hung from the branches, their glow making the place feel magical and otherworldly. "Beck, it's beautiful."

He moved to stand in front of me and went down on one knee. My hands flew to my mouth as I realized what he was about to do.

After taking a ring from his pocket, he held it toward me and said, "When I first met you, I viewed you as my enemy. My temper erupted, and I thought we'd never see each other again. But you were my perfect match—just as stubborn and determined as I was, never taking my bullshit. The more time we spent together, the more I viewed you as the opposite of my enemy, until I couldn't help but fall for you. You're everything I could've dreamed and more. Not only are you beautiful, but the fact that I can laugh with you one moment and make you moan the next is something I'll never take for granted. I love you and want to grow old with you, even if it means our T-shirt wars get even more ridiculous. Sabrina, will you marry me?"

"Yes!"

He slipped the gold-and-ruby ring—my favorite stone—on my finger, stood, and took my mouth in a rough kiss. It was hard and demanding, staking a claim on me.

And I loved every second of it.

When he finally pulled away, he cupped my cheek. "Do you think we can run off to Vegas and get married next month?"

"As if Emmy would ever allow that."

Many months ago, Millie—whose full name was Emilia—had asked everyone to use her childhood nickname again instead of Millie.

Beck moved closer, wrapping his free arm around my waist. "Maybe West can work his magic and get her to be okay with it."

"We live together, Beck. We can wait a little while and let Emmy and Aunt Lori have fun with our wedding."

He grumbled. "I suppose."

I laughed. "Well, a compromise—let's make a wish on the tree while we're here. If you want to use yours for a Vegas wedding, go for it."

He glanced at the big wishing tree. "You want to climb it and better our chances at it coming true?"

"Considering Zach fell out of it, and he's way more athletic than I am, I think not. Let's just touch the trunk."

We walked over and each placed a palm on the bark. I closed my eyes and wished for the future I wanted with Beck—our own house in Starry Hills with our two cats knocking stuff off counters, maybe even a kid or two playing in the yard with their older cousins, and regular crazy dinners with his family and my bestie.

Maybe even my own sister would show up one day. She'd tentatively responded to my messages to her last year, and we'd had an awkward correspondence since. Our relationship was far from perfect, and we were nowhere near as close as we'd been growing up, but it was a start.

Beck kissed my neck, and I opened my eyes.

Smiling at me, he said, "Wait here. I have one more surprise for you."

He went behind one of the trees and grabbed something, keeping it behind his back as he returned to me.

As I tried to peek behind him, I asked, "Now what do you have planned?"

He stepped back and produced a new pair of black cowboy boots. "I thought you could wear these while I take you against the tree."

Maybe to some, that would be scandalous. But it was far from the first time Beck had made love to me against a tree.

"Pity you didn't bring the lasso."

Heat flared in his eyes. "Next time, sweetheart. I can tie you up next time."

Soon he had my panties off, the boots on, and my skirt around my waist as he thrust hard into me over and over again, devouring my mouth at the same time.

When he finally stroked my clit and I cried out in

pleasure, the lights around us blurred, and I truly felt like I was in another world.

But I could be on the moon, and it wouldn't matter. As long as I was with Beck, I could live anywhere. Because he was my home, now and forever.

Bonus Epilogue

Beckett

A Little More Than Seven Years Later

Zach: My daughter is getting that look in her eye. Bring Charlotte to Amber's stand, stat.
Me: She's busy.
Emmy: I could bring Avery by. You know how all the younger kids love her.
West: She can't. She took our youngest home after he threw up.
Emmy: And you didn't tell me? I'm calling Avery.
Zane: I guess I could come entertain my niece. She loves me best.
Zach: Then stop texting and get your ass over here before Amber actually loses her temper.
Zane: Hm, maybe I needed a beer first.

Zach: Are you trying to get me murdered?
Amber: I'm here too, you know. <eye roll emoji>
Zach: But you love me too much to kill me. Right?
Amber: Oh look, customers.
Zach: Oh, shit.
Zane: Fine. I'm coming.

I stood with my two-year-old son, Lucas, asleep in my arms, watching as my five-year-old daughter grinned at me from atop a horse. Even though my teenage nephew, Wyatt, was by her side, ensuring nothing would happen, I still itched to go and place my hands on Charlotte to keep her seated.

Sabrina came up beside me, put an arm around my waist, and laid her head on my shoulder. "She'll be fine, Beck."

"I still don't see why I couldn't have been the one to lead her around the kids' course with the horse."

"Because you promised Wyatt he could do it. Don't ruin it for him."

Wyatt loved horses nearly as much as soccer. And at eighteen, he took his job watching any of his cousins seriously. There were a lot of them, but he had never scoffed at being too cool or old to play with them, even if they were so much younger than him.

"Still. Charlotte's just a baby, and I can't help but worry."

"She'll be starting school soon, so she's not that little."

"She'll always be my baby girl."

Lucas stirred, and I gently stroked his cheek to settle him.

Once he was asleep again, Sabrina said, "Although she might not be the only girl for much longer."

I stared down at her, blinking. "What are you talking about?"

Sabrina suddenly looked nervous. "I know we weren't going to have any more children, but the birth control failed, and I'm pregnant again. After this, you're most definitely getting snipped."

I placed a hand on her belly. "You're pregnant?"

She put her hand on top of mine. "Yes. I know it wasn't planned. But I'm already protective and can't wait to love him or her as much as Charlotte and Lucas."

"I'm more than ready to love another child, even if it means I have to get more storage for all the pictures I'll be taking with my phone."

She laughed softly. "You must have a few million of them by now, I swear."

"I'm better than when Charlotte was a baby." I'd been a proud dad, taking five hundred pictures a day the first few months and showing them to everyone, whether they wanted to see them or not. "But I'd rather have them than not. Besides, it's not as if I'm going to cover the walls with them like wallpaper."

"Even if we have more room these days, no, you wouldn't be allowed to hang them all. I love my children, but I don't want that much chaos. I'd miss our cozy home."

A few years ago, we'd moved into the house built on

the piece of land my parents had left me, and it was a hell of a lot bigger than the little guesthouse that had been our first home. I still remembered how happy Sabrina had been helping to paint our house and make the place ours.

"Whatever the pregnant woman wants, she gets."

She snorted. "Those are dangerous words, Mr. Wolfe."

"But I mean them, Mrs. Wolfe."

We stared at each other, smiling. I hoped she would make some of the same requests she'd made during her previous pregnancies, when she'd worn me out in bed. A lasso and boots might have made an appearance or two.

Eventually, Sabrina said, "I love you, Beck."

"I love you, too, Sabrina."

I had barely kissed her when Charlotte rushed over and tugged on my hand. "Stop kissing Mommy, Daddy. I want to get scones and hot chocolate. You promised."

Sabrina took Lucas—skilled, as always, in not waking him up in the process—and I crouched until I was at eye level with our oldest. "Hm, did I? I remember you saying we'd get some, and then rushing off."

"No, Daddy, you promised. Last night. At dinner with Aunt Lori."

When I picked her up, she squealed. I kissed her cheek and then nodded. "You're right. I did. But we have to take Mommy and baby brother with us to get them some scones and hot chocolate too."

She wrinkled her nose. "Lucas will make a mess."

I booped her nose. "You used to make messes too." Though she opened her mouth, I continued, "But your auntie Amber will be there along with some of your cousins. That should make up for it, right?"

One of Amber's children was Charlotte's best friend as well as her cousin.

She wiggled in my arms. "Then let's hurry! I need to tell Luna a secret."

Smiling, I glanced at Sabrina, her expression full of love and happiness. Even though her surprise pregnancy had thrown me, I couldn't wait to add a third kid to our little family. I definitely had more love to give.

As we walked, I took Sabrina's hand and listened as Charlotte enthusiastically talked about her pony ride.

I'd once thought I wouldn't have time for a woman, let alone a family. But in truth, I'd just needed to find the right woman to love. And now we had our children, our large extended family, and a bright future ahead of us.

After bringing Sabrina's hand to my mouth, I kissed the back of it and gave her a look that made her blush. She was all I'd ever wanted, even if I'd never known it.

Author's Note

I hope you enjoyed Beck and Sabrina's story! The hardest part of writing the first book in a series is to introduce everything. I dipped my toes in, but there's still a lot more to learn about the Wolfe family and Starry Hills in general. Because, yes, each Wolfe siblings will get a story. :) Next up is Weston Wolfe and Emilia "Millie" Mendoza's story, *Stay With Me Forever*. There will be even crazier text messages between the siblings, plus more of the BFF Circle (Abby, Millie, Katie, and Amber). And yes, you'll get cameos from Beck and Sabrina too!

And let's just say that West has quite the mouth on him in the bedroom. I can't wait for you to meet him.

While this isn't my first published book, it's my first small town contemporary romance (I've written nearly 60 books under a different name). I (mostly) enjoyed figuring it all out and came to love the characters I created as well as their town of Starry Hills. My plan is to have a book for each of the Wolfe siblings, and I did drop a few hints in this book for future stories. If you're wondering HOW Zach fell out of a tree and broke his leg, all will be revealed in time. :)

While I put a lot of myself into this book (even the flower petals on the discreet paperback cover are from my own backyard!), I wanted to thank Ashley and Illiana — two great beta readers who help me find typos and minor inconsistencies. Thank you!

And to all of you who've read this far, thank you from the bottom of my heart. Being an author is both the best and hardest job in the world, and it's only possible because of you all. I hope to see you in Starry Hills again, and if you want to make sure you never miss a release, then please join my newsletter at: **KaylaChase.com/Newsletter**

Until next time, happy reading!

~Kayla~

Stay With Me Forever

STARRY HILLS #2

He's a single dad who never wants to marry again. She's his little sister's best friend who can't stand him. But when a hotel reservation goes wrong and there's only one bed, things heat up...

After sixteen years away, I finally moved back to Starry Hills with my two kids, determined to heal the rift with my family and help with the family's winery business.

Slowly, my children and I are finding our place in Starry Hills. But then summer vacation arrives and my kids keep finding their way to *her* property.

Emilia "Millie" Mendoza, the wedding planner who is extremely close to my family.

Except she wants nothing to do with me. From the first time she saw me after I got back, she's glared and told me to leave her alone.

Which would be a lot easier if she didn't keep showing my children the kindness and attention they never got from their mother.

Every swim lesson, bedtime story, or word of encouragement chips away at my walled-up heart.

And then we're forced to work together at a wedding expo, they lose her reservation, and we have to share a room.

That one bed soon changes everything.

But making her fall apart with my hands and mouth is the easy part. Because Emilia has burdens of her own.

Ones that might keep us apart.

Except Emilia is the one I want to stay with us forever. And I'll do whatever it takes to win her.

Stay With Me Forever is now available in paperback.

About the Author

Kayla Chase writes sexy, feel-good romance full of laughter, friendships, and family. Her stories usually include crazy get togethers, fun festivals or events, and towns that feel like characters themselves. She also writes happy endings because real life and adulting can be way too hard.

She lives near Seattle but also grew up in California, which gives her lots of beautiful places to include in her stories (such as Sonoma wine country). While she's also lived in Japan and England, she has yet to figure a way to get her characters to those places. (But she does travel on a shoestring when she gets the chance!)

When not writing, she loves to read, jog on her treadmill, fit in some yoga, or try new recipes in the kitchen. More often than not, her cats derail her plans and make things, er, interesting.

272
146
607
361
51
21

1437.

Printed in Great Britain
by Amazon

36943993R00263